In The Blink of a

LOVING LILY SERIES BOOK ONE

BY

S.J. BATSFORD

COPYRIGHT

First Published – 27/05/2016
This edition published – 21/06/2021 by Batsford Publishing

Cover by S.J Batsford - 2021
Formatted by Sienna Grant - 2021

ISBN - 978-1-9196164-0-7
2ND EDITION

IN THE BLINK OF AN EYE

(Loving Lily series #1)

is a New Adult Romance, intended for mature viewers of 18+.

Strong language and sexual situations throughout.

CHAPTER ONE

Life swings in roundabouts. One minute everything can be going swimmingly,
then the next; all your plans, hopes and dreams can turn to dust.

Late August.

"Why am I going a month before school starts? Can't I just go to college here?" I ask, slumping onto my bed.

"No Lily, you can't; it's all paid for. You wanted to be a writer, and this is your best chance. Hey, look at it this way, you will *finally* get a tan." My mom, she thinks she's a comedian. She is constantly teasing me about looking like a vampire, and normally I'd laugh, but this time I don't find it funny.

"Do I have to live with Cora though? I know she is my nan, but I don't really know her." I press, not in the mood for joking around.

"Yes, you do. She's not getting any younger, and she

hardly knows you because I moved us to England. Plus, it'll be better for you to go early; so you can learn your way around, and explore a bit. Spend some time with Grandma, before school starts." She breathes heavily, exhausted from her rant.

"I'm worried about you though. You don't look well."

"I'm okay, I'm just worn out with work." She sighs, sitting beside me, looking drained. "You really wanted to go. What happened?"

"I know. I *was* looking forward to it when I thought *you* were coming with me."

"It's all sorted now. It would be a waste of money if you didn't go, and Grandma is really looking forward to having you." She's playing dirty, making me feel guilty.

Sighing, she gets up and leaves the room. "You need to hurry up, or you'll miss your flight," she shouts from the stairs.

"Are you sure you're okay?" I ask, following closely, taking a last look around my childhood home.

"Yes, yes, I'm fine. It's just the flu. Do you have your ticket and passport?"

I check again and show her that I have them. Pausing, I hesitate not wanting to leave the safety of my home. Stepping forward, she hugs me so tightly I choke up, blinking back tears as my throat throbs.

"I'll miss you, Mom. Love you so much." The crack in my voice breaks her resolve, and she sobs on my shoulder.

"I love you too. Always will." She holds my face in her hands, tears streaming down hers. "You best go. I'll speak to you when you land. Go on, get going, I love you." Blowing me a kiss, she pushes me toward the open door of the taxi, and shuts it as soon as I'm in. Smiling one last time, she runs inside with a quick wave.

I cry all the way to the airport, her tear-stained face etched into my mind.

I'm startled awake by the taxi driver, informing me that we've arrived at the airport.

Looking up at the airport sign, I take a deep breath, and push through the doors, pulling my luggage behind me. I'm so nervous my stomach churns.

Waiting for my flight number to be called, I observe those closest to me. A couple try unsuccessfully to amuse their kids, I smile my first real smile hearing them whine about having to wait. A young man sitting a few seats down, pulls my attention; dressed in a smart suit. He's talking on the phone, so his face is turned away from me, but he looks relaxed. While another bloke sitting next to him is typing frantically on his laptop.

Me, I'm bouncing my knee, chewing the inside of my cheek and trying not to freak out over a plane ride.

"Flight #927, to San Diego, now boarding." A bored voice calls through a loudspeaker. Jumping out of my seat, I grab my bag and walk towards the lady checking boarding passes, she is way too cheery.

Finding my seat, I sit quickly and pull the seat belt as tight as it will go, making sure to double check it's secure. I feel jittery, my nerves making me jumpy, like I've had too much sugar. The other passengers are going about their business, like everything is totally normal. Which I suppose it is, I'm just the nutter ready to jump out of her seat or throw up. I feel so out of place because I've never travelled alone before.

"Excuse me."

I'm interrupted from my musings by a young bloke

standing next to me, obviously the owner of the seat next to mine. I move my legs, so he can squeeze past, and I get a close up of a nicely toned arse. *Yum.* Shocked at my own thoughts, I look away, embarrassed. What the hell was that?

"Thanks." I look up and catch his smirk. *Shit. Caught.*

"You're welcome." I blush.

"Ladies and gentlemen, please take your seats, and secure your seat belts. We will be taking off shortly." Another cheerful voice announces. *Why the bloody hell they're all so happy to be trapped on this thing is beyond me.* Gripping the arm of my chair, I try to keep my panic at bay. Breathe, *breathe…*a hand touches my arm and I flinch, looking at the man beside me.

"Sorry. Are you okay?"

"A little scared, first time flying." I explain, giving him a tight smile.

"Ethan Barker," he says, as he extends his hand for me to shake. Peeling my fingers from the armrest, I turn to face him. His face is just inches from mine. *Wow, he's gorgeous.* My eyes take him in, *that's what you do when you meet someone new; you know to check they're not a psycho, right?*

He looked so tall when standing beside me, looking distinguished and sexy in his suit, I'm thankful the rest of him doesn't disappoint. His skin is nicely tanned, his light brown spiked hair shines, even in the dim light. My eyes fall to his strong square jaw, covered in a five o'clock shadow. His nose is so straight, leading my eyes to the most kissable lips I've ever seen. I have to force my eyes back to his, and my god, they are just beautiful. Hazel, with a touch of light green. Damn sexy.

He grins at me, raising his eyebrow. I realise he's waiting for me to introduce myself and shake his still outstretched hand. While I'm just sitting here like an idiot gawking at him.

Clearing my throat, I swallow, sliding my hand into his. "Lily, Lily Carter," I squeak, my voice failing me.

He smiles slightly, obviously pleased with my appraisal and releases my hand.

"Well, Lily. If you're scared of flying, why are you on an eleven-hour flight?" He asks, dialling up his smile, and it leaves me incapable of breathing. "Lily," he prompts.

Heat creeps up my neck as my cheeks blaze bright red. "I got into university; I'm moving in with my nan." I blurt, cringing at my verbosity. Taking a breath, I try to relax and stop acting like a bloody lunatic.

"Ahh, which one are you attending?" He rests his chin on his upturned hand, waiting.

"San Diego. It's the closest to nan's house." Uneasy with talking about myself, I quickly change the subject. "Where are you from? You're obviously American." I flush, cursing my loss of brain to mouth filter. My belly flutters when he laughs. I watch him, smiling, his eyes twinkling as he laughs deep and rough.

"I was born and raised in San Diego. Can't you tell by my tan?" He asks, sticking out a beautifully tanned, muscular arm; bringing my focus to how good he looks with his sleeves rolled up like that.

"Anyone can have a tan these days, sunbeds." I shrug, smirking, trying to play off my flustered state.

He laughs again, "you're funny. I love British people; the things you say are funny, but brutally honest. It's refreshing. I find a lot of people to be fake. Not all though." He amends.

"So, what were you doing in London, if you're from California? If you don't mind me asking, that is?"

"So polite. It's fine, I was in London on business, I work for my step-dad." Smiling, he swiftly turns the conversation back to me. "So, if you're just starting university, you're what? Eighteen."

"Yes, and you are?" I quirk an eyebrow, making him laugh. The cheeky bugger, he's not the only one who can get personal.

Wiping his eyes, he comes back with the worst attempt at a British accent I've ever heard. "Why, young lady, I'll have you know, I'm twenty-three years old." He even tips an imaginary hat.

I laugh so hard, tears run down my face. "I really needed that, thanks." I gasp.

His smile brightens. "My pleasure. You are most entertaining."

"So, what are you studying?" He asks after a beat, breaking the silence.

"Huh? Oh, creative writing, and dance."

"Wow, could I be talking to the next big author?"

I smile a huge smile. He has no idea how much that means to me; to have someone other than my mom believe in me.

"I don't know about that." I shrug.

We chat back and forth, like we've known each other for years. Only my yawn interrupts him. "Sorry," I mutter behind my hand.

"Am I boring you, Miss Carter?" His eyes twinkle, making him look younger than his twenty-three years.

"Never. I was panicking before you started talking my ear off." I giggle, making him laugh. I marvel at how at ease I am with him; I've always been so jittery around men.

"What time is it?" I ask, letting out another yawn. Looking down at his watch, his brows shoot up, and he smirks, leaning across to show me.

"Oh my god, it's two in the morning. We've been talking

for hours." *How had so much time passed without me noticing it?*

"We'd better get some sleep, we land in four hours," he whispers, looking around at the sleeping passengers.

Just like that, I tense, remembering where I am. *How did I forget I was on a death trap?*

Confused by my reaction to him, I lay my seat back, pull out my pillow and blanket and snuggle beneath it. Closing my eyes, I puzzle through my thoughts and feelings.

"Night Lily," he whispers, but I pretend to be asleep.

I'm jolted awake by the announcement that we're about to land, the light flickers on, to let us know we need to secure our seat belts. I groan as I sit up and stretch my aching back. Looking over at Ethan, I notice he slept through the announcement. I find myself scrutinising his face; he looks young and peaceful, and even more gorgeous when asleep. I grin, giggling quietly at myself.

Maybe it's a good thing that I won't see him again, I feel a twinge of disappointment, in the pit of my stomach at the thought. Shaking my head, I chastise myself for getting swept away in fantasies. *Priorities, I need to concentrate on school.*

I squeal when a hand touches my arm. "Jeez Louise....you scared the bejeezus out of me." I gasp, clutching my chest.

Laughing huskily, he gives me a 'you can do better than that' face.

I scowl playfully, "you scared the shit out of me. Better?" I ask blushing, looking around hoping no one heard me.

"You don't cuss much, do you?" He asks, his potent eyes twinkling at me.

"Not out loud," I admit.

"We need to put our belts on, we're about to land."

Making sure my belt is as tight as it will go, I death grip the chair once again, as my breathing accelerates. I brace my head against the chair and squeeze my eyes closed, praying it's over quickly.

"Lily?" Ethan taps my arm.

Opening my eyes, I look at him questioningly. Smiling sympathetically, he holds out his hand for me to take.

"Thanks." I smile weakly, taking his hand, enjoying the tingles that travel up my arm. Squeezing my hand, he winks, smiling that half smile I've come to realise, I really like looking at. *God, the wink combined with that smile; just, wow. Stunning.*

Sighing, I turn away. I consider myself average looking, like any other girl, I guess. A little on the pale side, but I like the way I look. I love my long dark, wavy hair and green eyes. I'm tall, but with curves, how that happened I have no idea.

The plane jolts as we come into land, I squeal and squeeze Ethan's hand so hard he winces.

"Sorry," I mumble, releasing him.

When the captain finishes his departing message, we stand and gather our things. My heart races and my belly churns with unfamiliar feelings. I'm happy to finally be here, and I'm thrilled to be getting off this death trap, but I can't help feeling a little sad, to be parting ways with Ethan.

Exiting the tunnel, we walk quietly beside each other, my heart racing the whole way. I spot nan as soon as we reach the gates. She looks much like mom, I pause feeling a stab of pain through my heart, though nan's dark hair has shots of grey through it. She is short, curvy and brown eyed; and she's waving both hands in the air. *So, embarrassing.* Smiling, I give her a small wave, before turning to say goodbye to Ethan.

"Someone's happy to see you." He chuckles, nodding over my shoulder.

I roll my eyes, smiling. "I haven't seen her since I was a kid. So yeah, I'd say she's over the moon to see me." We stand there awkwardly, staring at one another.

"I better go before she thinks you're here with me. Thanks for helping me out, I hope you have a safe journey home." I say, sticking my hand out. Pushing my hand away, his thick arms envelop me in a warm hug.

"You're welcome. Good luck with school and your grandma." He chuckles into my hair just as a throat clears behind me. Sighing at myself, I let go. Ugh, I really don't want to, he smells amazing; so clean and fresh.

"Hi Nan." I say turning, my eyes anxiously flicking between her and Ethan. "Erm, this is Ethan. Ethan, this is my nan, Cora."

"It's a pleasure to meet you, Ethan. Are you?" She waves between us.

Ethan chuckles, shaking his head.

"Told you," I mutter quietly.

"No. Mrs?" He asks, thoroughly enjoying my discomfort.

"Carter," she supplies sweetly, I blink stunned. *Is she really flirting*?

"No Mrs Carter. We're friends, we met on the flight," he answers, his eyes twinkling.

"Ah, you're a Cali boy." She exclaims excitedly, as if she already knew. I bite my cheek, trying to stop myself from laughing. *That's where I get my knack for stating the obvious.*

"I should go, and let you get home and settled. Lily, it was lovely to meet you. You too, Mrs Carter. Have a safe journey home." He mocks me, his gorgeous eyes amused. Waving one last time, he hurries towards the exit.

I turn, finding her grinning at me, knowingly. "I have to get all my luggage before we head out. Did you drive?"

She smiles cheekily, "yes honey. I brought the car, let's get your things and go home." She says sweetly, walking away. Rolling my eyes, I follow silently.

Standing waiting for my bags, my mind is still on Ethan. I grab my bags when they come around, it's a wonder I don't bump into people as we leave, I'm a mess. When we emerge into the blinding sunlight, I squint and shield my eyes with my hand. It's such a contrast to England's unpredictable weather.

"Wow. It's really sunny," I say, blinking my eyes against the spots dancing in front of them.

Tittering, she nods. "Yeah, it's sunny and warm. So you won't need that sweater." She points at the jumper I'm currently stuffing in my bag. "Most people wear shorts and t-shirts here the majority of the time. Rarely ever a sweater in sight, we will have to go shopping and get you some new clothes." Her obvious excitement for clothes reminds me of mom.

"I need to call Mom." I remember, feeling guilty. Being so distracted by a bloke to recall my promise.

"Call her when we get home," she huffs, lifting a bag, "these things are heavy. Whatcha got in 'em?" She asks grunting, as she pops the boot and hoists my cases inside. Her statement pulls the rug from under me, *home.* This is home now, not London with my mom, but here in sunny San Diego.

From the passenger seat, I watch the scenery whiz past; it's beautiful here, so vibrant and sunny. My excitement grows with every mile, I can't wait to explore.

Just the view between the airport and nan's has me itching

to go for a run; to feel the burn in my thighs, my feet pounding the concrete, my heart racing. I love it. Running is my therapy, it clears my head, sorts my emotions, but it also quenches' my love of the outdoors.

Mom and I always spent a lot of time outdoors, we'd go camping about three times a year. Our love of nature compelling us. So when time, and weather permitted it, we were out enjoying life and just being together, I loved it. The time out just the two of us. No TV or computer. Just me and her talking, laughing, cooking and playing cards usually twenty-one or bingo, nothing fancy. My thoughts jumble as we whiz through numerous streets.

I wonder if mom will come here for Thanksgiving. It's not something we ever celebrated at home, but nan does. What about Christmas? I don't think I could pull off a happy Christmas without her.

I blink as the car slows and we park outside a cute house. White trimming frames the cream outside; with a wide veranda wrapping around the side of the building. A white door with inviting flowers hanging from the wall, a white fence cuts off the property from the path. The garden is amazing, with loads of different coloured flowers everywhere; it looks exactly like the picture's mom had from when she was younger.

I feel a sharp longing for my mom. "Come on then Missy. Let's get these inside and get you settled into your mom's old room." She smiles happily.

I feel brighter knowing I'll be staying in mom's old room. Grabbing two cases, I head up the path looking around, I notice the street is pretty quiet and peaceful.

On entering, I absorb my surroundings; it's all open plan. The living room is larger than I thought it would be, and a lot more modern; with a big corner sofa dominating the room, a flat screen TV on the wall and a gorgeous ornate marble coffee table. The marble fireplace is stunning, definitely a feature in the room, with matching lamps sitting on side tables on either side of the sofa. It's not what I expected, it's beautiful and airy with tiled floors as far as the eye can see.

"Wow."

She laughs at my face, "what, because I'm old I can't like modern things?" She asks sarcastically.

"No, I'm just shocked. It's bigger than I imagined. It is beautiful, really. You have great taste."

She looks around the room proudly, assessing. Nodding slightly, she heads for the stairs.

I'm mesmerized all the way up, there are so many pictures. Some of Grandad when he was a young man, then older; mom as a baby, crawling, walking, then as a child riding her bike, climbing trees and swimming in the sea. The next ones capture my attention, she is standing with a friend in their prom dresses, they look beautiful. There are a few of her dancing, I smile she really loves ballet. When we pass some of me as a baby, I pause. There are so many, there is even one I've never seen; it's of mom, nan, grandad and me. I stop and look at it.

"Where was this taken?" I ask, staring at the picture.

"That was the last picture of us all together before your Grandpa died. It was taken on our last visit to London." She says, touching the frame wistfully.

"I don't remember him; he was a handsome man," I say proudly, and she giggles.

"Don't I know it? He was a looker when he was younger; quite the ladies-man. I didn't like him at first, but he wore me down," she whispers, smiling sadly at the picture.

Sighing, she moves on, and I follow slowly, taking in the pictures. They progress all the way up, mom and I gradually getting older; all of my school pictures up until I left, are present. I take them in, one after another, open mouthed.

"They're all there; just because I stopped visiting, doesn't mean I didn't care. I missed you both every day, I just couldn't fly that distance anymore," she says quietly, looking ashamed and leads the way into my new room, my mom's old room.

It's comforting being here, the room has been redecorated for me, but still has my mom's pictures and trophies on the shelves and wall. I wander over, looking at the photos, each of a much younger version of my mom, some alone, but in a lot of them she's with another girl.

"That's Tiffany Price; she was your Mom's best friend, until she moved to London. They did everything together, as you can see," she offers, looking at the photos on the wall.

I turn back looking at the rest, she looks so happy in the ones of her dancing; she was amazing. I laugh at the ones of her cringing as Grandad waves a fish at her. Camping on the beach looking messy eating s'mores with friends. One is of her at the swimming pool, mid-air about to splash a horrified looking Tiffany.

"Hi baby, how was your flight?" Mom asks as soon as the call connects.

"Hi Mom, I'm sorry it took so long to call; the flight was long, but the bloke sitting next to me kept me talking, so it wasn't that bad. I'm in your old room at the moment, unpacking."

"I bet it's changed since I lived there." She laughs, but it sounds sad, "so you met a guy on the flight?" She asks pausing, waiting for me to confirm or deny what she's thinking, I laugh at her obvious interest because I'd never mentioned men before.

"Tell me about him." She pushes and I grin, knowing where this is going.

"His name is Ethan, he was kind and distracted me from the flight," I say leaving out the parts that we talked for hours, and he's the sexiest bloke I've ever met. I smile, remembering his gorgeous eyes.

"Lily?" She shouts into the phone making me wince, I pull it away from my ear. "Are you there?" She yells again.

"Yeah, I'm here, if not deaf now. No need to yell," I shake my head giggling.

"Well? Was he?" She prompts. Oh crap, I drifted.

"Was he what?" I ask warily.

"Was. He. Hot?" She giggles, I'm so busted, she knows I was daydreaming.

"Erm, he was good looking, I guess," I say picking at the duvet, "You know the usual; tall, light brown hair, tanned, square jaw, fit and sexiest eyes…hazel with a touch of light green." I sigh, remembering how they twinkled.

"Wow. He made quite the impression," she snickers. I shake my head, grinning. I love these moments. "So, are you seeing him again? Where's he from? How old is he?" She fires questions at me.

I smirk, my mom is such a girl, I can imagine her jumping up and down clapping her hands like a teenager.

"He's from here and I don't know where," I add quickly, "and no, I'm not seeing him again, I don't even know him. Besides, I'm here for school and to spend time with Nan."

"What were you talking about then? If you don't know him?" She inquires slyly, when I don't answer she changes the subject, *thank god.* "So, did Grandma decorate my room for you?"

"Yeah, new bed and things, but your pictures, trophies and awards are still on the walls," I tease.

She groans, "I have a shrine!" She exclaims laughing, drawing a laugh from me too, because it does look like a shrine.

"Breakfast's ready," nan yells up the stairs.

"I have to go, Mom; Nan made breakfast," I say.

"Ah, blueberry pancakes and bacon. God, I miss Mom's cooking. Okay, baby, I'll speak to you soon. I've got to get back to work anyway; I love you," she adds quietly, making my eyes burn.

"Bye, I love you too."

"Bye baby," she whispers as the line goes dead.

"Lily breakfast," nan says from the door. I look at her, tears swimming in my eyes, my phone still in hand. She comes over and sits beside me wrapping her arms around me. "You talked to Lizzy?" She asks, understanding, clouding her words. I nod crying into her shoulder.

"I miss her so much already. I've never been away from her like this before, she's my best friend."

"It's okay, honey. I know what you mean, I missed you both every day. I don't understand why she moved all the way out there when her family and friends are here, I'm just so glad you're here."

Taking a deep breath, I wipe my eyes and smile. "Come on, let's go and try your famous blueberry pancakes and bacon," I say excitedly.

She looks at me surprised, grinning. "Lizzy's been talking about my pancakes and bacon."

"Yeah, they're the best apparently; I can't wait to taste them."

"Come on then." We walk downstairs arms linked.

"Sit."

I do as I'm told and wait patiently as she prepares my plate and sets in front of me. Taking my first bite, I groan, they're so fluffy. "Oh god, these are amazing." I mumble around a mouthful of pancake.

She chuckles, "there are more if you want some? Do you want more juice?" She asks getting up.

"I can get it; you sit down and eat." I wave her off wandering over to the fridge. I love her kitchen; it's truly amazing, with granite worktops, white wooden doors. I'm in love with the huge double door fridge freezer with an ice dispenser, though it does look expensive and I've always wanted to cook on a range cooker.

"So, what are you doing today?" Nan asks, pulling me from my kitchen envy as I sit back down and take my last bite. Standing, she picks up our plates and heads to the sink.

"I'll wash up," I say getting up, she refuses with a shake of her head and a wave of her hand.

"You cooked, please?" I ask again, feeling uncomfortable being waited on.

Holding up her hands in surrender she backs away and leans on the counter instead of sitting back down. "Okay, you win." She smiles, "so?" She prompts.

"Well, I think I'm going to go for a run, then shower and hang out with you?" I ask, and she nods agreeing readily.

"Is there a park or somewhere I can go for a run?" I ask.

"Yes, Balboa Park isn't far from here."

"Thanks, I shouldn't be more than a couple of hours. I'll have my phone with me if you need anything," I say heading for my room to change.

CHAPTER TWO

It feels good to be outside, the sun kissing my skin. It's really hot, but on the plus side, being in America does have the advantage of giving me a free suntan like mom said. As I run, I take in the familiar noises around me; my breathing, the cars, neighbours chatting and kids laughing. It all melds together relaxing me.

As I go through the gates of Balboa Park the noise level goes up and I stop, taking in the view before me. It's amazingly beautiful; gardens, flowers and ponds as far as the eye can see. From what I've read there are museums, attractions, restaurants and undoubtedly a lot more here. When I think of the word park, I envision grass, playgrounds, kids playing, dogs barking and people picnicking. Not ornate gardens and ponds. I have to admit though, the results are fantastic. Mother nature at her best, *serenity*, I sigh happily.

Dazed by the beauty surrounding me, I'm shocked when I run into a wall of hard muscle and fall flat on my arse.

"I am so sorry," I mutter getting up, I dust off my sore arse giggling to myself. "I wasn't watching where I was going, too caught up in the abundance of nature." I say, looking up at the bloke I just barrelled into.

Holy shit-balls. What is it with men here? Are they all built like brick shit-houses? Mr, Tall, tanned and toned smiles, he's gorgeous with dark, wavy brown hair. Just long enough for it to fall across his brow into startling green eyes.

"It's fine, are you okay? You landed pretty hard there," he asks, worry colouring his tone.

"I'm fine, really. You just gave me a sore arse," I blurt, without thinking, and gasp realising how bad that sounded, I slap my hand over my mouth. *Oh, my god, I did not just say that.*

He cocks an eyebrow as laughter bursts from his chest. I join in because it's one of those moments, when you either laugh or cry and laughing is better than crying. Right?

"Man, you should have seen your face, I've never seen a look of such horror," he wheezes trying to catch his breath.

I raise my brows, "I'm glad I can amuse you with my sore arse and potty mouth," I say boldly.

He smirks at me, "well, can I get your name? Or do I just call you potty mouth?" His eyes twinkling.

I stick out my hand, "Lily will do, thanks."

Smirking, he shakes my hand, "pleasure to meet you, Lily. I'm Mason, and you are definitely British. So, proper and so polite," he says causing my cheeks to heat.

"You too, and that's the second time today I've been told that," I muse smirking.

He laughs, "which part? That I'm Mason, that you're very British, or that you're proper and polite?" He smirks, utterly entertained.

"That'd be the latter. I'm not sure if it's a compliment or a slight on my character," I sigh, looking wounded.

He laughs again, "so glad I came for this run now," he

pants, wiping his face on his shirt. Giving me a glimpse of some cut abs. *Shit me, do all men look like this or is it just the men from San Diego?* I shake myself, startled by my thoughts. I never even noticed men at home, and now suddenly, I'm noticing their arses and abs? I need to leave.

"It was lovely running into you and chatting, but I've got to get back home," I mumble unnerved by my thoughts.

"Yeah, me too. My brothers are waiting further up the trail. Maybe we'll bump into each other again sometime?" He asks, bouncing on the spot.

"Erm, not literally next time though," I giggle.

Shaking his head, he chuckles. "I don't know; it was rather fun…" He smirks, looking thoroughly pleased as I flush again, damn it!

"Not fun for my arse, or my ego." I fire back, making him laugh.

He jogs backwards waving. "See you around, Lily," he shouts, sprinting off.

What a way to kick start my new life. Meeting two of the most, sexiest men I've ever met in one day. I grin as I make my way home.

When I get home I'm still grinning from my encounter with Mason. I find nan in the kitchen rubbing some sort of spice mix into the chicken in front of her.

I take a deep breath, drawing in the sweet scent of garlic and onions. "That smells amazing," I sigh appreciatively.

She grins at me over her shoulder. "My own recipe, we'll be having it with brown rice and baked potatoes, is that okay?"

"Sounds great. I'm going to take a quick shower, then I can help," I smile grabbing water from the fridge.

She beams at me. "It's wonderful having you here, honey.

I've missed so much of your life already," she says softly, sniffling.

On instinct, I go and wrap my arms around her, causing her to freeze momentarily, shocked, then she bear hugs me, and for a short lady, she's got some strength.

"It's okay, you couldn't come over and I don't blame you," I say realising my feelings toward her have changed since she told me why she could come over anymore. "Flying frightened the hell out of me. Plus, we have time together now, so don't worry," I say brightly, backing up.

She wipes her eyes. "Yes, you're right. I'm okay, you go shower, I'm just happy you're here," she says cheerfully, shooing me out the kitchen.

I bound down the stairs, fresh from the shower. Hearing voices coming from the living room, I head out that way.

"Here she is. Lily, meet Tiffany and Millie."

I freeze and blurt. "You were Mom's best friend, from the pictures, upstairs." I blush, cursing my mouth for running ahead again.

Snorting, she turns to nan. "You've still got those old photo's up?"

I watch her as she talks, she looks the same as she did back then; short, long blonde hair, tanned as is standard here apparently. She seems toned, so athletic. Her blue eyes sparkle with mirth as she talks. The few wrinkles around her eyes and mouth tell me she laughs a lot.

As I'm scrutinising Tiffany, I realise I'm also being scrutinised by Millie. She smiles shyly at me; she's a mini version of her mom, minus the wrinkles and with the addition of glasses.

"Hi, I'm Millie," she says stepping forward. "It's great to finally meet you, we've heard a lot about you over the years," she says quietly, she's the total opposite of her mom. She's quiet and unsure, while Tiffany is loud and confident.

"Hi, I'm Lily. Obviously, you already know that though." I chuckle, and she smiles, relaxing a little.

"Lily, why don't you go and show Millie the photos of Lizzy and Tiff while we check on lunch?" Nan urges.

I roll my eyes, I'm way too old for a playdate. Still, I do as I'm asked.

"Come on, let's let the adults natter," I nudge her playfully, giggling she follows.

"I like the way you speak." Her voice is so sweet, almost like a child's.

"Thanks, it's the way I was born," I joke, and she laughs this time.

"You're a lot like how my mom described your mom; funny, quick witted and smart," she says softly as we enter my room.

I point towards the pictures, walking over she scans them quietly. This is so different from my encounter with Mason, he was open and fun, our conversation just flowed, but here with Millie our conversations feel strained. I like her and she's probably really nice, maybe she just needs time to get to know me. It's strange, we're so alike and so different all at once.

"You know, I was never like this back home; I feel different here." I shrug, not sure what changed, but I'm realising I am a different person here.

"You're different from your mother," I say carefully.

"Yeah, I'm nothing like my mom. I'm quiet, plain, dull and nerdy," she laughs humourlessly.

I'm shocked; she's a beautiful girl and she thinks she's plain?

"That's not what I meant. Yes, you are quiet and shy but so was I. People used to say I was dull and a nerd because I liked to read and hang out with my mom," I shrug. "I'm hoping we can be friends though since the only person I know here is my nan." I pull a face making her giggle.

"I'd like that too." She smiles and looks back at the pictures.

"So, where are you going to school?" I ask trying to make her more at ease with me.

"The University of San Diego. What about you?" She asks, sitting on my bed.

"Same, I'm studying dance and creative writing. I want to be a writer." I smile nervously. "What are you studying?" I ask.

"I'm studying art, and creative writing too," she says excitedly, beaming at me.

The more she comes out of her shell the more I like her. We talk for a while before the smell of food brings us back downstairs.

"Hey Nan, are Tiffany and Millie staying for dinner?" I ask hopefully, I'm enjoying having someone my own age around.

"Yes honey, Tiff and I were just saying how it would be lovely if you two stuck together. You don't know anyone here yet and Millie usually keeps to herself."

Millie and I look at each other and burst out laughing.

"What are the two of you laughing about?" She asks with mock sternness.

"Nan, people don't 'stick together' anymore. They hang out or chill," I gasp, bending over to catch my breath. Millie is still giggling behind her hand, trying to hide it.

“Well, whatevs. You two should totally chill together,” she says, giving some real attitude for an older lady.

Millie's given up on hiding her laughter, she’s shaking as tears run down her face. Tiffany and I aren’t in any better shape, Tiffany’s got her head in her arms on the table; laughing so hard she’s snorting. I lean against the wall, holding my sides laughing so hard they ache. Nan just sits there with an innocent look on her face, as if to say, *what did I say that was so funny?*

“I should’ve moved here ages ago; I’ve laughed more since being here than I have in ages...and now…I know where Mom gets her attitude from.” Her smile is the brightest I’ve seen and her eyes shining with happiness.

Dinner is loud and filled with lots of laughter, nan and Tiffany talk constantly telling stories and by the time they leave I’m exhausted and aching.

“Well, I’m going to bed, I’ll see you in the morning honey,” nan says yawning.

Nodding, I stretch. “Yeah, me too. Goodnight,” I say kissing her cheek before heading to bed.

My phone wakes me the next morning, searching blindly I knock it to the floor in the process. “Ugh,” I groan, leaning over the side, I grab for it and fall out of bed flat on my face. “Ouch, h-hello?” I say annoyed, rubbing my head.

“Hi Lily, did I wake you?” A soft girlish voice comes through the phone, confusing me.

“Who?" I cut myself off as my brain kicks in. "Oh, hi Millie, sorry yeah. What time is it?” I climb back onto the bed wanting to go back to sleep.

"Um, it's eleven-forty-five. I'm so sorry, I'll let you go back to sleep, you're most likely jet lagged."

"No, it's okay. Honestly, I have to get up anyway. I didn't think it was that late. I need to go for a run," I yawn, rubbing my burning eyes. "So, what's up?" I ask stretching.

"I wanted to ask if you want to go shopping with me, Cora mentioned you needed Cali clothes," she giggles.

"Yeah, Cali clothes are needed, I actually need a bunch of stuff. Could we go after I've been for my run though?" I ask feeling my adrenaline kick in at the thought of a run.

She snickers, "yeah, you have way too many sweaters and boots," she teases making me laugh.

"Okay, I get it, I need summer clothes, but in my defence it's mostly cold and rainy in England."

After a quick shower, I bounce happily downstairs. Grabbing a granola bar and water from the fridge, I spot a note clipped to the fridge.

Lily,

Gone food shopping, didn't want to wake you, be back soon.

P.s Millie called about going clothes shopping. I've had money put into your account.

See you later.

Love Grandma.

Xxx

I gape at the note, she's put money in my bank account. Shaking my head, I grab my things as there's not much I can do now, it's done.

My thoughts drain away as I open the door and head out into the sun. Ah, a hot, sunny Saturday. The streets are filled with people today, and Balboa Park isn't much different. The only problem is, it's so bloody hot it saps all my energy and I have to take a break halfway through the trail. I sit under a massive tree and close my eyes, leaning back against the trunk. *It's a vast contrast to running in England. I do miss the milder weather. The heat is going to take some getting used to. Running in it is brutal.*

My brain turns to everything I need to do when I get back. *I need to message, mom and finish unpacking.*

"Well, well, well. If it isn't potty mouth." A voice breaks my thoughts.

I screech, heart in mouth. "Oh, you scared the crap out of me. You shouldn't sneak up on people like that, you could give someone a heart attack!"

"It's not my fault you were off in your own world. I wasn't exactly quiet on approach and I called your name twice," he laughs.

I cringe, "sorry, just thinking about my mom and how different it is to run here compared to England."

Sitting beside me, resting his arms on his bent knees, he swings his water to and fro. Looking at me from the corner of his eye. "And how does it compare? The weather I mean," he clarifies smirking.

"Well, it's definitely hotter here. Saps my energy faster, but at-least it's not raining. Suppose I'll get used to the heat," I concede grinning at him.

"Ah, the inner workings of potty mouths mind," he smirks.

"You'd better not say that in front of anyone else," I warn, looking around, I'm only half-joking.

"So, I know your name, that you're easily scared, you zone out a lot, you're a runner and you have a potty mouth. What else should I know?" He smiles cheekily.

I smirk, "oh, is it show and tell time?" I clap my hands squealing.

"Well, I'm Lily, as you know." I nudge him playfully and bat my eyes. "I'm eighteen and I moved here from England to go to college. I live with my nan, while mom is back in England working to pay for me to attend university in sunny San Diego. When I grow up, I want to be a writer and I love to dance," I say bouncing up and down, flicking my hair and doing my best flirty act.

"Oh God my sides," he groans, his arms holding his belly. "I asked for that, didn't I?" He asks and I nod smirking. "You should come with a warning, you know. *Lethal. Will, disarm with laughter*." He grins proudly, pleased with his joke.

I smirk. "Thanks, I think?"

"Don't worry, it was a compliment. I've never met a girl who outwitted me, or one that makes me laugh so hard." He taps my knee.

"So, your turn. Tell me all about Mason," I challenge.

"Okay, but there's not much to tell. I'm also eighteen, I live with my mom and dad. I have a younger sister, and older twin brothers. I'm also starting school at San Diego, I'm studying business and art, I play guitar and I can dance, but I don't often," he adds proudly. *Wow, he looks older than eighteen.*

"You're attending San Diego too?"

"Small world, huh? Good to know I'll be seeing you again, away from the running trails, that is." Thank God, I'll have two people I know.

I check the time. "Oops, I've got to get back. I have to go Cali up my wardrobe."

He snickers, "what? You don't wear an abundance of shorts, skirts and bikinis in England?"

"Well, no. I'd freeze my niblets off. It's been fun, I'll see you around." I dust off my arse, heading towards the trail again.

"Hey, since we're friends or whatever now, do you want to swap numbers? So, if I need a laugh you can text me?" He asks.

I hesitate, flabbergasted. "Yeah, okay."

I get home to find Millie already there, talking to nan in the kitchen; they turn as I close the door. "I'm sorry, I'll be ready in a few minutes, promise." I rush upstairs, taking two at a time.

I show the shower my arse, and change quickly into stone washed, ripped skinny jeans, I throw on a black strappy top, under a light blue shirt and shove my feet into my favourite pair of black flats. I vigorously brush my hair, pulling it up into a high ponytail and slap on a thin layer of foundation finishing up with a coat of mascara. Shoving my phone and purse in my bag, I'm ready to go. I'm in such a rush I nearly face plant the wall as I skid into the kitchen.

"Ready," I announce breathlessly. "Millie and I are going shopping, I'll see you later," I say kissing Nan on the cheek.

"Well, don't you look beautiful? Go on, have fun, and don't worry about money. There's enough in your bank account."

"About that, are you sure?" I ask carefully, not wanting to hurt her feelings.

"You're my granddaughter. It's my job and privilege to spoil you. Now, go have fun," she nudges us toward the door.

"Okay, okay, we're going. Bye."

Millie drags me around every clothing store they have at the shopping centre. It's exhausting and I hate the crowds, I do enjoy the food court though. With two big slices of pizza each, we snag a table that is just being vacated, the only available table in here and sit down, I sigh gratefully. We chat as we eat, I tell her all about my run-ins with Mason, even the one where I fall on my butt and make a fool out of myself, which of course, she finds hilarious. We also make plans for the next few days, I'm so excited to have made friends so easily. I even suggest asking Mason to hang out with us. When we're done eating, we spend another hour shopping.

"Okay, I'm done," I groan, weighed down with bags. I have tops, sandals, shorts, skirts, a bikini and matching wrap. High factor suntan lotion and sunglasses.

"Do you need a hand?" She asks giggling at my red face.

"Yes, please," I huff, rolling my eyes and happily hand over some of the bags as we make our way to the carpark.

Millie pulls onto my drive and I drag my bags out of the backseat, groaning as my arms protest. I drop them as soon as I'm inside the door making Millie laugh.

"Do you want some juice?" I ask, already heading for the fridge.

"Yes, please."

When the cold air from the fridge hits my face, I moan, wanting to stick my head inside.

"It's a bit warm today, huh?" Millie laughs as I run an ice-cold bottle of water across my forehead.

"I'm burning up here. Now I remember why I prefer colder climates."

"You'll adjust, in a few months."

I groan. “Really? Months? I hope there aren’t too many days like today.” I take a few sips of my water, enjoying the cold liquid sliding down my parched throat. “Do you want to stay a while and watch a movie?”

She agrees, and we start discussing our favourite movies, evidently, we both have eclectic tastes in movies and music. We laugh, talk and watch movies in between. Today has been so much fun I’m surprised when nan gets home.

“Hi girls, did you have a good day?”

I collect the popcorn bowl and glasses off the table, cleaning up a little. “Yeah, I got some new clothes, and we watched some movies. Do you want some coffee?” I ask, seeing that she looks tired.

“No honey, I’m going to take a nap then I’ll make dinner. Are you staying, Millie?”

“No, I need to get home, but thank you. I didn’t realise it was so late.”

“Okay, I’ll see you out. Nan, I can order in if you like? Saves you cooking, you look tired.”

Agreeing, she heads to her room. Millie stops when we get to the door.

“Okay, so I’ll pick you up for the beach tomorrow. Are you going to ask Mason?”

“Yeah, I’ll call him.”

“Are you sure it looks okay?” I ask pulling at my bikini top wishing I’d worn my old one.

“You look great. Stop pulling at it or you’ll fall out.”

I gasp clutching my boobs making her laugh and I smile.

“Where did Mason say he was meeting us, again?” She asks as we grab our towels.

"There he is," I point at the tall hunk of a bloke, giggling as Millie's mouth drops open. I pinch her side breaking her trance before drool hits her chin.

"Hey," she squeals.

"You were about to drool."

"I was not!"

"Sure, you weren't."

The beach is packed with young girls showing off their tanned bodies and blokes of all ages ogling them. I feel self-conscious in my two-piece, normally I'd wear a tankini and shorts but since I'm trying not to look like a vampire, I went with showing more skin.

"Come on you two, let's see those bods." Mason jokes as we near him trying to wrestle my towel away from me.

"No, I think I'll sit for a while and read."

"Lily, you're on a beach, there are other girls showing *way* more than you. Come on, how can you swim with that thing clutched to your chest?"

I sigh, looking around seeing that he's right, I'm just drawing more attention to myself by acting like an idiot. I'm spun around as Mason takes advantage of my distraction and whips the towel off me.

"Ta-da," he yells, and literally everyone stares, some even clap. I turn bright red and swipe his legs from under him. *Tosser,* I laugh.

CHAPTER THREE

From birth through childhood, the world is magical and new.
From bugs, to trees, and rain, to snow.
The world is colourful, sparkling and bright.
Adventure is found around every corner, waiting to begin anew.
Friendships blossom and bonds are made. True friendship is born, lying quietly unbroken.
With the years that pass and the battles we fight, the magic begins to fade, but let it be known that through life's struggles, heartache and pain come wisdom, strength and gain.
Keep fighting through the stormy times, for your friendships still remain.

Growling, I push the pen and paper away, frustrated. *It's stupid, if can't even write a short poem, how the hell I going to be a writer?*

Pushing back from my desk I head for the shower. It's

already nine-thirty, today I have to go and get my driving license. I'm a nervous wreck, but Mace assures me it's easy. So, if I fail, I'll never hear the end of it.

The whole drive to DMV is nerve wracking. *Please don't let me crash or throw up on the instructor.*

"Are you okay, you look a little bit green," Mason laughs from his seat as I try to get a hold on my nerves.

"I'm fine. Can you stop laughing?" I huff, making him laugh harder. Smiling shakily, I get out of the car. If this were the other way around and Mace was crapping himself, I'd be laughing, so I cut him some slack.

When my name is called, I squeeze Mace's hand and follow the balding, grumpy man. It doesn't take long but I'm sweating bullets and hoping I don't mess up.

When I pull the car to a stop where we started, I breathe a sigh of relief. The instructor gets out, hands me a piece of paper and walks off without a word.

"Well, that wasn't as bad as I was imagining." I sigh, taking the seat next to Mace, smiling now that I'm away from the instructor. I see the big fat PASS on the front and squeal doing a dance on my seat making Mace laugh.

"Told ya, you almost did as good as me. It's understandable, I am the best."

Laughing, I smack him in the arm. "You are not the best, I just let you think that."

"You keep telling yourself that, but I'm awesome," he says, throwing an arm over my shoulders, smirking and pulling me toward his car.

Life is amazing. I love spending time with my nan and getting to know her. We're a lot alike in some ways, being around her has brought me out of myself a little. San Diego is so beautiful, and I love it here. Every little thing amazes me as Mace and Millie shows me around their favourite places to eat and hang out. It's nice having a close friend's my own age to spend time with until school starts in September.

School starts tomorrow, and I've never been so nervous in all my life. The silver lining is, I have my two best friends with me. My phone buzzes and I smile, it's Millie.

Millie: *What are you wearing tomorrow?*

I grin at my phone, that's so Millie. She's gorgeous, a great person, and an amazing friend, but she thinks so little of herself. I'm glad to have her and Mace as my best friends. Shaking my head, I type back.

Me: *Don't know yet. Might go for skinny jeans, top 'n' light jacket.*

I busy myself picking my clothes and hanging them ready for the morning. I double check my bag, then jump in the shower, remembering to keep my hair dry because it's so long it nearly touches my butt. As I get out the shower and wrap myself in a fluffy towel, nan walks into my room looking around for me.

"In here, Nan," I say, emerging from a cloud of steam.

"Oh, there you are, honey. Do you have everything ready for tomorrow?" She asks, sitting on the bed.

"Yep, all set. I'm a little nervous though. So is Millie, she texted asking what I'm wearing tomorrow," I say laughing at the ridiculousness of it.

"I don't think she realises how beautiful she is, honey," she replies, sighing.

"Well, she should with the way Mason moons over her," I mutter, shaking my head.

"I wish he'd just tell her already; I know she likes him too, it's so obvious," I sigh frustrated with them both.

"Anyway, I just came to ask if you were catching a ride with Mason or Millie?" She inquires.

"I don't know, let me check," I reply, grabbing my phone. She wanders off knowing this could take a while, I smile at how much we've learnt about one another and how close we've become.

Me to Mason: *Are we still riding to school together tomorrow?*

I know it's probably pointless asking because, he said a couple of weeks ago, we'd ride together.

Mason: *Thought we'd sorted this? Does Millie need a ride too?*

Smirking, I roll my eyes at his hint.

Me: *Want me to ask?*

Mason: *If you want.*

This is so annoying. I think it's time to give them a kick up the arse.

Me to Millie: *Do you want to ride to school with me 'n' Mace tomorrow?*

Millie: *Yes, please.*

Me to Mason: *She said yeah.*

Mason: *Okay, I'll be there.*

Me: *Okay, thanks. See you tomorrow.*

Me to Millie: *You do realise he fancies you, right?*

Millie: *Why would Mason fancy me? I'm so not his type.*

Me: *Yes, you are!*

Millie: *Okay, whatever. Speak to you tomorrow. Need sleep. Night. :)*

Me: *This conversation isn't over! Speak tomorrow. Night. :p*

"Hey, how was your first day of American schooling?" Mace asks, leaning against his car.

"Well, it was as exciting as getting up in front of the whole class at the age of five, to introduce yourself and peeing your pants."

"You really peed yourself?" He laughs, his eyes comically wide.

I shake my head laughing. "Can't wait to see what's in store for us tomorrow," he says rubbing his hands together.

"Yeah, me neither. Have you seen Millie?" I wonder, looking around.

"She had her mom pick her up. So, we can just go," he mumbles turning away, but not before I see the hurt in his eyes. Sliding into his truck, I grab my phone.

Me: *Hey, why'd you ask your mom to pick you up?*

Millie: *It was weird riding to school with Mason.*

Me: *Think you hurt his feelings, he's quiet.*

Millie: *I didn't want to hurt him, I just don't know what to do, I like him a lot. What would you do?*

Me: *Take a chance. You may regret it if you don't & he finds someone else.*

Millie: *Maybe, I don't know. I need to think; you honestly think he likes me?*

Me: *Yes, he does. Want me to speak to him about it?*

Millie: *No! I don't know, maybe? What if he doesn't like me that way?*

Me: *No chance of that. Speak later.*

Stowing my phone, I think of the best way to broach the subject.

"Mace?" I say tentatively.

"Lils..."

"Do you like Millie?"

"Yeah, she's nice and a good friend. Why?" He asks, fidgeting nervously.

Huffing, I turn to look at him fully. "No. I mean, do you fancy her?" He freezes, looking like a deer caught in headlights.

"Look at your face. Are you blushing?" I snort rolling in my seat.

"You caught me off guard, that's all," he snaps.

"Hey, you don't have to tell me shit. You should know though, you're both idiots," I snap back, pissed at him for snapping at me.

He smiles weakly rubbing the back of his neck, embarrassed by his outburst.

"Sorry," he says, nudging my leg.

"So, do you?" I grin and he laughs, knowing I'm not going to give up until he tells me.

"Okay, okay." I raise my eyebrow, waiting.

He grins at me. "Yes, I like her, she's nice and cute, but it's complicated. My dad, he has plans. He wants me to date his co-worker's daughter. And since I'll be running his business someday…apparently, it's good connections," he says sarcastically. "Don't get me wrong, I love my dad and I love the business. I just want to choose who I date," he murmurs dejected.

"Well, that's bollocks. Why are you even putting up with it?"

He stays quiet, staring at the road.

"Come on, you know you can talk to me," I push gently.

Pulling over by the beach, he cuts the engine. "You want to walk?" He nods toward the beach.

I nod, shocked, he looks so worn. Normally he's all jokes,

quick witted, outgoing and happy. We walk along the shore silently for a while before he starts talking.

"My dad used to be easy going. He didn't have control issues, but as the business grew, he became a workaholic. Everything became about the business and where it was going, hence the connections," he sighs appalled.

"Why are you going along with this bollocks Mace?" His silence infuriates me and spurs me on. "He's your dad, not your keeper. Isn't he supposed to want the best for you? I mean, what the fuck. Using you as a pawn in his little game." My voice raises in outrage, and people start to stare at us, but I don't care. "And what about Millie? She genuinely likes you," I hiss, furious at his dad.

I turn, finding him staring at me with his mouth hanging open. I'm so angry, I don't care if I'm acting like a nutso. He's my best friend. He doesn't deserve to be treated like this.

"Wow. Your kind of hot when you're pissed," he teases, watching me pace. His lighter mood soothes my ruffled feathers.

I laugh, rolling my eyes, "Don't be disgusting," I shove him. "I'm pissed off because you're my best friend. Your dad has no right to do that. He should be supporting you whatever choice you make, not trying to lump you with some fake breasted bimbo," I rant, my face hot with anger.

"I know, but he's my dad. He pays for school; my car and I still live at home." He kicks the sand, frustrated. "I don't know what changed him, maybe things will turn out okay," he murmurs hopelessly.

"Uh-uh, no. He's not doing this to you. He can't. It's not fair." I go to kick a bottle lying in the sand, miss and fall on my arse.

He drops down beside me laughing, I rest my head on his shoulder and sigh, I hate feeling useless.

"What about your mom? What does she say about all this? What about your brothers? Can't one of them take your place? They're older, aren't they?"

Throwing an arm around me, he sighs. "No. My brothers can't take my place; Dad won't allow it, he loves them, but they aren't his sons. I'm his only son," he says quietly.

"I thought...I mean, I assumed. When you said they were your brothers?" I stumble over my words kicking myself for assuming.

"It's okay, I let you think that. I don't distinguish between full or half-brothers and most of the time dad doesn't either, but he wants the business kept within the family name," his tone bitter, I laugh as something occurs to me.

"I'm glad you find that funny," he snaps annoyed.

"No, wait, I just realised, I don't even know your last name," I snort, laughing again. We both laugh so loud people are staring at us again, moving away.

"My name is Mason Lee Scott," he informs me as we head back to the car. "Thanks, for letting me bitch," he whispers affectionately, ruffling my hair.

"Hey, watch the hair dude!" I laugh shoving him, he falls on his arse making me laugh so hard, I don't see him making a swipe for my legs, until I hit the sand laughing.

Getting home, I hang up my bag still pissed at Mason's dad. I hate him and I don't even know him, how could a father not want his son happy?

"Hi honey, good first day?" Nan asks cheerfully, smiling at me.

"Yeah, introductions and meeting teachers, all exciting stuff," I say sarcastically.

"What were you expecting? To jump straight in at the deep end?"

"I know, you're right. It's just that the start-up stuff is so boring. Why can't we just jump straight in?"

"As is the way of life, you have to start with the boring stuff and work your way up to the exciting stuff," she says amused by my disgruntled expression.

Trying to shake my mood, I help nan prepare tea, I watch as she explains how she does things. It has to be done a certain way, just like her grandma taught her. After tea, I go upstairs to read the email I know is waiting from mom.

Hi baby,

Just checking in.

How was your first day at school? Anything new to report?

How's Mom? Are you two getting along okay? I'm dying to know, are Mason and Millie together yet? Or are they still denying they fancy each other.

Anyway, write back when you have time. I haven't called because I'm still a bit under the weather and I have a sore throat. So, I can't talk too well.

Love you loads. Miss you.

Love Mom.

Xxx

I feel an ache in my chest every time I speak, text or email her; I miss her so much. My concern grows as I reread her email. She's still ill? Thinking about it, I realise she hasn't called me since the first week I was here.

"Nan, have you spoken to Mom on the phone recently?" I yell, jogging down the stairs.

Popping her head out of the laundry room. "We haven't spoken on the phone in a while, we've emailed though, why?"

Now I'm worried. "She just emailed me asking questions as usual, but she said she's still ill. She said she hasn't called because her throat's sore." I feel anxiety start to attack me and my breathing accelerates.

"Hey, what's got you in a tizzy?" She asks, sitting me on the stairs.

"I'm worried, she's ill and she's been avoiding my calls and just acting weird. Not just since I got here, but for a while now, she looked so tired before I left," I mutter, frustrated I didn't push harder when I noticed how poorly she looked before I left.

"Why don't we try calling her? I'm sure she's fine, perhaps she caught a bug and it's taking its time shifting," she assures rubbing my arm. Taking a breath, I nod and give her a shaky smile.

"Yeah, oh, wait. What time is it?" I look at the clock, "we can't call now, it's already two in the morning there," I sigh disappointed.

"Listen. Why don't you go for a run? Clear your head, by the time you're back you'll be tired and ready for bed. We'll call first thing, okay?" She smiles hopefully.

"Okay."

I wake covered in sweat and tears, my nightmare haunting me. Fighting my way out of twisted sheets, I sit on the side of my bed trying to wipe the image of mom's prone figure from my memory, I mentally shake myself and head for the bathroom needing a shower. My muscles immediately relax as hot water cascades down my back.

"It rang off again," I growl frustrated. "Why the feckin' hell isn't she answering her damn phone?"

"Lily. Language!" Nan scolds softly.

"Sorry, but why won't she answer her phone? I've called constantly for two bloody hours," I cry, throwing my phone on the sofa, pacing the living room.

"Maybe you could call her work? She may be in a meeting," she offers encouragingly.

"Yes. Thanks, Nan. Here it is." I smile triumphantly finding her work number and press call.

"Into U Designs, Natasha speaking. How can I help you?" Asks a cheerful voice.

"Erm, hi, Natasha. It's Lily, Elizabeth's daughter."

"Oh hi, Lily. What can I do for you?" She asks eagerly.

"Is my mom there, please?" I ask, biting my cheek.

"No, she's not here. Maybe you should speak with Diane. Hold for a moment, please."

"I'm on hold waiting to talk to her boss, she's not there apparently," I repeat to nan as she gives me a funny look.

"Hello Lily, Natasha said you were looking for your mom?"

"Hi, yeah. I can't get her on her phone. So, we thought she might be in a meeting."

"We? Oh, you're off in America with your nan, aren't you? Elizabeth is extremely proud of you."

"Thanks. Do you know where she is?" I ask again trying to hide my irritation, I know she is just being nice, but my patients have worn thin.

"No sorry, honey. She's not been in to work for over a week. She did call to say she was ill and wouldn't be in and we haven't heard from her since," she informs me.

Now, I'm starting to panic. I look at nan wide eyed, as my stomach churns anxiously.

"Erm okay, thank you, Diane. Bye," I mumble, laying my phone down on the arm of the sofa, my mind spinning with possibilities.

"Lily, what is it?" Nan asks urgently, clasping my hands.

"She's not there, she hasn't been in, in over a week. She called to tell them she wouldn't be in and they haven't heard from her since."

"That doesn't sound like Lizzy. She went to school even when she had the flu, she doesn't phone in sick for anything," she whispers worry filling her eyes.

"Yeah, that's what I was thinking too. She loves her job, she doesn't take time off, apart from if I needed her. She couldn't even get the time off to settle me here."

"What are we going to do Nan? It's not like I can check on her or send someone else to. We pretty much kept to ourselves, there's only her workmates." Tears prick my eyes as worry and anxiety swell inside me.

"What if the flu has turned into something serious? She has no one there, I should have stayed with her, I knew she looked off." I growl frustrated.

I try her phone again and get her voicemail. Hours pass with us sitting anxiously, me calling her near constantly, I must have called her a hundred times and still nothing.

Two days! *Two.* I have called, emailed and texted, nothing. I don't know what to do, there's no one to call. We are not eating or sleeping properly; I have been dodging Mason and Millie feigning illness.

I know they are worried and it's wrong, but all I can think about right now is finding her. What if she was in an accident? Or the flu turned into pneumonia? My thoughts and dreams plague me, my mind torturing me with numerous scenarios.

"Morning honey, did you sleep?" Nan's voice breaks through my thoughts as I walk into the kitchen.

Day three and she looks exhausted, her face pale, bags under her eyes and dark circles.

"Not really, did you?" Shaking her head, she nods to the pot of tea waiting for me.

I watch, detached as my hands prepare a cup and my legs carry me to sit across from nan. It's weird I'm there, but not. It's like I'm an observer. My phone rings, I get up slowly knowing it's Mace making his daily check-in.

"Hello?"

"Hello. Is this Miss, Carter?" A tired sounding man asks.

"Yes," I say and straighten, setting my cup down.

"This is Dr, Williams, I'm an Oncologist from St Thomas' Hospital. I'm calling regarding your Mother. Elizabeth Carter," he pauses, "She's here at the hospital, I'm sorry, she's incredibly ill," his tone is professional.

I feel like I've been kicked, I can't breathe. I'm shaking so hard I almost drop my phone. Nan looks at me panicked.

Licking my dry lips, I stand pacing. "What's wrong? She said she had the flu?"

"I'm sorry, but she doesn't have the flu. She has late-stage cancer, there isn't much we can do for her, other than make her comfortable in her last days," he says sadly. I stand in stunned silence, looking at my nan who looks baffled.

Then it hits me, my mom is dying. I let out a pained wail before collapsing, my body shakes as every painful word he just said hits me; tears stream down my face, I can't hear anything but those words repeating in my head. *I'm sorry. She doesn't have the flu. She has late-stage cancer. There isn't much we can do for her, other than make her comfortable in her last days....*

Wait, last days? What the fuck, how long has she been ill? I hear nan talking on my phone.

Shaking violently, I curl into a ball. "NO, no, no." I don't believe it, I can't. Ending the call nan cries softly, watching me, tortured by my anguished cries.

"Nan, s-she s-sent me h-here-so, I wouldn't see her d-die," I hiccup trying to see through my tears. Lying beside me, she pulls me into her arms, and we sob together.

"Ssh, honey, it'll be okay. We'll have to wait and talk to her; I can't believe she never told us."

"What are we going to do?" I ask wiping my nose on my sleeve, my heart aching.

"I don't know, Lizzy told the doctor she doesn't want us over there." She looks uncertain.

"*What?*" I explode jumping up, she flinches. "What do you mean? She said that?"

Nodding, she looks away. As anger explodes through me. How could she not want me there? Why would she want a bunch of strangers looking after her and not her own daughter? I storm into the living room trying to dispense my irrational anger. Nan follows sitting on the sofa, blinking back her own tears.

"He said…she," she chokes covering her face, the sight

hits my heart hard. This is not the strong and sassy woman I've come to know, is broken right now.

"Nan?" I whisper, crouching in front of her, removing her hands.

She looks at me. "He said she doesn't have much time left," she hiccups.

We cry together, holding each other heartbroken. I'm cold and in physical pain, time crawls as everything but our pain ceases to exist. Seconds turn into minutes, minutes to hours. I don't know how long we've sat here frozen, stricken by the reality of losing her and neither of us seeing her again. I blink, hearing the constant ding-dong of the doorbell.

She doesn't even twitch. "I've got it," I say, my voice hoarse.

Yanking the door open, I see the three concerned faces of Millie, Mason and Tiffany. Their faces change from concerned to alarmed on seeing me.

Mason rushes to me. "Lily, what's wrong? We've been calling you and Cora for hours," he blurts, rubbing my arms, panic tightening his features as I stare at him blankly.

"Lily, where's Cora?" Tiffany asks, gently touching my arm. I look down at her hand on my arm, turn and head back in. She's still where I left her curled up crying, my heart squeezes at the sight of her. Walking over, I kneel in front of her, her face is red, swollen, blotchy and wet. My eyes well up, clearing my throat, I touch her cold hand.

"Nan, Tiff, Millie and Mace are here." Sniffing, she wipes her eyes looking at them. She looks so vulnerable.

"Hi," she whispers softly, her eyes shattered; I feel helpless because there's nothing I can do to take away her pain.

Now, I have to find the words, to explain to my two best friends. To her best friend. I take a deep breath, squeezing her hand drawing strength from her, I stand and look at our friends.

"I got a call earlier." My voice cracks as emotion clogs my throat. Swallowing, I look at Tiffany knowing this will be harder on her. "You might want to sit, Tiff," I say gently. She sits slowly not taking her eyes off me.

"The call, Mom…she's ill. A doctor called from a hospital in London," I say, my voice wobbling; it's so much harder saying the words out loud. "She has cancer; she doesn't have long." I squeeze my eyes shut at Tiffany's whimper, almost breaking my resolve. I bite my trembling lip so hard I taste blood.

"She'd obviously known a while and didn't want to tell me, us." I correct myself, including nan in this as she was as clueless as me. "I realise now that she sent me here with the sole purpose to die alone." Saying the words out loud feels like swallowing razor blades. Both Mason and Millie step forward seeing me struggle. I hold my hand up to stop them, I need to do this.

"He said there's nothing they can do, just keep her comfortable in her last days. She doesn't want either, Nan or I there, to watch her deteriorate."

I hear Tiff and nan sobbing, but I can't move; I'm frozen, numb, staring blankly. I have nothing to give, my mind protects itself by shutting down emotionally and right now, I'm grateful because when I do feel, it will kill me.

I rouse slowly on the floor, sitting up I feel an arm drop from my waist. Shocked, I turn and see Mace asleep behind me. *What the hell?* It hits me so hard my breath explodes from my chest in a rush. My mom, the vibrant, smiling, strong woman who raised me, has cancer. *She's dying*. It devastates me all over again; she's everything to me. She's my best friend, my mom, and dad. *Why did I even come here?* I didn't need to, we could've come together, got her a new doctor. I've wasted months when I could have been with her, taking care of her. Instead, I've been sunning it up in California, while she's home suffering, alone.

I feel sick remembering all the emails and texts I sent, rambling on about how great it was here and how much fun I was having. Unable to stay seated, I walk to the window looking out, everything looks normal. The sun still rose; the world still moves, life goes on, but for me, one phone call changed everything.

Needing a break from my own thoughts, I head for the stairs, needing a release. I need fresh air to sort the jumbled mess of feelings and thoughts.

Passing Nan's room, I notice she's not slept there. Pausing, I rub my head trying to remember whether she was downstairs. There was me and Mace on the floor, Millie and Tiff on one side of the sofa. I don't remember seeing nan though, my heart rate skyrockets as I run back downstairs. Nope, not in the living room or kitchen. Panic creeps in and my mind blanks, *think, think, think. Where could she be? Where would I be?* Then the proverbial light bulb clicks on.

I run through the house like a mad woman, back upstairs and skid to a halt in the doorway of my room. I breathe a sigh of relief, she's there on my bed, curled up and clutching a photo to her chest, looking worn and sobbing in her sleep. I move around the room quietly gathering my clothes and change in the bathroom. My body itches to release pent up energy.

I creep back downstairs trying not to wake anyone, especially Mace, I need to be alone and I know he'll want to come with me. I breathe a sigh of relief as the sun beats down on me warming my cold skin as I stretch, feeling my stiff muscles release. Smooth, soothing music flows into my ears, not my usual choice, but today I wanted to feel close to my mom and classical was her favourite. I remember her humming it to me when I was younger, after a nightmare, or when I was sick.

So many memories bombard me, and I let them come, because while running it's okay. I'm moving, it's how I deal with my emotions, and at the moment I feel like they're on overload just waiting to spill over. I run on autopilot, my body navigating its way through the streets.

Like waking from a slumber, I notice I've reached the park, it's beautiful today. Packed with people, a combination of heat and the weekend brings more runners, cyclists, children playing and families picnicking.

Normally I run without music, preferring the sounds of nature, but today the noise is grating, instead of soothing. I want to scream, to release all the pent-up energy I feel coursing through me; it's been that way for days. It's like I'm on a non-stop adrenaline rush, making me feel twitchy, hyper, tired and snappy. I don't know what the hell I need but snapping at everyone isn't going to cut it.

Taking a break, I sit under my usual tree away from the main noise, close my eyes. I take deep cleansing breaths, hoping to clear my mind and decompress.

"Thank God, there you are." My eyes snap open wincing I blink, focusing on Mason as he stands over me looking relieved and out of breath. Glancing around, I'm dumbfounded, it's dark.

"I'm sorry, I must have fallen asleep, I was trying to quieten the mess up here," I say tapping my head. "I bet nan's having kittens, I'm sorry," I whisper again.

He plunks down beside me. “Yeah, she's worried, thinking all sorts.”

I immediately feel like shit, I didn’t want to scare her.

“It’s okay, I fired a text off to Millie when I saw you sitting here, under our tree no less.” He smiles sadly, I can just about muster up the energy to talk let alone smile. “I don’t know what to say, so I’ll just shut up and sit quietly. Just know that if you need me, I’m always here.” His face softens as he puts an arm around me.

And that’s all it takes, one small act of kindness from one of my closest friends, and I’m reduced to a blubbering mess. I clutch him as tightly as I can feeling fragile and broken, I sob all over him, rambling incoherently into his shirt.

Holding me to his chest and rocking me. “It’s okay, I’m here, you’re not alone,” he assures kissing my head. I nod, feeling grateful for having him as a friend, I’m glad to have someone there to hold me up.

Pulling back, I dry my face. “Thanks for coming to find me and for being there.”

CHAPTER FOUR

Over the next few days, nan and I try to come to terms with everything. I don't go back to school, I can't, I've only attended a few days so far. Thankfully, the university has been amazing about it. Mace, Millie and Tiff are constant pillars of strength for us as days pass with no calls, texts or emails from mom.

On Saturday we finally get to speak on the phone for a few minutes. It hurts so much more hearing her laboured breathing.

"Hi Mom," I whisper, swallowing past the emotion that's threatening to choke me.

"Hi baby, I'm so sorry. I know you're hurting, confused and most likely angry. I just didn't want you to have to deal with this, I don't want you seeing me like this," she coughs. "Please, all I want is for you to live life the way you want; be happy and fall in love. Look after your gran for me, she's been through so much already; be there for each other and know that I love you both," she wheezes, coughing loudly.

I sob quietly realising this is our goodbye. "Please, let me come home," I beg.

"No, baby. You need to be with Grandma. I'm being looked after, I promise. I've got to go. I love you. I've always been so proud of you," I hear her sob quietly.

"I love you, too. Bye." I say as the line clicks off. Dropping my phone, I crumble as pain ravages me. I hear faint, worried voices.

"Lils?" A voice calls faintly. *Mason?*

"Cora? She's not waking up."

"Mmm," I groan, my head fuzzy.

"She's coming around, don't worry, you caught her head before she hit the floor. Physically, she's okay." Nan whispers.

"It's too much. How are we going to?"

"I don't know, honey. It was hard but saying it. She's been through so much already," she hiccups.

I blink, I'm in my bed, still dressed. My head is banging. Getting up slowly, I head to the bathroom.

Looking in the mirror, I look and feel like I've been hit by a truck. My throat's dry and sore, my eyes are puffy and my hair's a rat's nest.

Splashing water on my face isn't enough, so I jump in the shower. After going through the motions of washing, drying and dressing. I trudge downstairs into the kitchen, Mace spots me, staring, his fork frozen mid-air. While Millie talks quietly to him.

Tiff and nan are at the cooker, preparing more food. They all turn as I sit, looking at me like I'm going to faint at any moment. I roll my eyes, grabbing some juice.

"I'm okay. I'm not going to streak down the street, screaming," I joke, my voice hoarse.

"Well, good, because I don't think the neighbours would like that much," nan says. I smile and get up to hug her.

"Are you okay?" I whisper into her hair.

"We're going to have to be, aren't we? How are you feeling? I've been so worried about you." She looks at me closely, taking in every blemish and blotch.

"I'm okay, numb, but trying to get through it," I whisper still feeling raw.

"Okay, then, let's eat, you need food."

"Wha…"

"Not now, Millie," nan interrupts her. Placing a plate full of pancakes, bacon and eggs in front of me.

Mason nudges her, shaking his head, she drops her gaze to the table eating quietly. I raise an eyebrow at them, but don't ask.

Shaking my head, I take my first bite, chewing thoroughly before swallowing. I still wince as it rubs my sore throat.

Mace looks up, hearing me wince. "You okay?" He asks, worried.

I nod, "yeah, just a sore throat," I croak getting up to look through the cupboards for cough syrup.

"Second cupboard, on your right," nan directs.

"Thanks," I sigh, feeling it's soothing effect, slide down my throat. They're all acting strange, glancing at each other then, at me. We eat in silence, it's so oppressive I'm relieved by the time we all move to the living room.

"Do you fancy a run?" He asks slapping his leg. I smile. Thanking him silently for knowing me so well.

"Yeah, I could use the fresh air and the exercise after that breakfast," I chuckle looking over at nan.

I need a break from everyone waiting for me to fall apart and waiting for the phone to ring.

I love feeling my calf muscles burn, the release of tension.

"So," Mason pants keeping pace with me.

"So?" I puff.

"Come on, Lils. No bullshit. I know you better than that. How are you really doing?" He veers toward our tree.

Sitting, I gulp water, taking a minute to appreciate the beauty surrounding me. Seeing life all around me, I just feel numb.

"Lils?" Leaning on my hands, I lay my head on my shoulder, peering at him wondering where to start.

"Okay, I've been better, I feel empty, numb. Sometimes I feel nothing, you know?" He nods, staying quiet, understanding I need to get this out.

"I feel like a part of me has died and I'm struggling with the need to be alone and wanting to be there for Nan. Problem is when I'm alone I think too much and it hurts worse. I just wish I could have been with her these past weeks. I feel guilty for all the emails I sent, I told her everything that was happening here. About you and Millie and how stupid it is that you two haven't got together." He chuckles at my jibe.

"She was so excited to know if you two had worked it out. She asked in her last email, but I never replied." I drift off.

"Listen. If you want to be alone. I can go over there or something," he points over at the swing set, I look back and forth between them and I giggle.

He's shocked by the sound. "And what are you laughing at, potty mouth?"

A belly laugh escapes me. "You, you're too big for kiddie swings and I told you not to call me that."

"Like you could stop me."

He nods toward the swings. “I bet I could go higher than you potty m...”

I’m up and running for the swings before he finishes, laughing. I hear him curse, then his feet rushing through the grass. We both jump onto the swings laughing like kids.

“Come on, let’s see what you’ve got,” he challenges.

I smile, poor guy has no idea, I’m great at this.

“Let’s go, but don’t cry when I leave you grounded while I’m up there,” I boast, sticking my tongue out at him.

“That’s rude you know,” he says, sounding like a child.

I snicker. “What are you, four? ‘*That's rude, I’m telling...*’” I taunt.

“Come on, no more stalling. Are you afraid?”

“Hell no. Let’s go,” I shout, feeling free for the first time in a long time. That’s the thing about our friendship, it’s so easy it’s like we’ve known each other forever.

On our return trip, we laugh and shove each other, trying to trip one another. Basically, acting like kids.

We walk through the door laughing and shoving each other.

Nan looks up surprise, smiling weakly at me. Seeing her, I sober immediately.

“Are you okay?”

“I’m fine, go take a shower, you both stink,” she says wrinkling her nose.

“Now, I know where you get it from,” he laughs, pointing at me.

I open and shut my mouth, looking at her in astonishment.

“Can you believe him? The king of attitude?” I ask, she grins at us tittering. Turning back to watch her home improvement show.

"Lily, can I talk to you for a minute?" Nan asks, perching on the edge of my bed.

"Sure, just let me throw on some clothes," I say around my toothbrush when I come out the bathroom, she's looking at a picture of mom and me.

"What's up? Where's Mace?" I try and keep the sorrow from my voice when I see the picture of mom holding me as a baby.

She looks at me, tears swimming in her eyes and dread washes over me leaving me cold. I swallow my rising panic and sit beside her.

"Mace went home a few minutes ago," she whispers, too softly. I nod, keeping quiet not wanting her to finish, but it's obvious she will.

"Earlier this morning while you were unconscious, I received a call from Dr, Williams." Grief and pain grip me by the throat.

"No. Please no. Not yet. She can't be. Please, tell me she's not," I beg, tears dripping from my chin. She just shakes her head, devastated.

"He said she passed away not long after coming off the phone with you, and that she went peacefully," she cries.

I curl into a ball on my bed as years of memories assault me. We cry quietly together each stuck in our own memories. Slowly I gain control over myself, putting my own emotions and grief aside to deal with later.

"Why didn't you tell me earlier? I left you alone for hours."

"You've been through so much the last few days." She hiccups. "And with you passing out and not eating or sleeping properly. I just wanted you to have a few hours as normal as possible. I was worried I was going to lose you too." She replies, her eyes begging me to understand.

"I'm not mad, just sorry that I left you to deal with it alone. I didn't mean to scare you." I mumble as she pulls me into a hug and we cry again, for the one person we both loved and couldn't be with in the end.

A cremation was performed in the UK days after she passed, at the behest of my mom. She wanted no one there, just a simple cremation then a ceremony here. It tore me apart not being there, but I respected her last wish and a week after her cremation her ashes arrived, and we got to work planning the ceremony here.

After everything was set for Saturday at two p.m. We had to sort out putting the flat on the market and find someone to pack up our things. Luckily, she had great friends at work that loved her.

Diane and Natasha went over with my permission to donate all the furniture and box all our personal items up to ship over to me. I have no idea what I'm going to do with it all, I just couldn't get rid of it all.

I'm not ready, I don't think I ever will be. I don't want to say goodbye. She was going to cheer the loudest at my graduation, and give me away at my wedding, I miss her so much already. Every day I go to pick up the phone to tell her something or to ask her advice.

Wiping away a stray tear, I look at the black dress I have hanging on the door for tomorrow. I cried when it arrived by courier, it was her baby, her masterpiece.

An off the shoulder dress, it falls just above the knee with a beautifully ribbed bodice. I smile remembering her design it. She was so intense when in the zone. Whenever she drew, she wore old sweats, her hair twisted into a messy bun with a charcoal pencil resting behind her ear. She'd hum as she drew, frowning in concentration.

She was so excited when the finished product was in her

hands, she loved it on sight. It's still a best seller. Diane sent it with her condolences, she thought it would be a fitting tribute to mom's talent as a designer and her love of fashion.

Breaking out of my thoughts, I go in search of nan finding her in her room picking out her shoes for tomorrow.

"Hey, do you need anything before tomorrow?" I ask from the doorway.

"No, honey, I'm all set. Are Mason and Millie coming here or meeting us there?" She asks, smiling weakly.

Dragging my phone out I text them.

Me to Mason: *Are you coming to ours tomorrow or meeting us there?*

Me to Millie: *Are you coming to ours tomorrow or meeting us there?*

As soon as I hit send, I get one back.

Mason: *I'm coming to yours first thing, and I'm driving.*

Millie: *Sorry, I've got to help mom tomorrow. She's all over the place. Will you be okay?*

Me to Millie: *Yeah, I'll be fine. Look after Tiff.*

Me to Mason: *Yes, sir. :)*

. . .

Mason: *Cheeky shit. :p*

I smile at his reply. "Mason's coming here first thing. He said he's driving. I don't think he trusts us to drive."

She shakes her head. "If I didn't know otherwise, I'd think you two were either together or siblings," she chuckles.

"Millie needs to help Tiff. She said she's all over the place." I sigh, knowing tomorrow is going to be horrendous.

"That's understandable, they were inseparable from kindergarten."

"I'm going to bed. I'll see you in the morning." I yawn.

"Okay, honey. Go get some sleep, I'm going in a minute too. Goodnight," she whispers as I kiss her cheek.

Heading back to my room, I find myself typing out a text to Mason.

Me: *Thanks for always being there for my nan and me. You're the best and I love you dearly (like a brother) xxx*

I press send, change and slide into bed, staring at the ceiling, thinking. Over the past two weeks I've been so angry at her for making the choice to die alone and be cremated alone. I felt she took away my chance to say a real goodbye.

My phone pings.

Mason: *Aww, that's sweet, you wuv me. I know I'm cute and lovable. :p Seriously though. I will always be there when you need me. I love you, too. (Like a sister) <- what's with that? xxx.*

. . .

I smile, I would have loved a brother like Mason.

Me: *Nan made a comment about how we act 'together'. Said if she didn't know otherwise, she'd think we were either together or bro/sis.*

Mason: *Oh god. Could you imagine you and me as bf/gf :/ weird, but I like the bro/sis option. Imagine all the trouble we'd get into. Lmao.*

Me: *Yeah, sort of freaked me out too. *Shudders* :p Mace, we get into trouble now anyway. Pmsl.*

Mason: *Oh yeah, I keep forgetting you already get me into trouble, you little rebel. Lmao. You better get sum Zzz's. Night, night. POTTY MOUTH. X*

Me: *Oh, no, you did not just call me that. I'm going to slap you tomorrow. Night, night, you pain in the arse. X*

The smell of blueberry pancakes wakes me. Mom's favourite.

God, I know I don't pray, much, but my mom always said, it didn't matter if I didn't go to church or pray all the time as long as I believed. So, here goes. Please, help me get through today. Give me the strength to help nan through this. Amen.

I feel stupid for praying to a silent room, but I need all the help I can get today.

Even getting out of bed is hard, but I push through. I can't be arsed to dress so I drag myself downstairs, when everything inside me just wants to go back to bed and pretend none of it is real.

Standing in the archway to the kitchen. I find nan staring out the window, her arms wrapped protectively around herself. Mason is cooking, in a frilly apron. I slap my hand over my mouth and try not to laugh.

In front of me is a tall, muscular, handsome man in a pink frilly apron. It's too good an opportunity to miss, I whip my phone out and just as he turns, I click capture. Laughing at his look of complete horror.

Looking from Mason to my phone, nan giggles from the window.

"You better delete that, right now."

"Oh, hell no." I dance toward him waving my phone in his face.

"Payback's a bitch Mason Lee," I sing dodging his attempt to grab the phone, I giggle running behind nan, she laughs looking at the picture.

"Come on, please? What have I done to deserve that?" He asks innocently, batting his eyes at me sticking his lip out. I get another pic.

"Fine. Do with them what you will. I won't be cooking breakfast for you anymore," he huffs, walking off.

I can tell he's not serious by his twinkling green eyes. "Well, there's always dinner and tea."

"That's it. Miss. Mouthy," he says, whipping off the apron and jumping the counter.

I screech and dart away barely escaping his clutching hands. Shoving my phone in my bra for safekeeping, I run for the living room, but I'm tackled to the sofa and pinned on my back, my arms restrained at my sides by strong thighs.

"Give me the phone or I'll be forced to tickle," he laughs, his hands poised.

"No, don't. The pics are payback for the name." I struggle.

"Oh, is that right? Those pictures are my punishment?" I giggle nodding.

"Well, I think this can be your punishment for taking them," he says digging his fingers into my ribs. I scream whipping my head from side to side.

"No. Please, stop, I'm going to pee myself," I screech trying to buck him off.

"Nuh-uh, this is your punishment for being a naughty girl. Say, I'm sorry, Mason," he says, settling more securely on me. I shake my head, unable to talk, gasping for breath between giggles, he stops to let me catch my breath.

"Say it," he insists, his fingers poised to torture me again.

"Okay, okay. I'm sorry!"

"Now, say, you're the best and I wuvs you so much." I laugh, repeating the words after him sarcastically.

"Now, say, you're the best and I wuvs you so much."

Shaking his head, he says, "No, no, you say. You're the best and I wuvs you so much."

I huff, "You're the best and I wuvs you so much. Now, get off of me, you heavy lump," I sigh as he finally gets off me.

"Come on you two, breakfast's getting cold," nan yells from the kitchen.

"Were you calling me fat back there, Carter?" He teases putting his fingers into claws.

"No. You just have a lot of muscle that's all," I say, shoving him, and he just grins cheekily at me.

"Oh, so you like my muscles? Do ya sass me cause ya secretly fancy all this," he asks, rubbing a hand down his chest.

I burst out laughing. "Don't worry, your safe big guy. You're so not my type." I giggle at his wounded face.

"So, what is your type then?" He asks, sliding into his chair not taking his eyes off my face.

"Don't know, haven't met anyone I think of that way yet," I murmur shrugging offhandedly, but the image of Ethan laughing pops into my head and the way I ogled him. *He's my type.*

"Oh, you're blushing. What haven't you told Mason?" He asks, rubbing his hands together, I throw a pancake at him. Laughing, he stuffs it into his mouth.

"Would you not refer to yourself as a third person? Tell him, Nan," I say, hoping to deflect their attention.

"No, I'm with Mason on this one. I want to know what made you blush like that," she chimes in. They high five and sit there staring at me. Making me squirm in my chair.

I roll my eyes at them and sigh. "It's a bloke I met weeks ago, I liked him, and he wasn't hard on the eyes either." I stand, ignoring them and washing my plate. Nan sits quietly listening while Mason keeps badgering me.

"Come on, you have to give us more than that."

"There's not much to know." I turn, leaning on the worktop.

"Where did you two meet?"

I sit back down ready to be interrogated. "Okay, we met on the flight here." I see her brighten out of the corner of my eye.

"Oh, the Cali boy?" She asks, smirking and I nod embarrassed. "He was a prime piece of meat too," she relays to him.

Mason howls hearing her use of what can only be described as a sexy voice. I cringe, not a thing I want to think about or hear.

"Nan." I protest, shaking my head.

"What? Am I lying? Ask her to describe him." She turns to Mason.

He looks at me eyebrow cocked as if to say, 'you heard the lady'. I groan.

"Fine. He was gorgeous. Tanned, light brown, spiked hair. Square jawed with a bit of scruff, straight nose and the most kissable lips I have *ever* seen. And my god, his eyes… They were hazel with a touch of green." I blush realising I went all girly.

"Okay. Are we done interrogating now?" I snap, before stalking off into the living room, hoping they'll drown it and leave me alone. No such luck. They follow me in and sit on either side of me staring. Freaking me out.

"What are you staring at?" I snap.

"You, Miss, Stroppy. I think you have it bad," Mace teases.

"I do not. I don't even know him. So, how can I have it bad? We only spoke for a few hours," I snap and slap my hand over my big mouth.

Shit. They aren't going to stop now. Bowing my head, I wait for them to bombard me with questions only one comes.

"So, when are you seeing him again?" This is Mace, nan already knows.

"I'm not. I don't know anything about him. Not much anyway and who gives someone they just met on a plane their phone number?"

"Maybe someone who spoke to a girl for hours. Men don't do that unless they're interested."

I see an opening and take it. "Oh? Is that why you're always talking to me? Cause you secretly wuv me?" I taunt.

"No. You're my best friend. A pain in my ass and it just so happens that you make me laugh," he quips. "Sorry Cora," he adds, sitting back relaxing.

"Okay, you *may* be right, but there's no point talking about it. There's nothing more to tell. I'm not going to see him again. So, let's just drop it," I snap irritated.

Staring at myself in the mirror, I take deep breaths. I can't believe it's time, I have to say goodbye. I don't know if I can do this. I feel panicky and so alone, it's oppressive, closing in on me and sucking the air from my lungs. I try distraction. I look at myself smoothing imaginary wrinkles. The dress looks amazing, the perfect tribute.

"Are you ready?" Turning, I see Mason standing by the door watching me. Looking incredibly handsome.

"My Mom would have loved you. I wish you could have met each other." I smile sadly at him.

"Me too."

"Thanks for distracting me this morning, I've been dreading today. I know it's not a proper funeral, but it's my only chance to say goodbye."

"It's a celebration of her life. She may have been cremated over there, but she's been here with you the whole time. Oh, and don't think that conversation is over!"

The drive to the church is quiet the silence only broken by nan's sniffles from the back seat as she cries softly. I sit next to Mace ringing my hands, breathing erratically. *I don't know if I can do this.* My thought scares me more than saying goodbye. *I can do this I need to, for mom.*

We arrive and stand at the church's entrance waiting for people to arrive, hoping people come. Everything passes in a daze; I shake hands and exchange words with people I don't know. More and more people arrive extending their condolences, telling me what a great person my mom was.

"Nan, do you know all these people?" I whisper stunned.

"I know, honey. Some are people Lizzy went to school with, dance and neighbours. She would have been shocked by the amount that want to pay their respects." She wipes her eyes, looking at everyone in awe.

"Wow. Your mom was well known and loved by the looks of it, you should be proud." Mace whispers. I nod, because I am proud of my mom, she was the greatest person I knew.

"Hi, I'm Kaysie. I'm sorry for your loss. I went to school with Lizzy, she was a wonderful person," a short redheaded woman says holding my hand.

"Thank you," I say robotically as the line goes on and on and my temper rises with every condolence.

"I don't know how much more I can take. Why the hell do people say, 'I'm sorry for your loss' anyway?" I hiss.

"Lily, honey, don't. You know they don't know what to say," she whispers softly patting my arm. I nod, refusing to upset her more than she already is. It's irrational, I'm angry, I just want my mom. I stifle a sob, chewing on my cheek as an arm slides around my shoulders.

"It's okay, Lils. It'll be over soon." This is why I love Mason. He's always there, no matter what.

I keep my head down. "I'm sorry. I'm a mess. It's a lot harder than I thought it would be," I hiccup.

"I know, I'm here. Just lean on me, you're not alone."

Turning, I hug him tight, squeezing his neck as his strong arms pull me tight against him.

"Thanks, Mace. I don't know what we would have done without you. I'm glad you knocked me on my backside that day," I say with a watery giggle.

I feel rather than hear him chuckle. "That was not my fault and you know it. You were spaced out and ran into me."

"Yeah, I was. Sorry, but you did get an awesome best friend out of it. So, you can hardly complain." I sass and he smiles at me nodding.

His smile dissolves, staring over my shoulder. I know instantly, it's time.

The Pastor motions us over, taking a deep breath, I grasp nan's hand, and we walk into the church together. People nod sadly as we pass, I nod back and turn away, I hate being the centre of attention.

We're sitting in the long front row and since there is only nan and I as family, I invited Mason, Millie and Tiffany to sit with us. It felt appropriate since Tiff was her best friend.

I stare at the photo of her, holding a teenage me from behind, laughing, happy; we were camping at the time it was taken. It's a beautiful shot of mom at her happiest. Seeing her face smiling happily at me hits me hard. A tear spills over as the Pastor starts the service. I'm not listening though. I stare at the photo wishing I could go back. Be with her again, hear her voice, see her smile. Tell her how much I love her.

"Miss Carter, do you wish to say a few words?" The Pastor asks. I blink looking at him blankly and stand robotically.

"You don't have to," Mason says clasping my hand.

"I'm fine, Mace. I have to say something in her memory," I say with a watery smile squeezing his hand. Straightening I breathe deeply. Shoulders back, chin up, deep breath and smile. You can do this.

Standing at the podium looking at all the people who came to pay their respects is staggering. I take another breath blow it out gently, I look at the picture again.

"Thank you all for coming. It shows just how much mom was loved. She wasn't just a mother. She was my dad and a best friend; she managed every role perfectly. When I was sick no matter the age, all I wanted was my mom. When I was tired, she rocked me to sleep, and when I had nightmares; she slept beside me. Without her, I will be truly lost." My throat closes my loss overwhelming me.

Looking over at her smiling face, I start again. "She loved fashion, loved her job. She designed the dress I'm wearing. I wear it today as a tribute to her achievements and love of fashion. We didn't have a lot of money, but she made sure I never went without. She was an amazing mother, and the kindest person. We were rich in other ways. Ways some people aren't lucky enough to experience, we were rich for having each other. That's what mom taught me. To be grateful of what and who I have in life. Today, as I say goodbye to her, I make a promise to cherish every moment, to appreciate the people I love and who love me and to try never to take them for granted. Thank you for coming." I take one last look at the picture before leaving the podium.

I walk back to my seat. The silence, throughout the church is deafening only broken by a few sniffles. I look to nan who is smiling and crying at the same time.

The wake is being held at our house, so we moved all the furniture to one side and set all the food on the dining table.

The countless faces, names and introductions are endless. The only enjoyable part of it is when people tell me sweet and funny stories about mom in her wilder days.

"Hey, Lily. Have you seen my mom? I can't find her," Millie whispers, making me jump.

"No. She's the only one that hasn't shaken my hand," I whisper back, we giggle.

"Come on. I'll help look and get a break from all the 'I'm sorry for losses.'" I roll my eyes.

"I'm sorry for your loss," she teases. I smirk at her smart-arse remark and stick my tongue out.

"You go that way, smart arse, I'll go out back and check," I say, pointing her towards the stairs.

My polite smile returns as I pass through the people gathered outside the back-door smoking and chatting. They all give me sad smiles as I hurry away.

"What the fuck are you doing here? Haven't you already caused enough trouble for this family?" Whoa, I stop before turning the corner. That's Tiff. I've never heard her sound like that before.

"Come on, Tiff. I just wanted to pay my respects like the rest," a male voice pleads.

"Yeah? Well, you didn't goddamn respect her when she was alive, why would you now?" Tiffany hisses back, the venom dripping from her words scares me a little.

What the…? I peek around the side of the house, sure enough, there is Tiff looking majorly pissed. Jabbing a finger into the chest of a tall man in an expensive suit. He stands there, head bowed, hands on his hips looking ashamed.

"Tiff, are you okay?" I ask, coming around the corner.

They both jump, but the bloke stares at me. He's tall, tanned and rumpled. Brown wavy hair and green eyes.

Tiff spins, "yes, sweetie. I'm fine. Just talking to an *old* friend of mine," she says, stressing the word old.

"Oh, um, sorry. Millie's looking for you. She's worried," I inform her. Rubbing my arm nervously. Hoping they don't realise I heard some of their conversation.

The way the bloke is staring at me though, is freaking me out. I look between him and Tiff waiting for an introduction. Clearing his throat, the man lifts his hand.

"I'm," That's as far as he gets before Tiff butts in.

"Lily. This is Alex. His sister Lilyanna, was a good friend of mine and your mom's." I'm shocked at her rudeness. Looking at Alex he looks shell shocked and a little scared, I don't blame him Tiff is scary right now.

"Hello, it's nice to meet you, is your sister here too?" I ask carefully, not wanting to set Tiff off again.

He shakes his head clearing his throat again and releases my hand. "You, too. I'm sorry about Lizzy. She was an amazing woman." I smile warmly at him.

But Tiff growls, huffing. My stunned gaze swings to her. What the hell?

"What's the matter?" I ask touching her arm gently.

"Nothing, I'm fine. Did you say Millie was looking for me?" She evades, grabbing my hand and pulling me away. Throwing an angry look at Alex. Who is still standing there open-mouthed staring at me?

"Hey, Lils. Millie thinks you've eloped," Mason yells across the yard heading straight to us as Tiff practically drags me along behind her.

I barely hear him as I swing my gaze back to look at Alex, whose gaze snaps to Mason coming across the lawn toward me. All colour drains from his face as Mason slings an arm around my shoulders.

What's wrong with Tiff? Maybe Millie should be worried.

She doesn't normally act like that. She's not rude, she's a sweet person.

I look back over Mason's arm, but Alex has disappeared.

"Well, that's the living room looking normal again. That was hard work," I moan, looking around proudly at our work. Mason huffs out a laugh collapsing onto the sofa.

"Well, it would have been much harder for you, if you had done any lifting." He nudges me.

"Well, excuse me, Mr, Muscles. How many hands have you had to shake today? My poor arms feel like lead weights." Pouting at him, I bat my eyelashes as nan comes into the living room.

"Well, I'm going to bed. You staying, Mason?" Nan asks.

He nods. "If that's okay?"

"Course it is honey. Good night, you two," she calls already on her way up the stairs.

"Do you want to watch a movie with me, Mr, Muscles?" I say nudging him.

"Hey, watch out. I'm sore from all the hard labour you've made me do and holding all those cougars off wasn't easy you know." His eyes laughing. I shove him in the ribs again.

"Okay, lady killer. What we going to watch?" I quip.

"Let's see what's on first," he says getting comfy holding an arm out for me. I snuggle into him loving our friendship. I never thought I'd be this close and comfortable with any man, without some sort of commitment.

CHAPTER FIVE

Ugh, what the hell is that? I sit up as the noise stops. I look at the clock, it's five a.m. fuck. It's too early to be awake on a Sunday.

I jump as the ringing starts again looking around, I try to find the offending object. Which turns out to be Mason's phone, wedged in the cushion of the sofa.

"Hello?" I ask, groggily.

There's silence from the other end. So, I look at the screen, then ask, "Is anyone there?" I ask considering disconnecting as an angry man answers.

"Who is this?" He demands on the other end. By his tone, I gather its Mason's dad.

"Erm, Lily. Hang on please?" I say, shaking Mason.

"Mace, Mace? I think it's your dad on the phone." He rolls over cuddling me, murmuring in his sleep and making me giggle.

"MACE!" I shout in his ear.

"Ah, what the hell? You scared the shit out me. What was that for?" He grouches rubbing his face. I fall into a fit of giggles at his reaction. Well, I was rudely woken up by his noisy phone. Why shouldn't he be awake too?

"Your phone, I think it's your dad," I gasp, handing him his phone. "I'll go start you some coffee, you're going to need it by the sounds of it." I get up still groggy.

"Dad?"

I don't catch anymore as I head to the kitchen. God, it's way too early to be up. Rude arse couldn't wait till a decent hour to phone?

I go about putting the kettle on for coffee and tea. Switch on the radio. While getting stuff out to make a full English. I haven't had one in ages.

Putting the sausages and hash browns in the oven. Whilst chopping mushrooms and getting tomatoes out the cupboard and eggs from the fridge, I hum quietly, my thoughts once again sporadic. Nan must still be in bed.

"What are you making?" Mace asks sneaking up on me, I jump shooting him a nasty look over my shoulder.

"What does it look like? It's breakfast."

He comes to look fully over my shoulder. "Are you sure? I haven't seen a breakfast like that before."

"Yes, I'm sure, you numpty. It's a Full English." I elbow him in the gut.

"Well, it does smell good. So, I guess I can give it a try," he grunts rubbing his belly.

"Oh, well, thank you, kind sir," I roll my eyes.

"You're welcome, my lady," he mocks, bowing and making me giggle.

"Okay, wise arse, was it your dad?" I ask, once again concentrating on what I'm chopping.

"Yeah, it was. He wanted to know where I was last night, who you were, whether you're my girlfriend and whether we were having sex," he laughs.

I drop my spatula, stunned that his dad would ask those sorts of questions. I remember what he said about not being able to screw around with anyone, but Jesus. He creases as I stare at him in astonishment and horror. I mean just, eww. The thought grosses me out. Mace is hot, but I've never thought of him that way.

"What did you say? I suppose it was quite suspicious my answering your phone half asleep and waking you up. He obviously knew you were there beside me." I allow feeling culpable. "I'm sorry," I add apologetically.

Shrugging, he grins. "Well, to be honest, it was quite funny. He was all flustered and pissed. Don't worry, I told him we're friends and you're more like a sister than a fuck buddy," he chuckles wiggling his eyebrows. I chuck a tea towel at him.

"Shut up, you arse." Shaking my head, I go back to my cooking.

"You know. I haven't forgotten about our conversation yesterday. I still want to know," he says amused. I freeze, looking at him over my shoulder.

"Which one? We had so many," I raise an eyebrow.

"You know what I'm talking about. The guy who got you all hot and bothered. Tell me about him. You obviously liked him. You noticed enough," he says ribbing me.

"Aww, come on. I won't be seeing him again. I only got his name, age and what he looks like. He works for his stepdad and that he's from here," I say placing his plate in front of him and sitting opposite him with my own, trying not to fidget under his incredulous stare.

"Then, tell me you don't like him, and you don't want to see him again," he challenges watching me intently.

"Okay. So, I liked him. He was hot. Yes, I would've liked to have seen him again. To see if the connection I felt was real." I curse, watching him out of the corner of my eye. A slow grin creeps onto his face. His eyes laugh at me, so I kick him under the table.

"Ow, that hurt." He rubs his leg.

"It was supposed to. Now, what do you want to know?"

"Everything you know but hold the swooning over his hot bod. You told me that bit." He shudders dramatically.

"Do I have to? I'll sound as pathetic as I feel," I whine, slouching in my chair.

"Yes, you pry into my love life, as it is concerning Millie. So, come on, Miss Mouth."

I growl at that name. "What's with the nicknames?"

He points at me smiling. "If the shoe fits. Now, stop changing the subject," he says getting comfortable.

"Okay, he's twenty-three. Works for his stepdad, like I said, but I don't know what he does. He's from here and his name's Ethan. That's all I know. Can we drop it now, please?"

His face is a combination of shock, confusion and curiousness.

"So, let me get this straight. His name is Ethan, twenty-three, works for his stepdad and he's from San Diego. He's tall, light brown hair, hazel eyes with green in them. Is that all of it? Was he in London on business?" He asks warily.

"Yeah, you got it all and yes, he was. I told you that already," I groan.

"Do you have a last name?"

"Yes, it's Barker. What's with all the questions Mace?" I grumble holding my head.

Mason looks back at me, his expression frozen in shock.

"You okay?" I ask moving to the other side of the table, crouching beside him. He mumbles something, but I can't hear it. Then laughs.

"Oh, my gosh. Are you okay? You're acting a little nuts."

"This is hilarious, I know him," he exclaims, abruptly sobering from his laughing fit.

"How do you know Ethan?" I whisper softly.

This just got awkward. How can he know him? He's what? Five years older than Mason?

Mason turns fully to me. Takes my hands like he's talking to a child and explains.

"I know him. If it's the same person and I think it is, I can't believe it. All this time you had a thing for my brother," he cringes, then laughs at my face. I fall on my arse, stunned. Eyes popping out of my head.

"What? What do you mean your brother? His last name is Barker, not Scott." I say feeling dumb for stating the obvious.

He pulls me up and drags me into the living room, sitting me on the sofa, clasping my hands in his much bigger ones.

He chuckles, "I know, this is unbelievable, but if this is the same man and I know it is; Ethan is my older, half-brother. My mom had Ethan and Niles at eighteen. Barker is her maiden name. Not long after, she and dad found each other again. They were together back in high school dad was nearly twenty-two at the time. My mom's younger, but they fell in love again," his speech rushed.

I'm stunned, "Twins?" I utter in astonishment.

"Yeah, twins. That's all you can come up with. You have the hots for my brother." He shudders, looking mildly sick.

I smack him in the gut. "Hey, it's not that bad and we still don't know if it's the same person," I say ruffling his hair.

"We could find out," he sings waving his phone in my face and I jump on him.

"Oh no, you don't. You are not calling him. What would you say? Hey, Ethan did you by any chance did you meet a girl named Lily on your last flight back from London?" I imitate him sarcastically.

"Well, I wasn't, but that's a good idea. Hang on," he mumbles distractedly, clicking away on his phone. I lunge for the phone.

"No. Mace. That will just make me look sad and pathetic."

His head swings my way. Oh god, he's smirking. That is not good, I can practically see the cogs turning in his head.

"Oh, come on. Would I do that to you? I was just going to show you a photo of him. You can tell me if he's a dreamy as you remember," he says, clasping his hands on his cheeks.

I clobber him with a pillow, "I never said the word dreamy. I said gorgeous." I stick my tongue out.

"Okay, let's see if my big bro is the man of your wet dreams." He laughs at his own joke.

"Eww, Mace. I wouldn't talk about that stuff with you before and definitely not if the man of said dreams is your brother. And before you jump all over what I just said. I didn't say I had any dreams about him. Wet or otherwise. Just that if, I had; I wouldn't be discussing them with you. I'd call Millie," I joke.

"I really don't want to know the content of your wet dreams about my brother, thanks. So, keep those little deets for your conversations with Millie," he grumbles cringing.

"Okay, here we go. This the most recent picture. You ready to see if we've found the man of your dreams?"

I roll my eyes. Leaning over I look chewing the side of my cheek. There on the screen is a picture of two men. Who look identical, but for a few differences?

One is shorter than the other, but no less hot. He has dirty blonde hair, brown eyes and a gorgeous shy smile. Next to him is a taller, buffer version with light brown hair, hazel eyes with a slight hint of light green.

Oh god, those lips. They're both smiling at the camera with their arms around each other's shoulders. I groan, burying my head in my hands, not looking at Mason.

"I take it from that reaction, that this is the same man you've been drooling over for weeks?" He snickers at my discomfort, and I nod. My head snaps up hearing tapping.

"Oh, my god. What are you doing? Mason." I jump on his back.

"You arse. What did you send? Please tell me you didn't," I demand pissed.

"More or less what you suggested earlier." He shows me his phone the text has sent.

Mason to Ethan: *Hey, E. Did you meet a girl called Lily on your last flight back from London?*

"I can't believe you did that. He'll think I'm nuts." I storm off into the kitchen, grabbing juice and snatching a glass from the cupboard and slamming it shut.

"Come on, Lily. I'm sorry," he whispers, looking genuinely sorry.

I spin around fully. "Well, it's a bit late for that now," I yell. "He's already got it. Ugh, he's going to think I've been talking about him," I rant. Mason looks so sad that I soften.

"I'm sorry. It's fine, maybe he won't remember me at all," I say hopefully. Feeling a twinge of disappointment at the idea.

"I'm really sorry, I didn't intend to say anything. I guess I got carried away," he whispers, looking like a little boy being scolded. I laugh at the sight of him, hands in pockets, head down scuffing his shoe nervously.

"How about popcorn and a movie?" I sigh, feeling like vegging out in my sweats.

"Yeah, why not? You can pick as a way of apologising for being an idiot. I would hate you to do something like that to me. I'm sorry," he apologises again looking sheepish.

I smile. "Okay, but you asked for it," I sing bouncing into the living room. I hear him groan.

I do an evil little laugh looking through the DVD's, I smirk seeing the perfect punishment, and pull-out Dirty Dancing. A man's worst nightmare.

Ah, sweet revenge. One hour, forty minutes of pure torture. I grin, setting it all up as Mason comes in with drinks and a big bowl of popcorn.

"Should we call, see if Millie wants to join?" Thinking how little time we've spent together lately.

"Yeah, go ahead. I've got to pee before the movie." I throw popcorn at him.

"Eww, I don't need to know that." He chuckles, jogging off. I grab my phone and ask her.

My phone pings.

Millie: *Can't sorry. Out with mom. Meet up tomorrow to catch up?*

Me: *Okay, miss you. Text me the time & place.*

I settle into the sofa. Grab the fleece blanket, cuddle down with the popcorn and press play.

"Come on, it's starting." I shout stuffing popcorn in my mouth.

"God, woman. Let a man pee in peace," he huffs skidding into the living room, jumping the side of the sofa and snuggles with me under the blanket.

Anyone looking at us would assume we were a couple.

"So, no Millie?" He asks hesitantly. I shake my head.

"Aww, come on. Did you have to pick the most chickiest film you had?" Lifting my head, I raise my eyebrow and give him my evil smirk.

"Okay, okay. I deserve it. I won't moan," he zips his mouth. I nod cause that's what I thought. Laying my head back on his chest.

"And to answer your question, no. She's with her mom, we are going to meet up tomorrow. Do you want to join?" I mumble, stuffing popcorn into my mouth.

"I don't know we'll see."

We settle in watching the movie. I'm just falling asleep when I hear the dreaded ding. Fear and excitement curl in my belly.

Mason and I look at each other there's no doubt it's his brother replying. He grabs his phone, while I hide under the blanket not wanting to know what he said.

"Come out. Don't you want to know what he said?" He laughs.

"Nope. I'm staying here," I mutter.

"Aww, come on. You know you want to know," he taunts.

"Fine," I sigh, "but read quickly." I bite my cheek.

He smirks at me. "Wow. Are you nervous?" He looks closely at me.

"No. Just want to get it over with," I mutter.

"Okay. Do you want to look? Do you want me to read it, or shall we look together?" He asks, I scoot over to him.

"Together," I answer quickly.

Ethan: *Is this a joke?*

Mason: *No.*

Ethan: *Why?*

I look at Mason, he looks torn. "I'm going to have to give him something or he won't tell me," he tells me.

"No. Mace, you can't." My insides feel jumpy, I feel queasy.

"I have to say something, or he'll hound me." I nod, I'm going to look like such an idiot.

Mason: *Cause, I think I know the girl.*

Ethan: *And how would you know that? When I haven't confirmed or denied it.*

Mason: *I answered your question, now you answer mine.*

Ethan: *Okay. Yeah. I did, again why?*

. . .

Mason: *As I said, I think I know her. What's her last name? Describe her?*

"What are you doing?" I hiss.

"Finding what he remembers of you," he replies smiling happily.

Ethan: *Okay. I'll bite. She was quite tall from what I can remember. She had long dark, wavy hair. Pulled back into a high ponytail. Soft, olive skin. Curvy, but not fat. She had amazing green eyes. Is that enough of a description?*

I stare at the screen unblinking. Mason doubles over laughing. I look at him confused.

"Oh god. This is hilarious."

"What the hell's funny about all this? It's embarrassing. Please stop," I plead as his phone pings again. We freeze. Mace looks, then turns to me his eyebrows raised in astonishment.

"What?" I demand, scrambling to see the screen.

Ethan: *So, now you go quiet? You started this. How do you know her? How do you know it's the same girl?*

Mason: *Her last name is Carter. Here's a pic.*

"What are you doing?" I yell, his phone pings again.

. . .

Ethan: *That's her! How do you know her?*

Mason: *We're friends.*
Ethan: *What do you mean by friends? She's only been in San Diego a couple of months.*

"Wow," he snickers.
"Stop being an idiot," I snip.

Mason: *We met the day she got here too. She literally ran into me and fell on her ass. We're friends. Why, do you want to know?*

Ethan: *Just wondered. Anyway, what's with all the questions?*

Mason: *Just wondered if you remembered her is all.*

Ethan: *Why does she remember me?*

"What shall I tell him?"

"You may as well tell him everything now. You've told him everything else," I snap angrily.

. . .

Mason: *Yeah, she does. I just figured out it was my brother she was talking about. Weirded me out.*

Ethan: *Why? What did she say about me?*

"This is just embarrassing," I groan into my hands.

"Don't worry, I got this" he says cryptically, I peek through my fingers.

Mason: *I can't tell you that.*

I roll my eyes, wow, genius.

Ethan: *You can't just not tell me.*

Mason: *She won't let me.*

"Mace." I thump him in the arm.

"Ow. What was that for?" He yelps rubbing his arm.

Ethan: *Okay…?*

Mason: *She's my friend.*

. . .

Ethan: *Hang on, I'm going to call you. All this texting is killing my fingers.*

I leave him to it not wanting to hear anymore, and head into the kitchen to make myself a cup of tea.

Holding my steaming mug, I wonder back towards the living room. Mason's hushed voice and stop, listening.

"Listen, it's not my place to tell you the details, but her mom died and she was a mess. I'm keeping her mind off it as much as I can. That's why I'm spending a lot of time here," he whispers.

I doubt I was meant to hear that. He's right. I have been a mess and I only just about coped because of him. He's been my rock. God, I love him.

Silence. "I can't give you that, but if you want to talk to her you can on my phone," Mace whispers nodding.

"Okay. Yeah, hang on," he comes out the living room, grinning from ear to ear holding the phone out to me. I look at it as though it's a snake.

"He wants to talk to you," he urges me to take the phone. I shake my head.

"I can't talk to him. This is your fault, you arse. What am I supposed to say?" I hiss at him.

"Just take it and say hi. I'm going out. I'll have your phone if you need me. See you in a few," he sings, handing me his phone before taking off laughing.

I take a deep breath, put the phone to my ear.

"Hello?" I say, sinking into the sofa.

"Hi, Lily. This is weird huh?" He asks chuckling.

"Yeah. You could say that. Small world too. I can't believe you're my best friend's brother," I snicker relaxing a little.

"Yeah. Who'd have thought it. Mason said you've had a shitty few weeks?" He asks hesitantly.

"Yeah. I lost my mom a few weeks ago," I say, breathing through the blast of pain.

"I don't know what to say, I suppose I should say I'm sorry, but I know that's not enough, from the way you spoke about her, you must be hurting." I feel warmth swathe me at his understanding.

"I didn't think I would see or speak to you again and here we are," he adds sounding happy.

"It's okay. Mace has been amazing to me and Nan. How have you been?" I ask, excitement taking over with every word he says.

"Oh, same shit, different day," he blurts, I laugh at the bluntness of his statement. Hearing his husky laugh, makes me tingle, mmm, still there.

"Would you like to go on a date with me?" His question breaks me out of my girly episode.

"Yes. I'd love to." I cringe at my eagerness. "You just want to talk my ear off again, don't ya?" I add trying to cover my awkwardness and laugh.

He chuckles. "Damn, you got me! Has anyone ever told you, you're mouthy?" He jokes.

"Yeah, actually. Your brother. He calls me names, obviously, you two share a lot of traits."

"So, can I get your number so I can text and call you instead of my brother?" There's hesitance in his voice, nerves maybe?

I rattle off my number. "Okay. I'll text you later on tonight then. I'm glad we reconnected. I've been thinking about you a lot since we met," he admits, making me grin like an idiot.

"Me too, but don't tell Mace that. I wouldn't hear the end of it. He's a pain in the arse," I blurt laughing.

"He is that, always was. So, what did you say about me to my brother, that weirded him out?" His voice lowers.

God, his voice, it makes goose-bumps race up my arms. Clearing my throat, I try to speak normally.

"Oh, that would be telling." I'm flirting.

"I know he won't tell you before you say you're going to ask him. You'll have to use your imagination," I say, my voice lowering.

"Okay, I think we'll have this conversation when I can see your face. See, if you blush it means I'm on the right track," he breathes heavily through the phone.

I see Mason come through the door. "I better go. Your brother just got back and I've got to kick his arse for sticking his nose into my business," I say loud enough so Mace can hear me, and I hear him chuckle.

"Okay. You go deal with him. Give him an extra kick for me and I'll speak to you later?" I look down to hide my face from Mason.

"Yeah, speak to you later, bye." Clicking the phone off. I take a deep breath and let Mason have it.

The following day we arrange our first date for tomorrow at seven, I have no idea where, but I want to look my best. So, I go for a dress which is rare for me, but it's a special occasion.

I'm a bag of nerves all morning Tuesday and the day is passing so slowly, it's painful. So, to pass the time I decide to go through the box of photographs from home.

There are endless pictures of me as a baby, growing up,

birthdays some with me with teeth missing. Wearing a tiara and princess dress. Some of dance classes and us camping. When the box is empty and I'm surrounded by pictures and memories. My face is wet with tears seeing years of precious moments.

By five-thirty I'm showered, shaved and moisturised.

Drying my hair, I leave it in soft waves down my back. I go subtle on my makeup, adding a light green eye shadow to go with my dress since it's still warm and I don't want to be sweating it off. My dress is simple; a flowing, soft green knee length material, it highlights my eyes.

Since I'm already tall I pick flat black ballet shoes and a leather jacket. I look more like a girl than I have in years.

"Wow look at you. You look beautiful." Nan smiles at me.

"Thanks, I was a bit worried I'd overdone it. I'm so nervous with this being the first date and not knowing where we're going. I haven't dressed like this voluntarily since I was little," I joke checking the time. It's six-forty-five, he should be here in fifteen minutes.

"Take a breath honey. I don't think I've ever seen you so jumpy," she chuckles as I blow out a breath still chewing my cheek anxiously.

I jump when the doorbell chimes and rush to open it.

And there he stands looking sexy in black pants, the fit does amazing things to his hips. A white shirt, open at the collar and a black leather jacket. His hair is rumpled making him look even more gorgeous. My belly flutters when I meet his eyes, they're exactly as I remember them.

"Hi," he says, his eyes sweeping over my outfit and widening a little at my legs. "Wow. You look amazing," he breathes swallowing hard.

The look in his eyes flusters me so much, my brain-to-mouth filter falters and I blurt my first thought.

"You look hot." I cover my face as nan and Ethan chuckle. I'd forgot she was present.

"Erm, thank you." His voice is soft and breathless.

Looking through my fingers I see his face is slightly flushed and realise I may have embarrassed him in front of her.

"Nan, you remember Ethan, right?" I ask pushing through my embarrassment.

"Yes, how could I forget? Good to see you again, Ethan."

"Nan." I warn.

"You too, Mrs Carter," Ethan smirks. "Are you ready to go?" He asks. I nod grabbing my bag.

"See you later, I have my phone if you need me," I give her a kiss bye and step up next to Ethan who smells phenomenal, taking his offered arm.

"Bye, Mrs Carter," he says politely.

"Bye. Have a lovely time you two," she cackles, making me blush again.

"You know, I'm glad I talked Mace out of coming here before our date. He would have been worse than my nan," I huff, making Ethan chuckle.

"You know they only do it because they get a rise out of you," his breath tickles my ear and I lose my footing.

He catches me to him, taking a deep breath. "You smell so good, like coconut." His gruffness sends a shiver through me.

Thankfully, we reach the car without another accident on my part. Sliding into his car I try to calm my breathing but having him that close has wrought havoc on my senses.

"So, where are we going?" I ask looking over at him.

"Well, you said your favourite food was Mexican, right?" I nod, forgetting that he has to concentrate on the road.

"Yes, it is," I say surprised he remembers.

"Well, a friend of mine and his parents own one of the best Mexican restaurants around here and since it's your favourite, I wanted to take you there."

The restaurant is beautiful. Red walls and dark wood everywhere. Beautiful tables and chairs with deep red velvet cushioning. We're seated at a table in a corner, extremely romantic and private. Tiny candles are lit in a bed of red roses, set along the middle of the table to create atmosphere.

"Wow. Ethan, this is beautiful." I smile blown away; he reaches for my hand.

"I wanted it to be special with it being our first date."

I squeeze his hand. "It is special, this is my first, first date. So, this tops anything I could ever imagine." I smile loving the feel of his hand in mine.

"Seriously? You've never been on a date before?" He asks, surprised as his thumb caresses my hand gently. I shake my head, staring at his thumb, my belly tightening.

"Well, I'm glad to be the first," he says softly as our waiter arrives to take our orders.

We share a big plate of cheesy nachos for a starter and end up choosing the same main of chicken enchiladas, rice with a sweet and spice pepper salad.

"Wow. That was fantastic," I say, wiping my mouth.

Ethan smiles, taking a sip of his beer. "Told you it was amazing here, but I've never had a more amazing meal than this one," his tone implying that it has nothing to do with the food.

Finishing up, we leave the restaurant, I feel a pang of disappointment that the night is ending so soon.

“I’m not ready for our date to end yet,” he whispers, I turn to meet his eyes taking in my reaction.

“Me neither,” I whisper back chewing my cheek.

“What would you like to do?” His voice lowers as he reaches for my hand, interlocking our fingers.

“I don’t mind,” I’m breathless wanting him to kiss me. My eyes drop to his mouth, plump kissable lips. Wet from the last of his beer. My heart rate spikes imagining what he would taste like.

“Lily?” His tone pulling me out of my trance, I look up. His eyes are dark, dilated, he’s right there in front of me as if he was reading my mind and agreeing. Slowly his lips touch mine. They’re like soft pillows and I sink into them, his scent enveloping me. His taste bursting over my taste buds as I lick his bottom lip.

CHAPTER SIX

<u>Two weeks later</u>

We're in my room talking and laughing about how I met Mason. Leaning into me, his big hand glides up my arm. Resting on the back of my neck. Looking into my eyes, his dark and smouldering. Lips parted, red and wet as he licks them.

"Lily," he sighs his breath fanning my face. *Please kiss me*.

"Ethan," I grip his thigh. His muscles bunch under my hand and gasps at the touch. Leaning in the rest of the way, his plump lips touch mine making me shiver. I slide my other hand through his soft hair, gripping it tightly as I kiss him back.

His kiss is hungry and the next thing I know, I'm astride his lap, both hands in his hair kissing him desperately. Our tongues gliding into the others mouth, tasting, he tastes amazing. Mmm, peppermint. I moan into his mouth.

Gripping my hips, squeezing repeatedly. "God, you're

sexy, I've wanted to touch you for so long," he growls into my ear kissing along my neck.

Shivering, I dig my nails into his shoulders. My lips gliding up his neck, licking behind his ear, he groans pulling me closer. Oh god, I can feel him, he's hard. Grinding on him I moan. I bite into muscle where his shoulder meets his neck, making him shudder and grunt.

He twists us with me still in his arms. I'm pressed into my quilt as Ethan settles on top of me, holding himself up on one of his arms. Feeling cold with the space between us, I pull him into me.

"Mmm," I moan, bringing his mouth back to mine. The man can kiss. I'm wet and tingling for him.

"I love your hair. It's perfect to hold onto." His voice gruff as he tugs my hair deepening the kiss.

My hands exploring his torso gliding over his bare, well defined pecs. When did he lose his shirt?

His body is gorgeous. My hand wonders across tight abs and lower. Sliding my fingers under the waistband of his trousers.

"Ah," he groans into my neck. I run a hand up his back over his bare skin. Soft, warm and toned. Delicious.

"Ethan? I need you." I stutter breathing heavily into his neck, nipping and sucking on his skin. Not sure what the hell I need, I feel like I'm burning up. Gripping his ribs, my nails digging in.

He hisses, sucking my neck harder. I feel his hand coasting up my rib cage.

Moaning, I push my chest into his hands. I feel electric sizzling through me. My breathing stutters out.

"Ethan, please?" I plead. His hand glides back down to my thigh hitching it around his hip.

"*Yes!*" I groan, I want. No, *need* more. He's torturing me, his hand slowly gliding up the back of my thigh. Leaving my leg shaking and tingling with his slow progression. Everything's intensified, I groan the closer he gets.

I'm rudely awoken by my phone alarm. Sitting up, I feel sweat clinging to my heated skin. Rubbing my face, I try to calm my breathing. My phone beeps on my nightstand. Blowing out a breath I grab it.

A grin kicks up the side of my mouth on reading it.

Ethan: *Morning. Did you sleep well?*

Me: *Morning. I slept amazingly, thanks.*

My body heats thinking about my steamy dream.

Ethan: *That sounds interesting. Want to tell me about it?*

Me: *Tell you about what?*

Ethan: *The dream that made it amazing. Was it a naughty dream about me? ;)*

Me: *You were one of the starring roles. ;)*

. . .

Ethan: *Really? Well, this conversation just got interesting. What was I doing to you?*

Me: *What lead you to think you were doing anything to me?*

Ethan: *Well, you said I was one of the starring roles. So, I know you were the other and you're rather reluctant to tell me what happened in this dream.*

Me: *Okay, you got me there. What do you want to know?*

Ethan: *If it was as hot as mine?*

Staring at the phone, mouth open. He dreamed about me, and a hot dream?

All the flirting via texts, and that kiss. Get me so, hot.

Me: *What was yours about?*

Ethan: *Mine was probably lewder than yours, I wouldn't want to scare you off.*

Shit. I'm in trouble. I'm hot and wet just from texting.

. . .

Me: *Don't know how to reply to that one, but mine was amazing...*

Ethan: *Lily Carter. Don't play with me. When can I see you again?*

Me: *I'm not playing. It was the best dream I've ever had. Soon, I hope. I have leave from school for a few months, to sort stuff out so whenever you're free.*

Ethan: *Good. I know we need to get to know each other, but I want to see you. Shit, it's been too long since I kissed you. You make me hot!!*

Fanning my face, I kick the quilts off. I'm hot, and in need of a cold shower, but opt for a cold drink instead, I jog downstairs in my jammies and get some water from the fridge.

Looking at the clock I see it's only seven-thirty, nan must be out already. I smile as I read her note. I get one every time she leaves the house and I love them.

I gulp down half the bottle thinking how everything's changed in a matter of weeks. Nan's coping better, I think. I still cry every morning missing her. Life seems empty without her; there's so much I want to share with her. Like my feelings for Ethan. I shake off my gloomy thoughts. Collapsing onto the sofa and switch to the music channels.

Another ping makes me jump. Shit. I didn't text back.

. . .

Ethan: *Did I scare you off?*

Me: *No. Sorry was getting a drink. I needed a cold drink, you made me hot. I want to see you too. That kiss was amazing.*

Ethan: *Shit.*

Me: *It's worse knowing what you taste like and coupled with that dream too.*

I flinch when my phone rings, Ethan's name flashing across the screen and I panic.

"Hello?" I answer gulping my water again wetting my dry throat.

"Hi, where are you?" He asks his voice husky and rushed.

"I'm at home, why?" I ask sitting up my nerves making me jittery.

"Because, I want to see you," he replies, his voice so deep it raises the hairs on the back of my neck.

"Well, my nan's at work so it's just me," I say breathlessly, cringing at how that sounded.

"I'll be there soon." He hangs up.

I look down at myself. Shit, I'm a mess, my hairs everywhere, I'm sweaty and still in PJ's.

I run up the stairs like a fire's been lit under me. I shower quickly and dress in a multi-coloured maxi dress. Brush out my hair, leaving it down on a whim. A thin layer of foundation, mascara, eye liner. A swipe of lip balm and I'm ready in record time.

Padding downstairs barefooted, I await my guest wondering if he'll kiss me again. I hope so.

I'm jarred from my thoughts by the man himself at the door.

Swinging the door open my mouth dries. He's wearing a soft, green T-shirt that stretches nicely over his chest, dark jeans, boots, leather jacket and sunglasses. He has a bad boy edge to him dressed like this, my gaze eats him up, traveling up to his gorgeous face and finding him grinning at me.

"Sorry, come in," I murmur, moving aside as he steps forward removing his sunglasses and flashing those beautiful eyes.

I shut the door, taking a deep breath and turn bumping into him. I groan feeling his chest graze mine. His gaze as potent as a physical caress. I bite hard on my cheek trying to resist licking his lip. He bites it teasing me. *Fuck.* I shake myself remembering my manners.

"Do you want something to drink or eat?" I ask, my voice breathy.

He blinks and chuckles. "So, polite. I thought you might have loosened up a bit since our first date is out the way. Water would be good, thanks. I'm not hungry, yet," he adds huskily.

Clearing my throat, I skirt him leading the way into the kitchen. Grabbing a bottle of water from the fridge my handshakes.

"Do you want a glass and ice?"

When I get no reply, I turn. He's leaning against the counter staring at my backside. Raising an eyebrow, I clear my throat. His eyes jerk to my face looking sheepish, but not sorry.

“Glass, ice?” I ask again, feeling off balance.

“Just the bottle since it’s cold. Thanks.” His finger purposefully brushing mine as he takes it.

“Do you want to sit?” I head towards the living room, needing to sit before I fall. We sit close together on the sofa, both nervous.

“Okay. Why are we so nervous? We’re fine on the phone and we got through the first date,” he asks looking at my lips. His pupils dilate as he leans toward me, my heart racing the closer he gets.

“Lily,” he groans. “I. Need. To.”

I cut him off gripping the back of his neck, pulling his lips to mine. Moaning as his soft lips meet mine. The heat of his hand gripping my waist sends shivers down my spine as his other hand cradles my face, his thumb skating along my jaw.

I turn fully sliding my hands into his hair deepening our kiss and licking his lip, he lets out a pained groan, wrapping my hair around his hand he pulls me so close I’m almost across his lap, his tongue twisting aggressively with mine.

He pulls back, panting, his face masked with such hunger, my insides tighten. *I jumped him!*

“I’m sorry,” I say still breathless from our kiss. His smell teasing my senses does not help, it's different from last night. Gone is the cologne today is all him, fresh, sweet and male.

“Don’t apologise for that, it was amazing. You just surprised me. I wanted to kiss you the moment you opened the door. I really like you, Lily. I know we’ve only been in contact with each other a couple of weeks and we’ve only been on one date, but can we see where this can go?”

He chuckles. “I liked you the first time we met. Now that we’ve spent time talking and I know you a little better. I think you're amazing and funny and smart and beautiful. That kiss." He blows out a breath smiling wickedly.

"Must have been all frustration from the dreams and the teasing," I giggle touching my swollen lips.

He groans burying his face in my neck. "Don't remind me, it was sweet torture. I'm already hot for you, I can only take so much," he growls as I bite his neck.

Swearing, he grips my hair and pulling my head back to look at him. His pulse beating rapidly through his neck, his eyes burning. My thighs tingle as the heat between us flares, my body aching so bad I'm burning. We collide in an explosive meeting of mouths and tongues. Both letting out groans.

I clamp my hands around his neck straddling him. Feeling a shudder go through his big frame as his hands fall to my hips securing me tightly against him. My hips moving of their own volition.

"Ah, Lily. Don't do that. Please," he pants as I rock against him.

"Why?" I moan, it feels so good, I move faster making him hiss. I freeze realising what I'm doing, I jump off him hiding my flushed face.

"I'm sorry, I didn't mean to do that. I don't know what came over me, it's all so intense," I mumble into my hands confused.

"No. Don't be sorry. I want to so bad, but I don't think we... You are ready for us to go too far yet. I mean I don't even know if we're together?"

I chuckle at how stupid that question is. "Okay. What does that mean? What is it you want from this?" I ask straight out. Sitting on the coffee table directly in front of him bumping knees.

"It means. I want to know if we're seeing each other. I want to see where this is going. I've never really felt any of this before. This craziness, the feeling's, the jealousy. What I'm trying to ask. Badly, it would seem. Are you my girlfriend? Because I really want that. I don't share," a growl escapes his throat.

Groaning, he rubs a hand down his face. "And now I sound like a damn teenager," he mumbles. Quirking an eyebrow, I take his hand.

"I don't share either, you have nothing to worry about with me and other men. If that's what you want, for me to be with you, then yes, I'll be your girlfriend," I giggle at how childish all this sounds.

"Now that we're both clear, come here." he says, wiggling his finger at me, unleashing a sexy little grin.

Scooting off the table I kneel between his legs, rubbing my hands along his thighs, watching his muscles tighten at my touch. I smile smugly, knowing I affect him as much as he does me.

I sigh as his palms glide up either side of my neck, his thumbs pushing my face up taking in all my features. His breath a whisper on my lips. Heat sears me, just a look and my heart beats out of control.

"God. You're gorgeous. Your eyes are stunning. And I love your hair, I've wanted to do this since the flight here," he whispers huskily running his fingers through my hair. My eyes close enjoying the slide of his fingers.

"Why didn't you do it the other night?" I whisper, surrendering to his touch.

"I didn't want to push you too far, but I can't resist any more," he mutters tugging my hair at my nape and kissing the shit out of me.

"Wow," I breathe, opening my eyes slowly finding him smirking at me.

"Well, that was well worth the wait," he breathes.

"Mmm... I wouldn't know…" I blush, feeling silly for being inexperienced.

"I know that, that was your first date, but have you been in a relationship before?" he asks, genuinely baffled.

I shake my head. "No. I was never really into the whole boy thing," I admit swallowing nervously.

"Really? This is your first relationship?" he asks, pointing at himself.

"Yeah," I fidget nervously looking into sexy eyes. "I pretty much kept to myself back home," I admit as he smirks smugly, I cock an eyebrow amused by his reaction.

"Like that, do you?"

Chuckling, he asks, "How is even possible? Guys had to have chased you."

"What's so funny? I'm being serious."

"Nothing. If there were, I never noticed, I spent a lot of time either with mom, we ran together. We loved the outdoors, so camping was a must and we both did dancing. Then of course, I had school and writing too." I shrug my shoulders.

"You like camping and running?" he asks astonished.

"Yeah. I run every day, mostly with Mason. I used to go camping with my mom as much as possible. We loved it," I reply feeling the bite of pain thinking of her.

"Why do you sound so surprised that I run and go camping?" I ask perplexed and he rubs the back of his neck sheepishly.

"I know, it sounds sexist and snobby, but most women I know don't like the outdoors and sleeping outside is definitely out of the question," he says with a serious face and I burst out laughing.

"That's the type of woman I pinned you dating… And since that is the case, what are you doing with me? Because while I like looking nice sometimes, I'm certainly no girly, girl." I scoff at the thought of constantly primping myself.

He relaxes back into the sofa with his hands tucked behind his head, making a big show of looking me up and down.

"Stand up, let me get a good look," he smirks cockily. Huffing, I stand cock an eyebrow, sticking out my hands, I twirl for good measure.

"Well?" I face him again finding him looking thoroughly pleased with himself.

"Well, on thorough visual inspection, I'd say you look pretty damn good, but I haven't seen very much, yet have I?" he asks raising his eyebrows suggestively, challenging me. My body visibly shivers, whether it's the innuendo or the deep rasp of his voice, I don't know.

A blush heats my chest and crawls up my neck. He looks thoroughly pleased with himself and my reaction.

"Well, I haven't seen much of you either, yet have I?" I goad.

His eyes darken as he stands, his chest an inch from mine. My breath hitches as desire swamps me.

"We can't have that, now can we?" His voice dropping as his fingers stroke along my neck and his other hand grasps my waist, guiding me to him.

Taking advantage, I run my hands up his firm chest, it's strong, hot and hard. I can feel every muscle through his T-shirt. His heart is beating a rapid beat beneath my hand. I look at his face gauging his reaction, his lips are parted and wet.

I run my fingertips slowly down and along his abs, teasing him. I trace every muscle before moving on to his hips. Pausing taunting him, before gliding up his sides and finally resting my hands on his ribs.

His breathing stalled somewhere along the way, and only recommences when he's sure my hands are finished.

He looks dazed licking his lips, his mouth descending on mine. Sliding my greedy hands beneath his T-shirt, I drag my nails along his back, making him groan and close his eyes briefly savouring the sensation. His lips barely touch mine, our eyes locked, breathing erratic and hearts pounding.

I'm dizzy, his scent intoxicating me. I snap first dragging a hand through his hair and pulling him into me.

I'm awoken by a bang and Mace shouting my name. I jump realising I'm lying on Ethan's chest, wrapped tightly in his arms on the sofa. We must have fallen asleep talking, making out and cuddling.

Shaking myself, I remember Mason who is now standing at the back of the sofa looking down at us with his mouth hanging open.

I hide my face in Ethan's chest, my movement, making Ethan tighten his arm around me burying his face in my hair and humming in his sleep.

"Ahem," I peek at him. Over his shock he's now smirking, arms crossed and eyebrow cocked.

"Well, well, well. What do we have here?" his amusement clear. When Ethan doesn't answer, he yells, *"ETHAN!"* Laughing when Ethan jumps up knocking me onto the floor.

"What the fuck man?" he growls helping me up off the floor.

"You okay, baby?" he croons, cradling my face. I see Mason's eyebrows shoot up out of the corner of my eye. I grin, brushing imaginary dust off my arse.

"Yeah, I'm fine," I reply and squeeze his hand. Recovering my senses, I turn on Mason.

"You feckin' dick. That was not funny. That's the second time you've caused me a sore arse," I seethe.

Mason and I burst out laughing at my outburst. Ethan stands there wondering what the hell we're laughing at. I take deep breaths, calming myself enough to tell him about how we met. When I'm done, he chuckles.

After standing there looking like idiots for far too long, I lead the way into the kitchen to make sandwiches for everyone.

"So, what's going on with you two? How was your date night?" Mace asks, looking between us. *That little shit!* He already knows, I told him as soon as I got back.

"It was amazing…" Ethan answers drifting off looking at me, his eyes pulling me in.

Clearing his throat, he focuses on Mason. "As for us…" His gaze flicks back to me, questions in his eyes, I nod turning away.

"Well, we're going to be together, I mean she agreed to be my girlfriend," he falls over his words. He catches me looking and smirks at my red face. I get back to my job grinning like an idiot.

"Your girlfriend? Really, and have you run that past Ashley?" he asks sarcastically.

Freezing, I feel the blood drain from my face, solving my blushing problem. This can't be fucking happening.

Turning, I look at Ethan, he looks guilty and pale as his gaze meets mine, and I know it is happening. Ethan. The bloke I've been kissing and touching has a fucking girlfriend. And he didn't think I needed to know that? *Why the fucking hell didn't you tell me, you arsehole?* I shoot daggers at him.

"Lily," Ethan says hastily, standing up and moving towards me.

"No. Why the fuck didn't you tell me you had a girlfriend? Why the hell did we even go on a date? Have you had a good laugh at my naivety?" I yell shaking.

"What the fuck E? You didn't tell her anything? You know the deal," Mason snarls, coming to stand by me, but all I can concentrate on, all I see, is Ethan's guilty face.

I want him to tell me why he didn't say anything and why he's been calling me his girlfriend? Why he even took me on a date? He sits down hard on the corner of the table blowing out a breath.

"I was going to tell her after I had spoken to Ashley and your dad." His guilty gaze locking on my face. I could smack him right now.

"Well, dad's not going to be happy it's all been arranged. You agreed," Mason grates out.

Ethan's face contorts as his anger rises. "If you didn't want us to be together, why the hell did you text me asking shit loads of questions about a girl I met on an airplane? Then tell me she remembered me. You know I don't want Ashley," he shouts back frustrated.

"Well, come on. What are you going to do? Break the engagement?" Mace yells back, my eyes feel like they're going to pop out. What the fuck?

"Okay, enough." I say, my voice deceptively quiet, my anger ready to boil over.

"You," I point at Ethan "leave now, I can't believe you even asked me out, let alone actually going through with it. You're engaged! And you," I say looking at Mace. "Do whatever the hell you want. I don't give a shit right now. I need a run. I don't need this shit right now."

"Lily, give me the chance to explain all this? I was going to tell you, I swear."

I stop dead and spin around.

"You swear? For a bloke who's spent all day telling me

how much he likes me. All our date telling me he enjoys spending time with me. How “different” his feelings for me are. That he’s never felt this way before. The same bloke who for the past two weeks hasn’t said a fucking word about the little matter that he’s *engaged!* I told you I don’t do this stuff and I told you that I don’t fucking share.” I yell feeling foolish. Embarrassed.

“Mason, can you give us a few minutes to talk alone, please?” Ethan pleads anxiously. Mace looks at me silently asking if I want to be alone with him. I nod my head slightly. I would rather have this conversation alone. This is all embarrassing enough.

CHAPTER SEVEN

"Okay. Just let me get this out before you decide if you want to see me again," he rushes holding his hands up, I nod waiting.

"I'm sorry. I wanted to talk to Alexander first, but obviously, Mason had other ideas. I don't know if Mason has told you about his dad wanting us to date his friends and co-worker's daughters, for connections and growth of the business, but that's what all this is in a nutshell.

Him wanting me to marry Ashley because her dad is his friend. I was fine with it until I met you. Then the possibility of having something more, something that I want. The deal with Ashley wasn't even an option after that.

I didn't think I would ever see you again, which was depressing. Then out of nowhere Mayo texts me and we found each other. I was so happy to have a second chance, to see you again and when you agreed to go on a date with me, I was ecstatic. The past two weeks… And then today..." He blows out a breath, looking amazed.

"Today was amazing, you blew me away. I wasn't lying when I said I have never felt this way before. Now I know for sure. It all just feels… *Right,* my feelings for you feel right. This is different.

I know it's too soon and with all this shit hanging over us… But I'm going to ask anyway because I want a chance with you. After the time spent with you, talking to you I can't see myself with anyone else. So please, will you just give me some time to sort this out?"

I gape at him; my thoughts and feeling are jumbled. On one hand, I really like him and want to try I'm curious to see where it will go, but on the other I want to slap him for lying to me and cheating on his fiancée.

"What are your feelings for me?" I ask, my curiosity winning out.

Smiling, he walks to where I'm leaning against the wall, standing close to me he takes my hand in his linking our fingers.

"Well, you make me laugh. When I speak to you either by text, phone call or like this. I'm happy and anxious to see you, itching to touch you," he whispers, running his fingers down my cheek to my neck. I know I shouldn't let him, but I'm helpless to stop him.

"You make me feel confused and tongue tied and hot, you tie me in knots and whenever you look at me my heart races. You are so beautiful, my heart aches looking at you." He places my hand over his heart, which is beating wildly under my hand.

"I've never felt any of that about anyone before. I feel like a kid at Christmas. I'm so scared I've messed up," he admits looking devastated.

"You light me up like no one ever has," I blurt before my brain can stop me.

His smile is radiant, blinding. He slides his hand up my back to my neck, his thumb stroking behind my ear.

"Can we get through this? I don't want to lose you. I don't want to marry Ashley. I want to be with you. So, I'll ask again. Will you be my girlfriend?" He waits anxiously, but I need answers first.

"How can this be sorted? Mace told me how relentless his dad is with this and you're already engaged… It's set-in stone." I feel sick at the thought of Ethan with someone else.

He pulls me to his chest, stroking my hair and my mind blanks. Just a smile, a touch, a kiss and I'm reduced to a bumbling idiot. This moment is no different, I'm unable to think of anything. Nothing exists but us, as I'm held captive by his gaze.

"I'll sort it. I'll get mom to talk to Alex. I'll leave the business if I have to, but I won't let him force my hand. I won't lose you, not now that I've found you," he states adamantly.

My head nods my assent even as my brain screams no. My mouth saying words my brain didn't process. "I want to be with you too. I feel all of that and maybe a few others."

My body heats just thinking about his body.

He smirks leaning down to whisper in my ear. "You're not the only one who feels those things. You're a beautiful, hot and sexy young woman, with a body to match. Believe me, I ache with wanting you." His voice lowers making me tingle.

Feeling dizzy I grasp his hips to steady myself but end up pulling him into me. Gasping when I feel him, he's right, he is aching, and hard too. Right now, his eyes are the deepest gold with flecks of green and orange, his pupils dilated, his breathing laboured, his heart thudding wildly and his face flushed.

I feel a niggling sensation in the back of my mind before

it shuts down and our mouths feast. His hand still on my neck, tightens securing me in place.

The other thuds against the wall beside my head, holding his weight as he turns his head to get better access to my mouth.

My hands slide into his hair, tugging, trying to get him closer. I moan as he opens my mouth, licking into my mouth finding my tongue.

I'm so lost in our kiss I don't hear the door until there's a loud fake cough.

"Erm… Guy's, I don't think Cora, nor I want to see any of that," Mason mutters sounding a little sick.

Pulling back, I look at Ethan he's smiling smugly, his cheeks flushed, lips red plump and wet. His hair rumpled from my tugging it. I blush breathing heavily, my lips tingling and wet. I'm pinned to the wall by six foot four inches of sexy, muscled, aroused male. While nan and Mace watch. God, could this be any more embarrassing?

"Hello, Ethan. You look as good as you did last time, I saw your fine ass. Everything going well then?" she cackles.

I gasp hiding my face in Ethan's chest. "Nan," I hiss, trying so hard not to laugh.

"Yes, honey?" She asks, laughter in her voice. "Could you come out from behind... Or in front of Ethan? So, I can hear you and not laugh at Ethan's back," I hear Mason laugh as well.

I groan. Ethan starts to shake with laughter, I jab him in the belly. "This is not funny Mister. See what happens when you distract me?" I grunt in mock frustration.

He holds his hands up in surrender. "Hey, you pulled me into you. Not that I'm complaining or anything," he adds quickly, seeing my eyebrow pop.

Grinning at him, I slide from in front of him to face my

nan, who is laughing silently. To my best friend, who looks like he isn't sure whether to smirk or throw up. I can't blame him after he just witnessed his brother pinning me to the wall.

The thought makes me smirk at him and stick my tongue out, before turning to nan.

"Sorry, about that Nan," I say my whole face burning red, my hands fidget behind my back. Ethan steps up behind me, his hands stilling mine interlocking our fingers and bringing them to rest on my belly.

"Hello, Mrs Carter. Nice to see you again." He squeezes my hands.

Mason is ready to keel over at this point. If he doesn't breathe instead of laugh.

"Oh, for god's sake. It is not that funny," I snap fisting our joined hands on my hips setting him off again. Rolling my eyes, I go to help her, picking up the shopping bags, she must have dropped when she saw… Well, what she saw.

"Can you stay for dinner, Ethan?" Nan asks, helping pick up the shopping. He looks to me for an answer, I look at him blankly. I'm not making this decision for him.

"Um, I would like that. Thank you," he answers. Not his confident, self at all, he looks at Mason questions in his eyes.

"Oh, she doesn't ask Mace anymore he's always here for dinner. He'll have his own room soon enough," I state, rolling my eyes again smirking at Mason, who smiles broadly at me from his chair before swinging his feet onto the table.

I smack them off. "Not quite though Mace. I can still kick you out without dinner if you don't keep your manky feet off the table." I quip, nan chuckles shaking her head.

"You'll need to get used to them behaving like five, year olds. Oh, and Lily's smart mouth," she sasses, I sputter at her statement making them all laugh.

"I do not have a smart mouth."

"Nope, just a dirty mouth. Isn't that right Potty mouth?" Mace teases, and I lunge for him.

"Oh, that's it. You've had it now Mason. Wait till I catch you. I'm so putting your girly pictures all over the neighbourhood near school," I sing chasing him around the kitchen once more before giving up. Panting, I lean against Ethan, who puts his arm around me.

"Told ya," I hear nan mutter, Ethan chuckles so I elbow him.

"Aww, come on. Don't do that, I was just kidding and I forgot about our deal," Mace pleads giving me puppy eyes.

"Oh, I don't think so buster. We had a deal. You broke it, so I get to show everyone your sensitive side. Oh, I bet Millie would love to see you in a pink frilly apron." I wave my phone giggling.

I show Ethan, who is now hanging over my shoulder. He bursts out laughing, "Oh, Mayo, pink is definitely your colour."

"Why do you call him Mayo?" I ask looking back at him.

"I'll tell you another time, I think you're torturing him enough right now. Why does he call you potty mouth?" he asks and I laugh remembering the day I met Mason.

"He can tell you," I say, Mace grins.

"Nan, is it okay if I invite Millie over for dinner too? We could have a movie and order in?" I ask hugging her from the side, just because. "Yes, it'll be nice to see her I haven't seen her in a while," she says sadly.

"Love you," I whisper kissing her cheek, she gives me a smile full of love.

"Love you too. Go call, then sit with that sexy young

man," she urges. I shake my head going into the guys, who've moved into the living room.

"Hey, Mills," I sing into my phone when she answers. "Hey, Lils," she sings back and we giggle.

"You busy?" I ask looking through my DVD collection. "Nope, just doing coursework. Why?"

"Do you want to come over for dinner and a movie night?" I ask nixing all the girly movies.

I can feel her overthinking it through the phone. "Come on, please? I haven't seen you in ages please, please, please? I miss my best friend," I beg because I really do miss her.

"Hey, Miss Mouth. I'm your best friend too!" Mason buts in.

"Oh, now, I'm definitely showing her the pictures."

"Mason's there?" she asks pausing, and I wait her out. "Okay, I'll come. Can you ask Mason to come get me, in about fifteen minutes?" she asks blowing out a breath.

"He'll be there with frills on. Bye," laughing, I hang up. Looking straight at Mason and making kissy faces and laughing harder as he lunges for me.

I jump into Ethan's lap, throwing my arms around him, hiding my face in his neck. He lets out a loud grunt catching me and tightening his arms around my back.

"Sorry," I mumble, my lips grazing his neck. He shudders pulling back to look at me.

His eyes dark, his passion renewed. Biting my cheek, I try to resist attacking his mouth.

"Oh, for God's sake. You two are making me sick mooning all over each other," Mace snips.

"Okay, let's wait till Millie gets here and let's see if you moon all over her," I smirk teasing him. Huffing he grabs his keys and leaves passing nan on his way.

"Honey, I'm going to grab a quick shower while it's

quiet," she says from the door winking over Ethan's shoulder at me. She's a crafty old lady my nan.

Ethan's hand starts exploring as soon as nan's gone. That's all it takes to ignite the fire inside me; I look at him feeling desire hum through me.

"Ethan," My voice husky and sexy. Just like that we're right back where we were before. Devouring each other, dual moans ring through the quiet room.

Twisting in his lap, I straddle him weaving my fingers through his soft locks taking over our kiss deepening it. I want him that bad, right now.

His hands glide down my back, squeezing and rubbing, I squirm needing to feel him. He groans as I moan at the pleasurable zing that hits me south of the waistline. It feels so good I do it again.

The pleasure increasing with every brush of his jeans, it's unbelievable, uncontrollable I'm desperate to feel him.

"Ah, baby. You need to stop doing that," he groans. I look at him, hoping he's not serious. His pained expression stops me immediately.

"I'm sorry, I…" I say, moaning as he nips behind my ear.

"No, it's just that you turn me on so much and my dick is about to burst. Here," he whispers pulling me down, grinding into me making us both moan.

"Ah, that feels fucking incredible," he sighs. My heart rate spikes looking at him, his head thrown back in pleasure, cheeks flushed, hair a mess. Red, wet, parted lips, his tongue just visible.

I'm mesmerized watching my hand glide down his pecs, feeling his muscles contract. My finger tracing his abs, him, hissing as my finger rub against his erection which is quite substantial and growing.

Opening his burning eyes, he licks his lips as his palm slides up my bare thigh.

Oh. Tingles sweep through me, my body tightening, trembling, needing more. I hold my breath pleading with him with my eyes for something anything.

"Breathe, baby." He whispers, looking at me through hooded eyes.

I lean down to kiss his parted lips. "Please, Ethan, touch me," I whisper.

"Where? Where do you want me to touch you?" He rasps.

Grabbing his hand, I place it on my chest covering my breast and moan as he squeezes gently.

"*Ethan,*" I gasp shuddering, he pinches my nipple causing me to grind on him. My head drops to his shoulder; I bite down as the next shiver rolls through me. Growling, he grabs my head, kissing me furiously.

"Fuck, we need to stop. Mason and your friend are going to be here soon and your gran is upstairs," he points out panting flushed and gorgeous.

I peck him on the lips once more before scooting off him, putting some much-needed space between us.

"Sorry, I got carried away," I say embarrassed, I've never behaved like that in my life. I'm mortified right now. It was incredible, but looking back, I attacked the poor bloke.

"Don't you dare apologise for that. You were amazing. I almost blew in my pants and I haven't done that since I was thirteen. It would have been embarrassing for me though, I would have had to sit through dinner with your gran, Mason and your other friend wet and sticky," he says, pulling a face making me laugh and blush at the same time.

Standing, he pulls his shirt down, trying to hide his erection. It doesn't work at all and I can't say I'm disappointed. I bite my cheek staring at him, or a certain part of him.

"You're really not helping here, babe," he growls at me. Looking up I blush, giggling at his exasperated huff.

"You did this. Help a man out would ya? How am I going to hide this?" He points at himself. I smile pulling him back onto the sofa in the corner.

"Here," I say putting a pillow over his…. Err... Problem and lay my head on it so it doesn't look suspicious. "You good now?" I ask, smiling sweetly at him.

"Not really helping the problem, but covering it, yeah," he groans, taking my hand, entwining our fingers, laying them on the back of the sofa.

"So, what time is kick out time here?" he asks distracting himself.

"There isn't one tonight. Movie night everyone crashes here. Are you going to sleep with me?" I whisper provocatively, purposefully licking my top teeth.

"*Fuck!*" His eyes wide, glued to my mouth.

"Lily, please, don't. I don't know how much more I can…." he pleads. Feeling my hand squeezes his thigh, he launches us off the sofa. Grabs my hand dragging me along behind him.

"Nearest room with a door?"

"Erm, that would be my room or the bathroom, but Nan's in there," I say breathlessly jogging to match his strides.

"Your bedroom, which way?" He asks, his words are clipped. "Upstairs, to the right, second door," I barely get the words out before I'm tugged up the stairs and into my bedroom.

Flicking on the bedside lamp, light bursts into the room as I hear the click of the lock. Turning, I gasp when I bump into his chest. I grasp his arms to stop myself tumbling, his arms slipping around my waist.

"Hi," he murmurs against my lips. I say something, I have

no idea what though, because I'm mesmerized by his mouth. Leaning in I lick his bottom lip, biting down. His breath stutters momentarily stunned.

His lips on my neck, his tongue teasing my skin, my body trembles swaying into him wanting, needing to be closer. My body ablaze with pleasure, my head falling back in surrender, in this moment I'm his.

His fingers twisting in my hair, moving my head for better access, his teeth sinking into my skin. I moan loudly, my eyes rolling back.

"Ethan, please. Do something…" I beg needing release.

He doesn't let up torturing me. "Ethan, now, I need you." He pulls back looking me in the eyes.

"Do you know what you're asking? We're not exactly alone here."

I nod knowing I'm ready. Not that I've held back, I've just never wanted to. His nervousness makes me smile.

"You're amazing do you know that? You're beautiful, sexy, funny, kind, hot, loving, sassy and mouthy, but I love you anyway…" He blurts, his eyes pleading.

I freeze at the words that slip from his lips; he looks as shocked as I am.

He doesn't look horrified though. I look him in the eyes, knowing what I feel to be true.

"I love you, too. I know it's fast and we have a lot to get through, but I want you to know that I feel the same way," I say and kiss him trying not to overthink.

Pushing him to the bed, I climb on top of him giving him everything I've got. I feel out of control, frantic, I need to get closer to him. To have all of him, now. Gripping my hips, he pulls me onto him fully, we both moan.

Wiggling I try to get comfortable. I still when he grunts

squeezing me tightly. “No. Don’t stop.” He hisses as I shift again, this time down.

Slowly, I reach for his fly, pulling the button, it pops open at the same time as his eyes. Looking into my eyes, he nods licking his lips, he falls back on the bed, trapping his hands under his head.

Letting me do what I want. I smile anticipation causing my hand to shake, he returns my smile watching and waiting to see if I back down. Well, you have another thing coming, Mr, Barker. I don’t back down and, in this case, I just don’t want to.

Leaning over purposefully putting my breasts in his line of sight. Licking my lips, leaving them parted and wet, tempting and slowly pull down his zip.

He gulps, groaning as I rub him through his boxers. Gently pulling him out, he hisses making me jump and release him.

“No, no. Give me your hand,” I place my hand in his, he slides my fingers around him showing me what he likes, groaning when I squeeze him a little.

“Keep going,” he says, letting go, his voice shaking.

His skin is like silk. He’s hard, long and thick and beautiful. I blush, realising I spoke out loud.

“Thanks,” he grins cockily. I squeeze harder, he loses the grin as I double my efforts to pleasure him. His eyes roll back and he starts to pant and moan.

In for a penny and all that. Grabbing a few tissues from the bedside table, I lean close to his ear. “Ethan... You're so hard. Come for me, baby,” I whisper my voice thick. Arching off the bed a shudder rips through him, groaning loudly.

“Lily,” he moans as he comes. I keep going, kissing him to mask his moans. Not wanting nan to hear.

Sagging into the bed, he blows out a breath and looks up

at me. “Wow. That was fantastic,” he breaths, a sleepy smile spreading across his face.

“You need to talk to me like that all the time when we’re alone. Just, wow,” he looks blissed out, I smile proudly.

I have a semi-permanent grin on my face as we walk hand in hand downstairs.

“You need to wipe that look off your face if you want to keep what we just did a secret,” Ethan whispers in my ear his voice thick. With a swift kiss behind the ear, he pulls me down the last few steps.

Luckily, no one’s there. Nan must still be in the shower and where the hell are Mason and Millie? I frown. We’ve been upstairs a while.

“I better check on Nan, then I’ll start tea, or do you want pizza?” I ask, sliding my arms around his neck, looking into the most gorgeous eyes I’ve ever seen.

“Pizza does sound good, but I’d prefer you…” He growls playfully pulling me into his arms, splaying his hands on my backside. I laugh at the corniness of that statement.

But as my hips touch his I feel how serious he is, my eyes widen. “How? You can’t be already,” I sputter feeling that he’s ready to go again. He gently closes my mouth, smirking at my reaction.

“Yes, I can. I told you, you make me ache.” He whispers kissing me softly.

“I had to put up with this, for an eleven-hour flight.” He says, his breath tickling my ear as he places my hand over his cock. Looking him in the eye I squeeze gently, the sexy little moan deep in his throat making me wet.

“I better check on my nan before you drag me back

upstairs." I giggle pecking him on the lips whispering "later" and running back upstairs.

"Nan?" I call knocking on her door, no one answers. Pushing the door open, I see her lying asleep on the sofa with the TV on low. Tiptoeing over, I grab a blanket and lay it over her, I notice the dark circles under her eyes, she mustn't be sleeping well. Guilt gnaws at me for not keeping a better eye on her. Kissing her cheek, I leave quietly shutting the door.

"Hey, no Millie and Mace?" I ask impatiently, the pizzas' ordered, movies picked, blankets and pillows set up. Popcorn, sweets and pop waiting.

"I'll call, hang on." Fishing out his phone, he frowns at the screen, swiping whatever's annoying him off the screen and puts the phone on speaker phone.

"Where the hell are you? It's been nearly an hour!" Ethan asks straight away. I hear music quietly humming in the background.

"We'll be there in about half an hour, we have things to talk about too," Mason snaps hanging up.

"Well, looks like it's dinner for two," he murmurs happily, pulling me onto his lap and kissing us both breathless.

"Mmm, are you staying for the sleepover or going home?" I ask looking at him my eyes taking him in.

"What do you want me to do?" he asks eyes smouldering.

"I want you to stay with me," I reply my voice low, sexy. I really want to sleep next to him and wake in his arms.

"Then, I'll stay. I want to feel you in my arms all night," he murmurs kissing my head.

I really want to ask what's going to happen when he tells his stepdad and Ashley, but I don't want to spoil our night. I don't like her already, but I can't be angry at her, she had him first and they're engaged.

She's the one wearing his ring. *Fuck.* That makes me the other woman; I don't want to be in this position, it's wrong and goes against everything my mom instilled in me.

Getting off him, I go to the window, pretending to look for the delivery guy. But of course, he's tuned into my mood swing, his arms slip around my waist, his chin resting on my shoulder and his breath on my cheek.

"What's wrong?" he asks, his eyes burning into the side of my face.

"Nothing, I'm fine." I force a smile, trying to sound normal, but having his arms around me is making me feel sick as my imagination conjuring images of them around another.

"You're not fine. You went from hot and sexy to sad and pissed. What were you thinking about?" he prods.

I stay quiet, he squeezes me tighter. "Baby, talk to me."

"What will happen when you tell your step-dad and *fiancée* about us?" I can't stop the disgust seeping through at the use of that word.

I don't even have the right to be disgusted. She had him first. I'm just his bit on the side. Homewrecker. Nausea surges through me at the thought of being branded that.

"I'll be right back," I blurt shrugging out of his hold and bolting for the bathroom, barely making it before vomiting the little food I've had today. I'm shaky and sweaty. Flushing the loo, I stand and look at the girl in the mirror.

"What the fuck are you doing?" I ask glaring at my reflection. A soft knock on the door snaps me out of the glaring contest with myself.

"Lily, are you okay?" Ethan muffled voice calls through the door.

I swill my mouth out with mouthwash. "Just get it over with," I mutter to myself.

Opening the door, I look up into the magnificently beautiful eyes of the man I've stupidly fell in love with.

"The pizza's here are you okay?" he asks, stroking my cheek.

I nod. "Yeah, I'm good now, thanks," I answer taking his hand, leading him to the kitchen, sitting I open a box and eat quietly.

"Okay, you need to tell me what just happened back there," he huffs dropping his pizza. I put mine down and take a deep breath. I need to be honest and tell him everything that's going through my head.

"Okay, here it is. First, what are you going to tell your step-dad and Ashley?" I ask bullet pointing what I want to ask in my head.

"Well, I'm going to tell them the deals off. That I've found someone I want to be with," he states simply, looking me in the eye he adds. "That I've found the woman I love and intend to marry."

My jaw hits the table and I stare at him dumbfounded. My face splits into the most radiant smile, I'm delirious, overjoyed, blissed out, ecstatic and speechless and that just doesn't happen to me.

"You… You just…" I sputter unable to finish my sentence. Cocking his head to the side, he smirks at my speechlessness.

"I just what?" he asks amused, I throw a piece of pizza at him.

"Oh, shut up. That's how you feel? That's what you want?" I stumble over my words, like an inarticulate idiot.

"That's what I want and feel, I was hoping you were

feeling the same?" he asks unsure. He looks incredibly nervous, anxious even for my reply.

"For God's sake. Put the poor man out of his misery," an exasperated voice huffs from the door. Turning I see an astonished Mason and a grinning Millie. Standing just inside the door holding hands!

"Well, come on, don't keep him waiting. He looks a little pale," Millie snaps me back to the here and now.

Looking at Ethan I see she's right, he does look pale, but I don't want an audience for this. Standing quickly, I grab his hand pulling him with me rushing to the stairs.

"Be right back. Save us some pizza," I call down, shoving him into my room, closing and locking the door.

The lamps still on and the bed, still rumpled from earlier. "I do," I blurt looking at his handsome face, aware of the depth of meaning to those words.

He releases the breath he's been holding. His eyes shine with happiness and his smile could light up the house, he rushes me, pinning me to the door.

"I love you, Lily Carter," he sighs relieved. Grasping his face, I say, "I love you too, Ethan. Now kiss me."

I may be a fool. Young and naïve, but love is a powerful inebriant, it intoxicates you, and if you're lucky, destiny will play you a good hand and you can stay drunk in love.

Walking down the stairs hand in hand, both must up, rumpled and happy. Whatever comes from all this, we'll weather it together, Ethan eradicated my fears of being his bit on the side with his speech earlier.

We stop dead in our tracks. Shocked at the sight before

us. My jaw hits the floor again. Shit, it's going to be sore later.

Mason is on the sofa with Millie straddling him, his hands are…. Well, one is on her arse, the other I can't see. It's Millie that is shocking the shit out of me. She has Mason's shirt up to his neck.

Her hands are exploring his muscled chest and is currently doing some major grinding on him. What happens next is comical and horrific (for them) all at once.

"Well, I can see I need to do more supervising here," nan's voice cracks like a whip.

Mason jumps almost knocking Millie onto the floor as Millie squeals, quickly adjusting her top confirming where Mason's hand was. She's beet red and speechless. Mace looks sheepish, but not sorry. I straighten my hair gently, mustering as much courage as I can while fighting embarrassment.

"We ordered pizza; do you want some?" I ask nan, surprised my voice sounds normal.

She cracks up, leaning on the sofa. "Wow, your faces," she chokes out, breaking the ice making us all laugh.

"Okay, you're all adults, technically, just no doing that, on my sofa. I've got to sit on it, for heaven's sake. Just don't tell your Mother I said that." She points at Millie, who hides her face in Mason's chest.

"Don't worry, Millie, I've been there. My Jacob was H.O.T. That was nothing compared to what we did," she says wistfully.

Oh, hell no. "Eww, Nan. No. Don't say things like that in front of me. I don't want nor need that stuff in my head, I need my ears syringing and my brain wiped." I mutter, shuddering in disgust the image of nan and grandad getting it on running through my head, they all laugh at my distress.

"How do you think Lizzy came along? Jake was *fine,* he looked after himself and, in the bedroom," she whistles.

"Okay." I shout literally gagging, "We get the picture... You *'did it,'* to have Mom, and Grandad was *'fine'* back then." I imitate her voice when she said the word fine.

"Oh, we *'did it'* more than just for Lizzy." She assures, biting her lip. Eww, I gag again. "Okay, pizza, movies and no sleep for me. Thanks," I cringe.

"Oh, come on. Are you going to not '*do it'* when you're older?" she asks exasperated. Blushing my eyes darting to Ethan, who raises his eyebrows, waiting for my answer.

"Erm, I am not discussing my sex life with you," I state flustered, my British accent coming stronger.

"Oh, you have a sex life, do you?" Nan asks teasing, I freeze trying to think. "Um, I..." I stutter feeling like a deer in headlights.

"Who wants pizza?" I ask rushing into the kitchen taking deep breaths. Well, that could have gone better.

"Hey," I look up at Ethan, finding him grinning at me.

"I totally walked into that, didn't I?" I sigh, my head dropping to my chest, my eyes not leaving him as he nods. "And it no doubt made her curious," I grumble sighing, he comes to stand in front of me, rubbing my arms.

"Hey, she's just teasing, but I've got to know now… You aren't going to deprive me in our marital bed when we get older are you?" he asks, trying to sound serious, but chuckles into my hair, I poke him in his delicious abs lowering my voice so only he can hear me.

"Don't push it buddy or you won't be getting anything in any bed with me," I giggle biting and licking his neck. He groans, "Okay, I'm sorry, baby, don't punish me like that please."

"Where's that pizza? Stop canoodling you two," nan yells, exasperated, I roll my eyes.

"We're coming!" I shout. Ethan freezes drawing in a breath.

"Ethan, you have to move for me to be able to reach the pizza." I quip, stopping at the look in his eyes.

"Don't look at me like that. My nan's just through there, with your brother and my best friend," I breath, rubbing my hands up and down his ribs.

"It's your fault for shouting that. Now, you're going to have to walk in front of me, so your gran doesn't see my hard-on," he groans adjusting himself.

CHAPTER EIGHT

I wake to the sun streaming through my bedroom window, I'm warm and comfy. Shifting, I bump into a wall of hard muscle. Turning over I see Ethan still fast asleep and bare from the waist up.

Yum. He looks so peaceful and relaxed, with a thick arm thrown over his head, the other lying on his chest, I have no idea if he has anything on. The thought makes me squirm. I must have fallen asleep before the good stuff last night, because I'm feeling a little neglected. My heart is racing, my boobs ache, my thighs tingle and I'm soaking wet.

Leaning over, I run my hand down his hard chest, so beautifully formed it makes my mouth water, I want to lick him all over.

Looking at his face guiltily, I rest on one arm and kiss his chest gently, he stays asleep, so I go to town licking and nipping his smooth skin. Leaving tiny teeth marks all over his magnificent body.

My fingers learn the contours of his nicely defined abs, stopping when I reach the edge of the quilt and stoke my fingertips along the edge.

He groans, abruptly grabbing my hand. "What are you up to?" he croaks, as I turn in the direction of his voice, his sleepily smile is heart-stopping.

"Just checking out the merchandise," I whisper, wiggling my fingers for him to lose his hold. He does, leaving me to explore.

His breath hitches when my hand slides over his abs. "Baby, you're going to get yourself into trouble. I don't know how much longer I can hold off pouncing on you," he groans, as my palm whispers over his morning wood.

In the blink of an eye, I'm on my back, with Ethan braced over me. His beautifully muscled arms showcased on either side of my head.

"What do you want?" he asks, our breaths mingling. I blink up at him knowing I don't want to have sex with him… Well, I do, but not until every thing's straightened out.

"I can't have sex with you, not yet," I whisper laying my hand on his chest, he looks at me guiltily, nodding. "Okay, I get that I don't want you rushing or feeling like what we're doing is wrong," he says sadly, sliding off me.

"No, wait! I didn't say we couldn't do anything at all, just not sex... Yet." I smirk, squeaking as he pulls me on top of him. "Okay, you take control, do what you want," he says, flashing me a wicked smile.

I flounder. "I don't know, Ethan. I've never done any of this before," I murmur embarrassed.

"Hey, it's okay, just go with your body, like you did last night." His eyes heat at the memory.

Shut off my brain and feel? I can do that.

I lean in forcing him to lay back on the bed, I sit back so I can get a good look at him. He's the epitome of male hotness. Gloriously bare, tan muscled chest. His happy trail guiding my eyes to his very happy package.

This image of him will forever be burned into my brain. An arm behind his head, the other resting lazily over his chest, leg bent as he’s sprawled across my bed waiting for me to play.

God, he's in the ultimate wet dream pose. An Adonis and mine to play with, I giggle at my thoughts earning a raised eyebrow from him.

“What’s the giggle for?” he asks his brow cocked.

“Nothing, just thinking how amazingly sexy you look sprawled across my bed,” I admit, biting my cheek. Feeling my excitement bubble, imagining all the things I want to do to him and with him.

“Good to know, since you'll be living with it a long time, hopefully,” he says, but his eyes are unsure.

“I’m all yours, Ethan,” I whisper against his lips, he groans taking my lips in a fiery kiss. My hands run down his chest, his hot flesh rippling under my palms.

I slide up and over him, my knees either side of his hips. Abruptly he sits up aligning us perfectly, crushing me to his chest. The smooth skin of his back begs for my nails, so I drag them lightly across his shoulder blades, his hiss of pained pleasure turns me on more.

His palm sliding under my top, slowly pulling it up and off, has me trembling and not just from nerves. I sigh as his chest rubs my sensitive, swollen breasts. “Mmm” I hum, wiggling closer.

“Ah, you feel amazing. Your skin’s so soft and these… I love,” he mumbles nuzzling my nipple, I squirm as his scruff tickles me. My giggle turns into a moan when he sucks it into his mouth.

“Ah, Ethan.” I arch into him, the dam bursting as flames lick my skin. I shudder, my stomach clenching hard, I bite down on Ethan’s neck trying to control my noise level.

“Did you…?” He looks stunned, I nod, feeling myself flush bright red, hiding my head in his neck.

“No, baby, don’t hide. Fuck. That was incredible. Amazingly *hot*." His growl connecting and revving my recently sated body.

"Is that your favourite word? You say it all the time,” I ask to distract him from my embarrassment. No, such luck with him watching me intently.

“Come here,” he pulls me into another scorching kiss. Broken only by a vibrating phone. “Ignore it.” He growls, stroking my tongue with his, rocking me against him. His phone goes to voicemail.

“Mmm,” I moan kissing along his neck, licking his collarbone with the tip of my tongue.

“Umm, that feels amazing,” he groans, a smile curling my lips as he uses the word again. I growl hearing, his phone buzzing again. Well, my moods gone from sexy to pissed in two point five seconds. Shuffling back off him, I pull on my top.

“Fuck. Who the hell’s that? It better be fucking good. Could you pass my phone off the dresser, please?” he huffs, rubbing a hand down his face sitting up.

Grabbing his phone, I notice the caller name, it's Ashley. I feel like I’ve been doused with ice water. Scowling, I hand it to him and disappear into my bathroom.

What the hell does she want? What if all this can’t be sorted? I sigh, looking at myself in the mirror. *What am I thinking getting into this mess? I have to go back to college soon.*

Questions swirl through my head wanting answers I can’t give. I can hear his one-sided conversation through the gap in the door.

“I’ll be back later today,” his voice is sickly soft. “No, I stayed with a friend last night." That stuns me and irrational anger burns through me. Just a fucking friend? Friends don't do what we've been doing.

My anger bursts free as I stomp over to the door, slamming and locking it for good measure. Jumping in the shower, I scrub my skin. I feel dirty remembering what we were just doing before his *fiancée* interrupted us.

How can he be like that? Sound so blasé about it. I only just feel the scalding water searing my skin, as tears sting my eyes.

It hurt to hear him lie about where he was and the way he spoke to her.

When I emerge from the bathroom, he's sitting on the edge of my bed, elbows on knees fully dressed. He looks at me warily, trying to gauge my mood. I'm glad I have a towel and robe around me, I feel the need for extra protection.

What we're doing feels all wrong and I don't know what to do or say. So, I walk to the window looking out, it's a beautiful day.

I know I'm going to have to make the decision, whether I can stick it out and fight for us or leave him to his life and his fiancée.

I need a run to clear all this crap out, I don't need this right now, I'm still grieving, then there's my nan and college.

My internal rant is broken by Ethan laying his hands on my upper arms and his head on the back of my neck.

"I know this is hard for you, I shouldn't have answered the call. I'm sorry," regret colours his words.

"I have to go, she's waiting for me, she needs to talk to me. We were supposed to go shopping, that's why she called," his whispered words make me sick, every single word coming out his mouth makes me gag. I need air.

Moving out of his hold, I grab some workout clothes and underwear from my draws. With jerky moves I manage to pull them on without showing my body. Grabbing my brush, I vigorously brush it, pulling it into a high ponytail.

"Lily?" his voice grates across my frayed nerves, I've already shut down emotionally.

"What?" I ask, not looking at him.

"I know you're hurt by all this, I'm sorry. I will sort it, I promise."

I spin, looking at him. "What, you're going to tell her today?" I ask hopefully, the guilt on his face quickly squishes it, he's not going to do it. Maybe he never will, why should he.

I feel dirty again. Turning around, I snatch my phone and earphones of the dresser, before making my way to the door.

"You said you've got to go, so let's go. I'm going for a run anyway, I didn't get to yesterday," my voice cold and purposefully devoid of emotion, he looks shocked and worried.

"Don't be like that. I've got to talk to Alexander first," he pleads, watching me. Ignoring him I make my way into the hall. "Come on then. You better get going, you have a long day ahead of you," I shout over my shoulder.

In the kitchen there's a note from nan saying she's already out.

Millie's just leaving as we walk in. "Hey, Mills, are you leaving already?" I ask, trying to sound bright and chipper.

Mace shoots me a funny look, then looks at Ethan. "Yeah, mom called, she needs my help with something. Can we catch up another day?" She mumbles, fidgeting uncomfortably.

"Yeah, tell Tiff I said hi," I say, hugging her. "Speak to you later," I say, going to grab some water from the fridge, while they all say goodbye. Ethan's eyes follow my every move.

"Okay, what's going on?" Mace asks, crossing his arms over his chest, looking between me and Ethan expectantly. I stay quiet, raising an eyebrow at Ethan.

Shoving his hands in his pockets, he sighs. "I've got to go; I got a call…"

"Yeah, I know, dad's been blowing up my phone for the past hour, wanting to know where you are," Mace interrupts, I watch as Ethan blanches slightly.

"He said Ashley was looking for you, that they couldn't get you on the phone, and you weren't at your apartment. He's really pissed E," his voice betraying his frustration, I look at him amused.

"What?" he asks, seeing my grin.

I shrug, "You've got that from me, you know."

"What?" He asks.

"That. The knack for stating the obvious," I grin, enjoying our easy banter.

He laughs, "Yeah, you sort of rub off on people," he jokes, making me flush, as my eyes shoot to Ethan, he looks amused, looking back at me with a raised eyebrow.

"Anyway, I'm going for a run, you want to join?" I ask Mace, ignoring Ethan.

He looks from Ethan to me. "Don't you two want to spend some time together?" he asks confused, then it all clicks. Me pissed and Ethan worried and nervous.

Before either can utter a word, I step in again. "No, Ethan has to go. So, run. Yes-no?" I ask impatiently.

"Lily come on. We need to talk about this, please?" I look at Ethan's pleading face, keeping mine blank. "It's fine, you have things to do... I'll speak to you later," I say nonchalantly, Mace frowns as Ethan nods, mumbling bye and leaves.

"What the hell was all that about?" Mace blurts as the door closes. "Nothing, are you going to change? You still have a few outfits here," I try joking, but it falls flat.

"Oh, hell no! I want to know what all that was?" he says planting his arse on a chair. "Mace... I can't talk to you about this, he's your brother."

"Yes, you can. I will even suffer the girlie and disgusting bits, promise," I laugh at his face and plonk into a chair.

"I don't know what happened, we were so close. Waking up this morning with him was amazing," I sigh happily, he waves his hand impatiently.

"Well, we were… Kissing and stuff," I stop as we both cringe. He looks pained, but nods for me to continue.

"Okay, we were… Anyway, we were both rather…. *hot,* and then the phone rang. We ignore it naturally, but it rang again and the mood was gone. He asks me to pass him his phone, I'm up at this point anyway, so I do, noticing it was Ashley. I gave him the phone and went into the bathroom," I shrug, playing with the label on my water.

"Okay, then what?" he urges.

"I heard some of his conversation from the bathroom, he told her he was with a friend."

He winces, looking at me sadly. "Lils, he couldn't really tell her he was with you, could he?" he sighs, like I should have known this was coming.

I glare at him. "I know that!" I snap.

"It's the way it made me feel. I felt dirty, and the way he was speaking to her, that pissed me off. What exactly is so important that it can't be missed today?" I ask, getting the feeling that there's more that I'm missing.

He looks away guiltily sucking on his bottom lip. That's

his tell, that nervous thing people do when they either don't want to talk about it or feel guilty or don't want to lie.

"And Mace, don't you dare lie to me! I don't like liars. I know there's something you're not telling me." I warn seriously. That's why this situation is eating at me so badly, I really do hate liars.

"Okay, but I don't think you're going to like it." He exhales.

"I probably won't, but I deserve the truth for once. I'm sick of the lies and secrecy. Would you want me to tell you the truth?" I growl angrily, feeling it simmer below the surface.

"Yes, I would, and I'm sorry for all this crap, I wish I hadn't opened my mouth yesterday. It should have come from E, not me. It just pissed me off how blasé he was. Saying you were his girlfriend," he looks me in the eyes, and I'm not so sure I want to know now.

"They're... Meeting the wedding planner today... To make sure everything is on track."

I feel all the blood drain from my body and my stomach lurch. I slap my hand over my mouth jump up. Running for the bathroom, slam the door. I retch until my stomach muscles hurt.

Why would he go through with this meeting if he was ending it? The obvious answer, he's a fucking liar!

"Lils? Are you okay? I'm sorry," Maces voice comes through the door muffled.

"I'm okay, I'll be out in a minute," I mumble, my voice barely audible, my throat sore.

When I come out, Mace is shouting. "She doesn't need this shit."

"I know, and I have to do that too. I won't give up, Millie. But this isn't about Millie and I. Lily doesn't need this. She just lost her mother. She's a mess and she's just thrown up after I had to tell her where you were and what you were doing."

"I had to tell her. She asked me out right, and I won't lie to her, I'm sorry, but I'm not losing my best friend over this shit," he shouts, throwing his phone at the sofa.

"Hey," I whisper, feeling bad for causing them to argue.

He swings around spotting me. "You okay? You're still pale," he says, holding his arms out for me.

I walk into his chest, wrapping my arms around his back. "I'm sorry. You shouldn't have to go through all this." He whispers softly into my hair.

"You ready to go for that run? I need to burn some energy," I ask, feeling my muscles twitch.

"Yeah, just let me change, two minutes," he sighs, heading for the spare room.

As we head out, we're both quiet, stuck in our own thoughts. *I wonder what he thinks of me being with his brother when he's with someone else. He never makes me feel judged even if what I'm doing is wrong. He's always on my side and for that I'm grateful, but does he resent me?*

I sigh, letting it go and enjoy the beauty that is Balboa Park. Families spending precious time together, friends playing, dogs barking and kids playing chase.

I notice a middle-aged couple, cuddling on a blanket. It makes me sad to know I probably won't ever have that with Ethan. Blinking, I focus on my pace.

"Race you back." Mace shouts, sprinting off. I look around realising we're nearly home. Feeling a burst of energy at the challenge Mace set down, I sprint after him at top speed, passing him at the last few yards.

"Even with… a… head… start, you still can't beat me," I laugh at his astonished face. "How the hell do you do that? I was way ahead," he pants, his hands braced on his knees. I pat him on the arm, "I know. Don't worry, I won't tell anyone I whooped your arse," I chuckle opening the door.

"Nan, you home?" I shout.

"Yes, I'm home, noisy," she says, coming from the laundry room smiling.

"Hey, Cora," Mace says, turning pink, I snicker at his face.

"Hello Mason. Where's Millie this afternoon?" she asks slyly, trying to hold back a chuckle.

"Erm, she's helping Tiffany," he mumbles, rubbing his neck, I laugh at his obvious discomfort.

"Okay, then. Shower and clothes in the wash," she says, holding her nose. We must really stink because we were out for three hours.

"Okay, back in a few," I say as we both plant a kiss on her cheeks as we go chuckling at her muttered, "Gross."

I feel marginally better after my run and a hot shower. It feels good to be snuggled in some comfy clothes. Sitting I take my time brushing my hair. It's long, thick and wavy, and I love it when it behaves.

"Lily, your phone is beeping and ringing off the hook," nan shouts up the stairs.

I sigh falling back onto my bed, knowing it's probably Ethan. I do not want to deal with all this right now.

I open my eyes when I hear the clearing of a throat,

finding Mason standing over me, my phone in his outstretched hand.

"It's Ethan, you have fifteen missed calls, and four texts. I think he wants to speak to you," he sighs when I huff, taking the phone and open the texts.

Ethan: *Mason said you've been sick again? Was it this morning that caused it?*

Ethan: *I know. I should have told you.... I'm sorry. I just didn't know how. I don't want to be the cause of anymore pain for you.*

Ethan: *I will sort this, I promise. I love you.*

Ethan: *Baby, talk to me. Please.*

I bury my face in my hands trying not to cry. Mace sits beside me, pulling me into a hug.

"Aww, Lils. I really want to punch him in the face for putting you through this, but I can't since the asshole's my brother," he states, gently stroking my hair, I give a watery chuckle.

"What am I supposed to say Mace? What am I going to do? We both said we don't share, but he's forcing me to. I don't want to be known as a home-wrecker," I whisper horrified.

"You are not a home-wrecker. Don't ever say that again," he says, anger bleeding through his words.

"I am though, aren't I? She had him first, they're engaged! I need to break this off." I say, my chest tightening, it feels like my heart is being squeezed in a vice.

"Maybe you should talk to him first. He may have already told her and is talking to my dad as we speak," he says, with forced enthusiasm, but his eyes are sad as he leaves me alone.

Taking a deep breath, I fortify myself for this conversation. My handshakes as I press call and wait for him to pick up.

"Hello?" I'm so shocked I don't speak.

"Hello? Is anyone there?" I'm frozen, this must be Ashley.

"Ash come on. They want us to pick now. Who's that?" I hear Ethan in the background.

"I don't know, they aren't answering."

"Wait! Is that my phone?" He sounds pissed and anxious.

"Yeah, it rang, so I picked up."

I hang up, dropping the phone, I feel tears leak from my eyes. Stupid idiot, I berate myself, as I grab a new set of running clothes, hurrying to put them on before running downstairs and out the door.

"LILS!" Mason yells up the street. I ignore him, pushing faster, needing to be alone.

I just run, forcing everything inside me to go cold, I can't do this anymore, we're done.

I don't know how long I've been gone, but it's getting dark. I've been wondering around aimlessly, and now I'm starving because I haven't eaten anything all day.

"Where the fuck, have you been?" Mason yells, when I finally stumble through the door. He looks at me furiously, hands on his hips.

"I'm sorry. I went for a walk, where's Nan?" I ask feeling like shit for scaring him.

"She's in bed exhausted, from worrying about you," he snaps still pissed.

I grab some juice and cookies and plonk onto the sofa, shattered. "I really am sorry. I needed to be alone."

After a pause, I whisper, "I called him." I spy him in my peripheral vision.

"I know, he called me when you wouldn't pick up. Ashley picked up the phone, didn't she?" he asks, his face softening.

"Yep, she did. I froze, then after hearing a short conversation between them, I put the phone down. I'm just sorry, he's dragging you into this," I say munching on my cookies.

"What did you hear?" He asks, and winces at the look I give him.

"Well, you tell me. What are they supposed to be picking out today?" I ask, my voice dripping with sarcasm.

"I don't know. What are you going to do?" he asks, sitting beside me, shaking my head, I cuddle his arm.

"I don't want this crap, I'm done," I sigh, feeling relieved. "Weren't you supposed to meet Millie?" I ask, confused.

"Yeah, I cancelled. I can see her tomorrow." He's so amazing to me, I don't deserve him sometimes.

"Aww, Mace…. I'm sorry. Go over there now. I don't want to mess things up with you two," I say, feeling like shit. I've been selfish again.

"It's fine, promise. You're my best friend. Fancy watching a movie? We can order pizza, or do you need to call

Ethan?" I think about calling him for a second but decide on an evening with my best friend and I grab the phone 'n' pizza menu.

"Movie and pizza, it is then. In your room though," he says, stretching, and I nod.

"Lilly? Ethan's here." Nan shouts.

"Who… Ugh, what time is it?" I mumble, shaking Mace.

"Mace wake up. We've got to get up, your brother's here," I yawn, rubbing my eyes.

"What time is it?" He grunts as I use his chest for leverage to look at the clock.

"Erm, nine… What time did we go to sleep?" I yawn again, stretching.

"I don't know about three. I better go downstairs," he says, rubbing his eyes, he looks at me.

"You okay?" he asks, I nod.

"I need a quick shower though."

"Okay, see you down there."

Walking into the kitchen. I see nan at the stove as usual and Mace and Ethan are having a glaring contest at the table.

"You two can pack that in right now. You are brothers," I snap sitting next to Mason.

"Morning, Nan. Have these two been doing that long?"

"Morning, honey. Yep, since Mason came downstairs. What's going on with you all?" she asks, looking between the three of us.

"Don't worry. It will be sorted after breakfast. Do you

need any help?" I ask hopefully, wanting away from the shit storm building at the table.

"No, thank you, honey, it's coming now, you stay where you are."

We all eat in relative silence.

"Okay, well… I'm going to go to Matilda's. Will you be okay, honey? Do you mind cleaning up?" Nan asks, looking apprehensively between us.

I get up hugging her. "I'll be fine, I don't mind cleaning, you cooked. Go enjoy yourself, love you," I add, her face lights up as she smiles lovingly at me.

"Love you, too, honey. You all be good now, you hear?" She says in mock sternness.

I turn on them as the door closes, ready to bang some heads together.

"Right. Let's get this straight. First; why are you two glaring at each other? Well?" I demand, hands on hips, waiting for them to speak.

"He caused all this shit by hurting you," Mason hisses angrily.

"That's between me and Ethan. You are brothers end of."

Looking at Ethan fully, my heart rate speeds up for the first time since yesterday morning, he looks exhausted.

"And you, what's your problem?"

Ethan throws a furious look at his brother before answering me.

"He slept with you... And he didn't even call me to let me know you were okay." He's furious. I gape at him.

I burst out laughing, "You… Think Mace and I…? Eww." I shudder.

"Hey! I'm not that bad," he laughs, trying to sound wounded.

"No. You're not, but you're like my brother. Sorry," I shrug, looking back at Ethan.

"As for not calling, he was busy dealing with the shit-storm you caused yesterday..." I pause, looking at Mace.

"Sorry Mace, I guess this has got something to do with you," I say apologetically.

He smiles, shaking his head and hugs me. "Just don't run off like that again, okay," I nod into his chest, taking in the comfort of my best friend.

"Yeah, I'm sorry for scaring you and Nan and for messing up your time with Millie."

"Whoa, hang on a second. What do you mean run off? Lily?" Ethan jumps in. I sigh, not looking at him.

"After I got off the phone, I needed time to myself. So, I went for a run," I answer meekly.

"No. When she got off the phone, she ran out of here in tears... Because you're an asshole," Mace shouts, letting go of me.

"Mace," I hiss.

"No, Lils. He should know what he's doing is causing you pain," he spits acidly at his brother.

"I know, okay. I'm sorry. I'm going to sort it." Ethan yells, pulling his hair.

"When? After the wedding? Did you try to tell her yesterday?" Mace yells, getting in Ethan's face.

I jump between them, pushing them both back. "Hey! No one is fighting, especially not in my house. So, just sit your arses down, before I kick you both out."

Eventually they both relent and sit down facing me as I pace.

"Okay," I blow out a breath, not having a clue what to say. I look at Ethan questions in my eyes, he gulps, not a good sign.

"Did you tell her yesterday?" I ask, seeing the answer written all over his face before he shakes his head.

Throwing my hands in the air, I mutter, "We're done."

"Wait! Lily. Let me explain please," he pleads, grasping my arms, I shake him off, I've heard enough.

"What is there to explain? You could have told your *fiancée* yesterday when you left me after…" I stop, looking at Mace, whose face contorts with anger.

"You didn't?" He hisses, surging to his feet, looking from me to his brother furiously.

I'm not sure who he's asking, but I answer. "No, not that." I say, affronted, he blows out a relieved breath.

"Good, because I would have smacked him in the face."

I giggle, patting him on the chest, "You don't need to defend my honour today, good sir," I quip, he chuckles bowing I laugh.

"Would you two stop. This is fucking serious!" Ethan shouts at us.

"Yeah, I know," I snap.

"I'm no home-wrecker, nor am I a slapper. But that's what I feel like now. If you wanted us to be together, you would have told her."

"I do want to be with you, it all got really complicated. Please, let me explain. Please?" He looks so pained and I find myself nodding.

Gulping he rubs the back of his neck; his eyes are anxious.

"When I met up with Ashley, she wanted to talk like she said. When… anyway, I agreed, I was going to tell her, there and then, that I couldn't go through with it, that I had met someone else."

Licking his lips, he looks at me sadly. "She, told me she's pregnant."

I gasp, stumbling, feeling my legs give out. Well, if it wasn't certain before, it is now, Ethan and I are never going to be.

"What the fuck E?" Mace yells, catching me.

Ethan looks at me in utter despondency. "I'm so sorry, I'm going to talk to Alex later today, then Ashley. I love you, Lily, please…." He's frantic, but those words make my stomach clench painfully.

"NO! Don't you dare say those words... They mean nothing! Don't bother saying anything to Alex and Ashley, because we're done. I won't take a father from a baby," I cry, covering my face, but not before catching the look of utter devastation on his gorgeous face.

"You slept with Ashley?" Mace asks, his voice shaking with rage.

"Yes, I am twenty-three Mason, and we were getting married."

"When was the last time you slept with her?" he growls and Ethan goes ghostly white.

Oh god, I don't want to hear this.

"I... I was with her that night, before you text asking about Lily," he murmurs quietly.

Sickness surges through me and I rush to the kitchen, my hand glued to my mouth. Hanging over the sink, my stomach heaves what I ate for breakfast.

"See what you're doing to her," Mason yells, pulling back my hair and rubbing my back.

"You okay, sweetie?" His voice is so gentle, like he's talking to a baby. I shake my head, I'm in pain, sick, aching, my head hurts. I work on taking deep breaths.

I straighten, turn, and there looking worried and remorseful is the man I fell in love with.

"You, disgust me," I spit.

His eyes widen and he winces. "After fucking your fiancée, you start chatting me up, texting me the same night. The things you texted…." I swallow, sick, threatening to choke me.

"It wasn't like that. I didn't know I would ever see you again." He argues, stepping toward me, but stops at my death glare.

"So, you thought you'd stick with an easy lay, over growing a set of balls and telling daddy, you didn't want to marry the woman."

They both wince at my words, I know it sort of applies to Mace too, but he isn't fucking one woman and thinking about another.

His eyes are wide and bleak. "Well, you can stick with your easy lay, because you aren't getting it from me. Thank fuck, I didn't go further. Shit, I'm stupid. Mom would be so ashamed of me right now," I sob.

"Hey! No, she wouldn't, this isn't your fault," Mason says adamantly, squeezing me to him.

"You've really fucked up asshole. I wish I had never sent that text. I should have listened to you. I'm so sorry, I brought all this shit on you." His voice thick with remorse, I can't even comfort him, because I'm a mess.

"No. This is on me, I should have grown a pair a long time ago, I'm sorry I didn't, but I am now. I can't marry a girl I don't love, even if she is pregnant with my baby. I'll be there for the baby but, I can't stay with her. I love you, Lily. I can't, won't give up on you, or us. I'm so sorry, I've hurt you. Baby, look at me please."

I stand back from Mace, not bothering to wipe my eyes, letting him see what he's done.

He's right in front of me, he gently takes my face in his hands.

"I'm so sorry, please. Please, forgive me. Give me the chance to sort this, I'll work to gain your trust and respect back, I promise. Just don't say we're done. I can't accept that. I love you, and once this is all over, I want to marry you," he rushes blinking back tears of his own.

I'm in shock, he's crying. I watch him struggle, wanting so badly to believe him.

"I want to believe you, Ethan, I..." His kiss shocks me. It's desperate, but gentle as he pours all his feelings into it. Longing, anxiety, anguish, remorse and love.

I whimper cut between wanting to melt into him and wanting to slap him. My mind and body waring with each other, my body wins out, melting against him without permission, everything dissolves, my world narrowing until it's just us.

My hands grasp his hair, kissing him back with everything I have, my body flush against him.

He softens his hold, his hands falling to my back. I moan as he lets go of my lips, only to kiss down my neck.

"Erm, E?" Mace coughs, snapping me back to reality, I stiffen.

What the fuck am I doing? Pulling my hands from his hair, I step back, putting some space between us, not taking my eyes off him.

He looks so hopeful, his gorgeous eyes shining, waiting silently. Laying his forehead on mine, he whispers, "I'm sorry, just give me another chance, I will do the right thing," he begs.

"Mace, can we talk alone for a while please?"

"Yeah, I'll be at Millie's, call me if you need me, okay?" I nod, understanding his unspoken promise.

"You, you hurt her anymore and I swear, brother or not I

will rip you a new one. Understood?" Mace threatens and Ethan nods, wide eyed.

"Wow," Ethan breaths as the front door slams.

"Yeah, he's kind of protective of me."

"No shit! He's never threatened me before."

"So, what are you going to do?" I ask walking into the living room and sitting.

"I have to talk to Alexander first, then Ashley, but… I have to be there for the baby. I can't abandon him or her like my dad did me and Niles. I hope you can understand and help me through all this? I'm scared babe." I feel sorry for him, hearing his voice shake.

My heart squeezes painfully at the thought of him having a baby with another woman.

"Are we going to be okay? With the baby and all?" he asks, looking vulnerable.

I don't know what to say, am I going to be okay with my boyfriend having a baby with his ex-fiancée?

CHAPTER NINE

"I don't know, we'll have to wait and see like everything else. Is Ashley going to be in our lives all the time?" I ask cringing at how bad that sounds.

"I don't know, I'll have to go to doctor's appointments, scan's, the birth. Then there's whatever we arrange so I can see him or her."

I look away, suddenly wanting to cry. He's having a baby…. I bite my cheek trying to quell my tears.

"Hey! What are these for?" he asks, wiping away my tears.

"It hurts Ethan. Would you like the thought of me with another bloke? What about having a baby with someone else?" I ask, knowing I sound childish, but I can't help the way I feel.

"No. I wouldn't," he sighs. "What are we going to do? I can't make this go away, and I don't want to. I know it's fucked up, but this baby is half of me too. I know it's selfish to ask this of you, you're so young, but I don't want to lose you. I've never loved anyone before and I love you, so much."

"I know, I love you too, but I've just lost my mom. Emotionally, I'm a mess. I know how I sound, but it really hurts, knowing you've slept with her that day, and now she's always going to have a piece of you."

In a rush, he pins me to the sofa, his knees on either side of me, his lower body pinning my torso. He kisses the shit out of me, my brain quietens as my body takes over. Moaning, I grab his hips tightly as he possesses my mouth, tongue stroking, teeth biting and… Oh god, he sucks my tongue into his mouth.

"Mmm," I moan wanting more of him. It's stupid, mad to make such a decision with my head a mess, but I need him right now. To soothe the hurt, to feel the heat we generate together.

"Ethan, I need you," I breathe, a minute passes before he freezes, looking at me, his eyes blaze with need. "Please?" I beg, squeezing his hips.

He blinks. "Is this becau-" Putting my hand over his mouth, I shake my head.

"No, this isn't because of anything other than the fact that I want you. I know you're still with her and it will make me a home-wrecker, but…" I stop seeing his face blanch.

"Don't you dare think that," his voice shaking with rage.

"It's what I am though, look at the situation," he growls, taking my face in his hands. "Listen to me, you are no such thing. I'm the one in the wrong, not you. Okay?" I nod, placating him. But inside, I know what I am and what I'm likely to be called.

"Now. Are you sure? What do you want from me?" he growls, barely leashing his hunger. "I thought you wanted to wait until all the crap was behind us. What's changed since this morning? You're confusing me," he breaths glancing at my lips, licking his own.

I lean up a touch, slowly licking his bottom lip, clamping my teeth around it and tugging. He growls tugging my hair in warning.

"I need you to talk to me in that sexy voice, the one that makes me so hot I forget about anything and everything other than us," I say slowly, my voice low, sexy.

"Holy shit. Keep talking like that and we won't make it upstairs." He groans as I squeeze his arse.

"Umm, you better move then, hadn't you?" I giggle at his shocked face. Wiggling from beneath him, racing upstairs laughing, I don't get far before Ethan catches up and pins me to the wall beside my door, grasping my hair, he tilts my head back and slowly lick from the base of my neck to my ear. "E," I sigh, arching into him.

We stumble into my room, kicking and locking the door behind us. Falling onto the bed, a tangle of arms and legs, fighting to get closer.

I pull on his jacket, yanking it impatiently off his shoulders, catching my drift he shrugs it off as I lift his T-shirt up, I struggle as it sticks to his heated skin.

My greedy hands run over every bit of toned skin I uncover. My eyes drink in his beautiful chest, leaning up I kiss above his heart sucking hard, leaving my mark.

"Ah, do it again," he moans, kneeling between my legs.

I do as he asks, but this time on his neck and bite down on his tendon making his body shake, "You're playing with fire."

"Then burn me… Please," I rub against him.

He yanks my oversized jumper off, finding me bare beneath, he growls, "You've been bare underneath that all this time?" I nod feeling the heat of his gaze.

"I love these," he whispers, biting my nipple, whimpering, I bow into him, holding his head to me. Chuckling, he sucks it into his mouth.

I cry out, heat engulfing me, hitting all the right places. Soothing, but intensifying the ache.

Dragging my nails down his back, I moan loudly needing more. Kissing his way up my neck, he sucks hard, marking me as his.

My patience snaps, I shove at his jeans, needing to feel him sliding into me. He halts, looking at me. "Are you sure? Once I take it, I..."

I growl, nipping his ear. "I want you to be the first Ethan, I need to feel you inside me."

"Shit. I want inside your hot, tight little body. To feel you tighten around me, feel your body tremble taking me…." My eyes widen as desire floods me, my core slickening in response.

He smirks down at me. "You like dirty talk baby?" Gripping his neck, I pull him to me, looking between his mouth and eyes, teasing I suck his lip into my mouth.

"It makes me so wet," I whisper, against his mouth. "Ah, shit. You're going to kill me," he groans, as his fingers weave through my hair, tugging my head to the side and sucking down my neck.

A sense of urgency steals over me. I reach into his open jeans, grasping him, stroking, I smirk when he jumps in my hand.

"But what a way to go," I say, stroking faster, his breathing changes with every slide of my hand.

Pulling himself from my grip, he slides off the bed, spoiling my fun. My complaint dies on my lips as he pulls my shorts slowly down and off, leaving me bare and vulnerable to his hungry gaze. His eyes roam up and down my body, scorching me.

“So, beautiful,” he breathes, running a finger down my belly. My muscles twitch in response, grasping his hand, I press it to my flushed skin, trying to entice him to explore.

“Please?” I beg, my hand exploring the tanned skin of his forearm, moving up, pulling him onto me, his weight pinning me into the bed.

His skin on mine is perfect. Impatiently I push at his jeans, wanting to see him naked.

“Baby, slow down, you need to be ready first.” He groans, as I take him in hand again.

“I don’t want to wait, I need you. I’m lying here naked, while you're still partly clothed,” I mumble, still trying to extricate him from his jeans.

Jumping up, he shucks his jeans and boxers, and there he is in all his naked splendour, blinking I look him up and down. Licking my lips at the fine specimen in front of me.

Wow. He’s magnificent. Muscles everywhere. Board chest, tapered waist, narrow hips, toned thighs and shit. He’s big.

“Mmm-hmm,” I hum biting my lip. He lets out a sound between a chuckle and a groan.

“Looking at me like that will get you into all kinds of trouble.”

Looking him in the eye, I part my legs, shivering as the cold air hits my heated skin.

His gaze is captivated by the slow glide of my fingers, as they dance over my skin, teasing, enticing, I crook my finger, calling him to me silently.

Crawling over me, he pinches my nipple, wrenching a pleasured cry from me. I pull him to me shivering when his soft tongue lashes my aching breast, his teasing, his voice and body has me on the edge so fast, my legs shake.

“Ethan, I need more, please?”

“What do you want?” He asks, still teasing my nipple, I groan, “Tell me what you need.”

I boldly take his hand, slowly sliding it down my belly. “I need you to touch me, here.” His eyes widen.

"You're soaking,” he whispers, kissing his way down my belly. Looking up at me, his mouth mere centimetres away, not touching, waiting, teasing. His eyes heat as he takes a long, slow lick, tasting me.

My body shakes. "Oh god, Ethan." I moan as my arms give out, clutching the covers. My body reaches for him, desperately begging for his touch.

"Mmm, you taste so good..." He hums, looking at me, his head hovering. The hunger in his eyes causes my body to tighten pleasurably as I watch him slowly lick his lips. My hips lift seeking him, my body begging him to end the torture. A grateful sigh escapes me as a finger slides slowly into me.

His eyes fall away as he sucks my clit between his lips. Scorching heat engulfs me, a sheen of sweat coats my skin as he works my body. My fingers pulling at his hair, I grind frantically against him.

His palm pins me to the bed as my vision blurs and my body trembles violently. The pleasure is almost painful. “*Ethan... I’m… Oh god,*” I groan loudly, grasping his hair painfully, grinding against him as I explode. “*Yes... Oh fuck, Ethan!”* I yell.

When I open my eyes, Ethan’s braced over me. His beautifully sculpted arms bulging. His tight body pressed against me, ready for business, if the erection laying against my hip is any indication.

Hot, hard, and twitching with the need to come. Sliding my hand down his chest, I trail my fingers along his belly, smiling when I reach my goal. His head drops as my fingers wrap around his cock, hearing him moan is the sexiest thing ever.

My preparation has taken a toll on him, so I take over, flipping him onto his back and climbing on top of him, straddling his hips. Rubbing against him, my clit rubbing against his bell-end, and along the length of his cock, feeling every ridge and vein throb.

Placing my hands on his chest, without a thought I thrust faster, losing myself in the moment. "I need to be inside you." Ethan breaths, clutching my hips, moving me faster.

"Oh shit, you're dripping all over me. Umm..." His voice drives me crazy and I circle my hips, sinking onto him a couple of inches. I gasp, heat blasting through me as he stretches me. I wiggle trying to dispel the twinge of discomfort. "Shit, babe. Don't move." Ethan grunts sounding pained.

I look at him, his face is flushed and tight, his eyes glassy and his chest is heaving. "I'm sorry," I try to move off him, but his vice grip on my hips stills me.

"No. No, don't... Just give me a second. God, you're tight and wet and hot, if you move right now…. I'll explode," he groans, feeling me getting wetter. His grip loosens, his hand sliding up, cupping my breast, tweaking my nipple.

I gasp, involuntarily pushing down harder on him. Trembling from the pleasure/pain. "Fuck. Lily... Am I hurting you?" he pants, unsure. Just looking at him makes me forget the discomfort. His muscles strain as he restrains the need to pound into me.

"No… I need more," I groan, clenching my muscles around him.

"Ah, baby... That feels amazing," he grunts.

Bending his knees, he urges me back. "Lean back, you've got a lot more to go." I groan, wiggling.

"You've got to be shitting me!" My body feels full, stretched to the max. And he's telling me he has more?

"You can do it, you'll love it when you get used to taking all of me," he says breathlessly.

"I don't think anyone could ever get used to taking all of you," I pant, wincing as I take a little more.

"You can, I'm all yours," he growls, pressing on my clit, while rolling his hips.

I circle my hips digging my nails into his chest. "That's it baby, take me. God, Lily." He moans, his head tipping back looking amazing.

My Adonis. My ultimate. Mine.

The last thought drives me a little crazy and I push all the way down, crying out and squeezing my eyes shut at the instant stab of pain.

"Shit. Lily, are you okay? Baby…. You shouldn't have done that," he admonishes me, his voice shaking. Taking deep breaths, I open my eyes to see his worried face.

"I'm fine. God, you feel amazing," I pant squeezing, his breath stutters.

"Ah, Lily. Shit. You feel…" he wheezes squeezing my hips.

"Babe. I've got to move, I'm ready to burst," he groans circling his hips. Causing sparks to shoot through my core.

I moan rocking on him. "Yes, Lily, like that…. Don't stop…" he shouts loudly, I smile at his flushed face, rocking a little faster.

Sitting up, he takes my lips in a hot kiss, I suck his tongue into my mouth, feeling his dick twitch inside me. He moans breaking our kiss, panting.

"I… So tight. I… Can't wait anymore, I need…" he gulps, his face tight, I nod, and I'm flipped to my back before I can blink, all without breaking contact.

Pinning my hands above my head, he starts to move in and out slowly, enjoying the tight grip of my body. The sheen of sweat coating his face drips down his temples, his breathing erratic.

"Ethan, faster." I gasp, the pressure of my impending orgasm causing my legs to shake.

He picks up the pace, but it's still too gentle. "Harder. It's okay, let go. You won't hurt me, take me with you."

My words snap what's left of his self-control. He slams into me. Hitting just the right spot. "Ethan," I yell, shattering. "Shit, Lily, baby." He groans into my ear, clutching me tightly as he comes.

I blink feeling relaxed, tingly and happy. I stroke Ethan's sweaty back. "Are you okay?" I ask gently, combing my fingers through his hair. Looking up his face is flushed and eyes shining.

"Yeah… I'm awesome right now," he breathes, making me giggle.

He twitch's and lengthens inside me. My eyes widen. "You... No way. You cannot be ready… *Again*?" I stutter astonished.

"I can and I am. I'm not that old you know," he says slightly affronted. I squeeze my muscles, making him gasp.

"Oh, I know. It's a good thing you have stamina. You're definitely going to need it. That was incredible," I sigh, blushing.

"How can you be blushing? After what we just did? It was amazing. It's never been like that before," he says, looking at me.

I look at him biting my cheek, wondering if he's telling me the whole truth, he's lied before… Well, omitted some details.

"I'm not lying to you, Lily. I am sorry though, you were a

virgin, I should have gone slower, been gentler, but you drive me crazy." Guilt written all over his face.

"No, I loved it the way it was." I smile happily.

"It did feel amazing being inside my future wife and mother of my kids," he says wistfully, then paling realising what he said. I close my eyes to the blast of pain, my bliss and relaxation gone just like that.

Pulling out, he moves off me to the side. "Shit," he mutters, I look at him puzzled.

"I just need time, okay? To get used to the idea of you having a baby with someone else. I'm sorry," I croak, turning into him. I'm shocked, seeing the look of horror on his face.

"Just give me time, I'll get used to it. I'll be there and stand by your side, through it all like I said. I promise," the words burst from me.

"No," he breathes and I blanch.

What the fuck? No? After everything he's put me through. He expects me to just be okay, with him having a kid with someone else.

"What do you mean no? Oh, so I'm supposed to just be okay with the fact that my future "husband" has fathered a baby with another woman? Well, it's not that easy, Ethan," I snap angrily. Jumping off my bed, I run into the bathroom and lock the door.

Splashing cold water over my face, I look at myself in the mirror. I'm a mess, my hair is everywhere, I'm flushed, my lips are red and plump. I blink as my eyes coat with tears. Taking a series of deep breaths, I try to calm myself.

My eyes widen to the size of saucers in the mirror, as liquid trickles down my thighs. "Shit, shit, shit." I hiss, pissed at myself for only just realising. We forgot protection.

I just had unprotected sex, with a man that isn't fully

mine. A man who is already having one unplanned baby with someone else. Fuck.

Panic chokes me, with every second that passes. What am I going to do? I take deep breaths, trying to think. Sitting on the toilet, head in hands, thinking. When my next period is due?

"Lily," I jump at the knock. "Come out, please. We need to talk, from the sounds coming from in there, you just realised what I did when I pulled out." He sighs, waiting. Well, I better put on my big girl panties on and go talk to him.

Opening the door, I pull my robe tight around me, like a shield. Looking at him hesitantly, he has his jeans on, but still bare chested, head in his hands, waiting. Hearing my approach his head snaps up.

"Babe, you got it all wrong, I know you need time, but right now we need to talk about what just happened. Are you on the pill or anything?" I shake my head. "I had no need to be," I state obviously.

"Okay, so what are the odds that you could become pregnant from this?" he asks gently. I bite my cheek, not wanting to be the second person to throw him through a loop today.

"It's okay, Lily. You can tell me; this is my fault not yours."

It breaks my heart seeing him beat himself up over this. It was my fault, I was on top, I was in control.

I grasp his face, forcing him to look me in the eye. His arms wind around my back, holding me securely as if to stop me from running.

"Hey. This isn't your fault. We were caught up in the moment, and I was on top if anyone is to blame, it's me. I forgot the Johnnie." Raising his eyebrows, he smirks.

"Johnnie?" he laughs.

"I mean condom," I say, turning a brighter red.

"I know, I'm just teasing. But this is still my fault, you were a virgin. I should have thought. Prepared."

I hug him to me, loving his caring words. "Let's just say then that it's both our faults," I reason. Brushing his hair back and kissing his nose. "And to answer your question, it's the perfect time for me to get pregnant." I wince at the thought of telling nan and Mace.

"I'm so sorry, Lily. What are we going to do? If you do get, pregnant?" He swallows hard.

"Well, it's going to be hard, but I won't be getting an abortion. I don't believe in those. Nan's not going to be pleased, nor is Mason. He's going to be pissed." I drift off, feeling the weight of everything that could go wrong with this weighing me down.

"What are you going to do? Are we still okay?" I ask anxiously awaiting his answer.

"What do you mean? What am I going to do? You don't think… I won't leave you either way. If we made a baby tonight, he's mine, Lily, you both are. *Mine*." He growls, flattening a hand possessively across my belly. As if it were already confirmed. Tears prick my eyes, at the furious longing in his eyes.

"I know, it's rushing, with you at school and we have all this stuff, but… I want there to be a baby. I want a son or daughter, born out of what we just shared. I want a baby with you…" he rushes breathlessly. Absently rubbing my belly.

"Ethan" I sigh, overwhelmed by love, longing for a mini-Ethan.

I grasp the back of his head, so he's looking at me. "I love you so much. I want a baby with you too. A part of you, to feel him or her grow and kick," I stop, catching my breath.

"But there are a lot of things going on right now. It's

just…" He pulls me so I'm straddling him and kisses the shit out of me, until I forget everything.

"Lily, I love you, and I know what you're saying is true, but it may have already happened, so how would you feel about trying for this baby?" He rushes out looking hopeful. I blink staring open mouthed at him.

"In the midst of all this. You want to actively try for a baby?" He nods, tightening his arms, as my heart beats rapidly, my brain throwing questions at me so fast, I feel dizzy.

"Yes, it's soon, fast and probably a stupid idea. But since it may well have already happened. Why wait? I know you're it for me, I will marry you. You will be my Wife and the mother of all my babies."

It's so hard to think. He makes it sound so simple.

"What about all the other stuff… Where would we live? When would we marry? What about school?" Questions flow from me in rapid succession.

"I'm sorting that. We can get married as soon as you want. We'll live in my apartment or buy a new house. Big enough for said babies. As for school, that's your choice, I have money, plenty of it. You don't need to worry…. I want to wake up every morning for the rest of my life next to you."

"Ethan, I want that too, you know that. But this seems rushed. You may have two babies due a couple of months apart. I'm only eighteen, I can be a royal pain in the arse. You don't know, you may change your mind."

He smirks, his hands moving over me, one holding my thigh, lifting me a little so I hover over him. The connection we shared sparking as I kiss his gorgeous mouth.

He breaks the kiss, pulling me back to him, sliding slowly onto him.

"Ah, Ethan," I breathe, as my head falls back, surrendering to him. He hisses, as my body accepts more of him.

Pulling my head up, he looks into my eyes. "Does this answer your question? I know all that and still, I want to put a precious baby inside my, sexy, gorgeous, pain in the ass, young, soon to be wife," he punctuates his words with thrusts of his hips.

My head lolls to the side, as I gasp for air. He lays open mouthed kisses along my throat, opening my robe.

"Ride me baby." He pants, laying back, clasping my hips. I use his thighs as leverage, to move slowly up and down, taking my time, making him crazy.

"Faster baby, I need to feel you come. I want you to drain me…" his voice dying as I slam down on him.

We're hot, sweaty and almost there, when his phone starts ringing. *No.* This can't be happening.

"Ignore, it," Ethan pants, moving me faster. "Ah, babe, I'm…" I'm cut off by the door slamming downstairs.

"E? You up there? Answer your damn phone!" Mace shouts, and to my horror I hear him coming up the stairs.

I scramble trying to get off of Ethan, to be flipped effortlessly onto my back. He puts his finger to my lips, grabbing our phones. Switching them off and start moving again.

"What are you doing? Mace is just out there…" I hiss into his ear.

"We're almost done. I'm not letting you out of here without finishing, I need to come," he hisses, when my insides clench involuntarily.

A loud knock has my eyes widening, even as Ethan moves slowly inside me. "I know you're in there. Get your asses out here!" Mace Shouts, banging again.

"Oh shit. I'm going to come, and your brothers on the other side of the door," I grate, trying to hold off.

Ethan chuckles, picking up the pace. "The faster you let go, the faster we can face him," he tells me, lifting, changing angles.

And god, it helps. "Yes… E, right there. Oh fuck, yes." I grasp his ribs, feeling them flex sets me off. "*Oh god!*" I groan loudly. Ethan grunts and whispers my name as he lets go.

"Eww. Please tell me I did not just hear what I think I heard," Mace groans, his gagging noises following him downstairs.

I laugh so hard at the horror in his tone, I snort. Ethan shakes laughing into my chest.

"It's not funny. How am I supposed to face him now, he's heard me come all over his brother?"

Ethan smiles smugly. "You were rather loud at the end there. '*Oh god!*'" He mimics.

"You arse." I hiss, pinching said arse to emphasise my point.

"Oh, you don't want to do that. Unless you want to go another round." He drives home his point by circling his hips, he's still semi-hard.

"God, are you a machine? Move your fine arse off of me, your brother is waiting." "Okay. But we're not finished here," he assures pulling out, kissing my belly.

Emerging from the bathroom, my room looks normal again. My eyes drift to Ethan, sitting on the edge of the bed, pulling on his shoes. He looks delicious, his face flushed with exertion, lips swollen and parted. His eyes shine at me, he looks happier than I have seen him.

"I just need to grab some clothes. Why don't you go

down and I'll meet you in a few minutes?" I blush from the look he shoots me.

"I don't think so. I think, I'll wait right here, and make myself comfy," his tone amused, as he scoots back making himself comfy. Hands behind head, knees bent and parted, his eyes burning intent on me.

Well, if he wants a floor show… I think slowly peeling the towel off, letting it drop to the floor. The gratifying sound of his breath hitching, is my reward. I look at him, and he hasn't moved an inch.

My gaze caresses his gorgeous face and body, not missing his substantial bulge. Pleasure rolls through me, it makes me feel more confident, I wonder how far I can push before he cracks.

Hiding a small smile, I walk over to my draws. Open the top one, purposefully keeping my back to him and pulling out my most, sexy underwear, bending I pull on my black lace thong and slide on my matching demi bra, which cups me perfectly and holds my ample breasts up. Tiny hairs on the back of my neck stand on end.

I know Ethan is right behind me. Smothering a smug smile, I turn into a fine chest encased in a thin shirt.

"Lily," he groans, his eyes lit with barely leashed hunger. He reaches for me at the same second Mace yells. For us to "move our asses." I rub his chest in mock regret.

"Sorry, baby, your brother wants us," I say sweetly. Laughing inside at the face he pulls.

"How am I meant to go down there and deal with whatever Mason wants, when you've done this to me?" he whines, placing my hand over his hard-on.

I lick my lips I give him a quick squeeze before letting go. Turning I bend down to retrieve some shorts and a top from a drawer.

My arse rubbing against him. He groans stilling my hips and smack my butt cheek firmly.

"When we're done down there, we're coming back to bed, so we can finish this, okay?" I nod, unable to speak.

"It's your own fault, I asked you to go down before me," I remind him breathlessly.

"And miss that show? Hell no! Come on, we better go before he comes back up," he says, giving my other cheek a smack.

CHAPTER TEN

We walk into the living room, holding hands, smiling.

"Finally," Mason explodes. "What the hell took so long?" he snaps.

My smile drops. "Who pissed in your cornflakes?" Ethan asks.

Turning I go into the kitchen giggling silently. Grabbing two bottles of water, passing one to Ethan, I down half mine.

"Well. I've been fielding calls from dad all morning. While you were obviously enjoying yourself," he snaps at Ethan, who drops the smirk he was sporting.

"What does he want?" Ethan asks, nervously, I watch from my perch on the counter.

"He wants to know where the hell you are. *Again.*"

"You didn't?" He looks nervously at me.

"No. I told him you were with me, but then we got into a fight, about where I've been and I accidentally told him, I… We were here." He cringes. Looking apologetically at me.

"Shit. Is he?" Ethan asks.

I start to panic as my brain goes to the worst-case scenario.

“Yeah, he’s on his way. That’s why I was so pissed off. What you going to do E?” Mason asks anxiously, watching Ethan pace.

“Well, this is as good a time as any to tell him I’m not marrying Ashley,” he shrugs, coming to stand beside me and throwing an arm around my shoulders and kisses my temple.

What the fuck were you thinking? I ask myself for the umpteenth time. *Giving your virginity to a bloke who’s with someone else. So, stupid.*

Watching Ethan pace and Mason suck his bottom lip in and out, I’ve gone from mild panic, to full on panic and berating myself.

What am I even doing agreeing to marry him? He’s still technically engaged. I’m eighteen for fecks sake. How could I have been so stupid to have sex with him. Unprotected, not once but twice? I shake my head, disgusted with myself, getting swept away in the moment and the magic of what we shared.

I run my hands through my hair as my legs bounce, fighting the need to run.

“Hey,” I startle, looking at Ethan, crouched in front of me.

“Hey,” I say softly, my voice wobbling.

“You okay?” He asks, laying a hand on my cheek, I nod not trusting my voice.

I’m so nervous, I’m nauseous. *What will his dad do? What will happen? What if it doesn’t work out? What if we can’t be together? What if I’m pregnant?* All these questions swirling around in my head, making me dizzy.

Blinking, I refocus on Ethan. Taking deep breaths, I try to

quell the panic that's choking me. Thoughts floating through my mind. Two words emblazoned. 'Single mom.'

"Lily, it's going to be fine, it'll be sorted in an hour, tops. Then we can move on with our plans," his assurance helps soothe some of my frayed nerves.

"What plans?" Mason interrupts, from his perch by the window.

"Erm…" I look at Ethan, at a total loss of what to tell him or how to explain.

"We've been making plans for our future, but this needs to be sorted first," he says vaguely. Mason looks from me to Ethan, opening his mouth to say something, we're saved by the doorbell ringing. We freeze wide eyed, looking first at each other, then at the door.

"I'll get it then, shall I?" Mason mutters stalking off, none too pleased.

"Baby, we'll be fine. You and me," he murmurs, stealing a quick kiss before standing.

I couldn't move if I wanted to right now, my legs are like jelly. My stomach churning, my palms sweaty, mouth dry and heart racing.

I look up in time to see Mason come into the room, with an angry yet familiar looking man. He zeros in on Ethan first, not even noticing me.

"Where the hell have you been?" he shouts seriously pissed.

"With Mason, here with Lily and Millie," he states obviously, I struggle to hold my giggle in, thinking he's spent so much time around me.

Three sets of eyes land on me. Shit, it must have escaped.

Ethan looks bewildered. Mace is smirking getting it, but his dad's face is a mixture of emotions. Shock, awe, bewilderment and anger.

"Wait! Don't I know you?" I ask, looking at him closely. Trying to pinpoint how and where I know him from.

Ethan interrupts, "Alex, we need to talk."

"You bet we do," he replies, his hands going to his hips, and it hits me.

"You were at my Mom's wake," I interject, confused I look from him to Mace and Ethan then back again.

"What?" Mace looks at his dad confused. "You were at the wake? Did you know her?" For a moment, I think I see panic in his eyes, before it's gone.

"Your Aunt Lilyanna was close friends with her," he says matter of fact, his green eyes bouncing between us.

"Back to the point. Why are you here Ethan? I know Mason is friends with Lily, but you?"

Ethan clears his throat, looking like a nervous little boy. "That's partly what I wanted to talk to you about Alex," he swallows hard.

After looking around nervously, he blurts, "I can't marry Ashley…" Looking Alex straight in the eye. Pride surges through me watching him.

"What the hell do you mean you can't marry her? It's all set. The wedding is two months away," Alex explodes, his hands flying in the air.

I feel like I've been sucker punched. Two months? He's meant to be getting married in two months.

"I know. I just can't…" Ethan replies adamantly.

"Of course, you can," Alex scoffs rolling his eyes.

"No. I can't. I won't marry a girl I don't love," he affirms.

"You have no choice, Ethan. She's pregnant with your child. You can't walk away from the mother of your child." He states unwavering.

"Dad," Mason tries to intervene.

"No. You stay out of this. You and I are going to have

words. Later," he yells at Mace, like he's a child, my blood boils, at the way he's "speaking" to them, they're grown men.

"Okay, that's enough! You cannot and will not speak to either of them like that in front of me," I fume, planting myself in front of Ethan.

Alex looks at me shocked and oddly, proud? "What has it got to do with you?" He asks arrogantly, raising an eyebrow.

"Dad," Mason yells. "Don't ever, talk to Lily like that again." He's vibrating with anger, standing between me and his dad.

Ethan's hands gently caress my hips. Looking at him I'm shocked to see desire flaming in his eyes, I turn away quickly.

Alex looks between us, Mason guarding me and Ethan at my back, his hands caressing me. "Please, tell me you're not…" he waves his hand between us, cringing.

I gasp. What the hell does he think I am?

"Dad... No. We are not altogether. Lily is my best friend," Mason says, between clenched teeth.

"Alex, you need to tread very carefully," Ethan grates between his, the threat clear.

"Oh, I get it now. You're going to leave your pregnant fiancée, two months before your wedding, to pursue an eighteen-year-old girl?"

"You know what. You know shit! This eighteen-year-old "girl," has most likely been through more than your average "girl" in a matter of months. So, don't make out like you know me. As for Ethan and me, I love him. I'm not going to stand here and listen to you talk to either of these two like you own them, like you, have a say in what they do, or who they love," I yell, my temper flaring.

"What's going on in here? Lily, honey, are you okay?" Nan comes rushing into the room looking worried.

"I'm fine Nan. Sorry," I say softly, embarrassed. "No.

You're not. What's all the yelling about? Who is this?" Her voice dying as she spies Alex.

"Well. If it isn't Alexander Scott," she says snidely, I look on shocked.

Mace and Ethan's heads snap in her direction too. Alex looks shocked and panicked. "Nan? How do you know him?" I ask moving to hold her hand.

Silence stretches, uncomfortably. "Oh, he's a big-time Vineyard owner, right Alexander?" she replies, her tone ice cold. Alex blows out a breath, looking at the floor.

"So, what are you doing in my house? Arguing with my granddaughter?" she demands coldly, and even I'm a little scared of her right now.

"I'm here for my sons," he mumbles pointing at Ethan and Mason.

"Your, oh gosh," she mutters, wobbling a bit.

"Nan." I yell horrified. Time seems to slow as I watch her hit the floor.

"Nan? Please wake up." I drop to the floor, placing her head gently in my lap.

"Shit. Cora. Someone get a damp cloth."

Ethan jolts out of his horrified trance and runs to the kitchen. "Here," Ethan hands me the cloth and drops down beside me.

"She'll be okay," he says reassuring me.

"Should I call an ambulance?" Alex asks, looking on guiltily.

I sputter, not knowing what to say. I glare. "How do you know my nan? Why did seeing you piss her off? She's never pissed." My tone accusatory.

He looks nervous. "Erm, that's a long story, as I said, my sister and your mom were close friends."

"Yeah, I got that part. But what the hell has that got to do with my nan, passing out at the sight of you?"

"I," he shifts on his feet as nan groans.

"Nan?" I wipe the cloth across her brow. She blinks, looking around confused. Until her gaze connects with Alex's.

"What the hell are you doing in my house?"

"My sons."

"Oh god," she looks stricken, looking from me to Ethan.

"Please…. Tell me you haven't?" she whispers to me.

"Haven't what?" I ask, she looks at Ethan.

"You haven't… slept with him or anything like that?" she whispers scandalized. It makes me giggle.

"Erm, Nan I'm not answering that." I blush bright red, looking at Ethan, who has a satisfied smirk on his handsome face.

"Lily, you can't be with Ethan," she says abruptly. I gasp, the thought of not being with Ethan causes my heart to tighten painfully.

"Nan, that's not an option," I state, my stomach churning nervously.

"She's right. You can't be with Ethan. Because he's engaged and going to be a father," Alex butts in.

I cringe as she gasps. "What?" Explodes from her like a bullet. She stands shakily, her eyes spitting fire. "So, not only are you his son," she jabs her thumb in Alex's direction. "A Scott no less, but you're engaged and having a baby? While messing around with my granddaughter," she rants, the venom in her tone compelling me to move in front of Ethan.

"Nan? That's not how it is." I say softly, holding my hands up.

"Oh? Then, how is it?" Alex asks snidely.

Nan spins back around. “You. Keep out of this. You’ve caused enough trouble,” she snaps at him.

His eyebrows rise in surprise, but he wisely shuts it. “Okay, Nan. Ethan doesn’t want to marry Ashley. He’s been trying to tell Alex for ages, he’s breaking off the engagement, he’s not playing with me, we love each other.” I reach back for Ethan’s hands and lay around my middle.

“Cora? I would never play with Lily’s feelings, I love her. I knew she was different the day we met, and I thank god, every day that we found each other again. I am breaking my engagement, but I will be in my child’s life.”

“Say something Alexander.”

I look at her confused and hurt. “Nan? What’s going on? What have you got against Ethan and I being together?” I cry, tears blurring my vision. Ethan turns me into his chest, shushing me and stroking up and down my back soothingly.

“It’ll be okay baby.”

“Ethan, you can’t abandon Ashley. She’s pregnant with your child!” I glare at him for using the abandon card.

“I know that, Alex. I’ll be there for the baby, but I won’t be marrying Ashley. Not when I’m holding everything I’ve ever wanted in a wife.” He kisses the top of my head for emphasise. I slide my hands around his back, burying my head in his neck.

“I love you,” I whisper and kiss his neck.

“I love you more.” He whispers into my ear.

“Would you two stop!” Alex yells startling us. “How can you be that way with him? He’s cheating on his fiancée, the mother of his unborn child to be with you?” His implied insult hitting its mark.

“Hey! Don’t you dare yell at her again. And don’t ever imply she’s anything but a good person. Embroiled in a bad situation. I won’t marry Ashley. For connections or any other reason. End of." Ethan's chest is rising and falling rapidly and he's glaring at Alex.

"Hey, it's okay. Baby, look at me," I say waiting for him to look at me. Finally, he looks at me, I place my hands on his face.

"I knew what people would think and say about me for this. It's fine baby. I don't care what he thinks. He's nobody to me. But he's your dad," I say, smiling weakly.

"I don't care after this. He does NOT get to talk to you that way. I'm a Barker. Not a Scott. You don't get to decide my life," he grates out between clenched teeth.

"Wait! You're not his son?" Nan asks.

"No. He's my step-dad."

"Thank you, Jesus," she breathes.

"Okay. We're just going around in circles here. Let's stick to the point and facts." I pipe up. Feeling drained, with all the different arguments and shouting going one, I have a splitting headache.

"Can we all sit down and discuss this like adults. Please?" I plead, sighing when they all nod.

Nan leads the way to the living room. I break off, heading towards the kitchen for water and painkillers.

"Are you okay?" Ethan asks, rubbing my tense shoulders.

"I'm okay. It's just more stressful than I expected, and what's with Nan and Alex? I've never seen her pissed off, let alone, cold to anyone."

"I have no idea. It's weird though... Let's just get this over with. Then you owe me alone time," he whispers kissing my neck.

"Erm, babe, you need to stop. Your dad and brother are just through there with my nan," I whisper breathlessly. Chuckling, he steps back.

“Let’s get this over with,” I huff stomping off, I hear him chuckle again.

In the living room Mace is by the window on his phone. Nan and Alex are having a heated whispered argument. Which stops abruptly when they spot us.

“Okay, what’s going on with you two?” I ask frustrated looking from one to the other.

“I’ll let him tell you.” Nan answers coldly.

“Erm, we… I,” he stutters looking around nervously.

“Oh, for god’s sake. Just tell them dad.” Mace snaps.

An uncomfortable silence settles over the room and Alex looks increasingly anxious.

“He called Ashley, she’s coming here,” she blurts, “Shit.” Ethan hisses.

I stand there in shock, looking at Alex, wondering if he’s lost his damn mind.

“You had no right to do that.” Ethan growls at him.

“Well, since it’s her future we’re talking about here, I figured she had a right to be here too.”

“Oh, so now we’re airing secrets?” Nan snaps standing.

“Don’t... Please,” Alex voice barely audible. The pleading look, on his pale face a sharp contrast to the arrogant, angry and pushy man I’ve seen so far.

“If you’re telling secrets, Alexander. I think maybe you should start with your own.”

“I know you’re angry, Cora. But this isn’t the time or the place for this,” he replies, placatingly.

“You have no right whatsoever to tell them what they are doing is wrong. You’re a coward and a hypocrite,” she snaps.

Silence blankets the room, we all sit there, occasionally looking at each other.

My phone ping's.

Mason added you to a group chat: Mason, Ethan, Lily.

Mason: *Can you believe all this over you two?*

Me: *I know! What's with Nan & your dad?*

Ethan: *It's weird. Why the hell would Alex phone Ashley to come here?*

Mason: *I nearly bust a gut when I heard her name.*

Me: *It's all confusing me tbh, I don't know how much more crap I can take today.*

Ethan: *I'm so sorry. I didn't want it to happen this way. Alex can be a real asshole sometimes. Sorry, Mayo.*

Mason: *Hey, I know he can be. I don't know how I'm going to tell him about Millie. He'll blow a gasket.*

Me: *I'll tell him. It's not right, and after today, I'm sorry, but I don't like your dad Mace.*

. . .

Ethan: *He was never like this when Niles and I were younger, he was kind and calm and playful.*

Mason: *Wow. What happened then?*

Our conversation is quashed by the chime of the doorbell.

Oh shit. I'm going to be sick.

"She's your guest, you answer it." Nan snaps at Alex.

My hands start to shake, as if I'm preparing for a fight.

They walk in with their heads together, whispering.

She's shorter than me, with shoulder length blonde hair, stick thin, heart shaped face and yep, fake boobs.

She has on way too much make up for my taste. She looks well bread though, in her designer clothes, unfortunately she also has that air of arrogance.

"Ethan? What the hell's going on? I haven't been able to reach you all day. Then Alexander calls. Saying you're all here, wherever here is?" She looks around, cringing.

Cheeky cow! I'm about to say something when nan wades in.

"Now. You listen here, Missy. Don't you dare come into my house, disrespecting me and my granddaughter. I didn't invite you here. So I suggest you find some manners right quick, or you can leave the same way you came in."

Alex looks embarrassed, whereas Ashley looks stunned by the short, plump woman telling her off. Go nan!

"What are we doing here? Who are these people?" She blunders on, not heeding nan's warning about being rude.

"You're here because Alex, can't keep his nose out of

things that don't concern him." Ethan sighs, finally speaking. My breathing slows as he gets up and faces her.

My nervousness is palpable I can't stop my hands shaking. I'm grateful when Mace grasps them, giving them a reassuring squeeze. I blow out a breath fortified by my best friend.

"Thanks," I say under my breath. "It's okay, I can't believe my dad." He mutters.

"Listen Ash. There's some things we need to talk about, can we meet at my apartment later tonight?" I stiffen, squeezing Mason's hand hard.

I don't want him alone with her. Why doesn't he just tell her?

"Why? What's all this about? Why is Alex calling me telling me to come here ASAP?" She asks annoyed. Ethan looks at Alex, frustrated.

"E?" She snaps.

"I didn't want to do this here." He growls frustrated. "Will someone just tell me what the hell's going on?"

"I…"

"Shut up Alex!" Ethan shouts. "You've done more than enough. Thank you."

"Okay, Ash, I… I can't marry you." Ethan winces, looking ashamed.

"*What?*" she screeches, making us all wince.

We look between them. She's turning red and in contrast Ethan goes pale.

"What do you mean you can't marry me? It's two months away," she says, waving her arms around.

"Come on, tell me why?" she storms forward and jabs him in the chest with her perfectly painted nail.

Ethan winces, just standing there. Which makes me spitting mad. Who the hell does she think she is? I go to stand, but Mace holds me down, shaking his head. "But…"

Ethan looks back, shaking his head, telling me no or to be quiet. But it's too late, Ashley turns on me.

"Who are you?" She asks coldly eyes narrowed. Oh, she's sprawling for a fight. Okay.

"Me?" I ask, pointing at myself sarcastically, standing. I hear a "shit." From behind me. "Who am I? Well, since this is my living room you're standing in, I suggest you find those manners my nan mentioned earlier. As for your question. My name is Lily."

"Oh, you're the girl Mason's been seeing?" I look at Mace and bust up laughing. He smirks shaking his head at me.

"Ah, no, I love him dearly, and he's all kinds of hot, but no. He's my best friend," I say, winking at Mace. He blows me a kiss acknowledging my compliment.

"Okay, I'm confused." She says, rubbing her head. Airhead. Comes to mind. I'm not a mean person, but I really don't like her, her air of self-importance ticks me off.

"Aren't we all," I mutter drawing a chuckle from Mace.

"If Mason is your best friend. Why is Ethan here and Alex and me? What do these people have to do with you not wanting to marry me? We were happy making wedding plans just yesterday?" she asks softly.

"I'm trying to tell you. I've… Met someone else," he blurts looking into her eyes.

"That's ridiculous. How could you have met someone else? What about the baby?" she whispers hurt. Oh God, my eyes widen and I fall back into my seat.

I need to run, I need air. My emotions are colliding inside me I need a release so bad. If I don't, I'm going to scream.

"Mace" I tug his shirt, looking at him, panic in my eyes. "What? Lils, are you okay?" he asks worried.

"I need… I need to go for a run, I..." I lick my lips, trying to put into words what I'm feeling.

"Okay, but now?" We look over at Ethan, who is trying to calm down Ashley, I notice how gently he's talking to her.

I'm about to turn away, when she flings herself into his arms, kissing him fully on the mouth, and he doesn't push her away.

I guess that's that then…I'm such a fucking idiot. My eyes are huge looking at Mace, he's gobsmacked too.

I've got to get out of here. I'm already out of my chair and headed for the stairs, as the thought registers.

"Honey."

"Lils?"

I hear nan and Mason calling, but I'm already safely locked in my room, whipping off my clothes, I yank my running clothes from my draws. Pulling them on with jerky movements.

Yanking my hair, painfully into a messy ponytail and yank on my trainers. Stretching so I won't have to stop when I get outside. Grabbing my phone and plugging in my earphones, I'm out within minutes.

Mason is pacing the kitchen angrily, while nan is at the table with her head in her hands.

I go and hug her, "I'm okay, or I will be. I just need a run, time to sort my head and feelings. I'm sorry to leave all this to you. Will you be okay?" I rush not wanting to be anywhere near Alex, Ethan or Ashley.

"It's fine. I'm so sorry all this is happening. Once you're gone, I'm kicking those three out," I giggle.

"Okay, I've got my phone, but it's in flight-mode. I'll see you later."

"I'm coming with you."

"No. Please, will you stay with Nan? Just until they go. She needs someone right now."

Blowing out a frustrated breath, he agrees. "I'm so sorry, Lily, I can't believe he did that."

"Okay, I've got to go. Text me later?"

Programming my music too loud, I head out, spotting Alex off to the side. He looks at me guiltily. I scoff at the thought. Arsehole, I think pushing through the door.

Taking off down the path, a nice breeze brushes my face.

My mind automatically changes pace, throwing thoughts at me.

Looks like plans have changed somewhat. Why the hell did I fall for his bullshit? Twice? What the hell am I going to do if I'm pregnant? Shit. Fuck. Shit, I'm so stupid. What am I going to do mom?

Looks like I'll be a single mother too. If it comes to that. It was plain as day where this is all headed. You, idiot. When she kissed him right in front of us all, he didn't push her away. Just the opposite, his hands go to her hips. Ugh.

Mom raised me alone, I can raise a baby alone too. Shit, I don't even know yet. It may all be okay. I don't want a kid born from all this shit, what a fucking mess that would be.

After giving myself a talking to. I head home, tired, sweaty, hurt and broken. The past few months have left me barely strong enough to get through life.

I do need to find a way to tell nan and Mace, though, I wince just thinking about it. Not going to be a pleasant conversation.

'You made your bed, now you have to lie in it'. Mom's words ring in my ears.

"God, I miss you so much." Stopping, I bend in half, absorbing the pain that always accompanies thoughts of her.

It's been hard, I have good and bad days. But I think about her every day. Sometimes, like now, when my emotions are all over the place, it catches me off guard, just how much I miss her. I could use her advice and support.

Sitting down I hug my knees to my chest, bowing my head as sobs overtake me.

The pain of seeing Ethan kiss Ashley. From all the crap that went down today and over the last few weeks. And missing mom so much it's physically painful. Just wishing I could call her and have her tell me it will be okay, that she's there for me.

I let myself grieve and cry until I feel better from my pity party.

Taking a series of deep breaths, I stand, wipe my face, shake off the sad thoughts.

I bolster myself. I can do this. I will move on.

With my positive thoughts circling, I start to feel mildly better, more in control of myself and my emotions.

I walk the rest of the way home, thinking happy thoughts.

I may be a mommy in nine months. I'll be fine.

CHAPTER ELEVEN

I walk into full blown warfare. "Oh, thank god, you're back, honey. Stop them, before they kill each other." Nan rushes to me looking frazzled and flustered.

Walking over I see Mason in Ethan's face, "I warned you to be careful. That she was fragile," Mason yells at Ethan, red faced and more pissed than I have ever seen him.

"I know that. I've seen it myself. I'm sorry," Ethan yells back.

"You keep saying that. But you keep hurting her. Making her promises, before you're able to fulfil them." Mason's tone is menacing, scaring the shit out of me.

"I know. I've messed this up, but Ashley is vulnerable right now..." Before he can finish his sentence. I hear Mason's growl, in a flash he's across the room, on top of him, his arm poised to strike.

"Mason, no!" I shriek, tears blurring my vision as I run to catch his arm.

"Lily?" he whispers, horrified, looking at me before getting up to catch me in a bear hug. I didn't know I needed until I was being squeezed.

"I'm sorry, I scared you, sweetie," he whispers hoarsely.

I didn't realise how upset he was by all this, and I should have.

"You didn't. I just don't want you hitting your brother. Not over me, it's not worth it." I look over his shoulder, my eyes connecting with Ethan's. He looks like shit, with his hair standing on end and his eyes red and swollen from crying.

"You okay?" Mace asks, setting me down. I nod, "As well as I can be. I'm sorry for leaving you and Nan to deal with all this. Everything just overflowed," I croak, blinking back yet more tears, I will not cry in front of him.

"Lily?" Just the sound of his anguished voice. Feels like nails on a chalk board. Summoning all the anger I can, I face him.

"What?" I ask, my voice cold.

"I'm sor…"

"Sorry? Yeah, I know. Me too." I turn to leave.

"Lily. Wait, please?" he pleads.

"God. You're like a broken record. I remembered those words last time the shit hit the fan, and I found out you had a fiancée." I spin yelling.

"How stupid was I, sticking with you after finding out that? From your brother no less," I pause, my chest rising and falling rapidly.

"After everything you said and promised. Just a few hours ago… I gave you…" I choke on my words.

I bite down on my cheek, to keep from crying like a baby. The sting of pain is nothing compared to the agony tearing through me at this moment.

"No. You listen to me. After this conversation is over, I never, want to see your face again. I may be emotionally fragile. But I'm a Carter, and like the strongest one I knew, I'm more than capable of raising a child alone." My words hit their mark, if the look on his face is any indication.

"Wait." Mason looks between us. His eyes narrow as he looks at Ethan.

"You didn't?" He growls, stepping toward Ethan. "Tell. Me. You. Didn't," he demands.

Ethan looks at his bother shame written all over his face and drops his head in answer to Mason's question. The next thing I know, Mason's fist is connecting with Ethan's face and blood squirts from his mouth.

"Mace," I grab hold of his arm. "Stop. Please, don't do this."

"Tell me the truth. Has he taken your... Virginity?" He looks at me furiously.

I nod grabbing his fist. "No. No more hitting, he's your brother."

"Like I give a shit. He took… He slept with you, and I'm going to go out on a limb here. From what you said… There could be a baby?" I close my eyes feeling bone tired.

"Yes," I whisper. "There could be a baby, but that's my problem." I point at Ethan. "I want nothing from you, you get me?"

"No. If there's a baby, I will be there for you and him or her."

"Oh, you mean like what you were going to be for Ashley? No thanks. I'll be fine. I may be a single mother, but I have my nan, Millie and Mace. Go be with your fiancée," I tell him, falling onto the sofa and closing my eyes.

"Lily?" I feel someone shaking me.

"What," I mumble not wanting to leave my comfy bed.

Turning I cuddle into a hard chest. Feeling warm and content. "Mm, Ethan."

"No, sweetie, Mason," he whispers. I blink looking down at him, I'm on top of him and my hand is under his shirt.

I jump off him, falling onto the floor. "Shit, Mace, I'm so sorry." I say covering my flaming face, I was touching him.

"It's okay," he says gently rubbing my back, and I giggle through my mortification.

"I'm sorry, Mace. I was dreaming," I sigh, wishing I could go back to my dream, away from the harsh reality.

"Yeah, I know. One minute you were asleep, then you were on top of me, kissing my neck, with your hand up my T-shirt. Moaning Ethan." He teases.

"God, Mace..." At a loss of what to say I change the subject.

"Aren't you seeing Mills today?" My head is banging, and my eyes are swollen and sore.

"Yeah. I called and explained. She said she wants to come over?"

"Not today. You go over there, spend time with your girlfriend. I just want to be alone, and I have to tell Nan I may be, there may be a baby coming soon."

"I'm so stupid Mace. I believed him when he said he wanted to be with me. That it didn't matter we forgot the condom. Convincing me to try for a baby, I got so swept up in the moment. Stupidly. I know."

"He asked you to try for a baby?" He asks, astonished I nod, unable to look at him.

"Wait. How many times did you…? Without one?"

"Twice. And I worked it out, it's the perfect time Mace," I cry falling apart, I look at my best friend expecting to see anger, anything, but there's only understanding.

"It's okay, you have your gran and you'll always have me," he murmurs softly, hugging me as I sob my heart out.

"I know and thank you. But if I am, I'll still be a single mom. How will I take care of a baby? I'm barely an adult. What the hell am I going to do Mace?" I sob, holding onto him tighter.

"Ethan will support you. He'll pay for everything."

"I don't want his money. I want the father of my child to be there, I don't want to do this alone. He said we'd get married. He said we'd live together. He said he loved me. I still love him, Mace," I whisper feeling empty.

I feel refreshed after my bath, yet at the same time I still feel unsure and drained. I just laid there for an hour and a half, turning everything over in my head. I head down to the kitchen, needing food since I didn't eat yesterday.

In the kitchen nan and Mace are talking intently. Probably about me, I throw them a weak smile. "I thought you were over at Millie's?" I ask Mace raising an eyebrow.

"I figured you needed me more today."

I shake my head amazed by him. "What would I do without you?" I ask hugging him around the neck.

"I don't know sweetie, but don't worry. You'll never find out," he replies, kissing my hand, urging me to sit and talk. Why couldn't Ethan be like Mace?

"Nan? I, erm, I need to tell you something."

She must see my struggle and places a hand on my arm.

"Whatever, it is, just get it out there, we'll get through it together. We're a family," Silent tears trickle down my face.

"I might, I mean there… I might be having, a baby."

"What?" She breathes, looking appalled.

"I'm sorry. It was a stupid mistake. Well, not the possible child, but the sleeping with him part," I clarify through a torrent of tears.

Nan's pacing and rambling incoherently. I didn't even see her get up.

I only catch snippets of what she's saying. She's mumbling about history repeating itself. Well, that's mom having me. Something about a father, and not losing me, like she did Lizzy.

"Nan, you're not going to lose me," I say, snapping her out of her rambling.

All this puts a new spin on growing up without a dad. Potentially becoming a single mother puts a new spin on a lot of things.

"Nan. I don't even know if I am yet. I just couldn't keep it from you, that's all."

"Honey. I think it's time for you to go back to school. I know you're still affected by your Mom, but with all this. I think you need a direction," she suggests as gently as possible. Mace nods, agreeing.

"I think you're right. Besides the more education I get done the better, just in case."

The past two weeks have flown by. Putting on a happy face is the hardest sometimes, but I've enjoyed school, even laughed and smiled some. Focusing my mind and pushing on with life, has been the best choice I've made since meeting him.

With the constant support of nan, Millie and Mace, I've gotten up every morning and gone through my daily routine.

It's been two weeks to the day since I've seen or spoken to Ethan. Just thinking of him makes me sick, but I miss him.

It's now time to confirm what I already know to be true. I'm pregnant, with Ethan's child.

Shit. Pregnant at eighteen... I guess I should tell him.

A knock on the bathroom door startles me. Mace ever the loyal friend is waiting to hear if he'll be an uncle soon. Wiping my face, I drag my arse off the floor.

"Lils, you done?" I take a deep breath. Thank god, nan's out.

I can't handle disappointing two people I love at once.

I'm going to be a mommy to someone.

"I'll be out in a minute!" I call.

Pull yourself together, this baby needs you. God, I'm going to be a mom.

Mason's perched on my bed when I emerge looking like a bag of nerves, his arms braced on his knees, legs bouncing.

"From the look of you, you'd think you were the one, pregnant."

"Aww, Lils... I'm not sure how to react. Are you happy or not?" He asks, excitement breaking his voice.

I smile. "It's not the best situation, or time, but I'm happy. Scared shitless, but how could I not be happy?"

Jumping up, he has me in his arms, spinning me around in a circle. I laugh wiggling out of his arms as soon as he stops, I really don't need to be sick again.

"So, what now?"

"God, Mace. I haven't the foggiest," I shrug, thinking. "I guess I have to tell Ethan."

"How do you want to do it, on the phone or face to face?"

I have no idea. I'm not sure I could see him. But I need to… To show myself that I can be strong. So, face to face it is.

"I'll text him to come here," I say, picking up my phone and tapping a quick text.

. . .

Me: *We need to talk. Meet me at my house in an hour.*

"Do you want me to stay?"

"Yeah, I think I'm going to need reinforcements," I joke, taking his hand. "You know, I don't know what I'd do without you," I choke, as the love I feel for him as my best friend courses through me.

"Okay, hormones. Calm down, we don't need a crying fest," he laughs, patting me on the head.

I jump when my phone ping's.

Ethan: *I'll be there.*

"Well, there it is. He'll be here in an hour," I say nerves shaking my voice. "I better get ready to see my baby daddy," I say sarcastically.

Mace chuckles heading out the room. "I'll be downstairs when you're ready."

While Mace is downstairs, I call Millie needed a girl to vent to.

"Hello," Millie answers, and I almost don't recognise her voice it sounds so cold.

"Hey, you okay?"

"I'm fine."

I frown, confused at her clipped answers and icy tone.

"I just called because I have some news," I try to sound happy, but I feel like I'm missing something.

"Let me guess you're pregnant?"

"Yeah, how?"

"Cora told my mom it may be a possibility. So, what are you going to do?"

"What do you mean, what am I going to do?" I ask baffled, this doesn't sound at all like the sweet girl I call my friend.

"Are you keeping it?"

"Of course, I am! And it's a baby not an *It*."

"I have to go..." That's all I get before the line goes dead. *What the hell just happened?*

I decide not to tell Mace about it for the sake of his relationship with her, but inside I'm shocked and devastated that she would be that way with me.

By the time I get out the shower and picked my clothes carefully. Black skinny jeans, white top under a long pink knitted jumper. Pink and white high tops, and I leave my hair down in soft waves. Not bothering with makeup. On the outside I'm ready, but inside I'm a jittering mess.

I take a series of deep breaths before heading downstairs, trying to stay calm, as I know stress isn't good for the baby. I chant repeatedly in my head. Mace is relaxing on the sofa watching TV, but jumps up when I walk in.

"Wow. You look amazing," he blurts, and blushes.

I giggle "Wow, did you just blush?" I tease. Smirking, he shakes his head.

"You're going to make my brother wish he hadn't chosen the Witch," my smile falls.

"Sorry," he winces.

"It's fine. Just a little raw right now. I have to learn to deal. I'm having his kid," I say. Trying hard to sound like I'm not dying inside. The thought of seeing Ethan on a regular basis and knowing he'll be married.

Mace leads Ethan into the living room. I'm sitting trying not to jump out of my own skin.

He looks good in a charcoal suit. White shirt slightly undone, his tie long gone. He must have come straight from work.

Mace sits beside me, grasping my hand.

Ethan looks tired and anxious. "Lily," he sighs.

My heart lurches, I blink holding back tears. Summoning all the strength I can, I straighten my spine.

"Have a seat Ethan," I manage in a bland voice, startling him. Who gives a shit?

Sitting on the edge of the sofa, he looks at me expectantly.

I take a deep breath and stand because I can no longer sit. Wrapping my arms around my middle. I look into the eyes of the father of my child and open my mouth, but nothing comes out. Heat sweeps through me; I feel weak and faint. Sweat breaks out on my forehead.

Please don't panic, please... Oh god, my vision blurs. I grab for the sofa, swaying.

"Shit, Lils," a garbled version of Mason voice reaches my ears.

"Lily?" Everything is fuzzy and sounds muffled.

"Ethan," I whisper my voice slurred.

"I'm here, right here. What's the matter with her?" He sounds anxious.

"She's not been well, E," Mace relays hesitantly.

"What do you mean she's not been well?"

Ethan sounds choked. “Mason?”

“I can’t tell you. That's for her to do,” he grates.

“Why?” Ethan demands, frustrated. “Because it’s her business. Don’t start with me, E. I’m still fucking pissed at you.”

He sighs, “I know, I don’t have the right to demand anything, but I love her, Mayo,” his voice cracks.

“Damn right you don’t. You made your choice. If you loved her, you wouldn’t have made a shit load of promises, taken her virginity, then went back to your fiancée,” Mason growls, lifting and placing me onto the sofa.

It’s weird listening to them talk about me.

“I know. I fucked up. It’s just that, Ashley needs me right now, with the baby coming and all.”

“Really? She does, does she? Well, so does Lily. But hey, that means shit, right?” Mace yells.

I groan. Feeling like shit, but finally able to open my eyes and move. The room’s silent, compared to a few seconds ago. I look over and see Mace looking guiltily at me.

Ethan as white as a ghost. “You… You’re?” Ethan stutters.

I shoot an annoyed look at Mason. “I’m sorry,” he mutters.

Ethan lick's his lips, running a hand through his hair before grasping the back of his neck and kneading it.

Clearing his throat, he blinks. “You’re pregnant?” He whispers, stumbling to the sofa, placing his head in his hands and cries.

Well, that’s a bit unexpected, I look at Mason, who looks shocked too.

“I’m pregnant, Ethan,” I say needing to say the words out loud. He nods, looking up at me. His face wet with tears, his eyes stricken.

"I-I'm so sorry. What are we going to do now?" He asks gripping his hair.

"You knew it could be a possibility. I'm keeping our child," I state, pissed at his stupid question.

"No, I meant how are we going to work a baby into all this? Ashley's going to be pissed." The last bit sets my anger ablaze.

"My baby is not being 'worked' into anything. You can see him or her after the birth and be a dad, but that's it. And frankly, I don't give a rat's ass, whether Ashley is pissed or not. I have more things to worry about right now.

Like, how I'm going to cope with a baby, college, and find a house. I'm eighteen and pregnant. Everything in my life has been turned upside down, but don't worry, I'll cope, you keep worrying about how Ashley will react."

"Don't worry, it'll be okay. You have me, we'll get through this," Mace whispers into my hair, holding me tightly as I try to pull myself together.

"I love you," I sob.

"Aww, are you going all girly on me? I love you too, sweetie. You know that. I'll be there every step of the way. You don't need to be scared."

A growl erupts behind us. We turn to see a very pissed off Ethan. I scowl at him. What the hell's crawled up his arse?

"What the hell's going on between you two?" he asks furiously.

My eyebrows shoot up, seeing where he's going with this.

"Well?" he snaps.

"Sorry, I'm just trying to work out what business that is of yours?" I say harshly.

Mace moves to stand behind me, sliding his hands around me, before coming to rest on my belly, where Ethan's baby lies. I jump looking back at him confused. He bends down, mouth by my ear.

“Play along, he’s seething,” he whispers. I press my face more into his, giving a slight nod. We must look very intimate, because Ethan’s vibrating with anger.

“Are you... And Mason?” he sputters angrily.

“That’s none of your business, E. You made your choice,” Mason reminds him, resting his chin on my head. I place my hands over his, where they rest. He laces our fingers squeezing.

“What about Millie?” Lily, you’re carrying my baby it is my business now.”

“Millie understands. Lily needs me with the baby coming,” he says rubbing my tummy.

“She’ll have me! That’s my baby, Mason, not yours. You will not play daddy. He has a daddy. ME,” he roars, red faced and gorgeous.

“You’ll be busy the next couple of weeks anyway with your nuptials. Then in eight or nine months, or however long Ashley’s got left, with your other baby,” I say goading him.

Mason’s chest shakes silently behind me. I know he’s laughing at his brother, but I have to hold mine in. It’s funny seeing him pissed and kicking himself, over his own choices.

“No... Shit. I know I’ll be busy, but he’s mine.” He points at my belly.

“I won’t let you take what’s mine Mason... They... He’s my baby. He’s half me and half... Lily.” My name comes out anguished.

“None of this is relevant right now anyway. I’ll let you know when he or she is here. When we’re settled, you can come and visit your child,” I say.

The finality in my tone telling him we’re done.

He looks frantic running his hands through his hair.

Looking between me and Mason. "Lily. Please, can we talk alone?" He pleads, close to tears again.

I look at Mace. "Go ahead, I'll wait upstairs," he says, pecking me on the cheek before heads upstairs.

I look back at Ethan, his eye shine with tears and pain.

"Lily, I'm sorry about what happened a few weeks ago. I'm so ashamed.... How I've treated you," he struggles, grasping for the right words.

"Yeah. Well, at least I learnt a valuable lesson from it all," I shrug like I don't care. But it's killing me not to rush to him and hold him. Kiss him, tell him I love him.

"I promised you... So much. I'm not proud of myself for it, and now you're pregnant and alone. I…" he's fumbling trying to explain.

"Well, it's my own fault really. I fell for it all, knowing you were engaged and becoming a father. I fell foolishly for the I love you' and the sweet nothings," I sigh disgusted at myself.

"No. It's not your fault, it's mine. You're not foolish, I wasn't lying, Lily, I do love you."

I scoff, "Yep. You love me so much, that when it came time to tell your fiancée, you love me and wanted to be with me. You ended up making out with her in my living room. Humiliating me in front of my nan, best friend and your dad. Who I bet is so happy you two made up so quickly? I wonder what he's going to say, when you tell him you knocked up your bit on the side?" I yell, swiping angrily at the tears cascading down my cheeks.

"Lily, I'm sorry, I've caused you all this pain. I didn't mean to, or to humiliate you. She caught me off guard, I was shocked. I do love you and I do want to be with you. It's so complicated right now. You wouldn't understand. You're too young to."

"You love me?" I ask acidly, without giving him a chance to reply, I go on.

"You want to be with me? She caught you off guard?" I scoff, "If that was the case you wouldn't have still been sucking face when I left. I can't believe I ever fell for your lies. You're pathetic, you know that? Oh, I'm too 'young'? I wasn't too 'young' when you were fucking me was I?" I yell.

He blanches paling.

I'm breathing so heavily I get dizzy again. Closing my eyes, I try to slow my heart rate and breathing.

I bend in half, as nausea hits me so hard, I throw up all over the floor.

"Shit, Lily are you okay?" Ethan rushes to me. "Ugh," I grunt dropping to the floor.

"*MACE!*" Ethan yells, making me wince.

"Shush, my ears." I mumble, as Mason comes skidding into the living room.

"Lily, you okay sweetie?" He's kneeling beside me, as I turn into him.

"Maybe it's time to take you to the emergency room?"

"I'm okay. I just got too worked up that's all," I say, sucking in deep breaths. "I'd love some water though," I say, weak from throwing up so violently.

Running to get it, he's back in seconds and lifting me off the floor.

"I think you should go," he says to Ethan, still holding me on his lap, as I slowly sip water.

"I can't, Mason. She's sick and it's my fault. You don't get it, do you?" He growls pulling his hair.

"What is it we don't get?" I sigh drained; he swallows hard licking his lips.

"I do love you, Lily. I meant every word I said when we… I meant every promise. I wish more than anything that I could keep all of them. I want this baby… Our baby," I slide off Mason's lap, still staying seated.

"If you wanted all that, you wouldn't have kissed her right in front of my face. You would have chosen me, no matter what. You would have chosen us." The last word a sob as I place a protective hand on my belly. A warm feeling spreads through me. It is that moment, I finally accept that I'm going to be a mom.

"It's been killing me staying away from you. Wondering if you were carrying my child. It killed me to walk away. I'm not sure I can do it again. Not now, no matter the consequences, and believe me, the stakes are high for me. You are both all I want. The only one I love and will ever love."

I'm so stunned that I feel for the tripe spewing from his mouth, that I just sit there. He must have taken it as a good sign, as he trudges on.

"I have to sort a few things out, but I will come back for you and him. You're mine. I was crazy to think I could go through with this. Please believe me. I love you both so much." His voice breaks.

"I'm sorry. I've heard it all before, and I'm not falling for this again. I'm not waiting around for you to do something I know you won't do." Laying my head back on the sofa, I close my eyes.

"Okay, So I've said it before. Come with me, please?"

"I'm sorry, Ethan, but no. This is it for us. You chose her… over me. You only want to come back because of the baby. You can still be a part of his or her life, after I give birth, but until then we're done." I say looking him dead in the eye.

"Please? Lily don't do this. I'm sorry, I should never have chosen Ashley over you. I love you." His voice cracks as tears fall from his eyes. It kills me to do this, but I can't have uncertainty anymore, not with a baby on the way. He made his choice. Now I'm making mine.

"Please, don't make this harder than it has to be. Just go, I'll call when the baby arrives," I'm trying so hard not to cry. I can feel my throat burning, my eyes stinging.

I sit looking at him memorizing his face waiting for him to leave, but not wanting him to.

"Ahh. What the fuck have I done?" He roars before leaving. Slamming the door. Taking my heart with him.

I bury my head in the sofa, as heart wrenching sobs break free. Fucking hurts.

"Come here," Mason whispers, gathering me into his chest. I sob so much, my throat, chest and eyes are hurting.

"That was brutal," Mace says, a little choked up himself.

"Did I do the right thing Mace?" I hiccup looking up at him.

"I think you did; you need to think of you and this little one. Not all the shit that's following Ethan around. He got himself into this mess, but shit, the look on his face before he left, pure agony. I can't help feeling for him, he's my brother. He made his choice though, and he has to live with that choice now." He sighs squeezing me tighter.

"It's such a mess and it hurts."

"I know, sweetie. We'll get through it. I'll even be your birthing partner. You can squeeze the shit out of my hand, whatever you want. I'll even do that funny breathing thing with you," he adds smirking, I laugh at the image.

"I love you and thank you." I kiss his cheek, settling back on his chest and falling asleep.

CHAPTER TWELVE

"Okay, you need to get out of this house." Mace barges into my room, placing water and some healthy snacks on the bedside table. He opens the curtains and the window, causing me to wince at the light.

"Mace, I'm tired," I protest.

I'm anything but tired, all I do is sleep, eat and pee. I just don't want to face the world. I'm pregnant, alone, and the father of my baby is getting married in the next couple of days.

"No, you're not, come on, let's go to the movies or bowling or shopping its nearly Christmas," he says enthusiastically, bouncing on my bed.

I smile seeing his boyish smile and behaviour. It's been nearly two months since my life changed forever and I haven't seen or spoken to Ethan since, he hasn't called me once, thankfully.

I wish I could get over it already. It's time to pull my head out my arse and start preparing for my little chunk.

Everyone's been great, but I see their pitying looks and sad faces. That's what I'm avoiding. So I take online classes because I quit college. No way am I walking around with a bump, with judgemental dickheads shooting me scathing looks. No, thank you.

The worst of it is Millie has been cold to me since I told her I was pregnant. We had a massive argument a few days after my blowout with Ethan, and we haven't spoken since.

I was doing fine, until his wedding crept closer, I heard Mace having an argument with his dad over the phone. He refuses to attend the wedding. Since the day I told Ethan about the baby, Mace has pretty much lived here. He refuses to go home, and it's caused a massive rift in his family, by all accounts. He won't budge though.

"Come on, please?" he begs breaking me out of my thoughts. I smile at his puppy dog eyes, but his pout makes me giggle.

"Okay, okay. We can go bowling, only if we can have pizza and spicy wedges?" I ask, my mouth watering. I love them. He rolls his eyes, smirking at me.

"You're going to look like a spicy wedge soon enough," he chuckles, as I scramble out of bed, racing to get ready.

"Be ready in five," I yell through the bathroom door.

"Okay, I'll meet you in the kitchen."

I'm glad Mason cajoled me into coming out, we're having a great time.

"Hey, it's my turn you cheat," I say around a mouthful of pizza.

"Can you put your food down long enough?" he quips raising an eyebrow.

"Yes?" I sound unsure even to my own ears. He laughs going to pinch a wedge.

"Don't you even think about it, buster." I growl.

"I wouldn't dream of taking it from Pooh," he smirks rubbing my belly.

"Is that what you're calling my little chunk now?" I ask smiling at him.

I get choked up every time he talks about little chunk. He's the only man I've ever been able to count on. He's always there for me no matter what, and he's been amazing through all this, he comes to all my doctor's appointments, hold's me when I cry and picked me up when I was throwing up everywhere.

"One day you'll be an amazing dad you know that?" I ask, he blushes sucking his lip in and out.

"Thanks, Lils, I'm enjoying going through this with you. You're going to be a great mother, and of course, I'm going to be an amazing uncle," he says puffing his chest out, and we both laugh.

"You already are. We're both lucky to have you."

"Aww, come on, you're going to make me cry." He clutches his heart dramatically, and bats his eyes, I laugh.

It isn't often we get all mushy, but pregnancy turned me into a big tit.

"I know, but seriously, I love you. For everything you've done for me and us. You're the best," I laugh as real tears enter his eyes.

"Okay, enough of the mushiness. I love you both, too, and I wouldn't want to be anywhere else, I wouldn't miss this for the world." His voice is gruff, and he's holding his arms out to me.

"Aww, you two are so cute," a girly voice coos. We turn to see a group of teenage girls. "You're a cute couple. Do you know what you're having?" Another asks, gobsmacked I answer her automatically. “No.” Mace keeps an arm around my shoulders and looks at the girl.

“Aww, I bet you’re both excited to find out if you’re having a girl or boy?” She sighs.

I’m about to tell her we’re not together, that Mace isn’t the dad. When Mace shocks the hell out of me.

“We are, not long now, though,” he sighs kissing the top of my head. My eyes bug out. What the hell’s he doing?

“It was lovely talking to you; you look great together. Good luck with the rest of your pregnancy, and the birth I hope it all goes well.” I blink still in shock.

“Thanks,” I whisper as they leave.

“What was that?” I ask, when they’re gone, looking up at Mason.

“What?” he asks innocently.

“You let them think we were together and this is your baby,” I hiss, not sure why I’m pissed.

“I’m sorry, I thought it would be easier than explaining that I’m just his uncle, and my dick of a brother is his father, who will be marrying another woman, who is also pregnant, in a few days.” He says angrily.

I forget sometimes, just how much this tears him apart.

“I’m sorry, I know you were just thinking of me,” I cry. Shit, I don’t want to upset him.

“Hey, it’s fine. It’s not your fault. I’m sorry. It's just what he’s done makes me so mad. You deserve better.” He bear-hugs me, kissing my temple.

“I don’t need better, I have you.” I hug him tightly.

“Yes, you do.”

Well, the day has arrived. He's getting married today and just the thought makes me sick.

I need to get out and do something. I refuse to sit here wallowing, it's time to move on.

Thankfully, Mason makes sure I don't have time to wallow. We hit the shops again trawling every baby store they have, buying little neutral coloured baby-grows, teddies and cute little booties.

I catch him looking at blue outfits, I laugh. "Are you hoping for a boy?"

He shrugs smiling. "Well, it would be easier to play cars with a boy, but if it's a girl, I'll have to learn how to make girly voices, for when we play dollies." He's serious too. I'm awed by the lengths he'll go for his niece or nephew.

We shop some more, splitting up to get Christmas presents. Yep, Christmas is just over a week away. We aren't celebrating it though. We didn't celebrate Thanksgiving either it didn't seem appropriate. We're just getting a couple of presents each.

I'm surrounded by Christmas decorations, music, busy shoppers and excited kids. But I'm not feeling it at all. Even the carol singers aren't making me feel warm and cosy.

We get back just in time for dinner. "Hey, Nan, that smells amazing," I groan salivating.

"Didn't Mason feed you today?" she asks playfully.

She knows better than that. Mace is like a drill sergeant when it comes to me eating enough.

"Not nearly enough." I groan, sticking my tongue out at Mason's scowling face.

"You know me better than that Cora. She had a full pizza and onion rings."

"Stop, I'm starving over here," I state as my tummy grumbles.

"You only ate two hours ago," Mace says laughing.

"Hey! I'm eating for two here. This kid is going to be a monster. He can obviously put it away like his uncle Mason," I say rubbing my belly.

Looking up I see them both staring at me. Nan has tears in her eyes, while Mace has a soft smile on his face.

"What?" I ask, feeling uncomfortable.

"If that's the case, then he's definitely a boy. I'm going to teach him so many things," he laughs evilly.

"You teach my kid anything naughty or nasty and I'll kick your arse," I say laughing.

"You two are like an old married couple. Shame you don't fancy each other," she mutters, heading for the stairs. Shocked, we look at each other.

"What was that about?" Mason is blushing.

"Aww, you're blushing," I tease.

"I have no idea, but she's seen how you've been there for me, you never waver, even though he's your brother," I croak biting my cheek. Freaking emotions.

"I don't give a crap, he fucked up and hurt you, then left you pregnant and married the shrew."

I reach out taking his hand, loving him more every day.

"What about your family? Your mom must be upset that you didn't go today, that you won't go home." I feel so guilty for the strain all this has put on Mace and his family.

"And what about Millie?" I ask hesitantly. He won't talk about what happened.

"Millie called it off. I told you this. It's not your fault. My family will get over it. Mom's too busy being pissed at dad and Ethan, to worry whether I'm home or not."

That shocks me, this is the first I've heard about it. "So, she knows, about me and the baby?" I ask softly, placing a hand on my belly.

"Oh yeah, and she was pissed at dad for getting involved, and with Ethan for being so careless with you. But mostly, she's pissed that she's missing out on your pregnancy because E's a dick."

"She is upset about missing my pregnancy?" I ask.

"Yeah. It's an important time. She'll miss all the pictures and stuff," he shrugs.

I feel a little guilty and sad for her, because she's stuck in the middle.

"We'll have to get her a copy of the pics and you can keep her updated," I tell him.

He smiles. "This will make her day. I'm going to call her." My eyes bug. I've never heard or spoken to his mom.

"Hello," her voice is soft and feminine. I smile. "Hi, mom." He smiles.

"Oh, thank goodness you called. Do you want to speak to your brother?"

And my smile's gone.

"No, I'm here with Lily. You're on speaker." There's a pause.

"Oh, sorry. Hello, Lily," her voice is gentle, motherly.

"Hello, erm, it's lovely to meet you, even if it's not in person," I ramble, she giggles.

"Yes, it is. I've heard so much about you. All good," she rushes. I giggle.

"Mom? We called for a reason." He sighs chuckling.

"Okay, sorry, go on honey."

"I told Lily how you're upset about missing out on her pregnancy, seeing scan pictures and things."

"Yes, it's very hard. I mean you're having my grandchild and I haven't even met you, and I know how hard and lonely it can be…." she breaks off. "Sorry, I just know. I've been there."

"It's okay, Mrs Scott. I have family and Mace has been amazing."

"So he should be, I brought him up right. I don't know what happened with Ethan, he's so confused and upset, not himself at all." I close my eyes as tears gather behind my lids.

"Mom?"

"Oh, I'm so sorry honey. I."

"Mom we called to tell you something and you're rambling," he sighs exasperated.

"Okay, go ahead."

"As I said, I told Lily about you being upset. She said we can get extra pictures when we go to the scan, and I can keep up informed on everything." Soft sniffles come through the line.

"Mom, are you okay?" More sniffing.

"Yes, yes. I'm okay. Thank you, darling. You have no idea how happy that makes me." Mace smiles, taking hold of my hand.

"Well, he or she is your grandchild. It would be unfair for you to miss out." I say simply, as muffled whispering comes through the phone, I look at Mason stricken.

"Hello?" Mace calls.

"One second honey." We hear a hushed one-sided conversation.

"No, I'm talking to Mason. No, Lily's fine. Nothing's wrong, I don't think that's a good idea. Okay, I'll ask."

"Mason are you still there?" She asks hesitantly.

"Yeah. We're still here. What's going on?" He asks pissed and I know what is coming, I can feel it and start shaking my head, no.

"Well, your brother's here, he'd like to know if Lily would talk to him for a minute?" She asks nervously.

Mason is livid. "He just got married, to the woman he left Lily for. It's his wedding day and he still wants her to talk to him?"

I shake my head again, this is horrible, but I don't want them fighting because of me. Taking a deep breath, I hold up my hand. "I'll talk to him, Mrs Scott," my voice is barely audible but strong.

Mason's head snaps to me. "You don't have to; you don't owe him anything." I smile, ever the loyal friend.

"I know, but I don't want your mom to be put in the middle of this, I have to talk to him sooner or later anyway, I am having his baby." I shrug.

"Thank you, honey. I know it's hard, here he is," she says.

Picking up the phone, I take it off loudspeaker and walk up to my room.

"Hello," I say sitting on my bed. A sharp breath sounds through the phone.

"Hi," he says and my breath whooshes out just from his voice. "How are you?" He asks softly, well that's a stupid frickin' question.

I grit my teeth together, "I'm fine, busy." What the fuck does he want me to say? "How are you?" I find myself asking, my manners taking over. I cringe disgusted with the whole situation. He's at his wedding reception right now.

"I'm good. Busy also…." he stops abruptly.

Ouch. Yep, he's busy getting married. Playing happy families and sharing pregnancy wonders with his new wife. While I'm alone, lucky to be sharing mine with Mace. Not the same at all, I can't tell Mace my hopes and fears, it's just different.

"Yeah, sounds fun. So, what do you want?"

"Lils…"

"Don't. Don't call me that." I snap.

"I'm, I. How are things going with…the baby?"

"Fine, as far as I know. We get to see chunk in a few days," I smile, I can't wait to see my baby, Mace is so excited.

"We?" Ethan interrupts thoughts, sounding none too happy.

"Mason's coming with me," I state obviously.

"So, my brother is going to see my child before I do?"

"Yes. He is, because he's been there for me through two of the hardest periods of my life and helped me through them. He's been here through the tiredness, puking, feeling shit and sobbing fits," I snap, my anger flaring.

"I'm sorry. I'm just pissed at myself for not being there. That's my child growing inside of you, and I've fucked everything up. You are alone in this, because I was stupid. I'm jealous of my own brother, he gets to be with you, see you and my baby grow. Soon he'll be able to feel my baby's first kick too, while I'm stuck here, not knowing shit.

I can't believe what I've done. Mom is so pissed at me, and rightfully so. I feel like I've done the same thing my dad did to her," his voice break's and I hear him crying. I tear up listening.

"This is tearing me apart. I want to be there for every little thing. My baby is going to know his uncle better than his daddy," he cries.

Tears are streaming down my face, I literally ache to tell him I need him, I miss him and still love him.

"I don't know what to say Ethan." I croak wiping my nose.

"Me either, I wish I knew how to fix this, but I don't think I can."

"I'll send an extra picture for you."

"Thank you. I know I don't deserve it, especially after today." Whoa. Reality check.

"It's fine, he's your baby too."

"Babe, what are you doing in here?" Oh, shit. It's Ashley.

"I'll be out in a minute, okay. I'm on the phone!" he grates pissed at her.

The sound of a door closing greets my ears, and there's an uncomfortable silence.

"Lily, are you still there?" he asks, his voice soft and nervous.

"Yeah. I'm here, you better get back. I'll speak to you in a few months. Take care, Ethan," I whisper hoarsely.

"Bye, Lily." His voice thick as I hang up.

Christmas day is here and it doesn't feel like Christmas at all, mom's not up jumping on my bed excitedly.

Mace is up though and cooking something that smells amazing. We don't have decorations up, nan and I decided we didn't want them up this year. We eat, smile tightly and open the few gifts we got each other.

I got Mace a 'Best Uncle' jumper, some new running shoes and a big, personalised teddy saying, *'Chunk and I love you, Uncle Mace'* He loved it.

I got nan a new cardigan, new shoes and a jumper saying, *'I'm the Grandma, and the Great Grandma'* It made her smile.

They both spoilt me, with bigger clothes, shoes, all sorts of mommy paraphernalia and money.

We ate dinner and watch old movies all day.

It's finally here, the day I see my precious little chunk, I smile rubbing my protruding belly.

"Lils, you awake yet? Come on, move it. I want to see Pooh…" he yells through the bathroom door.

"Okay, okay. Jeez, you'd think you were the one having a baby. Give a momma a chance." I grin at myself in the mirror, caressing my bump it's quite big for twelve weeks.

All through breakfast, all Mason does is jump in his seat. I smile shaking my head.

"Would you keep still? You're going to spill juice everywhere." Nan scolds him grinning.

"What time were you up? And how much coffee have you had?" I ask looking at him closely.

"Erm, about five? And maybe too much on the coffee." I chuckle, he's so hyper.

"I'm sorry I can't come. I can't take time off right now." Nan says sadly.

"It's fine, they only let one person in anyway, and storm over here isn't going to sit still until he sees chunk," I giggle.

"You ready? We're going to be late," he nags bouncing on his toes.

"Yeah, but I'm driving. You'll crash the car in the state you're in," I say, herding him toward the door.

"Would you keep still?" I chuckle, trying to concentrate on the road.

"Sorry," he sings at me happily.

Shaking my head, I pull into the doctor's office and cut the engine.

"Okay, you need to chill out! Take some deep breathes or drink some water."

"I am chilled out. I am a figure of serenity."

I laugh getting out the car. "Yeah, *serenity, of course."*

"Lily Carter?" I jump at the sound of my name, I'm so nervous. I look at Mace, standing shakily, he takes my hand as we follow the doctor.

"I'm Dr, James, how are we feeling today?" she asks gently, looking over my notes.

"I'm fine, glad to have gotten past the puking part," I joke.

She chuckles, looking up. "I bet, at least you have daddy here to help carry the weight." Shocked, I look at Mace, but he just smiles.

"He's not the baby's dad, he's the uncle," I tell her, because I can't lie to the doctor.

"Oh, I'm sorry. I just assumed."

"No, it's okay. Most people do, he's always there," I say, smiling up at Mace, he squeezes my hand.

"Okay, how about we see how this little one is doing?" She asks cheerfully, looking at Mason.

"Yes, please. He's really excited." I say teasing, he just rolls his eyes at me, smirking.

"Aww, he's an anxious uncle."

"Get yourself comfy and raise your top. This will be cold," she warns, but I still jump when she squeezes the goo on my belly. "Sorry, it'll warm up in a minute. Ready?"

I nod clutching Mason's hand. The screen comes on, it's all fuzzy for a few seconds. Then the face of my baby comes onto the screen. My eyes mist. That's my baby.

"Would you like to hear the heartbeat?" I nod, unable to speak.

The room fills with the sweetest sound of my child's heartbeat.

"Wow," Mace whispers, I look at him, seeing tears sparkling in his eyes.

God, he loves chunk as much as I do.

"Oh…" I hear the doctor murmur, and I panic looking at her.

"What's wrong?" I ask, my voice wavering.

"Nothing's wrong, but there are two heartbeats."

"Oh, my god."

I stare in shock out of the window while Mace drives. I'm still in shock. I thought it was going to be hard with one baby, but two.

Shit. What am I going to do now? Two babies twice the work and no daddy in sight.

"You okay over there?" Mace asks hesitantly.

"I don't know Mace. I think I'm in shock and freaking out a little bit. How am I going to cope with two babies?"

"Just take deep breaths, it'll be okay. I promise, I'll be there every step of the way," he assures.

"I know, but it's not the same. I'm sorry, I love you. You're amazing, but you're not their dad. I'm going to need constant help. You have school and eventually you'll have to go home." I breath, my life feels like it's spinning out of control, it's overwhelming me.

"You're still keeping them? Right?" He asks anxiously.

Honestly, I can't answer that right now, so I keep quiet. Closing my eyes, trying to stave off a massive headache.

Am I seriously thinking about giving up my babies? No. I can't, no matter how hard it'll be I can't do that. They didn't ask to be created, it's not their fault.

When we finally arrive back, I'm glad to see nan's not home because I need time to process.

"Are you going to tell Ethan?" Mason's quiet question brings me up short.

God, that means another hard conversation with him. I was hoping to not have to talk to him till the baby was born.

"Shit, I'm going to have to, aren't I?" I whine.

"Yep, you can do this you're the strongest woman I know." I hug him.

"Thanks, but right now I don't feel so strong. I feel helpless and scared shitless."

"I'd be worried if you weren't scared. You'll get through this and then you'll have two, cute little babies." His excitement sparks a warm feeling inside me. I can do this, I have to.

"Should I call him now?"

"Yeah. He'll still be at work."

"Do you want me to leave the room?"

"Do you want to stay?"

"I think this is between you and Ethan."

"Lily?" I close my eyes as his voice washes over me.

"Hello?" It's now or never.

"Hi, Ethan." I'm so nervous I'm shaking.

"Are you okay?" He asks, panic shaking his voice.

"I'm fine, I'm…" Shit, I don't know how to word this.

"Is it the baby?" I can hear his erratic breathing through the phone.

"No. Not exactly. We're fine. Healthy." An audible sigh comes through the phone.

"What's the matter then? You said you'd call when the baby was born."

"Well, I went to the scan today and…. Well, it seems, we... There are two babies," I stutter.

"Oh god," he breathes.

"Are you okay? I know it must be a shock. It never even crossed my mind. I suppose it should have since I'm a twin." His rambling makes me smile.

"Yeah. I'm shocked, but okay, I think."

"What are we going to do? This on top of everything else…" I know just how he's feeling. I was blown away too.

"We carry on the way we have, until the babies are born. Then we can talk. Listen, I just don't know what to say or do right now. How the hell am I going to cope with two babies?"

I'm sick of feeling unsettled, unsure. I had just got on an even keel and now this. It's thrown me through a loop.

"We need to talk about this, Lily. We can't keep ignoring it, I can help. I know this is hard, but you're not alone. I'm right here, I want to help, I want to be there for you and our babies. Please?" I feel myself weakening at the desperation in his tone, I want to say yes.

"I... I don't know Ethan."

"Please? I want to be there, to see you grow, to see my babies. Please?"

I know I'm going to need his help and support. "What about Ashley? She's not going to like this. Have you even told her about me and the baby... Babies?" The pause is telling. He hasn't even told his wife.

"No, not yet. We've been busy, I meant to tell her before the wedding, but everything was happening so fast, and I was upset about us."

"I wondered why she never contacted me. I suppose I have that to look forward too?"

"No. I'll talk to her at lunch, but everything was fine? With the babies?"

"Yeah. It was amazing, I should have thought there was more than one with how big I am for twelve weeks," I chuckle.

"When do you find out their sexes?"

"I'm having a 3D scan at sixteen weeks; I hope to find out then. My doctor said they are better at telling the sex's earlier than 2D scans."

"Wow. That's soon. I know this is a lot to ask after everything, but could I come to that scan? I would like to see my babies." I'd have to be a heartless bitch to say no to him, I can hear the heartache in his voice.

"Okay, yes. You can come, but you have to sort it so both you and Mace can be there. He's so excited, I won't push him out. He was amazing today."

He huffs, I know he's jealous, but he got himself into this mess. "Okay, give me the number and I'll call," he sighs. "I know it's wrong, but I'm jealous of Mayo; he's seen my kids before me, he knew there were two of them before me, he knew everything before me."

"This conversation is pointless. It was your choice, Ethan. You chose her. How did you think it would be between us, when you chose another woman over me? Then went and married her," I yell pissed at him all over again.

"I don't know. Just not like this. I'm going to miss so much of their lives, even though I'll be there as much as I can."

I laugh humourlessly, "You mean as much as Ashley will allow you to be." I snap.

"Hey. What's all the shouting about?" Mason asks, rushing into the room. I put the phone on speaker.

"Your brothers pissed off and jealous, because you've seen 'his' kids and knew about there being two first. He expected us all to play happy families, after he chose Ashley. Funny thing is Mace. Ashley still doesn't know about me or the babies," I rant.

"What the fuck, E? You still haven't told her? I thought you would have told her before marrying her," Mason yells.

"Yeah, yeah. We all know I'm a fuck up," Ethan says snidely.

"How can you be pissed about me being a friend and picking up your slack?" Mason fires back.

"Of course, I'm pissed. You're doing my job. Seeing my kids grow, seeing Lily…" He should not be saying this shit, he's married.

"Well, you made your choice. Don't go making Lily feel guilty for your choices, we're getting through this just fine." Mason is seething.

"Oh, you are, are you? What exactly is going on between you two?" he growls.

"That is none of your business. Not anymore."

I should have just told him nothing was going on. This will just cause more strife.

"Of course, it's my business. You're carrying my kids."

He sighs, "Okay…. This is ridiculous. You're my brother and their uncle, I'm glad she has you in a way. I'm just sad for myself, mad at myself. I know I made my choice, but that doesn't mean I like it."

CHAPTER THIRTEEN

The next morning, I'm woken by a consistent banging. Sighing, I slowly roll out of bed, it's my only speed these days.

I pull on a big comfy jumper and shuffle towards the door, shouting reaches my ears as soon as my door is open.

"Where is she?" It's Ashley, I can tell by the whine.

"In bed, she's pregnant, and it's early. What do you want Ashley?" Mace asks calmly.

"I want to see that little slut," she yells.

"Hey. Don't call her that, she's pregnant and the one alone in this. I'm calling Ethan, he's your husband, he can deal with you."

I listen intently. "Ethan? You need to come to Lily's. No, they're fine! Your *wife* is here yelling that she wants to see Lily."

"Yeah. Well, hurry up. I'm not going to be nice to her if she keeps calling Lily derogatory names."

"He's on his way, and none too pleased with you either," he says sounding smug.

"Mace?" I ask quietly, as I just came down.

"Lil's go back to bed. I'll be up in a minute, okay?" He rushes to me trying to coax me back upstairs.

"Aww, she fucking you too, Mace? Wow. Not much slows you down, does it?" She asks from behind Mason.

I laugh at her. She looks astonished. I won't let her rile me; my babies don't need the stress.

"No, I'm not fucking him. I don't need to trap a man into sticking by me. I've only ever slept with one man. Your husband." I don't know why I say it. It just pops out.

She screams lunging for me. Mace catches her, holding her off gently.

"You, little whore. You were just a quick fuck, he's my husband, he chose me," she screams, red faced, fighting to get at me.

"Calm down. You're pregnant," Mace hisses as she claws his arms.

"No. I won't calm down. She's *supposedly* carrying my husband's babies. He cheated on me with her," she screeches.

"That's something you should be talking about with Ethan. I may be carrying his babies, but that's as far as it goes," I say rubbing my belly.

"Oh, really? Like I'm going to believe a word out of your mouth, you little slut. Was it his money? Too bad you won't be getting a penny for either of those brats," she spits.

Gasping, I hug my belly protectively. "You really are a witch. Attacking defenceless babies," I choke.

"I don't care. They aren't even relevant, he's mine."

"This isn't about whose he is, you bimbo. it's about the babies. he's a father to all three of them," I yell, feeling dizzy.

Taking her chance, she lunges again, this time shoving me over.

"*ASHLEY!*" Ethan yells, we all turn, none of us had realised he was there.

Mason let's go of her and rushes to me. "Are you okay?" He's pale, sweaty and shaking.

"Yes, I think so," I say, rubbing my back, I hit the stair pretty hard. Mace shifts behind me lifting my top.

"Shit. It's bruising. I think we should go to the emergency room, get you checked," he looks frantic.

"I'll rest for a while, if I get any pain later, we'll go, okay?"

"See, I told you she was with Mason. How do you even know they're yours? She's trying out all your brothers, Niles will probably be next," Ashley spits, not even bothered that she's just assaulted someone.

I look at Ethan. He look's torn, not wanting to believe it, but the doubt's there in his eyes.

"What the fuck did you just say?" I stand shakily holding onto Mace's arm. He's shaking with anger.

I look at Ethan. "You believe her?" He looks from Mace to me. Unsure.

"Of course, he does, I'm his wife." She says smugly, as Ethan says nothing.

"Okay, then. Get the fuck out, and don't come back. Don't even call." My voice steady and calm.

They look shocked, as Mason's arm goes around my shoulders.

Ethan just blink's looking at me.

"What? I ask coolly.

"I, are they mine?" He whispers, and I have to physically restrain myself from lamping him.

Holding Mace back, I wobble to within an inch of his face.

"No. They're mine. They don't have a daddy, but they have an amazing uncle. Now leave and take your trash with you," I sneer in Ashley's direction before walking around them into the kitchen.

"You have the cheek to question her? You're no longer my brother, you're a waste of space," Mason's voice is arctic.

Leaning against the sink, I breathe deeply. Mace comes up behind me and pulls me into his arms.

"I'm so sorry, sweetie. I don't know what happened to him, but he is nothing to me."

"It's okay, I was expecting her outburst. He shocked the hell out of me though. How can he think? Believe her lies?" I hiccup, trying to keep the overwhelming emotions from swamping me. It's hard, normally I would just go for a run.

"You can cry. That was a vicious attack. He's going to regret this when he opens his eyes and realises what he's done." He sighs.

"His choice. He's not coming to the scan now, tough, as I said they may not have a daddy, but they have an awesome uncle" I sob.

"Let's not tell my nan what happened. She may beat the shit out of him," I laugh.

Chuckling, he kisses my forehead. "No. I think you're right, but I am calling my mom. She's going to kill him." He sighs.

I shrug, what can I do? It's his family. I shuffle back upstairs gingerly to lie down, my back is killing me because of that bitch.

Hunger wakes me from a restless sleep. I get up slowly, rubbing my back, it's sore. I take the stairs carefully.

I'm so caught up thinking about food, I don't see Mace at the kitchen table with an older woman at first. I immediately know it's his mom by her warm smile.

"Hi," I whisper as Mace stands to help me into a seat. Smiling, I thank him.

"Hello, Lily. It's a pleasure to finally meet you," she says softly.

"You too. Would you like a drink?"

"No, thank you, sweetie. How are you?" She looks sad.

I search my brain for an answer, coming up with nothing positive, I go with the truth.

"Well, honestly? Like crap. It's been a horrible day," I smile weakly.

Tears fill her eyes as she looks at me. "I'm so sorry. I'm so ashamed of Ethan right now. I don't know what happened to him. Since that day here, he hasn't been the same."

"It's not your fault. It's all been his choices. And he's choosing to believe what she's feeding him." I shrug, what can I say to his mom? That he's an arsehole? I may feel that way, but I'm not telling her that.

Shifting, I wince as my back protests.

"You okay?" Mace asks crouching beside me.

"Yeah, just back ache," I say.

"Let me see. Is it where you fell?"

Nodding, I lean forward slightly.

"Oh god, you have a massive bruise on your back," he gasps touching lightly, I shy away not wanting anyone to touch it.

"What happened?" Mrs, Scott gasps standing beside Mace.

"Oh, this is Ashley's handy work," Mason hisses. "I think we need to have you checked out."

"Ashley did that. Where was Ethan?" She asks horrified.

"Standing in the doorway, he didn't even ask if she was okay."

"I'm okay. I need the loo though." I rise, wincing again as I waddle to the toilet waving off Mason's offer of help.

While on the toilet I notice blood in my knickers, I panic and yell for Mason, not even caring that I'm half naked. He bursts through the door, panicked. His mom on his heels looking scared.

"Lils? What's the matter?"

"I'm bleeding," I screech panicking. "I need to go to the hospital," I say crying, he flies to me.

"Mom go call the number in her notes. It's in the kitchen, then start my car." He yells holding me. "It's okay, you're all okay," he whispers tears in his eyes.

"What if?"

"No. Everything is fine. They have your blood, they're stubborn little bu… Fighters," he smirks making me laugh.

"Hold onto my neck okay? Let's get your pants up and I'll carry you to the car."

I shake my head. "No, Mace, I'm too heavy," Scoffing, he lifts me up cradling me to his chest.

"See, easy. Now let's go. I'll text Cora from the hospital," he grabs my key and shuts the door behind us.

At the entrance of the hospital, I'm made to sit in a wheelchair. My Doctor is waiting for us as we arrive. "Hi, Lily. How are you feeling?"

"Hi, Dr, James. I'm not too good, had a fall today, now my back's hurting and I'm bleeding, so, I'm scared," I say softly.

Mason scoffs looking up from his texting my nan, I presume. "She didn't fall. She was pushed," he snaps, and her gaze shoots to him.

"Is that true, Lily? Who pushed you?"

"It was my brother's wife, Ashley Barker," his voice cooling as he utters her name.

"Is that right, Lily? If so, I think you need to report it," she frowns seeing my stricken face. "Let's check you out first, then we'll do an ultrasound, and see how the little ones are doing. Okay?" I nod, looking at Mace scared. I see Mrs, Scott behind him wiping tears.

"Dr, James? Can they both come in please? She's the babies' grandma."

Smiling, she nods, "of course."

Mace whispers a quiet "thank you," in my ear. I look at him questioningly.

"For asking if my mom can come. She would have been going stir crazy otherwise," he pulls a face, making me giggle.

"Thanks for being here, again."

He just shrugs. "Wouldn't be anywhere else."

"Okay, so tell me what happened?" Dr, James says.

"Well," I stop, unsure of how much to say.

"My brother's wife is crazy and turned up at Lily's house shouting her mouth off. Verbally attacking Lily. I was in the middle holding her off, when it all got out of hand, somehow, she got around me and shoved Lily over. She fell and hit her back on the stairs." Thank god, he left all the horrid details out.

"What was the reason for her attack on Lily?" She asks Mason.

"The babies. It's complicated, but the bottom line is; my brother is the father of the babies. He's also the father of his wife's baby, which is due just before Lily should have hers but with there being two." He shrugs and she raises her eyebrows looking slightly confused.

“He’s married?” She asks, there’s no judgement in her voice, but I can see her calculating the months.

“Yes, very recently. Bottom line he played Lily. He’s a dick. I know,” Mason mutters.

I think Dr, James just got more than she bargained for.

“Are you okay?” She asks kindly.

I nod as tears form in my eyes, hearing it laid out like that is worse than the gory details.

“I’m sorry, it just came out,” Mason whispers, clutching my hand, as she puts the scope thingy on my belly.

“Okay, here we go. There’s one heartbeat, it’s strong so that’s good, you want to hear?” I nod needing to hear their heartbeats.

I smile looking over at Mrs Scott as she’s crying.

Doctor James abruptly takes the scope off and wipes my belly.

“I’ll be back in a second.” My heart stops at her tone, she rushes out before re-entering with another machine.

“What’s wrong? Dr, James?” I squeak, looking from the monitor to her.

“Do you mind if we try a transvaginal ultrasound? It’s an internal scan that shows more and the images are better and clearer.”

“No, I don’t mind, but what’s wrong?”

“It may be nothing, but I can’t find the second baby.”

My heart lurches in my chest and I gasp as tears spill down my face. *Please God, don’t let this be happening, please let both my babies be okay.*

Mace’s arms pull me to him, squeezing me tightly.

“I’m just going to get some air,” his mom whispers, but neither of us respond.

“Lily? It'll be fine, they’ll find him.” His voice firm, even as tears coat his eyes.

I nod, unable to speak past the lump in my throat, I'm terrified.

We wait as she sets up, the wand is cold and uncomfortable, but al I can think about is my babies. I watch the screen praying everything is okay.

"Okay, here we go there he is, right behind his sister." A collective release of breath comes from us, the tension dissipating.

"Are you sure, they're both fine? Is there really a boy and a girl?" I smile widely, excited.

"Yes, they're fine. Both heartbeats are strong, and yes you have yourself a healthy boy and a healthy girl," she says, smiling. "Your little man isn't shy."

We laugh, relieved. I don't care as long as they're both okay.

"Thank you, what about the bleeding though?"

"That could have been from the stress. So, no more cat fights."

"Okay, as stress free as much as possible, got it," I salute her.

Stress free as it turns out, is harder to accomplish than I thought. Arriving home an hour and a half later. I find nan in the kitchen yelling at Ethan.

"What's going on now?" I ask startling them both.

"Oh, honey. Are you okay?" My nan asks, rushing over to me taking my face in her hands.

"I'm okay. In pain, but nothing I can do about that. What's with the yelling?" I ask, looking from one to the other.

"Well, I've kept my mouth shut until today, but not anymore. He's treated you worse than your father treated Lizzy. Letting his wife come here, saying the things she said about you, to you. Then to question whether he's the father of my great-grandchildren, you're lucky I'm being nice," she shoots him a look that could kill over her shoulder, Mace coughs behind me, but nan isn't done. "Then he lets his wife assault you in front of him, and he does nothing. You are the poorest excuse of a man I have ever met. I thought better of you." Nan's voice is so calm now a cold chill runs down my back and I wince.

"You know who my father is?" I squeak, moving into the room sitting down.

"What? Yes. I know who your father is. He's nearly as bad as him, but at least he never let Lizzy, or you get hurt."

I'm shocked, but I don't want to know right now, I have enough to deal with. I ache everywhere, I'm tired and just want to take the weight off my feet.

"Mace, could you get me some paracetamol please?" I rub my back.

"Sure," I don't look up as I wait, but I can feel his eyes on me.

"Here, sweetie. Maybe you should go lie down?" He asks, rubbing my back for me.

"You lot would implode," I chuckle, finally looking around. Mrs Scott is standing by the door quietly observing.

"I'm sorry, Mrs Scott, this is my nan, Cora. Nan, this is Ethan and Mason's mom. She came to the hospital with us."

My eyes zeroing in on Ethan for the first time. He's a mess, in the same suit he had on earlier, but now it's rumpled, his hair is all over the place. His eyes shock me most; they're a far cry from what they were the day I met him. There's no twinkle, no laughter in them, they're red, swollen and flat.

"Why are you here?" I ask, not taking my eyes off him as everyone else sits.

He just stands there, his eyes drilling into me saying nothing.

"Do you want me to clarify again, what we went over this

morning?" I say, my voice deceptively soft, still nothing. "Or would you like a DNA test when they're born?" All I get is silence in return.

"Do as you like, because as of this morning you lost all the respect, I had for you, it wasn't much, but it was a starting point. To stand by while Ashley called me horrible names is one thing, but to implying that I was sleeping with your brother, who by the way has been there for me and '*your*' kids since before they were confirmed. Says quite a bit about his character, don't you think? For a man you've accused multiple times, of sleeping with me and trying to take '*your babies*'. These babies are so lucky to have him as their uncle. I wish I'd have had an uncle like him."

Silence, not a breath is heard in the room. Mace kisses the top of my head, acknowledging my compliment.

"I can't talk about this in front of people, Lily. I'm so fucking ashamed of myself right now. I can't stand the person I've become. Even Alex laid into me for what happened this morning; I feel sick just thinking about it. I've made so many mistakes these past months, I know they're my kids, I know, and I don't know why or how I could ever question that," his voice wavers, but in that moment, my heart is hard to his suffering.

"I'll tell you how and why shall I? *You* fucked up so badly at the beginning, that *you* lost the one thing, that mattered most to you. Then *you* got jealous and angry at me for being there for my best friend. *You* saw things that weren't there, and *you* let Ashley plant shit in your head. She knows you love Lily, and she hates it. She's threatened by it, and in all that, *you* let Ashley cost you the relationships with four people you love." Mace chuckles humourlessly, standing behind me.

"You should have seen her face this morning. The

moment Lily realised you were questioning the paternity of her babies. She smirked, standing right beside you. Her. Work. Done." Mace finishes stripping him down in front of everyone.

His voice only wavering at the end. Getting up slowly, I move to him, holding him tightly. I know it's hurt him not talking to his brother, not seeing him.

"Mayo." Ethan's voice breaks.

I look at him, seeing tears running down his face. *Finally,* he's seeing what he's done. What Ashley's done. What he lost, what he should have never questioned. His brother's loyalty.

Mrs Scott is sobbing on nan's shoulder, seeing her boys fight must have been ripping her heart in two.

"Go to him, Mace, he's your brother," I whisper, kissing his cheek before moving away.

He looks wary, torn. Ethan moves first, pulling his brother into his arms.

I walk slowly and quietly toward the stairs. All my energy has gone.

"Lily?"

Sighing, I turn. "Ethan, I don't have the energy for anymore right now. It's been one of the worst days of my life."

"I'm sorry, I know you've heard it before, and probably sick of hearing it, but it wasn't supposed to be like this. I don't know what to do anymore. When Alex called me and told me that you were in the hospital. That, you may have lost one or both babies, I thought I was dying, it felt like I was. The pain, after everything I've put you through, and this morning. What Ashley did, I just, can you, will you ever forgive me?" He stammers, dropping to his knees.

"Ethan." I choke, tears slipping down my face. I thought

all the love I possessed for him, had gone after this morning, but no, it's still there.

Am I doomed to love just him for the rest of my life? Looking at me with pain and sorrow weighing heavily in his eyes.

"Please, I'm begging, don't cut me out of their lives. I know, I don't deserve it after what I said this morning, but I didn't mean it. I've been so angry and jealous. It's ripping me apart; I miss you so much and I want these babies more than anything. Not only do I already love them, but they are all I have left of you, of us." Sitting on the step, I rub my belly listening. "I'm sorry that Ashley hurt you, the three of you. I can't believe I just stood there. I couldn't move. God, you looked so beautiful, then Mason, touched you. I don't know what happened."

"Ethan, Mason would never do that to you, he's your brother. I would never, could never, do that to you either. No matter how angry I am at you, I couldn't hurt you like that. I can't see you because it hurts, it's not because I don't want you there or because I'm sleeping with your brother. Mace is like a brother to mee; we don't think of each other in that way. He's been there through the hardest times of my life, all this has hurt him as much as me. He loves you."

"I know. I've been an idiot," he mutters, watching my hand rub my bump. "Can I?" He asks, gesturing at my belly. He wants to touch me.

I nod, holding my breath; zeroing in on his hand as it draws closer, my breath leaves me in a whoosh as he tentatively places a hand on the side of my bump. His breath catching, he caresses me adding his other hand.

I could blame the pregnancy hormones for being turned on, but it could also be the memory of the words spoken, our second time together.

He's a married man.

"God, they're my babies." He blinks, looking at me in awe. His eyes burning with the same intensity, they had the night they were conceived.

"Ethan, don't look at me like that."

I stand, causing his hands to drop off my bump. He stays kneeling, gazing at me, his eyes dark. Biting his lip.

"You can't look at me like that. You're married and we're over." I say annoyed by my hormones, at myself and at him for still being able to turn me into an idiot.

I turn stomping up to my room, berating myself all the way, for letting him in again.

"Wait. Lily. I'm sorry. I can't help the way my body reacts." Spinning, I pin him where he stands.

"I know that, I can't either, but you're married. Everything's different now, you're not cheating on your wife with me. I won't let her attack me again and get away with it. I will not put my kids in danger."

"I don't want you or our babies in danger either, but it's no secret that I'm in love with you. She knows it, she saw it this morning. She knows if you hadn't sent me away, I would never have married her," he whispers, his voice seducing as he steps closer.

"Ethan don't do this, please, it's not fair. You chose to marry Ashley." I plead as he draws closer. His eyes dazed.

"Lily, I, just." He kisses me, searing my lips and for a moment I melt, weaving my fingers through his hair. Until I feel the cool metal of his new wedding band touch my jaw. Like a sharp slap around the face, I pull away. I look at him disgusted with him and myself.

"You're married," I hiss covering my face. "You can't keep doing this to me. Ever since we got together, it's been constant ups and downs, mixed signals. One minute you want to be here, the next Ashley need's you and you're gone. I thought since you chose her and got married, that all the upheaval would be over, but it's not and it never will be until I move on too." I sob, devastated again by the thought of never being with him.

Ethan looks stricken by my words. "Lily don't say that. I can't handle the thought of another man touching you." He growls possessively, pissing me off.

"Really, and what about me? I have to deal with thoughts of you fucking Ashley all the time. I have to move on. This changed everything." I snap, raising his ringed finger in front of his face for emphasis.

"I'm sorry. I won't cut you out of our son and daughter's lives, but as for this, no. This is wrong. There will never be 'us' again."

"Son and daughter?" He looks at me stunned.

Smiling, I rub my belly. "Yep, a boy and a girl," I say, happy that they're both there, safe.

Ethan grabs me, spinning around, laughing.

"What are you doing? Put me down before I'm sick all down your back," I slap his back.

Putting me down gently. We look at each other, happiness radiating from him.

"Thank you, for giving me these babies, and for giving me another chance to be their dad. I'm sorry for everything. I know you're right about us. It hurts, but you deserve so much better and, I hope you find it." His voice catching.

"Can we at least be friends?" He asks, placing a hand on my bump.

I nod, "yeah, we'll have these two soon. So, we're going to need to be."

A sense of serenity washes over me in the weeks that

follow our talk, I feel like we finally turned a corner and at last we accepted that we are over.

Well, all apart from Ashley, but I don't care about her feeling. Thankfully with all this Mason started going home again, although he's still there when I need him. I talk to Ethan quite a bit, always about the babies. I even visit, Isabella, Ethan's mom, once a week.

Mason and Ethan's relationship is slowly repairing in spite of what happened between all of us.

CHAPTER FOURTEEN

Ethan and Mason are both coming to the 3D scan with me. They're both so excited it makes me smile listening to them chat away about what the twins will look like, and whether there is definitely a boy and a girl in there. Their arguments over names make me giggle, their bickering carries on all the way into the doctor's office where I cut them both off.

"Behave the pair of ya or you'll wait in the car." They both quiet immediately, even though I wouldn't do that to either of them, but the warning works nicely.

"Lily Carter? Come on back, we're ready for you now," a cheerful nurse says. I smile, standing, glad to be dragged from my thoughts, I really need to stop worrying about Ashley and what she thinks.

Following her into the scan room, where Dr, James is already waiting for us.

"Hello, Lily. How are you feeling?" She asks, nodding to Mason, looking curiously at Ethan.

"Much better, thanks. This is Ethan, Ethan, this is Dr, James." I bite my cheek looking at him.

Smiling at me, he looks at Dr, James. “Nice to meet you,” he offers his hand.

“You too. Is this him?” She asks tentatively, looking at me for guidance. I nod, biting my cheek harder.

She scowls at Ethan, none too happy.

“Yes, I'm their dad. Thank you, for taking care of them a few weeks ago,” his voice sad.

“Oh, well, it’s my job, but you’re welcome. I hope it doesn’t happen again,” she says sternly.

“No. It definitely won’t,” he assures, looking at me.

“Okay, then. Jump up here, then Lily, and we’ll take a look,” she says, her eyes twinkling.

“I’ll just use the step and slide on if that’s okay. Can’t jump much these days,” I chuckle, getting comfortable, lifting my top.

I’m spell bound by the picture swirling on the screen. Two perfect little babies, facing each other, their little fists in their mouths; wiggling and kicking. Tears clog my throat, as I look at them, they have tiny noses. One baby waves a hand, making me giggle.

“She’s waving, mommy,” Dr, James says happily and I blink stunned, no one’s ever called me that before. It sounds strange, I look around wide eyed, my eyes connecting with Mason’s, he smiles.

I look at Ethan, shocked to see him actually crying silent tears, staring unblinking at the screen.

“Are you having a video?” She asks. I nod, unable to speak, or look away from Ethan.

He meets my eyes with a heart stopping smile and mouths ‘thank you,’ to me, smiling I feel the connection we once shared strengthen.

I have to admit I was worried about Ethan coming today, I thought for sure Ashley would cause problems. It makes me wonder if Ethan actually told her where he was going today. I push all thoughts of Ashley out of my head as I dress and instead embrace the joy of seeing my babies faces.

Since we got in the car Mace hasn't shut up. "That was amazing. Did you see their little faces? I think they look like me." He babbles from the back seat.

Ethan and I laugh, "You think so? I thought they looked more like me." He smiles, I shake my head at them.

"Okay, no fighting over my babies, they aren't even here yet. Can we just wait and see?" I ask giggling, I love that they are back to their old selves.

I relax enjoying the drive, occasionally I giggle listening to them argue and bicker.

Pulling into my drive, my heart sinks, and the smile is wiped from my face by the sight of an angry woman sitting on one of our veranda chairs.

"Okay. Stay in the car please?" Ethan looks at me pleading. First, I'm pissed; because why should I hide? This is my freaking house but looking back at her as she stomps down the front steps, I get it and nod.

"Mace stay with Lily. I'll deal with this, lock the doors when I get out." He looks anxious getting out of the car. Mace leans over locking the doors as instructed.

"It'll be okay, but can you open the window a little?" Mason asks, watching his brother and Ashley.

As soon as the window opens, we're blasted by Ashley's shrill voice.

"I told you I didn't want you to go." She's waving her arms around like a child.

"And I told you, that's not your choice. Those babies are mine too, I will be there for them and their mother. She's eighteen years old, for God's sake and you expect her to cope on her own, with twins. Without any support, financially or otherwise from the father of those innocent babies?" Ethan sounds really pissed off.

"YES." She yells. "She got herself in this situation by fucking a taken man."

God, she's getting louder. I look to see if any of our neighbours are out, breathing a sigh of relief that no one is yet.

"No, she didn't. I got her in this situation, and I was far from taken. I never wanted to marry you Ashley and you know it."

Shit. He didn't just say that. Oh god, he has just thrown fuel on her fire.

She comes barrelling towards the car, her face like thunder. I close the window quickly, glad now that the doors are locked.

She bangs on the window, making it rattle. "Get out here, you little slut."

I gasp as her words hit me like a blow to the stomach. Mace squeezes my shoulder.

She starts yanking on the door handle. "Open the fucking door! This is my husband's car."

Ethan's back appears in front of my window, obscuring me from her view. "Ashley, I will not let you harm them again. You almost cost me one, if not both babies with your last stunt. It won't happen again."

I can see through the window, that he's shaking with anger, but is restraining himself from physically removing her because she's pregnant. Her belly is small but noticeable.

"I don't give a shit. You married me, not her. Our baby is all that matters."

"You may not give a shit, but I do, and so does Lily, her family and mine. Yes, I married you, and we both know why, but all three babies matter to me. They're my kids." He grates, clutching the door handle tightly.

"But you chose me, and now you're always here or talking to her. You're cheating on me."

Is she for real? She sounds like a five-year-old stomping her foot. Which funnily enough, she just did. I giggle the same moment Mason laughs loudly.

"I talk to her about our kids, and I went to see those kids today. I'm not cheating on you. I'm being a good dad." He practically yells.

"Mace? I need to go inside. I need to pee," I squirm.

"Can you hold it a minute?" He asks anxiously.

I shake my head. The twins must be dancing on my bladder. If I don't go soon, I'm going to pee all over Ethan's upholstery.

Knocking the window, I try to get Ethan's attention, no luck. I look at Mace desperately and he whips out his phone dialling. Ethan's phone rings in his pocket, he pulls it out, turning he looks through the window, I open the window a crack.

"You need to move. I've got to get out I need to pee," I say hurriedly, and his eyes widen.

"Can you hold on a couple of minutes?"

I shake my head. "No. If I wait any longer, I won't make it, and I don't think you want pee all over your seat." I fumble unlocking the door.

Mace gets out, hurrying around to help me out of the car.

"Oh, you finally found your nerve to face me?" Ashley taunts.

"I'm not fighting you, Ashley. Just going to the toilet. I grew up a while ago. I don't even stomp my feet anymore," I snap, needing to hurry.

Mason chuckles, standing on my left side so he's between me and her.

"You little bitch. Don't you dare make fun of me, you beached whale," she screams.

Stopping dead, toilet needs forgotten for now. I turn eyeing her making sure I stand proudly head held high.

"Beached whale? You see this?" I ask pointing to my body, she just stands there.

"This is what real men like to sleep beside at night, not stick figures. I'm no beached whale *honey.* I'm pregnant, with twins, and when they come out, I'll go back to the way I was, because I take care of myself. I don't believe in starving myself for men to notice me," I chuckle looking her up and down.

Mason tries to stifle his laughter as does Ethan, but Ashley isn't amused. She lunges unsuccessfully for me. This time I'm ready and I have her by the hair. My strength over-powering her attempts to get a hold of me.

"Not this time lady. You almost killed one or both of my babies' last time. You'll never get that opportunity again. You may have Ethan, but you'll never take my babies." I growl at her. Her face paling, she actually looks scared. "Now, I suggest you leave, before I call the police. My doctor wanted me to press charges against you, so she also took an account of what happened and made a report of it. Just in case I changed my mind and went ahead with assault charges." I say watching her face pale.

"The police can retrieve those records from the hospital, then there are the witness statements from Mason, my doctor, oh and Ethan. So, if you ever come here again, or try to hurt me or my babies. I will press charges and you will be charged with assault." I let go abruptly, stepping back, I look at Ethan seeing he's as gobsmacked as Mason.

Smiling sweetly, I go inside and rush to the toilet.

Coming out a few blessed minutes later I'm surprised to see Ethan is still here sitting quietly at the table, while Mace and nan talk in the kitchen.

"Hey, Nan. What are you cooking?" I ask as my tummy grumbles.

"Spaghetti Bolognese. Why, you hungry?" She quirks a brow teasing, I'm always hungry these days.

Mace chuckles, I smirk, "Yes, we're hungry."

Chuckling, she switches off the cooker, plating up.

"Come on then," she says to everyone.

I hurry to sit down since my belly is grumbling rather loudly.

"So, where's the wife?" I ask, making a joke which obviously falls flat, as they all look at me as if I've lost my marbles.

"What, to soon?" I ask looking at each one of them, Mace smirks in amusement.

"She went home," Ethan says, hesitantly searching my face for something, anything. I purposefully keep my face blank.

Nan places a large serving in front of me making my mouth water, it smells amazing and I eat like I've never been fed.

"Thank you," I mumble, looking up I find everyone still staring at me. Mace looks surprised, nan anxious and Ethan sad.

"What?" I ask again, putting my fork down.

"Are you okay? With everything that just happened outside?" Nan asks, sitting beside me. I look at Mace.

"I just filled in the gaps," he shrugs.

"I'm fine, honestly. Sorry about the scene in the garden." I glance at Ethan, wondering why he's not with his wife.

“I’m sorry about her, Lily.” He whispers, looking down at his plate. I feel bad that he’s stuck in the middle.

“It’s okay, I’m sorry if I made it worse for you with what I said.” I’m not sorry I said it, just that it may have caused more trouble for him.

“She deserved it. She said some horrible things.”

I hate, 'I told you so’, but I knew she was a bitch, and that he’d regret marrying her.

“Anyway, when are we going shopping?” Mace asks, excitedly moving our conversation to a happier less awkward topic.

I look at him with wide eyes. Crap, I have been dreading this part. Where am I supposed to put it all?

“Slow down, Mace. I have to find a place to live first. Then we’ll go, I promise.” I say patting his arm. I’ve been sending my short stories to publishers but had no luck so far.

“Why do you need an apartment right away?” Ethan sounds puzzled.

“What?" I say, "I need a place for when our kids are born.”

Nan looks stunned. “I told you, you can stay here, that I’d help.”

“I know, but I need to provide for them, and it’s going to be cramped with me and the twins.” I sigh wishing I was more settled, older.

“How about we get a place together?” Mace blurts, and my head snaps in his direction. “Before you say anything, I have plenty of money saved, I’d pay my half. I’d be able to help with the babies. Please, just think about it?” I nod, still in shock.

“How do you have money set aside? You’re with me most the time,” I ask puzzled. He looks down.

"I've been doing freelance graphic designing, when you're in bed or I have free time," he mutters.

"What? How did I not know this? How long? Where did you learn to do graphic design?" Questions fly from my mouth rapidly.

"I haven't told anyone, but I've always liked doing that sort of thing. So I took online classes the past few months. I was going to tell you, but with everything going on," he says, looking apprehensive.

I feel bad for my selfishness, how could I not know something that's obviously really important to him?

"It's okay, there's been a lot going on lately. I mean, wow. A graphic designer? I'm really proud of you," I say, getting up to hug him.

"Wow. Mayo, that's amazing," Ethan says, but something in his voice is off, I look at him, his face crestfallen.

"Er, can we talk for a second, alone, please?" he asks, quietly, I nod following him to the living room.

"What's up?" I sit.

"I'll be providing for you and the babies." He blurts running his hands through his hair, I stare stunned at his outburst. "I know you haven't finished college with everything going on, so let me sort an apartment for you? I want to, please?"

"I don't know if that's a good idea, Ethan. It may be for the best if I live with Mason, he wants to help with the babies. I don't need your money, I have my own," I add quickly.

"I want to be there to help, I thought we'd been over this already?" He says, exasperated, running his hand roughly through his hair.

"You can't be there all the time. Through the night, you'll be at home with your wife and other baby." It comes out harsher than I'd meant it to. He looks away, sighing in defeat.

"Lily, I don't know how to make this right, I want to be there every step of the way. Night and day, but I have to be there for my other child and my wife."

My face hardens, "I know. That's why I'll be moving in with Mace, then I'll have some support." I say, my mind made up. "You can help support us if you really want to, but you can't be there through the night. You can't be there constantly, and that's not your fault. You have another baby coming, and he or she will need you too." I shrug smiling sadly.

"Okay, I get it. We'll go shopping once you've found an apartment then," he says a little more excited.

"Okay," I say giving in and shrug.

"Mace?" I shout, not taking my eyes off Ethan.

"Yeah?" He comes and sits beside to me.

"Looks like we need to start looking for an apartment." I say happily, as his face lights up.

"Really?" He asks, nervously looking at Ethan.

I nod, smiling, "yeah, once we find a place and move in. Ethan wants to go shopping for the babies. We'll need a room for them too."

"Okay, I've been looking and there are a few close to here, and a few nearer my mom and dad?"

I cringe at the idea of living anywhere near his dad. "Can we stay near here? We're all Nan has," I keep my voice purposefully low. Mason nods happily.

I'm excited for the next chapter in my life to start; just me, my babies and hopefully, a happy future.

The next couple of weeks, Mace, Ethan and I look for a 'house' near Nan.

I have to have a garden and drive for the babies, according to Ethan. I don't argue, since he'll be paying my half of the rent and amenities.

We strike gold, when we find a house just a few streets away from Nan's. It's a four-bedroom, detached house. With a garage and front and back gardens.

It has a big porch and I can see myself in a rocking chair in the summer, rocking my babies to sleep.

Well, it's March, and it's moving day. I'm so excited and so scared at the same time, I look around my sparse, bedroom sadly. I blink back tears. I'll miss feeling close to Mom. Plus, I feel guilty knowing I'm leaving nan alone.

"Nearly packed?" Nan asks sadly, from the door, I nod, smiling weakly.

"You know you don't have to move out. I'd love to have you all here."

Sighing, I sit on the bed, patting the spot beside me.

"I have to do this. I need to learn to cope with these two on my own. I know Mace will be there, I just don't think it's fair to ask you to have us all here."

"I don't mind. You're my granddaughter and they're my grandbabies," she says rubbing my big belly.

I laugh, "I'm only going to be a few streets away. You can visit anytime you want. I'm going to want the company anyway," I say hugging her.

"Okay, well, I better get some of this downstairs, the boys are going to be here in a few minutes."

"Nan, you don't have to. I'll ask Mace, Ethan and Niles to get it," I say.

Having never met Ethan's twin, I'm nervous.

"It's okay, I may be old, but I can carry a few bags," she huffs.

Holding up my hands, I laugh. "Okay. You win, I'll get this one then."

"No, you won't!" Three male voices shout together, making me jump.

"Jeez… Don't scare me like that! I could go into labour," I gasp.

They look at me frightened.

"Sorry, you just scared the crap out of me," I sit, trying to calm my heart rate.

"Sorry, we didn't mean to scare you. Are you okay?" Ethan asks, crouching in front of me.

I nod, my gaze flicking to Niles. Ethan catches on to my nervousness. Standing, he helps me up.

"This is my twin brother, Niles. Niles, this is Lily, and your niece and nephew," he adds rubbing my protruding belly.

Niles smiles shyly, "Hello, Lily. It's great to meet you. I've heard a lot about you." he says, smirking at Ethan.

"Oh really? Maybe we should have a chat later," I say, grinning.

"No. That's okay. You already know everything he does," Ethan says, smiling sadly at me.

My grin and jokes evaporate as an uncomfortable silence settles over everyone.

"And this is Cora, Lily's Grandma," Mace adds, breaking the silence.

"Hello, lovely to meet you. I hope you are all ready to do some lifting," she says, openly checking out Niles' muscles, making him blush.

"Nan! Ignore her Niles. She's made a sport out of making these two blush," I say, pointing at Mace and Ethan, grinning.

"It's okay, you'll get used to it. Cora has some serious sass." Mason grins, slinging an arm around Nan's shoulders.

"Oh, hush. He's a handsome young man, and I just love that blush," she says, walking up to him and pinching his cheeks.

A bubble of laughter breaks free, at the shy, embarrassed look he shoots Ethan.

"Alright, Nan, leave him alone, you're embarrassing him."

"Oh, let an old lady have some fun," she giggles at the scared look on Niles' face.

"Don't worry, Niles. She doesn't bite, often," I say, walking out the room, hearing his brothers laugh.

Downstairs, I make sure I haven't left anything lying around, double checking the laundry room for clothes.

"It's lucky you're only moving a few streets away with all this stuff," Mace jokes, lugging bags.

"Well, it's lucky I have all you strong men to lift all this stuff," I say sarcastically, rolling my eyes and gasp as I feel a baby move.

"Lils, are you okay?" Mason rushes overhearing my gasp.

"Yes, here," I say pressing his hand to my belly looking at his face.

"There, did you feel that?"

"No, are they moving?"

I nod, disappointed he didn't feel anything.

"Come on let's go," I say, leaving him to pick up the bags he dropped.

Minutes later, our cars are loaded, and we're on our way.

Nan's offered to help unpack, because Ethan and Mason

ordered a crap load of furniture online. Mostly the basics, like beds, a sofa, a table and chairs. Some kitchen appliances and TV. We still need to pick the soft furnishings, but they're not top priority apparently.

Pulling into our street, I smile seeing Isabella's car out front. It's been a while since we've seen each other. I'm really excited to see her. So I walk over to say hi but freeze when Alex steps out of the car too.

What the hell's he doing here?

Scowling, I look from Ethan to Mason, who appears at my side, obviously braising for an argument.

"Mom, dad. What are you guys doing here?" Mace asks, stepping forward to hug his mom. Smiling, she lets go and steps forward to hug me.

"We wanted to see where our son is going to be living. Hi, Lily. How are you, honey? Wow. Look at you." I giggle, pulling back.

"Hi, Isabella, I'm good, expanding by the day. How are you?" I ask, looking at Alex anxiously as Nan comes storming toward us.

"Oh, I'm great honey. Since we're here, Alex can help carry your things in," she says happily, looking at all the men with a raised brow.

"Let's go then," Niles says, clapping his hands.

He and Isabella are the only ones oblivious to the tension between Nan and Alex. Nan opens her mouth to say something, and I move as fast as possible to cut her off.

"Nan, can you help me get drinks please? While Isabella directs this lot?" I plead with my eyes; she nods as she walks toward me. I smile at Isabella, before walking into the spacious hall.

Inside is sparse, but spacious, the hall is nice, white walls and real wood flooring. On the left is an arch leading to the living room, my favourite room, it has a beautiful fireplace, bay windows, wooden flooring and two bookshelves built into the walls, on either side of the fire breast. It all needs decorating, but that's to taste.

The kitchen is across the hall and is gorgeous. It's recently been remodeled.

A huge five burner stove with two ovens, draws my eye straight away, I can see myself baking and cooking on it. Granite Worktops, dark wood cupboards, and a stainless-steel double sink. The finishing touch is a good-sized island. It has 'family kitchen' written all over it.

"Nan, can we leave the arguments in the past? Isabella doesn't know that you don't like Alex. He's been an asshole, but he's Mason's dad, he'll be here now and then to visit his son."

"Please?" I add.

Sighing, she agrees, "Okay, but only because you asked, and if he says or does anything else to cause trouble, I'll kick his ass myself." I giggle, knowing she's serious. But it sounds hilarious coming from a small, old lady.

For the next hour, there's laughing, shouting and banter between the men.

I order pizza for everyone as a thank you for helping. Isabella and Nan have been unpacking, arranging places for things to go with my supervision.

"Pizza's here!" I yell, after paying the pizza boy.

I smile when I hear bump, bump, bump coming down the stairs. Then Mace, Niles, Alex and Ethan come racing into the kitchen, pushing and shoving each other, all wanting to be the first there.

"Do men ever grow up?" I ask giggling, looking at Isabella and Nan.

"No." They say together, chuckling.

“I’m glad I’m having one of each then and not two boys. Especially with half their genes coming from them,” I sigh, pointing at them.

“Hey! There's nothing wrong with sibling rivalry, but our babies will be little angels.” Ethan smiles, and my smile turns into a laugh as Mace and Niles look at each other nod and grab Ethan. Mace has his arms locked behind his back as Niles headlocks him, giving a good noogy.

Nan and I giggle, as Isabella sighs exasperated. Alex is standing in the doorway looking at me, smiling. As our eyes lock, his turn sad, a silent apology in them. I nod acknowledging it, but still weary of him.

“Okay, guys enough, pizza’s getting cold,” I shout over the ruckus, and as quickly as it broke out it ceases, and everyone sits at the table digging in.

It’s so relaxed sitting listening to everyone chat about mundane things. I can almost forget the past and imagine we’re a real family.

As soon as the thought registers, Ethan’s phone rings.

Sighing, he fish’s his phone out his pocket, looking at the screen, his eyes swing to me sadly, before leaving the table to take the call.

I leave too, making my way upstairs, to unpack my clothes, to keep busy.

The situation is so fucked up. He’s married to her but is in love with me. They’re having a baby together, but so are we. So, I’m stuck in limbo. I love him but can’t have him.

I’ve got to move on and find a new path. Hopefully, I’ll fall in love again.

“Hey, you okay?” Mace interrupts my moping, sitting beside me.

Nodding, I lay my head on his shoulder. We sit quietly, mainly because I can’t speak right now without crying.

"I have to move on," I say, sounding like I'm being choked.

Picking up my hand, he squeezes gently, always my pillar of strength.

"Yeah, you do. You deserve better, and they deserve to see their mommy happy, laughing and content. Whether that's with someone else or not. It doesn't matter, but you have to let him go. He chose his path, and unfortunately you weren't the main feature. You'll always be tied together by these little people. So, it'll be harder than just cutting ties," he sighs putting his arms around me, holding me as I shake with sobs.

I calm myself, wiping my face. I move away and start pulling clothes out my bags. "Is he gone?" I ask, slamming draws a little too hard.

"Don't know, I wanted to check on you. It sounded like they were having an argument."

I roll my eyes because aren't they always? "Where is everyone else?"

"Downstairs," he says, sucking on his lip, just realising how bad that situation could be.

My ears prick up as we head downstairs. Everything's quiet, no arguing or fighting, which is good. Heading for the kitchen, we find Nan cleaning up the remnants of dinner, but no one else there.

"Where is everyone?" I ask, collecting the glasses from the dining table.

"They had to go," she hasn't even looked up. I know something is wrong with the way she's acting.

"What's wrong, Nan?" I look at Mason, who now looks worried.

"Ethan got a phone call from his wife, something about the baby. They all rushed off. I'll help with all the things that need doing here," she pats my hand.

I turn to see Mace looking conflicted. "Maybe you should go, they're your family too." I sit, grabbing another piece of pizza and forcing myself to swallow.

"I don't know, they're all there, they don't need me."

He's still trying to be a loyal friend. Getting up, I push him toward the door.

"Go. They're your family, you should be there with them. Thank you for being a loyal friend, but this isn't about loyalty. This is family, and your brother needs you right now."

Nodding, he grabs his phone and keys. "Will you be okay?"

"Yeah, we'll be fine. Phone if you need anything, and don't worry," I push him out the door.

CHAPTER FIFTEEN

Left to our own devices, nan and I busy ourselves emptying box after box, mostly treasures from my old life in England. It's nice to have parts of the life I shared with mom in my new house. My babies will know her, I'll tell them stories, and show them pictures of their Grandma Lizzy.

We unpack boxes of old pictures, including the special ones I've pulled together.

As it turns out my Nan is quite the expert with a hammer and nails. She hangs all the pictures of mom and me. Herself and grandad, nan and I, me, nan and Mace and finally some of Mace and me. I wanted memories everywhere. There are even some of Ethan and Niles, Isabella and Alex. All the twins' family are there in different shots. I even managed to get some of the babies only aunty Ava. Whom I haven't met, due her being away at art school.

"Nan, I think we deserve a break. How about we have a cuppa and some TV?"

"Okay, but you sit, and I'll make the tea," I shake my head sick of being treated like an invalid.

"Nan, I'm capable of making a cuppa," I protest grabbing two cups, she smiles holding up her hands in surrender.

"Okay, sorry." Smirking, I grab a couple of packets of biscuits and head for the living room.

We watch cooking shows for a couple of hours before ordering my favourite Mexican food, because these days I'm always eating something.

It's ten p.m. and Mace still isn't back. Nan's stayed as long as possible, not wanting to leave me alone.

"Okay, honey, I'm going to head home. As long as you're okay?" She looks unsure whether to leave me or not.

I nudge her gently, "I'll be fine, I'm a big girl now, literally," I giggle, rubbing my belly. "I'm going to be a mommy soon and I need to get used to taking care of myself." A genuine smile stretches her face.

"Good night, honey, I'll see you tomorrow?"

"Yep, call me when you get home, okay?"

"Okay, mom," she laughs, rolling her eyes. I laugh, she's so sassy, I love it.

Inside, I lock the door, heading for a nice hot bubble bath.

While soaking my phone beeps, I ignore it, letting all stress and tension go.

Wrapped in a big fluffy towel, I step into my room more than ready for bed.

My room is huge compared to any I've had before, with a massive bed.

Finally dressed, I crawl onto the softest mattress ever. Umm, fresh sheets… I immediately drift into a peaceful, but exhausted sleep.

"LILY?"

I wake with a start, hearing a yell from downstairs. I roll out of bed checking the time, it's two a.m. "LILY?" The voice is closer.

"I'm coming," I huff, moving as fast as I can.

Mason comes charging down the hall looking frantic. "Mace? What's wrong?" I ask, dread curling in my belly.

He blows out a breath hugging me fiercely. "Where have you been?" He asks, scowling.

"I've been here all night. Why?"

He frowns at me. "Then why didn't you answer your phone?"

"I was in the bath, then fell asleep; I was exhausted. Did you just get back?" I ask, moving downstairs to the kitchen, freaking heartburn.

"Yeah, I was scared shitless when you didn't answer. So, I left as soon as I could," he mutters following me to the kitchen.

I roll my eyes, "I'm a big girl Mace, I don't need watching constantly. You are allowed a life," I sigh rubbing my chest.

I take a good look at him; he looks drained and tired. "How is everyone? Is the baby okay?" I ask, praying he or she is okay. He looks pale and drawn. "The baby isn't…?" I feel ill at the thought of the baby dying.

"No. The baby is fine. She had a scare, high blood pressure or something. She was waiting in the reception area when Ethan got there apparently. But she needs a lot of rest, and someone to take care of her so…" Swallowing, he looks at me sadly, and I know I won't be seeing Ethan for a while.

"So, Ethan has to stay with her? He won't be making our shopping trip tomorrow, will he?"

"This hit him hard. He's blaming himself for all the stress.

He said he's going to be a better husband, that she needs to come first."

"So, not to sound selfish, but what about these babies? We're supposed to go shopping for them. What about the doctor appointment's he said he wanted to come to?" I know it sounds selfish, but I'm sick of our babies playing second best in his fucked-up life.

"He gave me a credit card for you to use, to get the babies things. I'll go with you to your appointments; you know I will."

My anger is at boiling point, and if I don't leave right now, I'll blow up at the wrong person. I leave the room silently, I need time away from everyone, not even Mason can help fix what I'm feeling right now.

I can't believe I let him in again, only to get pushed to the side-lines. Stupid, stupid, stupid! I'm so wound up, it's impossible to sleep. I wish I could go for a run, expel my pent-up energy. So as a poor substitute, I pace from one side of my room to the other.

That coward. He hasn't even called, or even text to tell me himself. Once again, I had to hear it from his brother!

I swipe my phone off the side table. Nothing. Fucking asshole. I need to get out of here for a little while. Chucking on some scuffs, I tie my hair haphazardly and snatch my car keys off the side. Storming back downstairs, startling Mace who's in the kitchen eating leftovers.

"Lils? Where are you going? It's after three in the morning." He looks at me anxiously as I grab a coat.

"I'm going for a drive. I'll be back in a bit; I just need some fresh air."

"It's the middle of the night. You're pregnant!"

Snorting I shrug, "I know. Maybe you should tell your asshole of a brother that. Because I've had enough of his bollocks, I'll cope on my own." I snap, slamming the door.

My chest restricts as I drive away from the house; I don't want to worry anyone, but sometimes I just need time to myself. Like right now, I need to let my anger dissipate before dealing with Ethan, or I may just slap the shit out of him.

So much for him wanting to be there for his babies, I scoff at the thought an squeeze the wheel tighter. I understand him needing to be there for his other baby and even her. I'm not a bitch, my mom raised me better than that, but I'm sick of my kids being pushed to the side.

"Don't worry, you'll always be number one in mommy's life," I say out loud rubbing my belly.

I drive aimlessly for an hour, before ending up at mom's bench. I pull my coat tighter around myself to stave off the wind.

Sitting I breakdown, telling her everything that's happened, how it's made me feel, how it's changed me for the better and worse. My hopes and fears. How much I miss her and wish she were here. I just wish I could ask her advice, and have her hold me because in that moment, I feel so alone.

"Lily? Thank god. I've been worried sick, I called Cora and everything. Where have you been? It's eight-forty-five," Mace looks pale and exhausted.

"I'm fine. I'm a big girl Mace. I can take care of myself. I'm going to bed, so you can call Nan and tell her I'm back and in bed. Night," I snap, walking past him up to bed.

I know he's been up all night worried and he cares, but last night something snapped in me and I just can't find it in me to give a shit right now.

"Lily, you awake?"

Groaning, I look at the clock, shocked to see it's twelve in the afternoon.

"Yes, I'm up," I shout, dragging my ass out of bed. Ready to put into motion the plan I came up with last night while sitting on mom's bench.

I need food, then it's time to put my plans into action. There's no way in hell I'm taking money from Ethan. I'll pay for them myself; he can stick his money. I have the money, our old flat sold for more than I thought it would. I was only letting him pay for things so he wouldn't feel like shit, but he can stick it now.

"Where were you last night? I was really worried."

"I'm sorry for snapping at you, but I've had it with your brother. He can be a dad when they're born, but until then, he'd better stay away from me. He can also forget about paying for this place and anything for my kids. I'll do that myself, thanks. You can give him his credit card back; I don't want or need it."

"It's okay, I know he's let you down again, but I'm still here; for all three of you. Plus, you promised to squeeze the crap out of my hand," he jokes, making me smile.

"Are we still going shopping today?"

"Yes. What do we need to get?" He answers quickly, smiling excitedly.

"I have a list, but first you need to take that card back. It isn't coming with us." There's no way that card will be used for anything.

"Okay, he's going to be really pissed off though," he sighs, dragging his phone out his pocket.

"I don't care much about his feelings. He can play happy families. When these two are born he can see them, but as far as I go, I don't even want to see him. Last night was the last time he gets to change his mind. He won't be coming to doctor's appointments, and he definitely won't be present when they're born. That's a special time, and I don't want it marred by his baggage." I feel better, lighter after saying my piece. Mason looks sad, but nods.

"If he has a problem with it, I'll deal with him, but this is it now. I'm sick of our kids being pushed aside like they don't count."

"I don't think he's doing that. I know it looks that way, but it's a messed-up situation. I'm just sorry you're at the bottom of the pile again."

"This isn't about me, Mace. There is no me and Ethan, not anymore; but these are his babies too. He helped make them, but all the responsibilities have been left up to me, because he has another life, another baby coming. I have to do this alone, and I've accepted that, but it's not fair for these two to have a daddy that will only be there when he can, or when he's not busy with his wife and baby. How is that going to be for them when they're older? Am I going to have to explain why their daddy can't come to see them today? Why their daddy doesn't live with them?" I hiccup, holding my tears in.

"I didn't want this for my kids. The constant wondering where daddy is?" I pause, needing to take a breath and calm a little.

"The worse thing is the questions will get harder as they

get older. I'm dreading having to answer them. How am I going to answer when they ask things like, why their daddy is with someone else, and not with us? Why they have a sibling the same age? Why they see more of their uncle than their own father?" I sniff, rubbing my face, tired of what ifs.

"It's all such a mess, Mason. I'm so angry at myself, I made so many immature choices. I know the cruelness that kids go through at school, but that's magnified when they don't have a dad at home."

"Stop. You need to stop worrying. It'll work it's self out. Ethan will be there, not as much as me, but you know I'm awesome, so…" I laugh at his smug face.

"Ugh, this is pathetic. I'm just going to go get dressed, then we'll go and you can drop that card off on the way." I kiss his cheek, whispering 'thanks' on my way out.

The drive to Ethan and Ashley's is tense and quiet.

"Did you call to tell him you were coming?" I ask, nervously, I don't want to speak or see him.

"Erm, no. I didn't want the argument, so I'm just going to pull up drop it off and leave him to his mood," he laughs.

"Wow. You are a genius. Quite the master plan you have there," I giggle, my mood brightening and my thoughts shift to the list tucked away in my pocket. I can't wait to get started, I sit there happily imagining all the pretty clothes I can get my daughter, and cute trains and cars I can get my son.

"Mace, will you help me do the nursery?" I ask softly, feeling sadness creep in again, Ethan was going to decorate their room.

"Really? Can we get the paint and things today?" He asks, bouncing in his seat.

Giggling, I hold my hands in the air in surrender. "Okay, okay. We'll get the thing's today, just calm down and concentrate on the road."

We pull onto the drive of a big house, surrounded by plants and flowers, it has *family* stamped all over it.

"Be back in a sec."

I laugh watching as Mason makes a mad dash to the door, it opens and Mace shoves his way inside. Minutes pass, and my thoughts turn to Ashley. *She lives in a dream house, she's married to the man I love, has his baby on the way and full attention, and she's she insecure?* I shake my head, disgusted, ungrateful cow.

I call nan while I wait, apologising for last night and explaining what happened. She's not pleased with Ethan. I also told her my plans, she seemed surprised, but happy so we arrange to go shopping at the weekend.

My smile evaporates when Mace storms out of the front door, looking thoroughly pissed off.

"Well, that went over like a lead balloon. He was pissed off as expected and will probably be calling you soon. I tried to explain it all, but he's upset."

Sighing, I squeeze his arm. "I'm sorry you're stuck in the middle. It's not fair on you, but I can't speak to him right now. Besides, I don't think Ashley would like me in her house," I smile slyly.

"Do you want me to drive?" I ask smiling as he fidgets in his seat.

"No, I'm good," he says taking deep breathes. We arrive safely in spite of Mason's agitated state.

"We'll go order the big stuff first, like the cot, pushchair and stuff. We also need to look for clothes, bedding and bottle things. Then, you can go mad getting paints or whatever. Okay?"

He nods, "I can't wait, this is so exciting." His boyish excitement is cute.

Halfway through we take a break to eat, so I can rest, my back is on fire and feet are killing me.

"Okay, so we have all the big stuff being delivered tomorrow. Are you going to be able to get all the decorating done in time for the furniture coming? I would help, but I'm not allowed by paint fumes and stuff," I grin, cheekily.

"Is it okay if Niles comes to help? That's a lot of work to get done tonight and tomorrow morning."

"Yeah, sure. As long as Ethan doesn't turn up." He nods, looking away uneasily.

The next shop is full of teddies and toys and clothes of all shapes and colours. Mace is in baby heaven he wants to buy everything. I hate to have to rein him in, but I only have so much room.

Niles and Mason are busy with the nursery. They kicked me out. Apparently, it's a surprise, so I busy myself ordering food and unpacking. I do as much as I can before my energy vanishes.

Making a cuppa I settle on the sofa, rubbing my belly and singing softly. I only have about nineteen weeks left, if I'm lucky. Just thinking about how fast that will go scares me.

The doorbell startles me awake; I must have drifted off. Grabbing my purse, I pay the delivery guy.

"Mace, Niles, foods here!" I yell setting everything on the table with drinks.

Music stops, a door banging, then dual thumping is heard

coming from the stairs. They crash into the kitchen shoving each other to get to the food first.

We eat, chatting and laughing, I love listening to the tease each other; it makes me wish I had a sibling growing up. Sometimes I catch Niles throwing sad looks my way, I understand it must be hard to do this in place of Ethan.

"So, is the nursery done yet?" I'm anxious to get a look, they've been up there for hours.

"Almost, just need the furniture now." Niles smiles at me.

"Impatient are you Lils?" Mace teases, he knows me too well. Scowling, I stick my tongue out making them both laugh.

A phone ringing interrupts my answer. We all look at each other, I shrug, because I know it isn't my phone, Mace is here and nan and I spoke earlier.

Niles pulls his out, his eyes flick to me before he answers, not attempting to leave the room.

"I can't right now I'm busy, I could come by later?" He sighs, looking really uncomfortable. "No. I'm at Mason's," he rolls his eyes at us. I fight the giggle that wants to escape. Mace looks at me, his eyes twinkling, shaking his head.

"I'm helping decorate the twins' bedroom," he says and cringes holding the phone away from his ear. Quite a few rather loud swear words come through the speaker. Even from across the table, we can hear him loud and clear.

"Listen E, that's between you and Lily. I just came to help with the nursery. I'm not getting in the middle of what's going on; you're my brother, and they're my niece and nephew. If you need me to drop by after I'm done here, then I will." I'm shocked by his calmness, he handled Ethan amazingly.

Bug-eyed, I look at Mace. He smirks "Ethan, Ava and I are the hot-headed ones, whereas Niles here, is as cool as a cucumber. He handles E the best, calms him and gets him thinking rationally."

I'm up bright and early the next morning, awaiting the furniture deliveries. I'm so excited to see it done. Niles turns up not long after I finish making breakfast.

"Hey, help yourself, thanks for helping out." Smiling, he sits beside Mace.

"I'm happy to help, you are family," he shrugs, and tears fill my eyes, I turn away quickly.

When we're all finished, I clean the kitchen while they get the nursery read for the furniture. When it all arrives, Mace, Niles and the two delivery men haul the boxes upstairs, I watch, supervising where needed.

Bored with sitting around waiting for them to finish, I pull the steriliser from the cupboard and sit cross-legged on the rug. Unpacking it, I read over the instructions first. I have no clue how one of these things even work.

"Hey Lils," Mace yells from the top of the stairs.

"Yeah," I call, trying to get the lid to click into place.

"You ready?" He asks from behind me making me jump and smack his leg.

"Dick," I snap as he laughs and helps my big arse off the floor and up the stairs.

"Okay, keep your eyes shut." Mace demands, walking me slowly down the hall, his hands covering my eyes. Giggling, I hold his arm in a death grip scared I'll fall.

"Okay, okay. Are we there yet, I don't want to fall!"

"One more step. Okay, open," Mace whispers, removing his hands.

Opening my eyes, I gasp, it's beautiful; their cots are

along the back wall, separated by the dresser/changing station. On the wall above that is a cute little toadstool night-light. All but one of the walls are designed in all thing's nature. Trees, autumn leaves, toadstools, animals, bird, butterflies. I'm gobsmacked, it's more than I could have wished for. Tears trickle down my face, I'm so grateful for all the hard work and love that has gone into this room, from their two uncles.

"Thank you both. It's., it's beautiful. More than I could have dreamed of." Smiling, they both hug me.

"What do you want done with that wall?" Mace points at the only blank wall.

Smiling, I go into my room getting the two main things I need. "Can you go get the box from the hall closet?" I ask Mace, hoping we can get my surprise up before he gets back.

Once he's out the way, I close the door. Smirking, I hand Niles the hammer, and quickly we get to work.

We finish just as Mace comes through the door, all puffed out and places the big box on the floor.

"Okay, are you ready to see what I'm naming your niece and nephew?" I'm so excited to see his face.

"Yes." He's been badgering me for weeks wanting to know. I smile pulling the first covering off.

Elizabella Rose Barker. Is beautifully scripted in a long frame above her cot. Their smiles are huge, their eyes are wet. Overjoyed by their reaction, I blow out a breath and remove the second cover. Mace gasps, shocked and hopefully happy.

On the wall above my son's bed is his name in the same frame and script as his sister's.

Sebastian Mason Barker. "Do you like it?" I ask, a little unnerved by their silence. Mace clears his throat enveloping me in a tight hug.

"Thank you. I'm, I just, wow. I'm honoured you gave him my name. I love what you picked, beautiful names." His voice is so strained I barely hear him. I'm so relieved I cry into his shoulder.

"We love you, Uncle Mace, but these hormones have turned me into a freaking basket case," I huff, and they both laugh at my disgruntled face.

My twenty-two-week scan finally arrives and I feel and look huge. My back aches like a bitch and I'm cranky, tired and bloated. So not good.

"Hi Lily, how are you feeling? You look tired."

Sitting, I rub my back, chuckling dryly. "Yeah, tired is an understatement. My back feels like it's about to snap and my mood swings could rival a tornado. But other than that, I'm fantastic." She smiles, nodding and ignores my sarcastic reply.

"Sorry, bad mood," I sigh, smiling weakly at her. I'm so ready for this pregnancy to be over. So I can meet my little angels and hold them.

"I understand," she smiles sympathetically. "Okay, everything looks good. You're gaining weight and eating right. The only thing I'm concerned about is that your blood pressure is a little higher than I'd like. We'll do some blood work to check your protein levels, but from now until I see you again, I want you on bed rest." Shocked, I just nod.

"When do I need to see you again?"

"I'll see you every two weeks now until the birth, have you decided if you're birthing naturally or C-Section?"

"Naturally, if I can, but if need be, I'll go for a C-Section." She nods, scribbling happy with my reply.

"What about medication do you want any?"

"None, if I can birth naturally. I assume I'll have to have an epidural if I had a C-Section?"

"Yes, that's right; but in the case of emergency, we'd need to put you out." Even with her light tone, I gulp frightened and I squeeze Mason's hand.

"Don't worry, I'm just making you aware of all your options, and what would happen in the event of an emergency. Now, who's your birthing partner?"

"Mason and my Nan," she looks at Mason amused.

"You're not going to faint, are you?" She asks, laughter in her voice.

"No, I wouldn't miss their birth for the world." Love and pride evident in his voice.

"He's been waiting impatiently for these two to come into the world," I add teasing him.

I'm glad the twins have such a brilliant male role model. I don't know what I would do without him. He's our constant.

CHAPTER SIXTEEN

I'm sick of being on bed rest, two weeks of watching crap TV and I'm done. I'm so tired of being waited on hand and foot by Mace, nan and anyone else who visits. Isabella visits once a week and Niles every other day. We've become quick friends, he's so calming to be around, but I love his sense of humor.

"How's the patient doing today?" Niles asks, sitting on my bed, handing me chocolates and spicy tortilla chips.

"Fed up, your brother is a pain in my arse. I don't know who's worse him or my Nan," I whisper, conspiratorially.

Snickering, he settles beside me grabbing the remote. "How about a movie?"

"Okay, but I'm not sharing my crisps. You can eat the chocolates." I snatch the crisps up and start chomping. I'm already as big as a house, I may as well enjoy it while I can. After these two are born, I'll be able to start working out again.

Laughing, we look through what choices we have and settle on a new comedy. About halfway through Mace comes in raising an eyebrow.

"What do we have here then? What am I, chopped liver?"

Smiling, I pat the other side of the bed. "Nope, there's always room for you. Plus, I need your chest to lie on, Niles is a bit shy around me," I chuckle.

Mason laughs lying flat on his back, so I can curl up as best as I can with my head on his chest.

"Our Niles is a little shy around the ladies. Ethan's the egotistical one." Mace jokes, and freezes as the words leave his mouth.

I feel like I've been shocked, I gasp, shocked. It still hurts even hearing his name. It's been weeks since his name has been mentioned. Feeling my emotions rise to the surface, I bury my face in Mason's shirt.

"I'm sorry," Mace says softly into my hair.

"It's okay. It just shocked me, that's all. I'm fine, let's just finish the movie."

Ah, I'm so happy to be out of the house. I bask in the feeling of the cool breeze on my face. Even if it's only for a visit to the doctor's office.

"Okay, your blood pressure is still a little high, but there isn't any sign of protein in your urine, so that's a plus. But the downside is you'll still need to be on bed rest, or it could turn into pre-eclampsia," I sigh, not liking the idea of being on bed rest again. I've read about Pre-Eclampsia though, and I know it's dangerous, not only for me but for the babies, too.

"Okay. Will that be until the end of my pregnancy now? Because I still have to go shopping for some things for the babies before they arrive."

"It will be to the end now; I don't want to risk it. Could you make a list so another family member could go? Or you could go, but you'd have to be pushed around in a wheel-chair," I cringe, and capitulate because there is no way I'm being pushed around the shopping centre in a wheelchair.

"Great, how am I supposed to prepare for the twins if I'm stuck in bed? I haven't even done my hospital bag yet," I huff, frustrated with myself for not having it ready.

"I can get whatever you need, and we can put it together in your room, but that means leaving you alone," He mutters, worrying his lip.

"I'll be fine Mace."

He shouldn't have to worry about leaving the house. He's eighteen and shouldering responsibilities that aren't his.

"I'm so sorry Mace," I say and burst into tears, covering my face with my hands. Damn hormones!

He reaches over, pulling a hand away. "Hey. What's all this about?"

When I stay silent, he pulls over. "What's wrong?" He asks, taking me into his arms, rubbing my back.

"You shouldn't have to worry about all this. You're eigh-teen and we aren't your responsibility. Ethan should be here, he helped make them, not you. He should be facing these responsibilities with me, not you. Not that I don't appreciate all you do, and have done for us, but it's not fair on you. You lost Millie because of this mess." I'm so angry and sad and worked up that my breathing is all over the place.

Mason looks startled at my anger.

"First. It wasn't your fault Millie and I didn't work out, so get that out of your head," he wipes a tear away and takes my hand in his. "I'm not sure what to say about Ethan shirking his responsibilities, but I've loved every minute of being there for all three of you, and as far as I'm concerned, all three of you are my responsibility. They're my niece and nephew, and you are like another sister to me, even before we knew you were carrying these angels." By the time he's finished, I'm a blubbering mess from the love I hear in his voice.

April passes with few problems, and a lot of resting. Boredom is killing me as June arrives, spring is in full swing and here I am stuck inside. It's driving me nuts, I haven't heard a word from Ethan since that day. I don't know what's going to happen when Liza and Seb are born since he hasn't even called to see how they are. I wish I'd picked a better father for my children, but life doesn't work that way. Hindsight's a bitch.

At thirty weeks I'm more than ready to meet my little ones.

Today I'm hoping Dr, James will talk to me about, my C-Section. I elected for it since my blood pressure hasn't gone down.

Since I'll only be allowed one person with me, nan and Mason decided between themselves that Mace would come in with me.

"Okay, so the c-section is set, unless I go into labour naturally beforehand. I need to get my hospital bag packed ASAP, just in case."

"Now that you can do mild exercise, we can go to the mall tomorrow. Get the stuff you wouldn't let me get." He rolls his eyes as I shudder just the thought of him buying my toiletries...

Our shopping trip is as eventful as always, it's weird whenever I go out now, every woman I pass stops me to feel my belly and asks some shockingly personal questions that amuses Mason to no end. Thankfully, we have gotten good at avoiding them. I either need to loo, or we conveniently have an appointment to get to. The amount of people that assume Mason is my boyfriend and baby daddy is hilarious, we usually just let them assume now instead of feeling like we have to explain.

Pregnancy is so invasive; I never knew it was this way. I constantly feel like my life is everyone's business when I'm outside.

Time passes so fast, yet so slowly, unfortunately leaving me enough time to think about Ethan and his inability to be there for his two other children. I have to force myself not to get angry over the whole thing and ruin the rest of my pregnancy.

I'm shocked and excited when thirty-six weeks rolls around; I'm a nervous wreck about the c-section but I really need these babies to be born. My back hurts constantly, I can't breathe properly, I'm huge and tired.

They are active little monkeys, and it fascinates me watching their feet and hands move across my belly. Mason of course, thinks it's amazing. We spend the last few days making sure everything's ready for the twins' arrival. I've packed and repacked my hospital bag a dozen times.

My thoughts turn pensive as the days fall away. The closer the birth gets, the more I think about everything that happened, everything that could have or should have happened. Everything I was promised. I also think about how far I've come as a person; I've learnt some hard but valuable lessons. I was so sheltered before I came here, I barely knew how to stand on my own two feet. I'm so thankful to have Mason and nan by my side through all this, their love and support means so much to me.

Sometimes I wish life turned out differently, that I had never met Ethan, but then I wouldn't have my babies and I quash the thought. Without him I wouldn't be having my twins, so for that I am grateful to him.

I wonder if he'll bother coming to visit them since I haven't heard from him in four months. I still miss him every day, even though I'm angry with him. I'm still in love with him, I know that and feel it sting every time he's mentioned. I'm disappointed that he hasn't been there for us like he said he would, I thought he was a better man, but I guess I was wrong.

One day he'll wake up and realise the mistake he made by not being a part of these precious moments. Not being there for his children's birth, to see their first moments in the world, and be one of the first people they see.

Tears trickle from my eyes. I can't believe how naive I was to believe him over and over again. To believe there would be an us.

"Lils, you in there?" Mason walks in before I can wipe my face. He looks at me, concern marring his face.

"I'm fine, just having a moment," I giggle, shaking off my sad thoughts.

"You ready for tomorrow? Are you excited?" Smiling, I nod, folding and refolding the baby-grow in my hands.

"Nervous, but excited to see them. Thanks again for being there the past few months. You're so amazing, and I'm lucky to have such an awesome best friend."

"I've told you before, there's nowhere I'd rather be. I

can't wait to meet these two," he sits, happily rubbing my belly, earning a powerful kick from one of the twins.

"I can't believe they're going to be born tomorrow. It seems surreal, I'm going to be a real Mom tomorrow," I say in awe as it hits me that I will hold them in my arms in a matter of hours.

He laughs at me shaking his head. "You've been a real mom for nine months; you just get to meet the two little miracles that you created tomorrow."

"Well, we better get some sleep, it's going to be a long day tomorrow," I say, feeling my excitement rising.

"Yeah, good night, mommy. See you bright and early."

I fall asleep smiling, thinking about my babies.

"Hi Mason, Lily, how are you feeling?" Dr, James asks making a happy entrance.

"Nervous, but excited and so ready to not be pregnant anymore," I joke, making them both laugh.

"I bet. We're just going to check your vitals and start your I.V, then you'll be prepped for theatre, okay?"

I nod swallowing my nerves. "How long will it take?"

"Usually around forty-fifty minutes. You look a little green, are you sure you're okay?"

"Just nerves."

"It's okay to be nervous, it will be over before you know it. Then you'll have your babies in your hands."

I don't know how, but she just calmed me immensely. "Thanks, that helped. "

Throughout the test and prepping Mace kept up a constant stream of jokes. Keeping my mind busy and making me and the nurses laugh.

Mason in scrubs makes me laugh so hard; they're a tad short in the leg and the top is so tightly fitted across the chest that I can see the outline of his nipples. We've been taking pictures all morning, but the picture of Mace in scrubs is priceless.

"Okay, I think I need new ones." He huffs, pulling at the top trying to stretch it.

"Okay. We're ready for you now. Oh, wow, do you need some bigger scrubs Mason?" Dr, James asks trying to hide her amusement.

"No. He's good. Let's go," I rush chuckling at his scowl.

"Okay then, let's get this show on the road." She holds the door as Mace pushes me in a wheelchair, Dr, James follows pushing my I.V. The theatre is big, clinical and sterile. Intimidating.

"Just sit on the side of the table and lean over this pillow. Dad, you can stand in front of her, so she doesn't topple." Mace looks stunned but does as asked.

"Okay, bit cold," he wipes something wet across my back. "I'm just going to administer the local anaesthetic to numb the area now, then I'll put the epidural in place. There will be a sharp scratch. It's really important that you don't move, so try not to jump."

I wince as the needle goes in, blowing out a breath and trying to keep still. I hate needles.

"All done, you can lie back now. I'll be here throughout the procedure to top you up if need be. How are you feeling? Any sickness?" Shaking my head, I look at Mace, who held out his hand smiling.

I'm covered in blue paper sheets, and one is clipped up obscuring the view of my bottom half.

"Okay, we're all set. Can you feel that Lily?" Dr, James asks, but I don't feel anything.

"No." Am I supposed to feel something? Has something gone wrong?

The heart monitor goes up with my heart rate.

"It's okay, I was just checking you couldn't feel before I start. It's good that you can't feel anything."

Blowing out a breath, I try to relax as much as possible. "Scared me there for a minute," I say, smiling at Mason, who has gone a little pale. "You okay?" I squeeze his hand.

Nodding, he sits in the chair the nurse just provided.

"Hey! You can't pass out. You promised you wouldn't wuss out. You said I could squeeze your hand as hard as I like."

He chuckles gaining a little colour. "That was when we thought there was only one baby, and you were birthing naturally."

"Hey! A deal is a deal, but if you want, we could swap… you can help do night duty instead." I hear a few giggles from nurses and a chuckle from the anaesthetist.

"How is that fair?" He tries to sound annoyed, but a smirk stretches across his face.

"Well, next time, don't complain."

"Okay, okay squeeze away."

"Nope. Don't need to."

"Okay, we're in. You'll feel a pulling now that's normal. Here comes baby number one."

I hold my breath as I wait, as does Mason. Then the loudest wale slices through the room.

"That's one loud little girl," Dr, James says.

Tears are pouring down my face, I'm a mom. I look at Mason, who has tears in his eyes looking at my daughter being cleaned and weighed.

"Here's comes baby number two." Another, smaller cry breaks through the air.

"He's beautiful, mommy." Wow. I have a daughter and a son.

"Here's your little girl. She has all her fingers and toes, weighing six-pounds and one-ounce and is nineteen point ten inches long."

I watch as she hands her to Mace, taking her, he leans down so I can see her. We watch her in awe.

She's beautiful, her face is pink and scrunched up, like she's going to cry. She has a tiny nose and heart shaped, red lips and a little bit of dark brown hair.

Another nurse brings over Sebastian at the very moment Elizabella opens her eyes. Mace and I gasp. Her eyes, they are almost identical to her dad's, but hers have a little more, green in hers.

"Wow, she has beautiful eyes," the nurse says, lying Sebastian beside me on my now free arm.

Tears flood my eyes as I stare at him, he's a mini replica of his daddy. It breaks my heart that Ethan isn't here to see them. His nose is the same, but smaller. His eyebrows, lips and hair colour are the exact same as Ethan's. I wonder if they have the same eye colour.

"He's a mini version of Ethan." Mason remarks, gazing from Elizabella to Sebastian.

"He perfect too. He weighs a little less than his sister, at five pounds, fourteen ounces and nineteen point eight inches long."

"But they're okay? No problems?" I ask, nervously. My heart overwhelmed with love for them both.

"None. They're perfectly healthy." She smiles walking away.

"Okay, we're done now, Lily. We're going to take you

through to recovery, once the anaesthesia has worn off, we'll move you back to your room. Mason will be able to stay with them."

This upsets me, I don't want to leave my babies.

Seeing my distress, she explains. "We need to keep a close eye on you until it's worn off in case of any complications. It may only take thirty to forty-five minutes."

"Lils, go get yourself sorted, I'll take care of these two till you get back. I won't let anyone see them until you're back," I nod reluctantly, kissing both my babies before they're both placed in plastic cots and I'm wheeled away.

"Miss Carter?" Blinking, I see a kind young woman in front of my face.

"It's time to take you back to your room now, so you can see those babies of yours." I agree happily, a smile breaking free.

I can't move yet, but I can certainly feel where they cut me now. The bed is raised slightly, then we're on the move.

On entering my room, I see Mason sitting in a big comfy chair holding both babies, talking quietly to them. He smiles as they push my bed through the doors.

"Here's mommy. I told you she'd be back soon…they've missed you, and they're hungry."

They finish getting me settled as both babies start wailing. Mace passes them over, looking away as the nurse shows me how to feed them both, it's hard, but with the help of four pillows we get comfy.

It's weird, but they get the hang of it and latch on happily sucking away. They cover me with thin sheets thankfully, I don't think my friendship with Mace extends to him seeing my boobs.

"Okay, if you don't have enough milk and they're still hungry, just press this call button and we'll bring you some formula." She places the buzzer by my hand on the bed.

I smile gratefully. "Thank you."

"No problem. They're beautiful, congratulations." She leaves the room smiling.

Mace comes to sit back down. "You know…I'll probably need your help with getting the hang of feeding when we leave," I say teasing him.

He turns pink looking away. "I don't know if…I mean, really?" He stutters, I laugh gently at the face he makes.

"Don't worry, I'll try not to need your services when feeding them, but if I do, I'll try not to flash you. We could always try doing it in the dark. Feeding I mean," I say, giggling at his now red face, he blows out a breath, relieved.

"Is anyone here yet?" I ask, wondering if nan's here pacing the halls.

"Yeah, Cora, Niles, Mom, Dad and Ava, but I wouldn't let them in until you were here. After you finish feeding them, I'll fetch them if you want."

I'm shock and sadness hit hard and squaring my shoulders and breathe deeply through the anger simmering in my veins. If Ethan doesn't want to be here, then that's on him.

"So, Ethan's not here." I say coldly, Mason looks at me, sadness and anger in his eyes.

"No. I don't know if anyone's called him, but I bet Mom told him the date of your c-section."

I shut down my feelings toward it, because right now I need to concentrate on my babies. When they're done feeding, I pull my gown back into place as Mace puts them in their cots.

“Before you get everyone, could you ask if I can put on a T-shirt and brush my hair? I know I can’t walk around yet, but I don’t want your family seeing me like this.”

Nodding he leaves quickly. Closing my eyes, I take a moment to absorb that I’m now a parent and responsible for two little people.

“They said yes, but you need to be careful, don’t sit up and I have to put it on you and brush your hair.”

“Okay,” we struggle, but manage to get my shirt on without him seeing or touching my boobs. Sitting beside me, he begins to pull the brush through my hair, slowly and gently, so gently I nearly fall asleep.

“Thank you.” He kisses my head.

I look up at him confused. “What for?” He clears his throat.

“For asking me to be here, it was the most amazing experience of my life.”

“Aww, Mace, I don’t know what I would have done without you. I thank god every day that you knocked me on my arse.” We chuckle quietly, not wanting to wake the twins.

“Hey, has Sebastian opened his eyes yet?” I ask, wondering what colour his eyes are.

“No, not yet. Should I pass them to you before I go get that noisy lot?” I nod eagerly, wanting to hold them again.

He places Elizabella on one arm, Sebastian on the other and grabs the camera taking a picture of me looking down at them.

“Do they know their names yet?” He asks, smirking.

“Nope. No one but you and Niles know, and I swore him to secrecy,” I stick my tongue out; he snaps a picture laughing.

“Go get them before I kick your arse,” I scowl playfully.

He laughs again, "You can't even move, so kicking my ass is out of the question."

I sit quietly looking from my daughter to my son. They're perfect, my little miracles.

Hearing scuffling, I smile as nan rushes to me, crying at the sight of us.

"Oh honey, I've been so worried. Oh, look at these beautiful little angels," she sighs, taking them in, running a finger down each of their cheeks.

Elizabella opens her eyes looking at nan.

"Wow. Her eyes are nearly the exact colour of yours and look at all that hair." She coos for a couple more minutes, before remembering the others. "Sorry, I'm hogging," I giggle as she moves aside for Isabella, Ava and Alex to see them.

Isabella tears upon seeing us. I smile, encouraging her closer. "Oh, look at them, they're beautiful." Sebastian opens his eyes slowly, looking at me.

"Oh god…" My gasp draws Mason, and the rest in.

His eyes are the exact same colour as Ethan's. He looks at me innocently, the spitting image of his daddy, so beautiful. Tears run down my face, blurring my vision as I stare into the eyes of my son. A perfect replica of the eyes, I fell in love with.

"Hi, I'm Ava. It's nice to finally meet you. Sorry, it wasn't before now. They're beautiful."

I smile at her. "It's fine, it's lovely to meet you, too." I say, looking at Niles.

Smiling, he steps around his mom and hugs me gently around the twins. Elizabella wails, making her uncle jump back, alarmed. Mace laughs, scooping Elizabella up and expertly rocking until she calms.

Isabella, Alex and Ava look on shocked. I smile proudly, they have a brilliant uncle.

"Well, looks like Elizabella loves her Uncle Mace already," I say, announcing her name.

A few gasps and a sob follow.

"Her full name is; Elizabella Rose Barker. And this little fella is; Sebastian Mason Barker." Sebastian makes a happy noise.

"Honey, Lizzy would be so proud of you. She would have been so happy to have a namesake…or half a namesake." She corrects herself chuckling, wiping her eyes.

My heart squeezes, I missed my mom so much today. I wish she could have been here to hold my hand, to see her grandchildren born. Teary-eyed I look around seeing a family.

"Has anyone called Ethan?" Ava asks innocently.

Isabella looks at her sharply, as Mason grunts his disapproval.

She winces mouthing, 'sorry' sitting quietly in a chair. I feel bad, she didn't know.

"It's okay, I was wondering that myself," I smile, when she sighs, relieved, and nudges Mace to let her hold Elizabella.

"No. No one's called him, we didn't want to upset you," Isabella whispers, as Alex rubs her back reassuringly.

Niles looks on pained, it must be hard for him, to be here and not tell Ethan.

"Maybe I should call him then, because he's going to be miffed. If he gets grouchy with me, he'll know about it," I huff, as Mace places my bag beside me.

"Should we leave?" Alex asks, looking longingly at Sebastian.

"No, but could you hold Seb please?" I ask, because I know he won't ask to hold him otherwise.

He smiles at me gratefully, cradling Sebastian in his arms, looking at his tiny face.

I have to search his number, it's been that long since I used it. I put it on loud speak when it rings.

"Hello, Lily. What do you want?" Ashley's nasty tone comes through the speaker.

Taking a deep breath, I close my eyes summoning all my manners.

"Hello, Ashley, I'm calling to speak with Ethan. Could you put him on please?"

"I'm sorry, but he's busy right now. I'll be sure to tell him you called though."

Isabella gasps at her rudeness.

"Put Ethan on the damn phone, Ashley." Alex snaps, and I'm shocked at the venom in his tone.

"Alex? What are you...?"

"I. Said. Put. Ethan. On. The. Damn. Phone."

She huffs. "It's not a good time, he's busy decorating his son's nursery," she announces smugly. I hide behind my hair, not wanting anyone to see how much that shot hurt.

"Either you put him on the phone, or I come to the house to talk to him, and I'm telling you now, he won't be a happy bunny when I tell him about you answering his phone and not letting his family speak with him," He whisper-shouts, to not startle Sebastian.

"She's not his family!"

"No, but I am and so is his mother, his sister and his two brothers."

"Hold on a sec." She snaps. "It's your family. They need to speak with you," her bitchy tone grating.

"Hello," everyone looks at me. I squeak trying to clear my throat.

"Hello?"

"Hello Ethan."

"Lily? Ash said my family needed to speak to me?"

"Yes, we do. I, I just wanted to let you know that…you became a father at twelve-twenty this afternoon."

Silence, then a thump. "Hello?" I look at his family confused. "Hello, Ethan. Are you there?" Still nothing.

"Did any of you warn him that today was the day they would be born?" I ask curiously, they all look at each other, then at Niles as if he should have. Poor Niles.

"What? Just because he's my twin doesn't mean it's my responsibility."

"And no one thought to mention this before I just dropped it on him?"

"Ethan, are you back? I'm sorry, no one told me you didn't know they'd be arriving today."

A choking sound comes through the phone, then sniffing. Shit, he's crying. I look at each of his family members, they're all upset hearing his heartache. Right now, I'd love nothing more than to go into the bathroom and cry.

"I'm here," Ethan's voice barely audible. I feel helpless, wanting to comfort him, but then, I don't. He's hurt me so much.

"We have a daughter and a son."

"Are they okay?" He asks, his voice wobbling.

"They're both perfectly healthy and doing great."

"Was it a normal birth?" His question shocks me. How little does he know?

"No, they were born by c-section."

"But I thought you said they were healthy?"

"They are it was an elective c-section. I had some complications at twenty-two weeks. So I elected to have a c-section instead."

"What?" He explodes, making both Elizabella and Sebastian cry. Ava and Alex immediately pass them to me.

"If you're going to shout and scare the twins, then I'm putting the phone down," I snap, trying to hold my anger in.

"Sorry, is that them? Crying, I mean?" Mace, Niles, Alex and Isabella chuckle. nan's not so easily swayed.

"Yeah, who else's babies would it be?" I shake my head, smiling at my angelic little babies. Who are both looking for the owner of the voice? I realise they probably recognise his voice.

"Visiting time is over guys," a nurse says, popping her head in. Nan sighs handing Elizabella back to me and kissing my head. They all kiss me and the twins as they leave.

All but Mace, who can stay overnight because he was my birthing partner. Everything is so quiet. We each have a baby. We just sit watching them, watch us.

My phone beeps, I reach for it blindly, not taking my eyes of Seb. Mason chuckles, getting up, he hands it to me.

Ethan: *Can I come and visit my daughter and son please?*

I look at Mace holding Eliza, then at Seb watching me curiously. It's not fair what he did, but he's their dad and they come first.

"Ethan?" Nodding, I look at Mace. "He wants to come and see them, doesn't he?" I nod again, tracing a finger down Seb's cheek.

"How do you feel about it? About seeing him?"

"I don't know Mace, he's hurt me so much, but he's their dad. And like it or not, they're going to need him."

Agreeing, he rocks Eliza murmuring quietly to her. I have to let him come see them. He's allowed to come now because he's their dad.

Me: *Yes. You know the hospital. I'll tell them you're coming.*

My phone immediately beeps.

Ethan: *Thank you. I'll be there in ten mins.*

"Well, looks like daddy's on his way. Shall we change these nappies and put on some nice clothes?" Mace smiles, swapping Eliza for Seb.

"I'm sorry, I love her, but I have no clue how to do girlie clothes, and I'm not doing her bum she's got girl bits."

I laugh. "I love you, Mace. Don't worry, we got it, don't we baby girl? Could you just pass me a nappy and some pretty clothes for the princess please?" Eliza makes a happy noise kicking her legs, making us both smile. Until I feel warm, wet fluid trickle down my leg.

"Oh, you did not! You wouldn't do that to Mommy." Mason bursts out laughing at my disgruntled face.

Pressing the button, I finish making her pretty while I wait for a nurse. Mace has Seb changed in minutes, those classes really paid off.

A pretty young nurse comes in with kind eyes.

"I think I need a clean sheet, she just peed on me." The nurse looks at my face, then Mace who's sitting in a chair laughing so hard he's crying, to the two innocent babies and chuckles.

"Okay, let's get you sorted," she comes in taking Eliza wraps her up and places her in the cot. Grabbing a fresh sheet, she helps me out of bed and into a chair. While she strips and makes the bed again, all within minutes.

“Thank you. I’m expecting their dad any minute. While I’m up, can I get changed?”

“Of course. Do you want to go wait for him while I help Lily change?” She asks Mace shyly.

Placing Seb gently in the cot, he kisses them both before leaving.

“Is he related? He really loves them, doesn’t he?” She asks, grabbing clothes.

I opt for sleep pants and a tank top, they’re loose and comfy.

“Yeah, he’s their uncle, their dad's brother. He’s my best friend, and yes, he’s loved them since I found out I was expecting.” I can tell she likes him because she goes all swoony and flushes.

I sit, waiting quietly for Mace and Ethan to arrive, feeling hopeful. Wondering what the future holds for me and the twins. Hoping Ethan will be a good dad to them. Hoping I’ll do a good job raising them alone. Hoping I find love again.

CHAPTER SEVENTEEN

Mace pops his head in, eyes closed, asking if I'm dressed. I laugh assuring him I am. So he opens the door wider letting an anxious looking Ethan in.

Wow, it's been a while since I've seen him, but not long enough for my body to behave the way I would like it to. Flushing, I look to see if Eliza or Seb are awake. They are and just like in the womb, they're both kicking up a storm. Ethan stands in the doorway waiting for me to speak first.

"I'm going to get a coffee. Do you two want anything?" I ask for a hot chocolate, as Ethan asks for coffee. Neither of us look at Mace, his eyes burn into me.

"You have to come in the room to see them."

"I'm sorry, Ash…"

"Don't." My voice is quiet, but firm. "Do not bring her in here." Agreeing, he comes closer.

The twins start to cry. "Can you get them for me? I can't move around right now." Shooting me a nervous glance, he takes his first glimpse of his daughter and son. He stands frozen, stunned.

"Wow, you're more daddy's double than Uncle Niles, but

don't tell him I said that." He chuckles, starting at Sebastian in awe.

"Look at you, my little princess," he whispers, choked up. He kneels down between them, touching their hands. It's the most beautiful moment, seeing them connected is amazing. Grabbing the camera, I snap a shot as both the twins grab his fingers. Watching him with them, I can feel the love emanating from him.

"I'm sorry, I've missed so much. I love you guys, so much. You are the most precious gift I've ever had," he whispers, kissing them both on the head. "What have you named them?" He asks, not taking his eyes away from them.

I'm nervous, I hope he's not mad about Sebastian's name. "Elizabella Rose Barker and Sebastian Mason Barker."

Looking at me, he smiles. "I don't think I could have chosen better. Thank you for giving them my last name."

"Ethan," I sigh. "I may be mad and hurt, but they're your kids too. They should carry their father's name. they come first above all else." Smiling gratefully, he picks up Seb holding him close.

I hear him whisper. "I love you, my little Sebastian. You really are my double." He chuckles, looking at me. "Let's just hope you're only my double in the looks department."

Handing me Seb who cuddles right into my neck, sighing and dropping off to sleep.

He lifts Eliza kissing her cheek, he sits on the bed looking at her. I've heard there is a special bond between a father and daughter, but Ethan looks enchanted by her.

"She's somewhere in the middle. But you're going to have your mommy's hair by the looks of it," he says, raising her the same way he did Seb.

"I love you, my little Lizabelle. My little girl, wow. Is she the youngest or oldest?"

I blink back tears. "Erm, she was born first and a few ounces heavier than Seb. She came out wailing, where Seb gave a small cry, but not an ear splitting one like she did," he laughs, looking at Eliza.

"Are you going to be a firecracker like your mommy?"

"Hey! I'm the quiet one, like Seb. She obviously takes after her daddy."

Our happy banter is interrupted by an unhappy Mason.

"Lils, I just got a call, one of my sites has been hacked and I need to sort it out, but the nurse said if I go, I can't come back until morning. I can't leave you alone, I promised to be here for you." Ethan winces, it's unintentional but a direct hit.

"We'll be okay, don't worry."

"But you need help, you can't walk around or pick them up yet."

"I can ask the nurses to help. If I can't cope alone, they'll put them in the nursery until morning."

"No."

We all jump at Ethan's sharp tone and the twins cry simultaneously. Lucky for Ethan, it's feeding time, or I'd be really pissed at him.

"They're hungry, could you fetch the nurse, please?" I ask Mace.

"I'll stay. I don't want them in the nursery, anything could happen to them."

I don't want them in the nursery either, but I don't think it's a good idea for him to stay here.

"I don't think that's a good idea," I mutter, arranging the pillows for the twins' feed.

"I know, but you can't look after them alone. You need help right now, and I'd like to spend time with them." His sincerity and his pleading gaze weakening my resolve slightly.

"What about Ashley? She can't be alone either, or she'll be really angry, I won't have her making a scene in front of the twins. Does she know where you are right now?" He winces, just thinking about it.

"Yes, she knows I'm here, and yes, she'll be mad, but they need me right now. I'll ask Alex to stay the night. He offered to stay with her so I could come here." Shocked, I stop fiddling with the pillows and stare at him.

He chuckles at my face. "Yeah, that's what I was like when he turned up at my door and offered, but there it is."

A nurse comes in, Mace knows the drill and stays in the hall. She sets about settling Eliza and Seb on the pillows. So intent on what we're doing, we forget Ethan's there until it's too late.

The nurse leaves without handing me the blanket. I look up to see Ethan staring at us in awe. Embarrassed, I try to reach it myself. It's just out my reach.

"Could you pass me the blanket, please?" I don't look at him, I try to cover myself with my hands, but my boobs are huge. They were big before, but they're just embarrassing now.

Thankfully, he passes it to me silently, not removing his eyes from my chest.

"Ethan," I try to get his eyes off my chest. Things are awkward enough without him staring at my exposed chest.

"Sorry, that's amazing. Does it hurt?"

"Not really, it's more weird than uncomfortable, but they hurt if I don't feed them regularly." Crap, I can't believe I said that. My face turns bright red, amusing him.

"Still embarrassed? How is that even possible when you're holding our children?" Shrugging, I feel Seb release me. I hand him to Ethan for winding. If he wants to stay, he's going to have to learn.

He looks at me, his eyes huge, he looks terrified. "Lily, I've never done this before." He sounds so scared, I smile.

"Me neither, but I had to learn. So, put him over your shoulder, pat and rub his back gently." He does so gingerly, making me giggle.

"He's not going to break, just be gentle." Smirking, he carries on while I sort myself and wind Eliza.

"Wow. You're really good at this," he smiles.

"I had classes," I shrug, thanking god that I was able to attend them.

"Are you sure it's okay if you stay tonight?" I smile hearing Eliza's burp and kiss her soft cheek. Contentment washing over me, making me hopeful that I can be a good Mom.

I look up to see Ethan staring at me, love shining in his eyes. I look away, it's just too painful.

"If it'll cause too much trouble then go home," I say, it comes out sharper than it was meant to, but the unfairness of the situation, and emotions swirling inside me right now take precedence.

Shocked by my sharp tone, he blinks, staring at me.

"It's no trouble. I'd like to spend some time with them," I nod, texting Mace, letting him know it's safe to enter now.

He enters gingerly, but seeing me fully dressed, he comes and takes Eliza, holding her close humming like he did earlier.

I love that he loves the twin's so completely he needs to hold them. Ethan doesn't look so pleased with his brother's fierce love and connection with his daughter.

"Ethan's offered to stay, so you don't need to worry about

us. You do what you need to and I'll see you bright and early."

"Are you sure you'll be okay?" I know, he's worried about leaving us alone together.

"Yeah, I'll be fine. He wants to spend time with the twins," nodding he passes Eliza to me, and approaches Ethan expecting him to hand over Seb.

He looks torn, then reluctantly passes Seb to his uncle, Mace walks over to the window, talking quietly to Seb.

"Now, Sebby, Uncle Mace needs to go to work. You need to take care of the girls for me okay? You be a good boy and I'll be back in the morning."

I turn to mush watching them, the fact that Seb seems to be listening intently to Mace is so cute.

Chuckling, Mace kisses his cheek and whispers. "Good boy." Catching us watching, he shrugs, smiling and hands him back to a dismayed Ethan. "I'll see you in the morning. Call if you need me, okay?"

I nod smiling, I sigh as Ethan scowls angrily at Mason's retreating back. I can see he still harbours jealous feelings where his brothers concerned.

"Do you still have a problem with Mace?" I ask, my voice quiet but harsh. I won't allow anyone to harbour bad feelings toward Mace. He's amazing. He has always been there when I needed him.

"No. Just upset that he's closer to my kids than I am. I know it's my own fault, and that's why I'm angry at myself, not him." I feel better knowing he's finally taken responsibility for his actions.

"I wish I had done and said things differently. But I did what I thought was for the best at the time. I knew you were more than capable mentally and physically to take care of yourself and these two, but Ashley, she isn't. "

A sharp laugh escapes me. "You thought I was mentally and physically capable of taking care of twin babies at the age of eighteen? After all, that I'd been through mentally and emotionally the past year? I lost my mom just before you walked into my life and turned it on its head. You were my first boyfriend, lover, friend with benefits or whatever the hell you want to call what we were."

"I know, but you're stronger than anyone your age, because of that. I didn't mean it the way it came across, but Ashley isn't strong. She's mentally weak and physically needs someone, me."

"Wow, so because I wasn't needy enough, I got pushed to the side-lines to raise our children by myself, thanks." I say scathingly, shaking my head. "Wow, because I take care of what I need to instead of bitching and trapping someone into marriage, I get left alone with no support whatsoever?"

Thoroughly pissed, I get up to put Eliza down, forgetting that I'd just undergone surgery. I gasp at the pain that radiates through my belly.

Luckily, I'd placed Eliza on the bed before getting up, or I might have dropped her. I close my eyes, trying to breathe through the pain, while holding onto the bed.

"Oh God, Lily, are you okay? You're not supposed to be out of bed." Huffing out a breath, I ask him to put Eliza in her cot through gritted teeth.

God that hurts. I wish I hadn't gotten so worked up now. Gentle hands hold my sides trying to take the weight off me.

I freeze, his hands are on me and really close to my breasts. My breath is frozen in my lungs.

Clearing his throat, he moves his hands down. "Sorry, I, I didn't mean to. Er, it just happened. Here, let's get you back into bed, you're not supposed to be moving around yet."

I must have fallen asleep after getting back into bed because I wake with aching boobs.

I watch Ethan holding Sebastian close murmuring quietly. The sight is so heart-warming I snap another picture. It's so beautiful I stay quiet, watching them, until Eliza wails for her feed and Seb follows like a little sheep, startling his dad.

"Let me just get this right, then you can pass them over, they're hungry."

"God, you weren't joking about her vocal cords," he cringes, making me chuckle.

"I'm ready now. I'm sorry, I'm not going to be able to cover up. If you're uncomfortable, you can wait in the hall." He shakes his head refusing to leave.

"It's fine, as long as you're okay with it."

I shrug, he's already seen everything.

We manage to get a few hours' sleep between feeds, burping and changing nappies. Ethan's picked it all up quite fast and seems more at ease with holding them now.

But by the time nine a.m. rolls around, we're both exhausted. Ethan looks rough in his wrinkled clothes, messy hair and bags under his eyes.

"Wow. Who knew parenthood was such a rough ride?"

I giggle. "Yeah, well, we do have twins. Would you be able to stay long enough to watch the twins while I shower?" I ask nervously, still not comfortable with asking anything of him yet.

"Yeah. I just need to call Alex." He seems nervous. Is Ashley so bad, that even her husband is scared of her?

"Hi Alex."

"Yeah, they're fine," his face breaks into a smile and he chuckles.

"Yeah. It was hard work, but I loved every minute," he says, looking directly at me. I try not to see any double meaning in what he said. Not wanting to feel hopeful, but it's there anyway.

God, will I always love him? Will I always hold out hope for us? I hope not or I really will end up alone.

"Is Ash up yet?" I blanch involuntarily, blocking out his call, I stare at my beautiful babies stroking their soft cheeks.

They're so beautiful. Seb looks up at me still feeding. The same eyes as his dad's. I wonder if they'll ever resent us for the choices we made. I wonder what the future holds for us. Hopefully, Ethan will be there for them, even though he has another family. I must be a glutton for punishment, or an eternal optimist.

"Okay, just tell her I'll be back in a bit." The strain in his voice causes me to look up. His eyes are apologetic.

"Everything okay?"

"Yes." His quick answer sets off my anxiety.

"Are you sure? If it's too much trouble you can go, I can wait till Mace gets here."

"It's fine. Just…".

While I wait for him to continue, Eliza and Seb release me, thankfully. I cover myself quickly, I don't want to have an unpleasant conversation with him while my boobs are out. I bundle them up, preparing myself.

"What is it Ethan? You're making me nervous standing there looking like I'm going to rip your head off. Is everything okay at home?" I manage to hold my wince this time.

He looks guiltily at me. "It's just, Ash. She, erm, wants to, to come and meet the twins?" My jaw must be on the bed. I'm so shocked I can't even blink. My brain is so silent, it's scary. Is he actually asking if she can come here?

"Why would she want to meet your 'brats'?" Sarcasm laces my words.

He looks even more afraid now, than he did before, if that were even possible.

"She said er, since they're my babies, she should get to know them. With, her being their step-mom." He actually winces this time.

My anger rises, so rapidly and strong that I feel it burn in my belly.

How dare she call herself their step-mom. Who the fuck does she think she is? There's no way in hell she's getting anywhere near my kids.

Knowing I can't and won't shout in front of the twins, I press the nurse's button. Minutes later a nurse comes into the room questions in her eyes.

"Could you take the twins to the nursery for a while please?" I don't look away from Ethan, who gulps and pales.

"Of course. Is everything okay? Do you need any help?" She stutters, tuning into the frigid atmosphere between me and Ethan, I nod looking at her pale face.

"Yes, everything's fine. We just need to talk and I want to take a shower. What time is the doctor coming?" Appeased, she pushes the button again and two other nurses come in, she tells them to take Seb and Eliza to the nursery.

"She should be here in about an hour," she informs me before hustling out the room.

Turning back to Ethan. I take a deep breath, because I'm fucking furious that she has the gall to ask to see them, let alone call herself their stepmom after nearly killing them.

"You've got to be fucking kidding me?" My anger explodes, he cringes, standing there silently not saying a word.

"After everything she's said and done. She has the

fucking nerve, not only to ask to see them, but to call herself their stepmother. After everything I've been through because of her and you. You ask me if she can come here to see my New-born twins? You want me to allow her to involve herself in the most, happiest and special time of my life?"

I'm breathless when I'm done. My head feels like it's about to explode. He looks shocked and ashamed. But is he ashamed of himself or the situation? I don't care. I can't believe he even asked.

"I know, it's a lot to ask, but she will be in their lives too," his voice is pleading.

I'm so astonished I laugh.

"You think after she nearly killed them, that I would let her anywhere near them? If *you* want to see them, then *you* can. However, she will never see them."

"Lily, come on, be reasonable here. How am I going to be able to see them if Ashley can't? We live together, she's my wife."

For the first time, him calling her that doesn't make me cringe. It's an odd thought, but hopefully it's a sign. Maybe I can finally move on.

Shaking off my thoughts, I struggle to stand wincing from the pain radiating through my middle.

"Be reasonable?"

"*Reasonable*? Were you *reasonable* when you left me pregnant, after making crap loads of promises, only to snog your fiancée in my living room? Were you *reasonable,* after everything you'd already put me through, to accuse me of sleeping with your *brother*? Was it *reasonable* of you to still ask to see our kids, after questioning their paternity? Only to desert us *again*, when Ashley stomps her foot? You've never been there for me, or our kids. Before they were born, I hadn't seen or heard from you in months. *I* had to call *you* yesterday to let you know you were a dad."

A nurse comes rushing in looking alarmed. "Miss Carter, are you okay? Do you need assistance?" She looks warily at me shaking, breathless and angry, to Ethan shocked and ashen.

I cringe, realising all the nurses probably heard everything I just said.

"I'm okay, are the twins okay?"

She nods, looking unsure. "Do you want me to call some-one?" She asks, lowering her voice. I look at Ethan shaking my head. I assure her everything's fine, she nods, throwing Ethan a scathing look before leaving.

Dead silence greets my ears.

"Lily, I don't know what to say? I never meant for any of this…."

"Well, neither did I, but I'm the one stuck with the raw end of the deal. I've given up so much since meeting you, and now I have to watch you play happy families with your wife and another child. Who are more important to you than our babies? And before you say anything, I'm not saying your other baby isn't important, because he or she is. But you shoved Seb and Eliza aside when Ashley stomped her foot not once, but twice. You questioned their paternity. Then we hear nothing from you for months. Not even a text to see if they're okay. Your brother was there through everything. The sickness, the tears, every appointment, even their scans and most importantly their birth. He was even the first to hold Elizabella."

I see my point has been made from the look of utter devastation on his face.

"To make myself perfectly clear. She cannot come here to see my children. She cannot spend time with them. She cannot see them, and she definitely can NOT call herself their stepmother. She is nothing to them. Have I made myself clear enough?"

Nodding, his eyes go over my shoulder and he pales again. Turning, I see my nan and Mason in the doorway. Both carrying balloons, teddies and flowers. And both have matching expressions of astonishment and anger.

"Where are the twins?" Nan asks, stepping into the room. Mace places, everything he's carrying down and rushes to me helping me back into bed.

"They're in the nursery." My mood shifts from angry to misery, as tears fill my eyes.

"Lils, what happened? Are you okay?" Wiping my eyes, I feel like such a baby for crying.

"I'm okay, I'll let Ethan explain what happened." Looking at Ethan, he looks tired. Sighing, he sits down rubbing his face. Looking to me, but I'm not going to make it easy on him.

Ethan goes on to explain every miserable word.

"You've got to be kidding me?" Mason hisses, growing angrier with every word out his brother's mouth. Nan has yet to speak, I think she's in shock.

"Look, I know I shouldn't have said anything right now, but she has a point. She's my wife. She's going to be there when I have the twins over." I'm so stunned by his reply I stare open mouthed.

"I'm sorry, but you think you're having the twins in your house overnight. With the woman who despises them and nearly killed them?"

"She didn't mean to harm them. She apologised for pushing you. What more do you want? And of course, I'm having them overnight, they're my kids too, Lily."

Puzzled, I look at Mace, who looks equally confused.

"What apology? She never apologised. I know they're your kids, Ethan. Believe me, I never *forgot* that fact, but if you want the twins overnight. When they're older, you can have them at your mom's house. Just not around her. Until then, you can visit them at our house."

He looks gobsmacked, and if it wasn't such a serious conversation, I would have laughed.

"Come on, Lily. You've got to be reasonable here, I can't stay at my Mother's house every time I have my kids. Ashley's my wife, she's not going anywhere. That plan just isn't realistic. You're both making my life ridiculously hard. I can't choose between my wife and kids… I won't."

"I'm not trying to make life hard for you, and I'm not asking you to choose. I just won't allow her near my kids. She's done nothing but try and take you away from them since she found out about them."

"No, she hasn't. She was shocked in the beginning and reacted badly."

"Oh, is that all. Okay, then you tell me why I hadn't seen or heard from you in over four months, if it wasn't her idea?"

"It wasn't Ashley's idea. I thought it would be easier for all of us to have time apart. Ashley needed me…"

"Wait." My brain clears, focusing only on one thing he just said.

"You left me with the responsibility of taking care of…as you keep saying, "our" babies? Your choice?" He nods, shamed.

"You self-centred wanker. What about us? We needed you too. I was bedridden for weeks. I've been scared out my mind, worrying about Seb and Eliza. Worried about how I'd cope. As everyone likes to point out my age, I'm *nineteen*. Your wife is in her twenties."

"Wow. How stupid am I? You break promises, treat me

and our kids like crap, question their paternity. Like an idiot I keep letting you come back, expecting you to do better, to be there, and you have the nerve to ask for more?"

"Yeah, I'm an asshole, but the reality of the situation is, I'm their dad and Ashley is my wife. Soon the twins will have a brother or sister, who I want them to know. So, we need to work out a better arrangement than this, because it just isn't going to work."

"Just leave, Ethan. When we're home and settled you can visit. Alone. I want nothing more to do with you. So, you can tell your *wife* not to panic because, I wouldn't want you if she hand-delivered you to my door."

Mace and nan seem stunned. Ethan sits staring at me, I ignore him turning to my nan and Mace.

"I'm going to shower. Can you ask the nurses to bring the twins back? I won't be long." My voice is flat, emotionless.

Mace nods mutely, leaving the room. Getting up slowly I kiss nan and slowly make my way to the bathroom, closing the door quietly behind me.

God it's good to be home, it feels like forever since I've slept in my own bed. Looking down at Sebastian and Elizabella, smiling at their alertness; they're looking around from their twin beanbag seat.

"Welcome home, my little cuties," they both kick their legs happily.

No sooner have I sat down the doorbell rings. "I'll get it. You stay there," Mace rushes off. He has been quiet the past few days. I guess he's still upset over what happened between me and Ethan.

"Oh, look at them..." Isabella gushes, rushing over and

kneeling beside them. She's kept her distance, probably heard about the blow-up.

"Alex isn't here with you?" I ask curiously, she pulls her eyes away from her grandchildren and looks at me. She tells me he's in the kitchen with Mason making drinks.

I decide to give Isabella a few minutes alone with the twins. She's amusing them with baby voices and tickling their hands and feet.

I pause in the hall, hearing hushed tones.

"I know it's not right, but you need to talk to her. Ashley is raving mad about not being able to see the twins. What Lily said about not having them at their house just threw gasoline on the fire. She's talking about lawyers and taking her to court for custody…"

"Whoa, hang on a second, what grounds does she have?" Mace hisses.

"I know, I'm not happy either, but Ethan is vulnerable right now. She's taking full advantage, trying to make him hate Lily. She's trying to say she's unfit and unable to take adequate care of them alone. The fact that they're married and have a stable home won't help if she manages to get Ethan to take Lily to court."

I feel sick and extremely angry. If I lose my babies. She won't love them, she doesn't even want them, she just wants to stick it to me.

I walk into the room stone faced.

"Over my dead body will she get my kids. Who the hell does she think she is? If she thinks I'm going to sit back and let her walk in and take my kids, and play mommy, she must be cracked in the head."

Walking into the living room, I grab my phone and dialling before Mace and Alex have time to step through the door.

"Nan are you busy?"

"No. What's wrong? You sound angry."

"Can you come to mine? I'll explain when you get here."

"I'll be right there."

I take few deep breaths, before turning to see them all regarding me with wary looks. Mace is sucking on his lip, Isabella's not sure whether to call and warn Ethan or not.

"What are you going to do?" I look Mace in the eye, so he knows I'm serious.

"Well, first; I think I'll call your brother. Then, I think it's time to put little Mrs Tantrum in her place."

When nan arrives, she takes one look at me, seeing how angry I am and sits next to me.

After explaining what I overheard, let's just say, I've never heard her cuss so much. I take the twins upstairs, making use of the monitors. I don't want them hearing or sensing any anger.

I take a calming breath and I press the call.

CHAPTER EIGHTEEN

"Hello?" Well, if isn't Mrs Tantrum herself.

"Put Ethan on the phone." I'm past pleasantries with her now.

"He's a little busy right now, but if you want to discuss the twins, I'm more than happy to talk."

"No thanks. If Ethan isn't available, I guess we'll just talk through lawyers." My sharp tone, plus the fact that I know about her threat of legal proceedings catches her off guard.

"Here he is," I smirk at her quick acquiesce.

Nan is grinning like a fool, but his mom and Alex look uneasy and Mace looks like he doesn't know what to do. He's caught between his brother and best friend, poor guy.

"Lily?"

"You can put me on speaker, so Mrs Tantrum can hear, that way I won't have to repeat myself." I wait while he does so, "so, I've heard of your wife's plans to try and take my children out of my care. That she thinks I'm unfit and unable to look after them alone."

"Lily, I…"

"No. You listen carefully, because I will only say this

once. I've had it with your excuses to last me a lifetime. Just listen and hear me loud and clear."

"Let's start where it all kicked off again shall we? About three days ago. Let me guess, you went home and told little *her* what I said to her question, or demand to see my kids and she didn't like it? Well hear it from the horse's mouth lady. You are not, nor will you ever see my kids. After all you've said and done to them, I don't want you anywhere near them. As for what I heard today, you want my kids removed from my care into yours? Let me tell you, it will never happen. And I'll tell you why….

After I finish with this call, I'll be contacting the hospital for the records of when you… Mrs Barker, assaulted me whilst I was pregnant. Then I'm going to have a nice chat with the police, and have you charged with assault. Then a lawyer will be contacted, to not only make sure you can't have my kids, but to make a will to ensure that if anything were to happen to me, that my nan would be soul guardian of both the twins. Now, before this morning I was willing to play nice for the benefit of our kids, but to be quite honest, I don't think they'd benefit from being around either of you for long periods of time. It hurts me to say that and especially in front of your parents, Ethan, but since marrying her you aren't the man I fell in love with."

I look at all the people in the room, there expressions range from stunned to devastated and proud. Mace is stunned, nan proud. Isabella is devastated and Alex is a mix, somewhere between proud and devastated.

"Lily, wait. I was never going to take you to court. Jesus, this has gone too far," Ethan voice is panicked.

"Yes, we were. She's trying to stop us from seeing your kids. She can't do that."

"Would you shut the hell up!" Ethan bites out and Ashley quietens immediately.

"Can I just point a couple of things there, *Ash*? First; I'm not trying to stop Ethan from seeing his kids, just you, and yes, I can stop you from seeing them since you're no relation. Add the fact that you're a danger to them."

"I'm their stepmother."

"No. You. Are. Not. You're nothing to them. You're just a woman their dad married out of obligation."

Her gasp makes me smile inside. I know it's petty, but I'm sick of sitting back and playing nice.

They argue in the background, her whining about what I said and him telling her to go into the other room and let him sort this mess out.

"Lily?" His voice is hesitant, placating, trying to calm me down.

"Yep."

"Listen, there's been a huge mistake. I was never going to take you to court. This is just getting out of hand. Listen, I'll do what you suggested at the hospital. I don't want all this to be dragged through the courts. I'm sorry, this is a big mess. How did it all end up this way?" He sounds so tired, for a minute I soften.

"I wonder the same thing every day." I sigh, sitting as everyone vacates the room.

"I never wanted this to happen. I'm sorry about everything. I know you've heard it before. God, I must look so weak, being so easily manipulated by my wife. I don't even know it's happening until the damage is done and I'm having to deal with the aftermath. I'm not making excuses; it's just she makes it all sound so logical. Well, until she runs into the force of nature that you are." He chuckles, making me laugh too. I can't help it, I have a sunny disposition, mostly.

"Well, I'm a mother now, I can't afford to let people walk all over me anymore." I realise my mistake as he winces. "Ethan, I…"

"No, it's okay. I'm ashamed to admit it, but I have done that, but I never meant to. I loved you…" I gulp at his use of the past tense. Even though I'm angry and hurt at all the things he's done, I still love him and hearing him say he *loved* me hurts like hell.

"Listen can we talk about this later? Your mom and Alex are here, along with my nan, and the twins are waking up." I manage to squeak, my throat tight.

"How are they? Can I come and see them please? I've missed so much already."

"Ethan. I don't know if that's such a good idea right now. Your wife is pissed and if you announce you're coming here, then she'll flip her lid."

"I'll talk to her. Please, I just want to see my kids. It's been three days already, we can talk."

I soften, knowing a yes is coming, because no matter what, I still love him and crave seeing him. God, the moment he holds one of our babies… I melt.

"Okay, but if she causes any more trouble, that's it." I hear him blow out a relieved breath. He must have been crapping himself thinking I'd refuse him. I'm not the type of person who keep children from their father.

Ethan and I sit in comfortable silence, watching the twins snooze in their cots.

"This place is amazing," he looks around at the animals and all their things.

Smiling, I nod. "Yeah, Mace and Niles did a good job."

He looks at me, so drained and tired, I push the plush stool off the rocking chair over for him to sit.

"We shouldn't be fighting over them, you know. This should be the happiest time of our lives," he states, looking at them wistfully. I agree, all I want is a peaceful life with my kids.

Since our conversation we've settled into a happy, tranquil routine. Everything is going well and I have hope that we got over our last bump in the road. Well, life just doesn't seem to work that way for me.

Ashley has to have an induction, she's a week overdue, so Ethan stays with her constantly. I understand, but the twins miss him, they cry every day at the time he normally arrives. I can't sooth them and it's not like they an talk and understand. So I sit with them in my arms as they cry and I cry praying this isn't the precedent for the future.

We're sitting watching TV when Mason gets a phone call later that evening, he's an uncle again. The twins have a little sister, not a brother as they were told. They named her Evie Marie Barker. It's a beautiful name, and I'm happy for him and his family.

I have horrible dreams of them all around Ashley, Ethan and their new baby, one big happy family. I'm standing outside with Eliza and Seb, they don't see us or don't care. My heart breaks for the twins with every day they don't see Ethan. Ava's been around a few times. Niles more than most, he loves the twins.

Ethan has been absent as I knew he would, spending time at home with his wife and new daughter. Nan's not happy, but what am I supposed to do? Life goes on. It's his choice not to come and see his children, I can't and won't force him.

Thankfully, my days are filled with check-ups for the twins, daily mommy duties and my writing which is coming along nicely. I'm enjoying my new role and routine; the twins are the best parts of my days and while I'm sad when they go to bed I know I need that time to be me.

After a week Ethan starts making his visits again; I keep my distance when he's here, I'm still too mad at him and I refuse to upset the twins by arguing with their dad in front of them.

Weeks pass with Ethan radiating happiness; I don't begrudge him his happiness, but I can't help feeling sad and lonely, it's just hard to see it. Don't get me wrong, waking every morning to my twins' smiles is amazing, it erases the sadness, filling me with happy memories of seeing them grow and learn. Like now playing with their tiny feet as they chew on their hands makes my heart melt.

Being their mom, is the most rewarding experience of my life, but the loneliness when they go to bed is unbearable, even Nan and Mace have noticed. So, when nan comes over and we have a small cookout, it lifts my spirits some watching Mace bond with the twins is amazing their faces mesmerised by their uncle Mace. I snap pictures capturing precious memories.

When the day of my six-week check-up dawns; I wake feeling refreshed and positive. Deciding it's time for me to move on, maybe make some more friends. I get up and stick my head in on the twins, they are asleep holding each other's hands. Smiling I rush back to my room for a quick shower.

I'm nervous about leaving the twins for the first time; Ethan has never had them alone and as much as I know he can take care of them I still feel apprehensive. I dress in a light pink, flowery summer dress, off the shoulder with matching flats. I look pretty good and to say I just had twins you wouldn't know it unless you knew me before. I'm pretty much back to my normal size, apart from a little baby fat. Unfortunately, my boobs are still huge, and my butt is very much noticeable, but today I'm concentrating on being and feeling positive. After a small amount of makeup and a vigorous brushing of my locks, I like the result.

Happily walking downstairs, I see Ethan talking to Seb and Eliza. Smiling, I drop to the floor kissing both their cheeks.

"Okay, I'll see you both in a little while, be good for daddy."

"If they get hungry, I expressed milk this morning. It's in the fridge just ask Mace; he's in the study. You know where everything else is. Thanks for doing this." Receiving no answer, I look back at Ethan; who is staring at me dazed, his eyes dark and shining, *is that desire?* Oh, hell no. I can't be pulled back into him.

"Ethan?" I snap, his eye shoot to mine from my body. Blinking, he licks his lips swallowing hard.

"Sorry, got it. Milk, fridge. Mace, study." Nodding, I grab my bag, phone and keys.

"I have my phone if you need me, I shouldn't be long."

He walks me toward the door, "Okay, we'll be fine, don't worry." I look back at him nervously and catch him eyeing my butt.

"Ethan. Stop staring at my arse."

Smiling guiltily, he holds his hands up in defence. "Hey, I can't help it, you're walking in front of me. God, your body has changed since having the twins. You sure don't look like an eighteen-year-old anymore."

"That's because I'm nineteen now." I say sarcastically walking out the door.

After my check-up, I walk slowly to my car happily absorbing the rays. I text Ethan to let him know I'll be home in a little while; I just need to grab a few things for the twins.

Walking around the supermarket alone, it feels weird, I'm usually with Mace or nan and the twins. It's refreshing to do normal things again without being babysat. I grab the nappies and wipes and head for the cashier, thankfully there aren't a lot of people here, I'm getting anxious being away from the twins so long.

On my way out I smile at the old couple coming in and wait as they come in first. Unlocking my car, I get in and throw the nappies and wipes onto the passenger seat.

Turning the key, I frown when nothing happens, "you have got to be freaking kidding me." I growl at my car frustrated, hitting the wheel.

Grabbing my phone, I search local mechanics and press call for the closest one.

"Ever auto repair."

"Hi, my car won't start and I'm stuck outside of Assenti's grocery store." I say riffling through my bag for my purse.

"Okay, I'll send someone to you now." He says sounding more bored than I am sitting here.

"Thank you, do you how long they'll be?" I ask opening the window, it's so hot sitting here.

"Shouldn't be long Miss," he says and sighs heavily.

"Okay, thanks." I say awkwardly, I hear another voice in the background and wait.

"Have a good day," he replies sounding a little brighter.

"You too," I mumble trying not to laugh.

Putting the phone down, I grin shaking my head; it must have been his boss.

Pulling up my texts I text Ethan an update.

Me: *I'll be later than I thought. Car won't start, sorry. I've called the local garage; I've got to sit here and wait.*

Ethan: *It's fine, are you okay?*

Me: *I'm fine, just stuck at the store. I hope you're okay to stay a little while longer. How are Seb and Eliza?*

Ethan: *Okay. It's fine they're my kids too, stop worrying. They're adorable, perfect. We're watching cartoons.*

Me: *Okay, if you're sure. They'll be here soon so I shouldn't be long.*

Getting out the car, I relish the breeze on my heated skin. I'm glad there aren't many people here, I bet I look suspicious just standing here leaning against my car.

I sigh in relief as a beat-up tow truck pulls into the lot. I watch as a tall, lean, young guy walks towards me; he wasn't what I was expecting. Blinking, I swallow hard, I don't mean to stereotype but I was thinking an older more rounded guy would be coming to my rescue; not that I'm complaining, not at all. He's gorgeous even in his grungy uniform; he barely gives me the time of day, glancing at me he mumbles a quick "hi," then his head goes under the hood. *Okay then.*

As he works, I check him out, his hair's so dark, it's almost black and his shirt sleeves are rolled up showcasing tanned, muscled arms. They're sexy, telling me he spends a lot of time outside, those biseps look like they'd be comfy to snuggle into. *Oh man, am I really drooling over a guy's arms?*

"Your battery's gone; it'll need replacing. It'll only take a couple of hours at the shop and you'll be good to go," he says, wiping his hands and turning towards me. His eyes take a slow trek from my legs all the way up until his eyes meet mine. His widening as he smiles.

"Hi Lily, right?" He smiles and I frown confused, "you don't remember me, do you? We went to school together."

Blinking, I nod and really look at him; his eyes a rich chocolate brown, angular jaw, he has some scruff, but I don't recall him. I was going through a rough time, so I probably wouldn't.

"I'm sorry, I don't. Were you in any of my classes?" I feel bad for not recognising him.

"No, but I was friends with Mason. Well, I was until he left; I'm Jackson Garcia." His name rings a bell, but only vaguely. I shake his outstretched hand.

"Sorry, I went through a rough time while I was at school. How are you?" I ask embarrassed.

He nods, in understanding. "Weren't you pregnant?" He blurts, clearing his throat he rubs his neck as it turns red. "I'm sorry. I didn't mean to say that. I'm doing good; how are you?" Smiling, I cringe inside remembering how I was after my mom died. Then everything with Ethan and finding out I was pregnant...

"It's okay. Yes, I was, gave birth six weeks ago," I say pushing past the awkwardness, he looks shocked, looking me up and down.

"Wow. You look great…I mean to say, you just had a baby," he looks away his face getting redder by the minute.

I giggle. "Thanks, I had twins though, not just one."

"Wow." He breaths, his eyes showing their appreciation, I blush under his gaze. Clearing his throat, he lowers the bonnet of the car. "Anyway, you need a new battery. I can take it in and have it back to you in a couple of hours or so."

Sighing, I grab my bag and shopping from the front seat.

"Do you need a ride home?" He asks, taking my keys.

"Yes, please, if you don't mind."

"Not at all; let me just hook this up, then we can go."

We chat all the way to my place, laughing a lot. He tells me funny stories about his family and friends and I tell him about the twins and Mace. He asks about the twins' dad and I tell him the short, simple version. That we didn't work out, but he still sees the twins. Pulling up outside my house, I'm sad to say goodbye, it was nice talking to someone outside of Mace and nan.

"I'll bring it back in a couple of hours, don't worry," he assures me smiling. I nod and grab the door handle. "Lily?"

Turning, I'm drawn into his gorgeous eyes, "yeah?"

"Would you, er, like to go out sometime?" He sounds nervous, rubbing his neck again I see he is nervous. I'm shocked he'd want to go out with me, since I'm a single mom and all.

"Yeah, yes. I'd love to. You have my number on the paperwork, text me when and where."

His smile lights up the truck, and my dormant heart flutters. Biting my cheek, I say bye and rush up the path, waving before going inside. Blowing out a breath, I lean against the door, closing my eyes. God, it's been ages since my heart's beaten that wildly. Smiling, I feel my excitement bubble, I can't wait for this date.

"What's put that smile on your face? I thought you'd be pissed about your car." Ethan's voice breaks my thoughts and my giddy mood. *Shit, can I get a break?*

Opening my eyes, to see him holding Seb over his shoulder, looking at me bewildered. I'm not sure whether to tell him or to keep it to myself. I guess he'll be okay, since he's married and happy. Why shouldn't I be happy too?

"Erm, it'll be fixed and back in a few hours, needs a new

battery," I mutter, avoiding eye contact and going to take Seb. He hands him over, but I can feel his stare. I know he's not going to give up, not when he can tell I'm purposefully changing the subject.

Sighing, I concede, I'll have to tell him sooner or later. "I just ran into an old friend of Mason's from school, he was the mechanic who picked up my car. Erm, he asked me out," I whisper, feeling bad.

Ethan looks stricken, which makes me feel worse. I shouldn't have told him.

"Ethan…" I'm not sure what I can say, I have to move on, he has. He's married for God's sake. He should have known, I wouldn't be alone forever.

"Are you going to go out with him?" He asks softly, not meeting my eyes, he's staring at Sebastian who's kicking and squirming.

"Yes, I am." This is so awkward. He looks close to tears, it's so painful I tear up just seeing his face.

"Where's Eliza?"

He swallows twice, pointing toward the living room. Not able to bare his pain anymore, I go in search of my little girl. I smile, taking in the sight of Mace and Eliza, snuggled on the sofa watching cartoons.

"Hey, you two." Eliza looks around at my voice. "Aren't you supposed to be working?"

Smirking, he shrugs. "What can I say? I love spending time with my niece and nephew and it just so happens that they love cartoons too." He coos at Eliza, who looks at her uncle and bats him in the nose. I laugh, she's such an uncle Mace's girl.

Ethan still hasn't come into the room. So I sit by Mace and keeping my voice low tell him about running into

Jackson and that we have a date. He looks happy, then winces as I tell him about Ethan's reaction.

"I think he's upset, but what am I supposed to do Mace? He's married."

He nods sadly, "I know, he just needs time to come to terms with it. You deserve to be happy though. So, when's the big date?" I smile and kiss his cheek; he's always got my back.

I place Seb flat on my knees and play with his feet while he chews his fingers.

"I don't know yet he's going to text me. I'm really nervous Mace, I haven't been on many dates and only with…" I don't finish my sentence as Ethan comes in looking mad.

"Mason, can you take the twins upstairs please? Lily and I need to have a talk." His voice cold and unyielding, surprised Mace looks at me. I nod, if he's going to rage, I'd rather the twins be out of the room.

"You wanted to talk, so talk," I say, as Mason's footfalls fade.

He has no right to be mad, he's happy with his wife, why can't I be too?

"Don't you think it's a bit soon to be dating, after having the twins?" His condescending tone pisses me off.

"Ethan, I'm going to say this once, so you better hear me," I say, slowly standing, I look him in the eye. "What I do romantically is none of your business. My kids will always come first, but I deserve to be loved too. Whether that's by Jackson or someone else is my choice. If it turns into more, then great. You need to get over this, you're Seb and Eliza's dad, not mine," I try to keep my voice even and censor my words, so I won't hurt him.

"It is my business though, they're my kids too. I don't

want them being confused by their mom introducing them to different partners," I don't think he realised what he implied until my face hardens.

"Well, lucky for them, they don't have a mother that jumps from one relationship, or bed to another." I know, I hit my mark as he winces and looks away.

"Okay, that was out of line, and I'm sorry; but I don't know how to deal with this. I thought we'd just got things smoothed out, on an even path and now you throw this at me."

"Ethan, you don't have to deal with anything. What I do and who I see is none of your concern, this shouldn't affect you, you're with Ashley. You are happily married."

I'm so tired of repeating myself. It seems I'm the only one of the two of us who remembers he's married. Exhausted, I sit and close my eyes.

"You know that's not true, and you know why it affects me."

"Which part do I know isn't true? And believe me, I really don't know why it affects you. You're married and you've been blissfully happy the past few weeks."

The sofa dips beside me, but I keep my eyes closed.

"What you do will always be my concern and you know why, it's not a secret. I have been blissfully happy, because I have three beautiful children."

"I can't keep doing this; it's not fair of you to keep implying that you love me, that my love life has anything to do with you. You don't love me Ethan, if you did, you wouldn't be married to anyone but me. You're confused. Yes, I'm the mother of two of your children, but that's it."

"No, that's not it. I do love you. It hurts to even think of you looking at another man, let alone dating one."

"What do you expect me to do? Be alone for the rest of

my life? While you get the best of both worlds? That's not fair and you know it." I huff, opening my eyes slightly.

Rubbing his face, he looks at me pleadingly. "Just give me some time to come to terms with it. I know you deserve to be happy, and I know it's unfair. But I love you and no matter what's happened between us, you love me too. I know you do; I can see it in your eyes."

Reaching out he strokes my face gently. It feels so good, I close my eyes mustering the strength to pull away, it's wrong. I jump feeling warm, soft lips touch mine, my eyes flash open meeting his now dark ones.

"Please, Lily, just..." He's breathless, staring at my mouth. My heart is beating fiercely; my mind a whir of confusion, I want to kiss him because he's still the man I love, but I know we shouldn't, he's not mine. It will only complicate things more.

His eyes flicker closed and he kisses me again and moans, the moan that drives me crazy. For a second I forget everything and kiss him back urgently, revelling in the taste of his mouth and tongue. I moan as his scent invades my senses, sliding my fingers through his soft, wavy hair. More than anything I've missed doing this, every time I see him, I want to run my fingers through it.

"Lily," my name a moan as he pushes me flat on the sofa, settling on top of me. My body automatically accepting his.

His hands run up and down my sides, greedily. I pull my mouth away needing to breath, he moves down my jaw and neck to the generous swells of my breasts. God, it feels amazing to have his weight on top of me, his mouth on my heated skin, his hair running through my fingers.

We freeze at the shrill sound of his phone ringing, looking at each other shocked, and disgusted on my part.

"Ignore it, please; I need a few more minutes just being

me and you. I can't be sorry for this; I've wanted to do this for months. I miss you more than I ever thought it possible to miss anyone."

"Oh my God, please get off me," I look away. What the hell am I doing? "God, I feel so cheap," I whisper my stomach lurching in disgust at what I just let happen.

"Lily, you're not cheap, we love each other, this is what people in love do." He strokes my face, but I cringe away, blinking back tears, I hate myself right now.

"People in love aren't usually married to another person. People who are in love and do this, aren't cheating on their wife in the process. We can't do this. I won't do this."

"You'd better call whoever's call you just missed." My voice is shaky, but firm. I won't be the other woman again. He got married, and that left no room for us. As a result, I must move on and find someone for me.

Sighing, he grabs his phone from his pocket, looking even more guiltily at me.

"Hey, yeah, sorry, I was busy…with the twins." I look away, not even wanting to look at him.

"Yeah, she's back. I'll be home in a few minutes then. You, too, bye." I squeeze my eyes closed. Hearing him profess his love to her cemented my resolve and breaks my heart.

"Lily." Shaking my head, I stand and quickly wipe my eyes.

"It's fine, go."

"Lily, we need to talk. Are you still? "

My phone rings this time, smiling shakily, I answer. "Hey, Jackson. Yeah, I'm at home, I don't have a car remember," his smooth laugh is seductive. I look out the window, blushing.

"Your car's done; I can bring it by now if you like."

"That would be great, Mace probably wants to say hi too."

"You told Mace about me asking you out?"

"I tell Mace most things, but we live together and he wanted to know where my smile came from, so…"

"I'm glad I made you smile. Is it okay if I come by then, and catch up with Mace?" He's hesitant to assume anything.

"Yeah, I'd like that, but the twins are here so it may be noisy." I bite my cheek, hoping he'll be okay with the twins because if it's not, that's a deal-breaker.

"I'd love to meet them. I love kids, so I think we'll be fine."

My relief and happiness is so evident I feel Ethan shooting daggers at me.

"Okay, then I'll see you in a while. Bye." Turning, I see a very pissed off Ethan, arms crossed tapping his foot impatiently.

"I thought we agreed it was too soon for you to start dating?" Whoa. I didn't agree to shit.

"Hang on a second, I didn't agree to anything. You made your feelings known and I heard you. I won't bring loads of men into the twins' lives, but that doesn't mean I won't date. Jackson is a nice bloke and we're attracted to each other. I want to see if we could have something."

"But you're still in love with me. How can you go out with some other guy?" *The gall.*

"Erm, you seem to forget that you said you loved me when you were with Ashley. Got me pregnant and promised me the world then left without a backwards glance to marry her. And now you ask, no, you decide that it's too soon for me to date." I stare open mouthed at him my belly burning with anger, "I can't believe it, how can you think you have the right to decide I shouldn't be able or want to go out with another bloke. Yes, I still love you, but you live and sleep with your wife every day. You've got some balls. You have your happily ever after, why shouldn't I have the chance at finding mine?" I yell, surprised at his level of selfishness even though I shouldn't be at this point.

"Just leave it alone please?" I plead, as hard as it is to let go, I need to, for me. He agrees but doesn't look very happy.

"You need to go; Jackson is on his way over and it'll be awkward if you're here."

I want my fresh start to go as smoothly as possible, and Ethan will be territorial and possessive. It'll just make things harder than need be.

"Okay, but I'm saying goodbye to my kids first." His face as hard as his voice, stomping up the stairs.

I follow slowly to give him space. "Bye my little angels, daddy will be back tomorrow to see you both. I love you." He kisses them both handing Seb to Mace.

Picking up Eliza we bring them back downstairs. I fidget as my nervousness increases; Mace will want to talk about what just happened with me an Ethan, but I'm not ready to tell him I fucked up again.

I keep checking the window to see if Jackson is here yet, making Mason smirk looking at Ethan. I jump a mile in the air when the doorbell rings; my eyes the size of saucers looking from the door to Ethan and back again. Mace laughs, finding it hilarious. Ethan has a face like thunder.

Rushing to the door, I pause before opening it and take a deep breath. Opening it I see he's showered and changed into clean clothes; he also looks nervous. I drink in the sight of him for a second; thick thighs encased in fitted, worn jeans all the way up to his tapered waist and broad shoulders. He is beautifully, and his T-shirt hides nothing.

He grins at me, and my long-neglected sex drive revs

back to life, I practically drool. An impatient clearing of a throat behind me makes me cringe. Ethan's being purposefully rude, obviously not liking my reaction to what he views as his replacement.

"Sorry, come in," I step aside as he moves forward. I catch a faint whiff of him as he passes. Mmm, he smells amazing. Musty male, with a subtle hint of citrus to it. I sigh audibly and my eyes widen, I turn pink hearing Mason's chuckle. Jackson looks at me over his shoulder, smiling his eyebrow cocked.

"Hey, Jackson. Nice to see you man." Mace breaks the silence and they do the bloke handshake thingy.

"You, too. How you been?"

"I'm good, been busy since Lily had the twins."

As if on cue, they cry for attention. Instead of heading for the door Ethan heads over to the twins, squatting in front of them, he murmurs quietly to them. They quiet down immediately, the sound of their dad's voice soothing them.

"Come on through, would you like a drink?" I ask anxious to leave the room and Ethan's anger behind as the atmosphere becomes increasingly uncomfortable, with my ex and father of my kids in the same vicinity as my prospective new boyfriend. One hostile and the other, oblivious, for now. I give Mace a desperate look to get rid of Ethan.

"Water please." Jackson turns, smiling warmly at me as he follows me into the kitchen. Mace goes to try and vacate his brother.

"Is it me or is that guy a little hostile towards me?" Jackson asks, leaning against the island. I sigh, feeling bad for bringing him into a hostile situation.

"That's Ethan, Mason's brother and, er, the twins' dad. He's just being an arse. I'm so sorry, just ignore him, please."

"Are you and he still?" He's so adorable, I want to kiss

his sexy lips. They look delicious, drawing me in and holding me hostage. The longer I stare, the more I want to kiss him. Involuntarily my tongue licks across my bottom lip.

"Lily?" My head snaps around at Mason's amused voice. My face burns like I've been caught doing indecent things. I haven't, but my mind had. My only excuse is that my body is sexually deprived.

"Yeah?"

"The twins are hungry, and I don't have the equipment to satisfy them," Mace laughs pointing at his chest. Jackson chuckles making my face redden even more.

"Okay, I'll, er, go do that then." I stutter, rushing from the room. Picking up my crying babies. I place them in the Moses basket I use to transport them around the house and escape upstairs to feed my little angels.

CHAPTER NINETEEN

When I return, I find Mace and Jackson laughing in the living room, enjoying their catch up.

Mace spots me and smiles. "Where are the twins?"

Laughing, I roll my eyes. "They need sleep Mace. They'll be awake again soon enough."

He sticks his lip out, pushing to his feet. "Well, since I won't be getting any cuddles for a while, I think I better get some work done." He sighs heavily.

I laugh as he leaves, sitting in the corner of the sofa I pull my legs up beneath me. Now that we're alone my nerves kick in, and butterflies break free.

"So,“ He sits forward, bracing his arms on his thighs.

Looking at him, I lean my head on my hand, waiting to see what he's going to say.

"So?" I prompt when he just stares at me.

"Are you and Ethan still together?"

Shaking my head, I sit up. "No, we had a brief, relationship. It was stupid, and a lot of bad crap came from it, barring the twins. I've moved past that and he's married. So you have nothing to worry about. Jackson, I would never have agreed to go on a date with you if I was with anyone else."

Blowing out a relieved breath, he smiles the brightest smile and relaxes into the sofa.

"So, when you're not saving countless damsels in distress' what do you like to do?"

He chuckles, turning and giving me his full attention. "Well, I play guitar, not sure I'm that good but I enjoy it. I also like to read, mostly horrors. Love movies, just not too many chick flicks, like Dirty Dancing." He shudders.

"Hey, Dirty Dancing is a classic." I giggle at his pained expression.

"Okay, tell me what your favourite food is?" I ask, facing him, getting comfortable.

"That's easy, I love sea food. What about you?"

"Any Mexican food. When I was pregnant with the twins, I ate it constantly. It's why I was huge."

"I can't imagine you huge."

"You wouldn't want to either," I joke, holding my arms out in-front of me and blowing up my cheeks.

He laughs shaking his head. "No way were you that big. You look amazing." His face turns a little pink.

"Thank you, but I really was, but there were two of them."

We regale each other with funny stories, his of his family here and spending time in Spain, and mine of memories of my mom and exploits with Mason.

I learn so much about him in the space of a couple of hours; he's so funny, witty, charming, but he has a quirky side. He is also loyal, loves his family and would do anything for them at the drop of a hat. When he talks of them, there is so much love in his voice I could melt right into the sofa.

He is everything I'd love to have in my life, plus he's gorgeous. *How could I not have noticed him at school?*

Before leaving he confirms our date on Friday. I am so excited to spend more time with him.

He said wear old clothes, but his don't look old and grungy like mine.

He's the perfect gentleman though, never mentioning how bad I look. Opening my door, he holds out a hand to help me out of his truck. My foot catches on something, so I yank my leg and almost smack him in the junk with my knee.

"I'm so sorry," I gasp, as he jumps back dodging my wayward limb.

Relieved and at a safe distance, he laughs. "It's fine, next time I'll wear a protective cup," he chuckles, taking my hand as we walk.

"I…I'm not usually so," I drift off seeing him laughing his arse off. "You arse." I smack his arm laughing.

He stops when we get to a wooded area, turning he takes both my hands. "I thought with us being *only* nineteen, we should act our age, hence the old clothes."

"Okay," I say looking around apprehensively.

"Come on, let's get suited up."

"What?"

"You'll see," he yells, sprinting off and I give chase, laughing. I lose him in all the trees, so I slow to a walk looking around a little confused as to which way I came.

"JACKSON?"

"Follow the colours." I look around confused, not seeing anything, then paint splatters centimetres from my feet making me jump and scream.

“What the feck?” I whisper, then paint starts hitting the ground in a line, so I follow and end up outside a small hut.

“Inside you’ll find what you need,” Jackson’s muffled voice breaks the air.

Opening the door, I peak Inside, scared something will jump out and kill me. When nothing happens, I breathe a sigh of relief; laid out on a table are overalls, protective wear, goggles, a paint-gun and ammo. Excited, I hurry to get changed, I’ve always wanted to try this, but mom never wanted to.

“Are you coming out?”

I don’t answer, instead I peek through the window, spying him crouched ready to fire as soon as the door opens. He’s so engrossed in watching the door that he doesn’t see or hear me slide the window open a little. Giggling, I aim and fire hitting the tree right by his nose. He jumps and falls on his arse, laughing.

“That was a dirty trick!”

“Yeah, yeah. Like you weren’t waiting for me to step through the door.” I shoot repeatedly, and while he’s distracted, I make a run for it.

We play until we’re almost out of ammo, weaving and dodging each other, laughing like kids. I hit him in the thigh so close to his nuts he freezes, giving me the opportunity to shoot again. I laugh as paint splatters across his chest and he fake dies, holding his chest and dropping to his knees letting out a god-awful cry.

“Okay, truce. Let’s go eat.” He says getting to his feet and brushing the dirt off.

“You just don’t like to lose,” I laugh pulling off my goggles and sitting.

“You were so going down, but we’ll agree to disagree.”

“Yeah, whatever,” I laugh patting his chest, “I’m starving,

thanks for thinking of this, I haven't laughed this much in ages."

"You're welcome, I've had a great time. It's not a romantic restaurant, but I saw an old diner on our way here."

"It's perfect, but we need to clean up first. You got paint…" I wipe neon pink paint down the side of his face and run. Laughing, he gives chase, lunges and takes us both to the ground, laughing hysterically as he wipes paint down my cheeks, into my eyebrows and on the end of my nose.

At the diner we order two massive burger meals and milk-shakes. I feel my age for a change, this date was unexpected but amazing. People stare at us covered in neon paint. The rest of our date is spent eating, laughing and talking.

After our first date we make plans to see each other more, so every Tuesday, Friday and Saturday Jackson takes me somewhere different. There are rules to our dates, I must act my age, no adult talk and I have to smile and laugh as much as possible. So far, we've been to the movies, the zoo, an arcade, a fun fair and a bowling alley and I've loved every minute of it. We get on so well and he makes me feel like no one ever has, I come first.

Sunday is usually my lazy day in this house with the twins, but Jackson came over with toys for the twins, so we've played instead. I watch him play with them and my heart does a happy dance, he is so amazing and patient, and fun. He's such a great bloke, quiet a change from my last one, he's romantic, attentive, my feelings for him have grown and it's a relief to finally be free of Ethan tangled web.

Things wind down when the twins go down for their nap, so I can relax and have a cuppa.

I find myself staring at Jackson as his arm muscle bunches when he brings the cup to his mouth, then his mouth moves.

"Huh?" I blink shaking myself.

He chuckles, rubbing the back of his neck. "I asked if we were a couple now?"

"Erm, do you want to be?"

"Yeah, I mean, I, er really liked you in school, but since getting to know you better. I mean I'd really like us to be." He rubs his neck nervously.

Smiling, I sit next to him. "That was a rough time for me. I'm glad we've had this time to get to know one another, it's been amazing, the best. I need to ask though, are you okay with me being a single mom? You should know now that the twins come first. So I need to know you're okay with that."

Taking my hand, he links our fingers and brushing his thumb over the back of my hand.

"I'm more than okay with it. It's how it should be, they're your kids and I like spending time with you and them. I really like you Lily and I'm *really* attracted to you." His voice seductive again.

"So can I kiss you now that we've established that we're a couple?"

Instead of answering, I place my hand on his whiskered cheek and bring my lips to his gently. Feeling how soft they are, has my body heating so fast, I feel lightheaded. My eyes slide shut as his hand catches the back of my head, securing me, taking control as he deepens our kiss. Moaning, I melt into him, our tongues sliding across each other's, tasting.

His taste is spicy with a hint of mint, from chewing gum? Pulling back slightly, I keep my eyes closed, breathing heavily.

"Wow," he blows out a shaky breath, I smile. God, he's so cute.

"For such a big bloke you're really cute. I mean, with all your muscles, I," I snap my mouth shut, blushing.

He laughs. "You've noticed my muscles, huh? You are so adorable when you blush." He kisses me on the nose.

"Do you want to stay for a while?" I ask.

"Yeah, if that's okay."

"How about a movie? We could ask Mace to join and crack out some popcorn?"

Nodding, he agrees and smiles at my enthusiasm.

Grabbing my phone, I text Mace.

Me: *We're going to watch a movie with p-corn, you in?*

Mason: *Yep, be there in a few. I'll grab the p-corn and drinks. You're not going to be all smoochy through it, are you? :p*

Me: *No, what would make you think that?*

Mason: *Maybe because of the way you've been eye fucking him since he walked through the door.*

Gasping, I turn my phone away, making sure Jackson doesn't see. Unfortunately, I turn bright red.

"What did he say to make you look like a tomato?"

Shaking my head, I hide my phone behind my back and bite my cheek as he smirks scooting closer.

"Tell me, please?" He asks softly, batting his eyes. I shake my head again, leaning back.

The playful look that enters his eyes sends a thrill through me, and I squeal jumping up, trying to run for it. Squealing again when strong arms scoop me off my feet, pinning me to his hard chest.

Breathless, he whispers in my ear. "Tell me."

Heat zips through me, a thrilling side effect of his closeness and his breath skating across my neck.

"No," my voice wobbles.

I'm still dangling in the air, pressed against his hard chest.

"I could tickle you, I guess. Or I could just do this," my feet meet the floor as he spins me around. His hand diving into my hair, my eyes go to his lips, then slide closed as my hands grasp his shoulders.

Just as quickly as I was snatched up, I'm let go and my phone is in his hand. *Shit.* He's reading my message. His laugh snaps me out of my stupor.

"Hey. Give it back. You distracted me, that's not playing fair," I whine, but laugh.

"I never said I played fair. If I want something, I go to any means to get it." That voice again, I flush not missing the double meaning. *Message received loud and clear.* I shock him by grabbing a fist full of his shirt and plant one on him.

He catches on quickly and his hands sweep down my sides, squeezing my hips. I loosen my hold on his shirt and run my hands over his well-defined chest.

My hands find their way into the soft hair at his nape and pull myself flush against his body with a moan.

Behind us a throat clears, but by this point I'm so used to Mason walking in on me at inappropriate moments. I pull back slowly, blinking I smile up at Jackson as he smirks wickedly at me, flashing me the dimple on his left cheek.

The last few weeks have been pure bliss, Jackson and I are well into the honeymoon period of our relationship, much to Mace disgust and amusement. I couldn't tell you the amount of times he's walked in on us make out on the sofa, or in kitchen.

Life has settled into a somewhat normal routine, Ethan see's the twin's most days, but when he doesn't, he calls to talk to them through the phone. The twins are three months old now and babbling from the moment they wake to the moment they give up the goat and sleep.

Even though Jackson and I have been together a few months, we have been taking it slowly, getting to know each other before we take our relationship to the next level, but I'm so ready for him to pin me to my bed, I ache to feel his weight on top of me. It's been torture over the last few weeks, our make out sessions, the teasing touches and the interruptions have driven me mad.

So tonight, I'm planning on spending some quality time *alone* with my boyfriend, while Ethan has the twins overnight at his mom's. Ethan's still cold toward Jackson, but I expect nothing else from him, and Jackson doesn't seem bothered by him.

"Are you *sure* you're okay with them staying out?" Mace teases, for the thousandth time, he knows I'm scared shitless.

"Will you stay with them tonight? Make sure Ashley doesn't go over?" I plead, he sighs looking none too happy but he worries about the same thing, knowing her she will ignore my wishes.

"Okay, but Ethan's not going to be happy." He agrees and kisses my head.

"If she does show up, call me and we'll be straight over."

I'm really panicking over this. I don't want Ashley anywhere near the twins, she's dangerous and volatile and she hates them.

"It'll be okay, let me go call mom."

Jackson arrives as Mace leaves to call his mom. He chuckles seeing me in a mess over the twins staying out.

Pulling me into his chest, he kisses my hair. "Everything will be fine, they'll be with their dad and besides, Isabella will be there. You should be more worried about what I'm going to do to you tonight." Oh god, I love it when his voice drops like that. I grasp his ribs digging my nails in.

"I'm not worried, but you should be. I have plans for you

mister." Cocking an amused eyebrow, he drops his head, so he talks against my lips.

"Really? I can't wait," we break apart as an angry grunt comes from behind Jackson.

"Hello, Ethan." Jackson says, not looking away from me. Okay, maybe he is a little bothered.

"Jackson, Lily. Are the twins ready? I'm in a rush." His snappy mood makes me scowl. "What's stuck up your arse?" Jackson chuckles as does Mace, Ethan however, does not.

"Look, I have to get the twins to moms. Then I need to get some stuff for Ash, so if you could hurry up, I'd appreciate it. I don't have all night to listen to you two moon over each other."

I don't like his attitude. "Well, if it's too much trouble then go do what you need to for your wife and maybe you can have the twins when you're in a better mood and have time for them," I snap and walk off going to sit with my babies while they sleep to calm down.

Sitting in the rocking chair, I listen to their breathing taking deep breaths myself.

"I'm sorry, okay? I'm still adjusting to you and Jackson. It's hard," Ethan says from the doorway, looking at him I can see he's upset, but there was no need for that display back there.

"Ethan, you need to get over this, you've been married almost a year. I won't put up with you treating me like that just because I've finally found someone to love and who loves me. We have children together if you want them overnight, then don't come here acting like a wanker."

"Okay, yeah. I get it and I deserved that. So, can I still have the kids even though I was a dick?"

I sigh. "You know you can, but don't make them feel like they're a burden to you. Ever."

"They aren't and I'm sorry it came out that way. Okay, I'll get the stuff in the car and then come back to get my little angels. Don't worry, we'll be fine. Have a good time…" He winces at the implied meaning behind it from what he overheard.

After Ethan reluctantly agreed Mace could go and help out. The house is quiet, too quiet; Jackson and I are finally alone, I relax as Jackson's arms slide around me from behind.

"They'll be fine you know," he whispers into my neck, nodding, I lay my head on his chest I love that he's so much taller than me that my head only just reaches his shoulder.

"Do you want to go out or stay in to eat?" He asks, kissing my neck and making me shiver. Turning in his arms, I poke his chest with my finger.

"We're not going anywhere, I have plans for you tonight. I don't want to wait anymore, I know we said we'd wait because I rushed before, but I think we've waited long enough."

Reaching up, I wind my arms around his neck and place kisses all over his face and down his neck, biting the tendon between his neck and shoulder he groans squeezing me tighter.

"Okay, do you want to eat first?" Shaking my head, I lick up his neck and suck on his ear.

"Lily," moaning my name, he takes my mouth in a hungry kiss backing me up against the nearest wall. His hands fisting my hair, pulling it back as he lays open mouthed kisses along my neck, and the tops of my breasts.

My hands run down his back and grasp his amazing backside. It sticks out slightly, perfectly round, tight buns. Enough to make me crazy wanting to touch, to squeeze every time he turns. But, my God, when he bends over.

He grinds into me harder as he pulls the top of my dress

down, palming my breast, feeling its heavy weight. I moan as he pulls my hard nipple into his mouth.

"Oh God, *Jackson.*"

He groans as his name slips from my lips, his hand following my every curve, grasping my knee and hitching it up onto his hip, opening me to him. The firm glide of his hand, making its way back up and under my dress has my breath stuttering.

"Please," I moan in his ear, rocking into him. His hand reaches and kneads my cheek, slapping gently, enough to sting. I bite his neck, sucking on his skin hard, marking him as mine.

"God Lily, I need you."

Pushing his chest, I flip our positions pinning him to the wall. His breathing speeds up as I push his shirt up and over his head. Drinking in the sight of his bronzed, toned chest and belly.

He has a beautiful tattoo stretching up his side, the design is intricate, and has; ***encontrar el amor verdadero, es amarse a uno mismo*** *s*cripted through it.

Kissing down his chest, I trace his tattoo with my lips and tongue. His muscles tighten and he moans, his head falling back with a bump against the wall as I tease each nipple with my tongue.

Dropping to my knees, I look up into his chocolate eyes, dark and burning with heat. His chest rising and falling rapidly, lips parted and wet.

I dance my fingers slowly along the waistband of his jeans. Licking my dry lips, I pop the button, lowering the zipper slowly. Taking my time revealing tight black boxers.

I pull his jeans and underwear down, uncovering him. He's gorgeous, thick and long with veins running along the length of him and pierced. Leaning back, I take in the sight of him, he's a masterpiece.

He loses his shoes and clothes while I admire him.

The full picture is beyond words, he's better than any male characters in books. I've learnt in theory how to do what I'm about to do. Let's just hope it wasn't exaggerated.

Taking a steadying breath, I run my hands up his thick thighs. His body shudders in pleasure, looking into his beautiful eyes, I lean forward and lick from the base to the glistening tip. He hisses as I kiss his piercing. His taste bursts on my tongue, clean and salty.

"Sweetheart, you're killing me here." His hands tangle in my hair, clenching. Taking pity on him, I quit teasing and suck on the head, hard, making him growl.

"That's it, put your hand around the base. Ah, just like that. Lick the tip again."

I curl my tongue around the head, sucking gently. Shuddering, he pulls me closer.

My hand moves in even strokes, while engulfing as much of him as I can with my mouth. He twitches in my mouth as I trace each vein with the tip of my tongue.

His big body shudders when he touches the back of my throat. I relax, breathing through my nose so I don't gag.

"Ah, si, así corazón," his voice slurred, as he speaks in Spanish. God, it's such a turn on. I have no idea what he said, but it sounds good.

His voice and the sound of moans make me so wet; I squeeze my thighs together and hasten my pace, sucking harder. I run my hand up his abs feeling him.

"You need to stop. God please stop, I don't want to come yet."

Pulling my mouth away, I stand shakily, he pulls me into a kiss his teeth nipping at my swollen lips.

"We should take this to your room, I don't want any interruptions when I'm licking every inch of your body and I really want to strip you out of this dress. I've been dreaming about your gorgeous body bare and writhing under me for weeks."

Smiling, I take his hand and lead him to my room. I lean against the door a little nervous, he sits on my bed wiggling his finger.

"Come here, mi amor." That accent, I shiver moving toward him. He smirks seeing me stumble and kisses my belly as I stand between his legs. I grasp his face bending his head back and kiss him with all the pent-up hunger from the past few weeks.

His hands slide up my bare legs, thumbs stroking circles on my thighs. The tips of his fingers dip beneath my thong sliding it down, I gasp at the rush of cold air hitting my heated centre.

Stepping out of my thong, I kneel on the edge of the bed, straddling him, causing him to lean back a little grasping my hips.

Missing his skin on mine, I pull my dress over my head. His look holds so much desire I tingle.

"You're sexier than I could have ever dreamed."

He takes my engorged nipple into his scorching mouth and my head falls back in surrender.

My legs tremor beneath me threatening to give out, so I lower myself onto his lap, whimpering as his piercing rubs my clit. He groans biting my nipple and sending a rush of wetness between my legs.

"Maybe I should suit up before this goes too far?"

I nod, getting up, my eyes glued to his backside as he collects a box of condoms from a bag I didn't see. He turns, and the look he shoots me is electrifying. Jackson in all his glory is a sight I'll never forget. Any and all men are eclipsed by him, not just his body but *him,* I've slowly fallen in love with him; he owns my heart. His patience and steadfast way of dealing with things is amazing especially with the twins, they love him too. He's so playful with them and talks to them constantly.

So, before we go any further, I want him to know how I feel about him, I don't want there to be any doubts about us.

"Come here for a sec," I say patting the bed beside me, my voice shaking a little with nerves and love.

His brow furrows, as he drops the condoms and comes to sit beside me, taking my hand.

"What's wrong? If you're not ready, we don't have to." I place my finger on his lips to quiet him, smiling.

"No, it's not that. I'm ready, more than ready. I just want you to know, that this, it's more than just sex. I wanted you to know, that I, I love you." He looks stunned. "I know we've only been together a few months, and you may not feel the same, but I couldn't help falling in love with you. You're amazingly sweet, and the way you are with the twins… They adore you Jackson and so do I. I couldn't help falling love with you. I'm sure there's plenty I'm forgetting, but."

"Aww, sweetheart. Of course, I feel the same. How could I not? You're unlike anyone I've ever met. I was a little scared to say it, I mean, you were in love with Ethan for so long, and I know you were still so when we started dating. You have no idea how happy I am right now. You're all I want Lily, and I would never do what he did to you. There is no one else for me; it's just me, you and the twins, that's it."

I sniffle, wiping my eyes. *God I'm a mess.*

Chuckling, he pulls me into his chest and I go willingly, pressing my face into his neck, placing little kisses along his jaw hoping to rekindle our earlier mood.

Reaching his lips, I pause, looking into his eyes, hoping he can see I love him, with no reservations. I *need* him to see he's not a replacement. He's the one.

I pull him to me, his body fits mine perfectly, deepening the kiss, he takes over, surrounding me. I feel consumed, safe. Loved.

He settles himself on top of me, pinning me, knowing exactly what I want and need. I hiss when the cold metal of his piercing nudges my clit, his cock sliding easily through the wetness gathered between my legs, sending shards of pleasure through me.

"Oh God, harder, please, I need you. I want to come."

Humming in agreement, he sits back on his heels and I whimper at the loss of his body.

Shaking his head, he grabs a condom, ripping it open with his teeth. I groan watching his hand roll it down his magnificent cock. Watching me watch him, his eyes flaring with desire.

I grab his neck, dragging him back to me shamelessly grinding on him, he watches as he lines himself up.

"Don't close your eyes. I want to see them as I slide into you the first time." He tells me his eyes focusing on mine, nodding I fold my arms around his neck.

My eyes hold his, as he pushes slowly into me, one blessed inch at a time. Moaning, I struggle to keep my eyes open as ecstasy engulfs me.

"God, you're tight."

Sweat runs down his temple as he pushes in just another inch. Sucking in a breath, I moan at the stinging stretch, feeling every push and retreat parting my tight muscles.

"Am I hurting you?" He asks, worried, his voice strained.

"No. God don't stop. You're massive, *fuck*. I love feeling

you stretch me." I breath feeling myself burn for more of him. "*Harder,*" I demand, grasping his backside, urging him on.

Hearing me, he pounds into me harder and faster. His breath bursts from his chest, with the exertion. I scream as my orgasm takes hold, pulling me under and I come so hard I see stars. *God it's been so long.*

I sigh, happily and peel my eyes open seeing Jackson braced over me, jaw clenched, holding back his own orgasm.

"*Holy fuck.* I nearly came just watching you. That was amazing, but I need to move. I don't know if I can hold on, you're so tight and wet."

"Just let go, I need to feel you."

He pulls out to the tip, pausing, then slowly sliding back in, making me feel every inch of him, every vein, every throb of his cock.

"Jackson," I groan frustrated, digging my nails into his back and hitching my legs higher.

The faster he goes, the more I hear my wetness. Every thrust of his hips bring more.

"Oh God, Jackson, Yes, I'm coming. Fuck, yes." I scream.

He pounds on faster, one hand gripping my hip while the other is clenched onto the headboard for leverage as he slams in and out of me. Growling, he pushes my leg to my chest and goes impossibly deeper.

"Jackson." I cry, feeling him hit my cervix.

"Fuck, I'm comin."

Holy…watching him come, his eyes wide, muscles straining as sweat rolls down his neck.

"Lily," he sighs, falling on top of me gently, I stroke his hair and back, smiling, content.

"I'll be right back," he says, pulling out gently, I whimper at the loss, but ogle his glorious backside as he walks out the room.

I relax into the bed feeling happy and sleepy. “I hope that smile is for me.” Jackson is leaning against the doorframe in all his naked splendour. Smirking, I pat the bed beside me wanting him closer.

I sigh when his cool skin touches mine and curl into his side, laying a kiss above his heart. I rest my head on his arm, looking up at his handsome face, grinning.

“Are you okay? You look a little dazed,” he asks amused, giggling, I poke him in the belly.

“I’m fine, just happy. Are you okay?”

Stroking my cheek, he smiles. “I’m fantastic.”

“That was unbelievable,” I sigh rubbing my cheek on his chest, as he runs his fingers through my hair.

“I’ve never came that hard in my life. I was worried I’d torn the condom, but it was fine.” My face goes pink and I bite my cheek.

“The moment you were fully inside me, I’ve never felt anything like it, the connection. I know it sounds corny.” I hide my face in his chest not wanting to look at him after saying that. It sounded so much better in my head.

“Hey, don’t hide. I felt it the same, I just don’t say girly things out loud.” We laugh, kissing.

“Seriously, I’ve never felt that before. I felt the connection before I was inside you though. I think knowing you love me changed everything, I was able to relax knowing you’re mine,” he smiles. “There you go, I said something girlie. Just don’t go telling anyone, okay?” Giggling, I kiss up his chest.

“It didn’t sound girlie, it was perfect. You’ve made me so happy, the happiest I’ve been since I moved here, baring the birth of the twins. I love you so much Jackson. I’m glad my car broke down that day.”

"Aww, sweetheart. You and the twins have made my life so much brighter. Thank god, I came to fix your car that day and not Gary. I love you," he yawns.

Crawling further onto his chest, I pull the quilt over us. Falling into a peaceful sleep, his strong arms around me. I'm safe, content and loved.

CHAPTER TWENTY

I can't wait for the twins to get back; I've missed them terribly and waiting was making me nervous, so I start making sandwiches. When Jackson walks in barefooted and shirtless, my blood heats so fast it's a wonder I'm not drooling.

"Cariño, you keep looking at me like that, and your ex will walk in on you being pinned to the wall, with your skirt around your middle."

His description leaves me wet and wanting; I look at the clock wondering if we have time. Groaning, he grabs me from behind tickling me.

"As much as I'd enjoy the quickie and seeing his face. I don't think Mace, nor the twins want to see that. I wouldn't want to scar them with the image of their mommy screaming my name. Plus, this is all mine, I don't want him seeing any more than he already has," he growls, stepping back.

Jumping onto the island, I motion him between my legs. I take his mouth as soon as he's in reach. We may not have time for a quickie, but kissing we do.

"Well, it looks like you two had a good night. Didn't worry too much, did you, Lils?" Mason's amused voice interrupts our kiss.

Pulling back, I stick my tongue out at him. Ignoring Ethan's angry scowl, I move toward my little angels, who are babbling away in their car seats.

"Have you been good for daddy?" My voice automatically going into that baby voice that I used to hate, but always do now. Kicking their legs, waving their arms and jabbering as if in answer.

"Oh, mommy has missed you both so much. Let's get you into to the living room so I can munch you both." Three chuckles resonate behind me.

Jackson and Mason stay in the kitchen and do their bro hug thing, talking about cars and bikes.

Ethan follows me carrying Eliza, while I've got Seb.

As soon as we're there, I whisk Seb out of his seat, cuddling him close, drawing in a deep breath. I love the baby smell.

"How's my little man? Have you missed mommy?" He lets out a happy shriek and pulls my hair.

Giggling, I pull it out his fist before it ends up in his mouth. Jackson walks in sitting beside me and gives Seb his fingers to suck on. I pass him over and grab my princess from her seat. Kissing her cheeks and blowing on her belly, she shrieks wriggling.

"And have you missed mommy? Or have you been spoilt for attention?" She clobbers me on the nose. Jackson laughs softly as a sleepy Seb snuggles into his bare chest.

Ethan huffs, not happy at all. "They were fine. A little off with the bottles, but we got there in the end."

Nodding, I turn my attention to Eliza, she looks just as

sleepy as her brother. Her eyes drooping as she lets out a big yawn.

"Oh, that's a big yawn for a little princess," Jackson coos, stroking her cheek, while patting Seb's bum as he sleeps. She latches onto his finger, cuddling his hand to her and closing her eyes.

Ethan shoots me a look of thunder. "Can we talk privately for a minute, please?"

I place Eliza on Jackson's chest, beside her brother where she happily snuggles in and drifts back off. Smiling at Jackson, I fortify myself to deal with Ethan's mood.

"Come on then, out with it," I say, not waiting for him to start, I know there's an argument brewing, I can feel it.

"Why is he still here?" He keeps his voice low, but I hear the anger behind his words.

"Because I asked him to stay the weekend, he is my boyfriend."

"But what about the twins? They're in the next room." He hisses, disgusted.

"Yes, they'll be in the next room, and?"

"You can't."

"I can't what? Have *sex* with my boyfriend? Let me ask you something. Do you have sex with Ashley while your daughter's in the next room?" His face is comical, but I manage to hold my laughter.

"I, er," Biting his lip, he looks away knowing I have a point.

"Why is he allowed around the twins when Ashley isn't? You never asked me if I was okay with it, like I did you before you bit my head off."

My head spins from the sharp change in direction. I'm astonished he has the balls to ask.

"He doesn't hate the twins. He didn't try to harm them

before they were born. He isn't a crazy asshole. That's why there was no discussion."

"Ashley isn't crazy. She was upset about what happened between us. She's my wife, she should be in their life. He's just someone you're sleeping with."

The feckin' gall of him. Seeing red, I yell. "He isn't just someone I'm sleeping with, you knob. I love him. We're together, so get over yourself." Shocked, he blinks looking away.

"Maybe I should go," Jackson says, behind me. Spinning, I see he's fully dressed, looking over my shoulder angrily.

"No. I don't want you to go. If anyone should go, it's him. Ethan, you're the father of my kids and I'll never keep them from you, but what I do and who is in my bed has nothing to do with you. You're going to have to come to terms with Jackson and I because he's going nowhere." I stand in front of Jackson, pulling his arms around me.

"Fine, but we need to talk about Ashley seeing the twins. I can't keep up with what happened last night. I can't keep leaving my wife and daughter every weekend."

"Fine. Have the twins every other weekend, but I'm not budging on Ashley seeing the twins. She's dangerous and I don't trust her breathing the same air as them."

"We'll talk about this when we're alone, but the conversation isn't over." Huffing, he walks out slamming the front door.

"Wow, remind me to never get into an argument with you, you have a comeback for everything."

Chuckling, I turn wrapping my arms around his neck. "And don't forget it buddy," I kiss him until we're breathless.

"Thank you, for defending me, us," he whispers against my lips, his head resting on mine.

"What else was I going to do? Stand there and let him

demean us? We're together and he's just going to have to suck it up."

"Mmm-hmm," he hums, pulling me into another kiss.

EPILOGUE

Two years later.

I stand staring at my reflection; I can't believe it's my wedding day.

I look elegant in an Ivory A-line chiffon gown; it has lace sleeves and back, a medium length train falling down my back and my hair is curled, left cascading down my back with a small tiara rests atop my head.

My hands shake slightly as I straighten the bodice, my engagement ring catching my eye. It's gorgeous a vintage square cut platinum band with a stunning green diamond, surrounded by white diamonds.

I remember the day he proposed like it was yesterday; we were at Balboa Park with the twins, Mace and nan having a picnic. Mace and I were discussing his latest high maintenance customer, who didn't have a clue about web designing.

He strolled right up to me taking my hand and leading me to where nan was playing with the twins, Mace dutifully follows a knowing look in his eyes.

Looking back at Jackson, 'who was on bended knee'

holding out the most magnificent ring I've ever seen. Looking up at me, his gorgeous face shining with love and hope.

Gulping, he said; "Lily, from the moment I saw you on campus, I knew you were special. The way you made my heart race. I just never got the chance to ask you on a date before your world was turned upside down; for which I am eternally grateful for now, because without that phase of your life, you would never have made the two most amazing children I've ever met. I love them with all my heart as I love you. Will you make me the happiest man alive and agree to marry me?"

Tears trickling down my face, I agreed, laughing at his relieved expression. Standing, he slid the ring on my finger, it fit like a glove. Pulling me into a passionate kiss. As Nan and Mace clap causing the twins to join in, making us all laugh.

It was one of the most magical days of my life. This one will undoubtedly top it, today, I become Mrs Lily Anne Garcia.

"Lily, are you ready?" Turning, I look into eyes identical to my own, smiling.

"Yeah, is everyone here?" My voice shakes slightly, showing my nerves. There's a mass of butterflies attacking my stomach.

"Everyone's in place apart from the bride."

Nodding, I look back at the mirror, feeling dizziness wash over me, I sway a little and Alex rushes to steady me looking concerned.

"Are you okay? Do you need some water?"

"I'm okay, I should have eaten this morning, that's all."

"Should I go get you something?"

"No, I'm fine. Thanks for doing this, after everything that's happened the past year, with Isabella." Blanching, he looks away. “Have you spoken at all?” I ask hesitantly, I’ve been reluctant to broach the subject with Mace or Ethan. But something needs to be done. It’s been over a year! And they’re both miserable.

“No, she won’t speak to me. I’ve tried, the boys won’t even see me. The only reason Mason is here today, is because it’s your big day.” He shakes his head, smiling sadly at me. “It’s my pleasure to do this, I’m honoured to have been asked. I didn’t think you’d want anything to do with me when you found out.”

He sounds so sad and my heart does go out to him, but he has to face the consequences of his actions. I’m the only one who has forgiven him, but it took me a while to get over the lies and secrets. I was really mad when nan told me, mad at him, my mom and nan, but kids have a way of making you look at the world differently.

Plus, I couldn’t judge them when Ethan and I did a similar thing. Relationships, lust and sex complicate things. They can motivate people to do things they wouldn’t normally do.

“Dad, you need to try and fix things with everyone, but right now, why don’t you start with Mace? He’s here, and he’s a big softy around the twins.” A smile wipes the sad look from his eyes.

“I still can’t believe how much you’ve grown up in the last two years. Your mom would be so proud of the young woman you’ve become.” I tear up at the mention of my mom, today she would have walked me down the aisle.

“And I can openly admit to being the twins’ real grandad. I’m so grateful you’re giving me a chance to be the dad I should have been when you were born. You have no idea what today means to me. I’m so proud of you, all you’ve accomplished and I love you.”

I'm a mess of tears and runny makeup when he's done. It's every girl's dream to hear her daddy say those things, but even more so when she never knew who he was.

Hugging me tightly, he chuckles. "You've ruined your makeup."

"It's okay, I'll fix it. I love you too. I'm just sorry that your life was torn apart by how I acted."

"You had every right to be mad, I left your mom pregnant and alone. I ignored the fact that I had created a life and tried to act like I hadn't betrayed my family. It was a long time coming. I'm just happy to have patched things up with you."

Pulling away, I look in the mirror cringing, I no longer look elegant, more like a zombie bride. Sighing, I clean under my eyes and reapply my eyeliner and mascara.

"Okay, let's do this, before they come hunting." I say, smoothing my dress and picking up my bouquet; beautiful Calla Lilies a mix of white and purple passion, bound together with a white satin ribbon.

Blowing out a breath, I take dad's arm and we head out the door. I squeeze his arm as we pass through the arch wound with lilies the same colour as my bouquet. My breath leaving me in a rush when I catch a glimpse of him. Jackson's smile broadens on seeing me, love shining brightly in his eyes.

The aisle procession is a blur, all I concentrate on is my groom, trying to quell the urge to run into his arms. A smirk kicks up the side of his mouth, his eyes daring me to do what I'm thinking. But before I embarrass myself, dad places my hand into Jackson's and kisses my cheek.

"You look gorgeous." He whispers, leaning his forehead on mine.

"So do you. God, I love you so much," I sigh, cupping his face and kissing his cheek.

Looking into my eyes, his, shining with emotion. “I love you too, cariño.” His voice giving away his every emotion.

“Ladies and Gentlemen.”

I neither hear, nor see anything after that, until Jackson squeezes my hands, saying my name.

“Lily, every moment we've spent together has been so special; from the moment I first laid eyes on you, you left me breathless and dazed. You knocked the wind out of me. I was heartbroken when I lost my chance with you, but then fate brought you back to me. You are the love of my life, my soul mate, and the mother of our children and future children. I love you with everything I am.”

Tears drip from my eyes when he finishes; what he said with so much love and devotion in his eyes makes my heart ache with love.

A flutter of nerves kicks-in as I realise it's now my turn, and everyone is waiting. How can anyone top the beautiful words he just said?

“Jackson, the day you rescued me and fixed my car was one of the luckiest days of my life. You really are my knight in shining armour, because since that day you've been saving me over and over again, just by being yourself. You've done what I thought impossible, you healed me and made me a better person. You took away the hurt and grief and replaced it with the purest love. With everything I am, I’m yours. And I love only you.”

Smiling softly, he mouths, ‘I love you,’ and once again everything fades into the background, as I stare into the eyes of the man I’m desperately in love with.

“Jackson?” Blinking, he looks at Mace holding out a ring.

"Sorry," he mutters, Mace smirks staying silent.

"Lily, I give this ring, as a symbol of my love, honour and commitment." He says as he slips the ring onto my finger. Once in place he kisses my ring. A collective "aww," comes from our family and friends. A sense of calm washes over me.

I take the ring Mace hands me and with shaking hands. I take Jackson's left hand, placing the ring just before the knuckle and look into his beautiful eyes, repeating the same words to him.

Strengthening our bond and love. "I love you," I whisper, kissing his wedding band.

"With the power vested in me, I pronounce you, man and wife. You may kiss your bride," the Pastor announces happily.

Smiling wickedly, he pulls me into the sexiest kiss of my life.

Pulling away slowly, he leaves me breathless and hungry for more. Pink in the cheeks, the Pastor clears his throat and announces us for the first time.

"I give you, Mr and Mrs Jackson Miguel Garcia." Turning, we look out at our nearest and dearest, smiling and clapping. The twins bounce happily in the laps of my dad and nan, who eventually got past what went on with Mom.

"Are you ready to dance with your husband, Mrs Garcia?" A shiver travels down my spine, as his deep voice whispers over my neck. A burst of happiness flows through me at his use of my new name.

Turning, I wrap my arms around his neck, feeling the love I have for him burn in my chest. He always takes my breath away, but today he leaves me dazed and drooling every time I look at him.

His dark hair trimmed and spiked; his magnificent body encased in a vintage grey suit with a dark purple tie and white shirt. He's the epitome of male yumminess and he's all mine, *forever.*

"Your wife wouldn't want to be anywhere other than in your arms, pressed up against your hot bod." I say cheekily, chuckling as he kisses me swiftly, before clasping my hands and escorting me onto the dance floor.

His hands slide around my waist as a sensual Spanish beat pulses through the room, I forget everything but him as his hands drift down my back, arching me into him.

He spins me, so my back is to him and we dance a dance that shows our love and passion for each other.

His hands run up my sides, brushing my breasts, arousing me. Closing my eyes, I enjoy the feelings, letting him lead me. We glide across the floor in our own world, there's only us. I know he's as aroused as I am by the bulge against my lower back, my hips move against him as he glides his hands up my arms. His lips finding my neck, his breathing ragged. This first dance as man and wife is everything we are together. He may be American, but he has heated Spanish blood and when he's like this, it's the sexiest thing I've ever experienced.

When the last stains of music fade, I'm face to face with my husband breathing heavily, and wanting him so badly I ache. Applause breaks out around us, his wicked grin making me giggle.

"You look flushed, cariño. Did you enjoy your first dance as my wife?" The heat in his eyes, my breath hitches and my knees go weak, everything about my husband arouses me. With his shirt sleeves rolled up, his damp hair. The sweat on his upper lip, tempting me to taste, his face shining with love and passion. I get why women have a thing for Spanish men, mine is freaking hot.

I actually moan softly, my thoughts torturing me. He smiles smugly and pulls me in for a short steamy kiss.

"Later, mi amor," he whispers, kissing my neck. I need a breather, so I excuse myself and make my way to the bathroom.

Looking in the mirror, I see a flushed, sweaty, happy woman looking back, even my eyes are shining.

Wetting a towel, I dab my heated skin. Trying to calm my raging hormones, the combination of Spanish music, Jackson and dancing like that makes me so hot. *Damn, I have one sexy husband.* My eyes close, I feel blissful.

When the bathroom door opens; I smile, keeping them shut. Male arms slide around my waist, but they feel wrong and his scent is also wrong. My eyes pop open and it's not my husband staring back at me, I go cold, all heated fluttery feelings are gone. I immediately pull away from him, spinning to face him, anger pulsing through me.

"What the hell are you doing, Ethan?"

Am I overreacting? Probably, but I don't care. He shouldn't be here, he wasn't invited, and he certainly shouldn't be holding me like that. Like he has the right to, like I would want him to.

"I need to talk to you, I wanted to beforehand, but your dad was there. That was quite a show you both put on."

"What would we have to talk about on my wedding day? The only thing we have to talk about is the twins. That wasn't a show, we were dancing!"

"You may as well have been fucking him on the dance floor. That's what it looked like."

The disgust colouring his words, makes me so angry I

could slap him. I'm shaking with the effort of holding back. How dare he ruin my wedding and make something as beautiful as what Jackson and I just shared into something wrong and vulgar.

"Who the hell do you think you are? That was *Spanish* dancing and it's meant to be sensual and loving. My husband is part Spanish you knob. It's part of his heritage." I scream, my eyes stinging as my face burns with rage.

"I…"

The door bursts open, and there's my husband, looking pissed off.

"What's going on? I could hear you over the music. Everyone could." Coming to me, he rubs my arms, looking into my eyes. "You okay?" Blowing out a breath, I nod, leaning my head on his chest.

"What the hell is going on? What are you doing in the bathroom with my wife?" He asks through gritted teeth, as he turns on Ethan.

"We're talking that's all."

"No. You came in here. I thought it was you by the way," I assure Jackson, before continuing. "And wrapped your arms around me as I was wetting my face, then made our first dance sound sordid." My chest heaves with my every breath.

"What the fuck? She's my wife, you don't get to touch her. You weren't even invited and just so you know, I couldn't give a shit about your opinion on our dancing."

Jackson's eyes blaze with anger. I can't say I blame him, with what Ethan pulled after finding out we were engaged.

"I think you need to leave, and if you *ever* touch my wife again. I'll knock your teeth down your throat." Looking from me to Jackson, Ethan pauses, seeing the rage in Jackson's eyes and leaves quickly.

Blowing out a breath, I turn and press my face into Jackson's chest, clutching his lower back.

"You okay?" I look into his beautiful brown eyes and let all the crap go. Leaning around him to lock the door, his eyebrows shoot up as a sexy smile curves his delicious lips.

"What are you doing, Mrs Garcia?" His hands run up my sides from my hips.

Pressing against him, I grip his open shirt and pull him down to my lips. Letting him feel the heat we generated on the dance floor.

His hands grip my butt, squeezing and pulling me into him, securing me against the bulge in his trousers. My hands delve into his hair, my dress is pulled up, his hands exploring. I hum as he lifts me, his hands gliding my legs around his waist.

Turning I'm pressed against the wall, freeing his hands to start a slow assault on my satin and lace covered chest. Moving my hair aside and kissing down my neck. Pulling my dress, exposing more skin, licking, teasing. I shiver, my breathing erratic.

"Amor, te necesito."

"Soy tuya, tómame." My Spanish still rusty, but I do know how to tell him I'm his.

Sliding my dress further up my thighs, teasing me with the feel of his palms warming my skin, electrifying me with every touch.

"Please, Jackson, hurry. I need you, too." My head falls back. I surrender to him.

"We can't make love here. I want to make love to mi *Esposa* for the first time thoroughly, and in a bed."

"Please."

"I can make you feel good, but I won't take you in a bathroom." Relieved and slightly disappointed, I crush his mouth to mine.

His fingers slip under the edge of my white thong, sliding into my heated flesh. Moaning, I grind myself harder onto his fingers, my whole body lighting up as he works me.

Pulling my lips away, I pant into his neck, my lipstick catching his collar.

"*Jackson,*" my words slur with pleasure as my climax hits me fast and hard. Shuddering, I suck his neck.

"Feeling better?" The strain in his voice telling how much it took for him to hold back. Sliding down the wall, I feel every hard inch of his tort frame shudder as I rub against his swollen cock.

Smiling, I drop to my knees, tugging his fly and zipper in one smooth motion. Groaning as the cool air washes over his heated skin. Licking my lips, I pull him free and take the tip in my mouth, sucking gently.

"Ahh, cariño," sighing, he slides his fingers into my hair, directing me as his other palm slaps against the wall to stabilize himself. My hands clutch his backside, feeling it flex as he thrusts into my waiting mouth.

"Lily," his speech slurring, he's so hot, it's only minutes before his body tenses and his orgasm takes over. Pulling him further into my mouth, his piercing brushing the back of my throat, he trembles, moaning incoherently as his warmth explodes onto my tongue, filling me with a surge of feminine power.

"Better?" I ask, finishing straightening his trousers and shirt. Looking up his arm is still braced on the wall, his head lowered, and eyes shut, a sleepy smile gracing his handsome face.

"Much."

Pulling me to my feet, we share a sweet kiss.

"We'd better get back; they're probably wondering where we are." He chuckles, pulling me along behind him.

Entering the reception room, everyone looks happy, none the wiser dancing and chatting. The kids are all playing and laughing.

"And where have you two been?" Mace whispers in my ear, making me jump, turning, I smack his arm.

"Do you have to sneak up on everyone?"

"Not everyone, just you." Laughing, Mace and Jackson fist bump.

Mason's face turns serious as he looks back at me. "Ethan's here," I nod, turning to him. Jackson slides an arm around my waist.

"Is he still here?"

He nods behind me. I spot him holding Eliza and Seb, bouncing them happily.

Growling, I pull away from Jackson and storm over to them. "Dad, could you take the twins to get some cake please?" Hesitantly, he takes the twins from Ethan and walks away. Jackson and Mason come up behind me, as I drag Ethan by the arm into the hall.

"What the hell was that back there? Haven't you caused enough trouble? Have I not made myself clear? There is no more us. There never will be, I've just married the love of my life, I'm blissfully happy with him. You're the twins' dad as I keep saying and that's it. I'm sick of going over this. You're married, I'm married. You may be miserable, but that's not my problem, it's yours. I will not leave Jackson, I love him." I yell.

Ethan looks sad. "I know, it was stupid and selfish and I'm sorry. It won't happen again, I'll back off. You're right, it's my own fault I'm miserable and I'm happy that you've found happiness. I'm going to go, tell the twins goodbye, I'll see them soon." He turns and leaves without another word.

"Are you sure you'll be okay?" I look at my daughter and son conked out on nan and dad's laps. They look so angelic right now, but when they're awake, they are into anything and everything.

"We'll be fine, Mace and I have it under control. If we need help, I'll call Ethan and Alex." Mace and Jackson smile as nan placates me. Placing Sebastian beside dad, she stands.

"Okay but call if you need us. We're not far," She nods, chuckling and hugs me tightly.

"Just relax and enjoy the night alone. You won't get any peace on your honeymoon, these two will be keeping you both busy."

"We wouldn't want it any other way and besides, my family is looking forward to meeting them, and of course my beautiful new wife." Jackson nuzzles my neck, his arms sliding around my waist.

"Okay, then. I think it's time to get these two home and leave those two to."

"*Mason!*" Nan's hand covers his mouth. "Do *not* finish that sentence." Jackson is laughing so hard he's shaking.

Everyone gathers outside as we leave, waving and wishing us well. I smile sadly looking at the twins one last time, before we get into the vintage Rolls Royce.

Holding hands, we run through the hotel lobby laughing, we steal kisses in the lift and stumble into the suit breathless and happy.

Walking over to the window, I look out enjoying the nights sky.

"Alone at last." Coming up behind me, moving my hair to the side and kissing along my neck, arms winding around me, hands cupping my breasts, tweaking my nipples.

Moaning, I grind into his hardening cock as his one hand starts a slow glide down my belly, rubbing me through my dress.

"Are you wet for me, Mrs Garcia?" His voice strained.

"*Yes,"* I'm breathless and more than ready to be possessed by my husband.

Slowly undoing each button down my spine, he makes sure to brush my heated skin the whole time. The mixture of his heated breath and the cool air hitting my sensitive skin, making me shiver and moan. Wanting to feel him closer, I wind my arms around his neck. Turning my mouth to his, licking his bottom lip, I bite down and suck.

Groaning, he pulls my dress off my upper body, running his hands along my white lace bustier.

"*Lily,* turn around and step out of the dress, I need to see you." Hiding a smug smile, I step out of my dress, bending slowly, I pick it up and place it over a nearby chair, my ass rubbing against him.

"You little tease." He groans, stepping closer, I fall to my knees in front of him. His hands are as quick as lightening clasping my waist and pulling me to my feet.

Shaking his head, he steps back, his heated gaze taking me in slowly.

"You look fucking incredible."

Wetting his lips, his finger drifts between my breasts and across my quivering stomach, settling me on the bed beneath him, he makes his way down my body, kissing as he goes. Pausing he looks at me with those intense, gorgeous eyes and whispers "I love you Lily, always."

I sigh happily "I love you too, Jackson, forever."

The End

ACKNOWLEDGMENTS

For all who believed in me and helped me achieve my dream. Thank you.

To my Husband for putting up with my frustrations and encouraging me not to give up. Thank you, I love you. And of course, my kids, thank you, because without you and Dad I wouldn't have inspiration.

Thank you to my friend and virtual twin Laura Martinez for putting up with my bitching.

A special thank you to Sarah Queen for helping me refine the last sentences at the end.

Love ya lady.

Thank you to my beta readers Kimberly O'Connell, Kym Michelle, Denielle Hoppe, Milva Chin and Sarah Queen.

And thank you to my proof reader's Sarah Queen, Scottie Mohler.

Thank you to all my friends who read my baby and gave constructive advice. Without you all, I would have gone mad, you're all awesome! And finally thank you to everyone who liked, shared, commented and posted about this book.

Especially my main pimpers Karen Dillon, Kaye Springett and Zai Floriza.
And a massive thank you to Aidan Willows for formatting this monster for me.
Each and every one of you are amazing!

The Loving Lily Series continues with Ethan's story, With a Beat of my Heart.

Blurb

When tragedy strikes, Ethan is forced to re-adjust and learn lessons he thought he'd mastered long ago.
As life goes, with darkness comes light.
Secrets are revealed, lives torn apart…
He thought losing Lily was hard…
Well, it has nothing on what is at stake now… To lose everything he holds dear and have to start again, is excruciating.

"Life's a bitch and then you marry one."

Truer words have never been spoken.
Everything is dark, shadowed, there is no light, until I meet her. She is his light, salvation, and strength, as he struggles to cope with all the changes in his life.
It's said, God never puts more on your plate than you can handle, but with Ethan's plate overflowing will he survive all the challenges life throws at him?

Website
Wattpad
Instagram
Blog page
Amazon Page
Facebook Author Page
Loving Lily Page
Goodreads
You Tube
Bookbub
Twitter
Tumblr

BOOKS SO FAR

Loving Lily Series:

Book 1 ~ In the Blink of an Eye
Novella ~ Making Memories
Book 2 ~ With A Beat of my Heart
Book 3 ~ The Eve Of Forever ~ Novella

Sweetest Love Series:

A Life For Riley

Standalones

Co-write:
Laura B. Martinez
A Chance on Love

S.J. Batsford is a British indie author and writer of the Loving Lily Series.

She always liked to write but struggled with learning difficulties then and now. Her love of romance novels eventually led her to push through the fear of failure and try. She has loved writing romance ever since.

Her first book; In The Blink of an Eye was published in July 2016. It's the first in the series.

The second book, With a Beat of my Heart, is now available on Amazon as well as a short Christmas novella, Making Memories.

She recently finished writing the next book in the Loving Lily Series, Embracing Destiny.

As many other authors, she is always looking for new ways of challenging herself with future projects.

She plans to work on different books throughout the numerous sub-genres within the romance.